Till DEATH Us Do PART

Till DEATH Us Do PART

Reverend PENNY STEPHENS

QUERCUS

First published in Great Britain in 2025 by

QUERCUS

Quercus Editions Ltd
Carmelite House
50 Victoria Embankment
London EC4Y 0DZ

An Hachette UK company

The authorised representative in the EEA is Hachette Ireland,
8 Castlecourt Centre, Dublin 15, D15 XTP3, Ireland (email: info@hbgi.ie)

A CIP catalogue record for this book is available
from the British Library

HB ISBN 978 1 52944 142 0
EB ISBN 978 1 52944 1 444

1

Typeset by CC Book Production
Printed and bound in Great Britain by Clays Ltd, Elcograf S.p.A

Papers used by Quercus are from well-managed forests and other responsible sources.

For Jonathan, Eleanor and Ben, with thanks and love.

PROLOGUE

Harriet

Death at the wedding – how tactless. Inconsiderate, to say the least. Impolite, certainly.

Glorious flowers cascading in hues of gold and green over the arched doorway to the church; Rolls-Royce carrying the bride and groom to the reception, purring as advertised; kisses and toasts: all to be expected.

But this?

Harriet looked at the body crumpled in the corner of the tree house. She could hear the chatter and laughter from the marquee, the clatter of glassware and the hum of the generator. She had sidled out to have a break from all the politeness and complicated tableware. The other guests at her table were pleasant, but she wanted a breather all the same. It wasn't easy being back here.

She knew the garden from childhood visits, before the rift. Knew the pathway through the trees to the farmland beyond. Knew the hiding places and the scratch of brambles as she'd crouched behind the piles of felled timber. She had sketched her memories of the landscape, the walled gardens and the raspberry canes. But she wouldn't be painting this.

She moved tentatively towards the man. He lay curled up on the wooden floor, his back towards her. She felt weirdly detached, distanced – refusing to acknowledge, even to herself, who it was.

His suit was dark; his thick hair was dark too. His face was turned away – perhaps he'd simply come up here to sleep off too much booze. But she didn't really think so. The heel of his shoe was worn and scuffed, the angle wrong somehow.

She crouched behind him and reached to touch his arm. Suppose it was an asthma attack and he needed help? He'd had those as a child.

Music from the festivities and sudden sounds of cheering contrasted with the stillness in the tree house. She knew before her fingers touched the fabric of his sleeve. She knew before she saw the grimace of his stilled face and the stickiness of his reddened shirt, the hilt of a knife embedded there.

She reached for it, even though there was nothing to be done.

Shouting came from below – someone yelling about where the toilets were. She felt cold and afraid, sick and vulnerable. She was the one with the biggest reason to kill him.

What to do? Get out? Get help? No. She should run.

She heard someone calling her name. They were climbing the stairs.

CHAPTER 1

Clare

Clare was confident that Anna would excel herself as a brides-maid. Her daughter had been one before, five years ago, when she was only six. She had danced the night away, twirling across the dance floor with her dad and others. Clare had a lasting memory of David carrying their daughter in from the car, a flurry of petticoats in his arms. Anna was fast asleep, satin shoes grubbied and dangling, her face serene.

This time, she was older. Poised. Last week, she had told her grandmother about their time in Italy, with precision, reeling off facts about the duomo in Florence.

They had returned in good time for the wedding and were making a weekend of it. David was bringing Tom from home, after dropping off the dog with their friends. They were trav-elling separately; Clare's responsibility was to deliver Anna to the house for Operation Bridesmaid.

As they approached the mansion, Anna was wide-eyed, absorbing each detail. Ranks of trees lined the long drive and a sweeping curve of crunching gravel led to the front door, which was open as if in surprise.

Clare had not expected the place to be quite so grand.

Inside, they could see the spacious hall with chessboard floor tiles, an elegant table or two at its edges. The house felt solid: Queen Anne gracious with a smooth façade. Clare pressed the bell beside the large doorway and waited, not wanting to walk in unannounced.

Anna was excited but composed, with no chatter. She knew that Susan, the bride's mother, was an MP. Anna, now in Year 7, was regularly in touch with their own MP, expressing her and her classmates' views on global warming, wildlife and anti-slavery measures.

Clare had briefed Anna that today Susan was off duty, acting as mother of the bride rather than a prominent MP and junior minister. Even so, she was nervous that Anna meant to make the most of the day in every way, asking Susan lots of questions.

David had worked with Susan and said she had a reputation for being nice. Colleagues in the Home Office had found her brittle at first, yet more congenial over time. Clare wondered whether the new minister was just shy, beneath the necessary networking. Her husband gained Susan's trust faster than most colleagues, due to his long-standing friendship with her daughter. He and Jess had met years back, on a trekking holiday.

David was the one sent in to raise trickier topics with the new boss, and there had been plenty of those. Susan had controversial views and no shortage of opponents. At times, there had even been concerns for her safety. Clare remembered that Susan's family had been targeted too, and Jess was worried by it.

Jess was great, energetic and always ready for a spot of football in the garden or a game of sardines, a favourite with Anna and Tom. And she had asked Anna to be one of her bridesmaids, which increased her popularity still further.

Clare could hear chatter coming from inside, beyond the empty hall. Or not so empty, as there was a box of flower sprays here, a pile of shoes there, and just beside the door a wheelchair, folded and waiting.

'Anna . . . it must be Anna. Hello, darling.' Susan swooped towards them in welcome. The mother of the bride and rising politician gleamed: her foundation had a glistening tint, her smile was glossy-lipped. 'And you must be Clare? A vicar, I hear. How exciting.'

'It's lovely to meet you.' Clare smiled. 'And on such a happy day, too.'

'Well, so far, so good. Let's hope everything stays that way. Anna, I think you know all about how to keep the bridesmaid show on the road, don't you?' Susan scarcely paused for breath. 'I'll take you upstairs to meet the others and get ready. Excuse me for stealing your daughter, Clare. Do make yourself at home – drinks are in the kitchen, through to your left.'

Susan swept Anna off, and Clare lingered in the hall. One wall held a mosaic of photos – she saw a youthful David in a couple of group pictures. It made her smile to see him. He was wearing a posh jacket and held a glass up in a toast. Jess's twenty-first, perhaps? He was a few years older than Jess and her contemporaries, but they had definitely met by then. He had taken extended leave from work to travel in Nepal, and she had joined a trek he was on, making it round the Anna-purna trail. With others from that group they had completed another Himalayan trip, and gone climbing in Wales. They had been friends ever since, and Jess was now a friend of Clare and the children too.

There were several pictures of Jess – with a pony, jumping an alarmingly substantial fence at full stretch; at graduation, scroll in hand and mortarboard at a jaunty angle. There was one of her as a child with Fabian, her brother: both mud-splattered and grinning. Another of them standing on deck, with the outline of Cromwell's castle on Tresco behind them. Tall, sporty siblings, Jess with her trademark high blonde ponytail, they looked ready to sail the world. Clare wondered how the bride would do her hair today. She thought Susan might prefer an elaborate style.

There were photos of family holidays throughout the years, taken in a variety of exotic, and probably very expensive, destinations. This must be Jim – with the same blue eyes as his son. In later photos, Jim was in a wheelchair, Susan leaning in towards him, with champagne flutes in their hands. Clare reckoned that one was taken at Glyndebourne, and was that ornate interior the Orient Express?

'I see you're getting to know us,' a voice behind her said, making her start. 'I'm Jim, Susan's husband. Jess's dad. Welcome to Greenwood House.'

Clare felt self-conscious that she'd been caught examining the photos so closely, but didn't miss a beat in exchanging pleasantries. Church life included plenty of those. Jim's handshake was strong. He invited her to take a look at the other family photos arranged on a table beneath a painting of horses grazing. Was that a Stubbs? Whatever next. Perhaps a Picasso in the downstairs loo.

Jim wheeled himself over to show Clare a picture of David at a summer barbecue, croquet mallet in hand. She couldn't believe how young he looked, even though he was older than Jess. Next to that photo, she saw a delicate charcoal sketch of Jess, captured in teenage absorption, reading in a window seat.

'This is so lovely,' Clare commented, pointing towards the sketch. 'There's such a peace about it.'

'That was done by Jess's cousin, Harriet. She's quite a successful portrait artist now,' Jim said, briefly indicating a photo of a girl with her back to the camera, sketching a landscape view. He turned away from the pictures and gestured towards the far side of the hallway. 'Let's go through to the garden and get some air.'

Clare followed her host as he propelled himself through a set of double doors into an expanse of drawing room with William Morris wallpaper, and out to the terrace beyond. Below them lay a sloping garden, with a collection of marquees and a man carrying a tray in the distance. Scents of lavender and rosemary greeted them.

'So, you snapped up young David,' Jim continued. 'He never seemed the religious type to me – does he still support Man U? Terrible waste.'

Clare wasn't sure whether it was her husband's choice of wife, football team or faith that Jim deemed unsatisfactory. In any case, she assured him that Man U was indeed still David's team, but that their son had the sense to be a Chelsea fan.

'You'll meet our vicar,' Jim continued. Clare wondered if he'd even heard her reply. 'Decent woman. Does a lot in the village. Her husband was army. Now, I'm not one for God-botherers, but I must admit, I like her.'

Clare was spared from having to make a tactful response to this, as Anna appeared with a couple of smaller and energetically squeaking bridesmaids. On their heads were circlets of flowers, and their purple silk dresses rustled as they moved.

'Well, you look very fine, young ladies. Give us a twirl,' Jim greeted them.

One of the younger girls obliged, briefly, then they led Clare out of the room with them, as if to take her upstairs, before changing their minds and scurrying away. She was not sorry to leave Jim; there was something unsettling about the father of the bride.

CHAPTER 2

Clare explored the garden and grounds while Anna was having her hair tended to by a stylist wielding straighteners. She'd looked very capable, like she'd marshal wayward bridesmaids without any trouble.

She noticed a red-haired man standing just beyond the terrace, beside a well-manicured hedge. He gave a small wave of hello and Clare walked over to greet him.

'Hi, I'm Rufus Winslade.'

Clare thought how clean-cut he looked, and eager to greet her, like a dog on point. He was wearing a sharp suit with a yellow patterned tie.

'Hello, I'm Clare. My daughter is a bridesmaid, and very excited about it. They're all busy getting ready, and I'm busy making myself scarce.' She shot him a conspiratorial grin.

'My girlfriend is a bridesmaid too. Athena and I are long-standing friends of the family, as well as being politically connected.'

'How lovely,' Clare said, immediately aware of how insincere she sounded. 'So, do you work with Susan?'

This youth, with his focused stare, seemed scarcely old enough to be a 'long-standing' anything. Rufus proceeded to explain that it was Athena who worked for Susan, as a special adviser. She had known Jess at university, and initially worked for Susan on a summer internship, before becoming her parliamentary assistant and then landing the special-adviser post, once Susan was appointed a Home Office minister.

'Perhaps you two know my husband, David Brakespear?' Clare offered. 'He's worked with Susan at the Home Office, and possibly with Athena, too.'

Rufus's enthusiasm to make her acquaintance intensified. Clare tried to be generous, but ambition dripped off him.

'I'm keen to be involved in Susan's change programme and I want to help her move forward on her agenda effectively,' he proffered. 'Priorities, planning and performance: that's what I deliver. As your husband does, too, I am sure. Targets and tech. We must be clear and transparent, focused and forceful—'

Clare was saved from any further slogans by the arrival of a rotund chocolate Labrador, which came bounding down the path. The dog greeted her with energetic tail-wagging and backside-wiggling. She bent down to stroke its soft brown fur, pleasantly warm from the summer sun. She wanted to make this moment last, to delay having to stand up and engage in conversation with Rufus again. Unfortunately, the dog meandered off, realising no treats were available, so the matter was taken out of her hands.

'Your husband's work is famous, of course,' he said, rather intensely.

Clare doubted this, but listened patiently as Rufus carried on his flattery of David. She was amused as he commented that David's achievements were recognised chiefly by those 'in the know'. A group that encompassed Rufus, clearly.

'I look forward to connecting with your husband later,' Rufus continued. 'We can discuss how I might sharpen up Susan's effectiveness in delivering strategic momentum.'

'Oh, are you working for her, too?' Clare asked, mildly.

'Yes, though currently in an unofficial capacity. But obviously we talk often. The plan is for me to become part of the team once Susan has a Cabinet portfolio.'

'That sounds interesting,' Clare said, wondering whose plan this might be, and suspecting that it would be news to Susan. 'What is it that you do now?'

'Fingers in various pies. Some consultancy roles, investment advice and political strategy work, mainly,' Rufus breezed back.

Clare concluded that he probably wasn't doing very much at all and was dead set on landing a paid role alongside Athena as one of Susan's growing tribe of special advisers.

What made these advisers quite so special was often elusive.

Eventually, Clare escaped Rufus and his deluge of self-promotion, as he spotted Jim on the terrace with a newly arrived couple and set off to investigate.

She snuck away, following the garden path between blocks of low-cut privet, and walked through a brickwork archway into a walled garden with an inviting range of glasshouses and sheds.

The tubby dog was there, heading down the path in front of her, nose to the ground. The vegetable rows were laid out precisely and the apple trees looked plump and rounded, their branches curved upward as if playing cat's cradle. The dog lingered at a bench.

An orange dress emblazoned with aquamarine swirls stood out against the greens of the garden. The large woman wearing it also sported a trailing scarf with tasselled fringes of aquamarine and gold. She was laughing heartily, absorbed in conversation with a bearded younger man. He was dressed casually, with heavy work boots on his feet. Clare saw he held a broom; perhaps he'd been giving the pathways one last sweep before the festivities began.

As Clare joined them, the woman greeted her vivaciously.

'What fun to be here! I'm Celeste, and this gorgeous chap is Martin. He's looking after Greenwood's gardens for Susan and Jim, these days.'

Martin smiled too, his brown eyes warm, and murmured a gentle-voiced greeting.

'I've not been here for years,' Celeste continued. 'And it's such a thrill to be back. Martin is all grown up, now – love the beard, Martin – but I remember him when he was just a little boy. He and my daughter, Harriet, were thick as thieves, back then. Do you remember those pony races with Harriet and Jess?'

'I do, Mrs Zetland. It was great having Harriet here. We missed her, after . . .' Martin trailed off, stuttering to a pause.

'Darling Martin, don't worry. There's nothing to be embarrassed about.' She turned to address Clare more directly. 'It's marvellous to be back here, and so kind of Susan and Jim to invite me. I'm Jess's aunt, but I haven't seen her for years. Family problems, you see, but let's not dwell on those.'

'Family issues can be so difficult,' Clare offered, curious to know more. Her words went unheard, Celeste being well into her stride.

'Anyway, after that unhappy episode, I've carried on.

And – do you know, darlings – I've been OK. And I still am. Still sculpting – that's what I do – and I'm still travelling. There's so much to see and to enjoy. And it's just fabulous to be here again. And fabulous to see you, Martin.' Celeste reached her arms out expansively, as if ready to dance with the garden. 'And now Jess is grown up, too. The last time I saw her, she was a teenager mucking out stables and making eyes at you, Martin – and now she's a doctor, getting married!'

'Yes, and – speaking of the wedding – I'd better get myself ready; I can't go dressed like this.' Martin grinned as he indicated his clothes and excused himself.

Celeste hugged him warmly, then leaned forward to Clare, conspiratorially. 'Now, enough about me. Tell me all about *you.*'

Clare immediately liked this woman and her zest for the day ahead. Celeste looked thrilled when Clare explained her connection to the family, and Anna's bridesmaid duties.

'Oh, you're the vicar!' Celeste enthused. 'Susan told me all about you. Isn't your husband a spook or something?'

Clare was quick to agree that she was indeed a vicar, but assured Celeste that David was nothing as exciting as a spook. He was simply a civil servant who had covered security policy from time to time.

Celeste was not so easily convinced, raising her eyebrows, archly. 'It's the dull ones you need to watch, darling. Didn't George Smiley tell his wife he worked for the coal board?'

Discovering a shared enthusiasm for thrillers and detective novels, they strolled from the walled garden across the lawn to explore the marquees, discussing how Agatha Christie might have used this setting, and enjoying the relaxed ambiance.

A van was being unloaded, and a generator hummed. A drum kit and amplifying equipment were being taken into a side entrance of one of the tents. Perhaps the music would be modern, but the rhythms of a wedding always felt traditional to Clare.

'I feel so glad to have met you,' Celeste said, grasping Clare's arm with both hands and gazing into her eyes. 'I just know you'll understand. It's wonderful to be here, but I feel nervous about today too. There's someone who I think may have been invited and he reminds me of the worst time in my life . . .' Her voice trailed off and for a second she looked lost to her memories, her eyes vacant and faraway. Then she shuddered theatrically and rearranged her face in a smile. 'Anyway. Darling, pray for me, won't you, in case he does come? We'll all need it.'

Clare assured Celeste that she would do so, and the moment of intensity passed.

CHAPTER 3

An affronted cat stalked across the landing. Clothing was draped over the bannisters, and Taylor Swift's voice blared from a speaker, singing angrily about 'Bad Blood'.

'Clare!' called Jess. Her hair was pinned up and she was wearing a tightly belted silk dressing gown. No ponytail then, Clare thought. 'Come and have a drink! Doesn't your Anna look gorgeous!'

Jess was as much of a live wire as ever. She introduced Clare to a number of people around the room, finally gesturing to a woman in a beaded dress, who was one of her senior brides-maids. 'This is Suki, Ahmed's sister. She teaches at a big school in London,' Jess explained.

Suki greeted Clare warmly and remarked how well Anna had been doing at keeping an eye on the little ones, who were currently hunting the cat.

Clare wondered how Suki navigated her relationship with Susan, who had been at loggerheads with the teaching profession during her time as minister for schools. Now, obviously, wasn't the time to ask.

Jess was animated, almost manic in her movements, passing glasses around, picking up clothes and moving cards and photos from place to place in the room. Her face had an edge to it, her cheeks drawn in.

'What a crazy day! I'm so glad you're here, Clare. At least it's not raining.'

'Well, you're marrying Ahmed, not the weather.' Clare smiled. 'And you look so well on it.'

'Mum's happy it's a church wedding, and Ahmed has been so brilliant about everything. I want to enjoy it, but I have to admit I'll also be relieved when it's over.' Jess shifted her phone from the dressing table into her pocket. 'Suki, your family are coping with enough today. I'm going to recruit Clare to help with my lot. She's a vicar, so she has to be nice. Clare, can you chat with my diva aunt, please? You're so good with everyone. She's one for drama, and we don't need any more of that.'

'Of course. And every wedding has a bit of drama,' soothed Clare, sitting herself down next to Suki on the window seat and not mentioning that she had already met the enthusiastic Celeste.

'Ahmed and I have plenty of our own aunt issues,' commented Suki. 'They'll love you, Jess, don't worry, but royalty wouldn't be good enough for Ahmed.'

Jess's face tightened further, and then she laughed in a staccato tinkle. 'I know! I'm one lucky woman. Sorry, guys, I just need to sort something out next door.' And, with that sudden about-face, she was gone.

'She's so tense,' murmured Suki. 'I hope she can relax a bit.'

Clare agreed. Jess seemed brittle, overplaying the happy-bride role, which was strange when she was normally so at ease. But then, it was a big day, with aunts to navigate, and Clare knew a lot of people went a bit peculiar under wedding-day strain.

All the bridesmaids were frocked up and looking relaxed. Suki was tapping at her phone, while also having the finishing touches put to her elegant hairstyle. She was chatting to a cheerful young woman who Clare learned was Athena, girlfriend of Rufus the Ruthless, as she had privately named the self-promoting young man. Athena was friendly, complimenting Clare on her scarlet-flowered dress, asking after David and their journey, and mentioning how much she enjoyed working with him.

Then Susan appeared in the doorway and announced that Athena was needed in the bedroom for a moment, as 'something had come up'. The sharpness in her voice made Trixie and Tinky lift their heads from the ranks of nail-varnish bottles they were assembling. Susan pushed a smile towards them and began complimenting them on their grown-up looks, moving effortlessly into the politician's conversational skillset.

Anna watched, alert to Susan's shifting behaviour.

Clare joined in the chat, discussing the imminence of the bridesmaid photos and how lovely a setting the garden would be for them. Susan apologised for the disappearance of the cat, who had proved disappointingly resistant to the prospect of a manicure or fur-styling, despite Trixie and Tinky's most persuasive efforts. They considered the possibility of kittens.

After a while, Clare excused herself, giving Anna a kiss and saying she would see her at the church with Dad and Tom.

She knew that her daughter wouldn't have missed the tone of anxious energy in Susan, and murmured to her that everyone gets a bit uptight at weddings, to which Anna responded, in a world-weary tone, 'I know that, Mum. It's fine.'

Clare made her farewells, telling Susan she would see her at the service and wishing her well. Susan's dress was regal, a deeper purple than the bridesmaids', with lilac feathers at the cuffs. No doubt a fantastical hat would join the ensemble. Clare had been careful to say that she looked wonderful.

As Clare walked towards the stairs, a woman carrying hairbrushes passed her and pushed open another door on the landing. Clare caught sight of Jess, phone in hand, waving it towards a startled Athena.

'Can you believe it?' The bride's face was stricken, and her arms were moving jerkily, brandishing the phone as if she was about to hurl it at someone. 'Can you believe it?' she snarled again. 'I wish he was dead.'

Athena was nodding as if to placate Jess, while also waving the confused hairdresser away.

The hairdresser backed out and closed the door. She smiled wryly at Clare, who had halted, shocked by the scene.

'Always drama at a wedding, isn't there?' the young hairdresser commented, in the tone of one who had seen it all before, then she headed towards the room where the bridesmaids were waiting, to check on them instead.

Yes, there's always drama at a wedding, Clare thought, but not generally death threats from a murderous bride. Well, not until after the speeches, anyway.

Who had disturbed Jess to such a degree? Surely not Ahmed, on their wedding day. Athena would certainly be putting her

18

social and political skills to good use, getting Jess into bridal mode again.

Downstairs, the brown Labrador thumped his tail on the floor and lumbered to his feet to greet Clare.

'All OK up there?' Jim asked, as he manoeuvred his wheelchair from the open sitting-room door and came towards her.

'There's lots of hairdressing happening,' Clare said. 'And some happy young bridesmaids. Although Tinky and Trixie are sad that the cat wasn't keen on having its claws painted.' Least said, soonest mended; Clare thought it would be better if Jim didn't hear about any upsets.

Jim breathed in deeply and looked worried for a moment. 'All I want is a happy day for Jess, without any politicos stirring up trouble for Susan.'

'Of course, and everything looks so well prepared. I met . . . Martin, was it? Tidying up in the garden. And the marquees look great. This is such a beautiful setting and it's so convenient having the hotel next door. I think many of the guests are booked in there. We're staying and it's lovely.' She knew she was chattering on, but she could tell appearances mattered to this family and she wanted to make Jim feel better.

'Thank you, Clare.' Jim looked at her, steadily. 'I think you understand how much this means to me – having Jess happy, Susan able to enjoy the day, and everyone here. I don't want anyone to spoil the occasion.'

'Well, weddings can make us all a bit tense,' Clare replied. 'But I'm sure we'll have a brilliant day.'

Conscious that she might win a 'Blandness of Britain' award, Clare retreated towards the open front door. 'I'll head off to the church. I'm meeting David there; he's bringing our son,

Tom. David's looking forward to meeting you again, Jim. Thanks for everything. See you later.'

She left, wondering why Jim's words made her feel so uneasy. She hoped no one would cause trouble today.

CHAPTER 4

Clare found her husband and son in the churchyard, exploring and waiting for things to get going. Her children were familiar with churchyards. Aged nine, Tom already had years of experience making Easter gardens in them and hunting for chocolate eggs, or playing hide-and-seek with his elder sister amongst the headstones.

As they strolled on the grassy pathways, Tom told Clare in some detail about his school friend, Angus, who got to carry a dagger at a wedding. David had clearly heard all about this exciting weaponry in the car, but nodded appreciatively as the story was recounted.

Tom reliably informed her it was called a dirk, and it was Scottish. Angus had also had to wear a kilt, though, which Tom regarded as embarrassing. But a dagger in your sock was undeniably cool.

Clearly her son was unconcerned about being less involved in the wedding than Anna with her bridesmaid duties, but he felt disappointed that there would be no daggers for him or anyone else today.

Clare noticed the clusters of new arrivals in the car park that the church shared with the neighbouring hotel: some hatted women, and one or two men in morning suits. Groups of younger men and women were now chatting animatedly by the lychgate, their clothing bright in the sunshine. One younger woman in a darker green dress stood a little apart, watching everyone, then checking the contents of her bag. Clare also spotted Celeste, the chatty woman she had met in the garden, still resplendent in her swirl of kingfisher colours.

Celeste linked arms with the woman in green and headed up the path towards the church porch. Ahead of the women walked Ahmed and his best man, presumably.

'David, mate, great to see you,' Ahmed called. The tall, bespectacled groom looked smart in his formal morning suit, complete with white carnation in the buttonhole. 'This is Gwyn, my best man.'

'Good to meet you. And, Ahmed, it's your big day!' David said. 'Congrats. How are you doing?'

'All the better for knowing you're here. And here's my other best mate,' Ahmed announced, high-fiving Tom and smiling at Clare.

They were interrupted by Celeste, who swooped in. 'You must be Ahmed,' she declared. 'I'm Jess's aunt, Celeste. And this is my daughter, Harriet.'

'Hi,' said Harriet, adjusting the strap of her bag.

'Jess will be so pleased you've made it,' Ahmed said, greeting them both and tugging at the neck of his shirt. 'And I've been looking forward to meeting you. Thank you so much for coming. I am delighted you're here.' He moved his glasses up his nose, betraying his nervousness.

Clare wondered what the big deal was about attending the wedding of a cousin or niece, but maybe Ahmed was just being polite, and Celeste had certainly been tense about some aspects of returning to Greenwood. Presumably Ahmed knew about all that and was simply being kind. Clare also wondered if he knew how tense his bride was, and why.

Other guests strolled up from the car park and gathered on the path to the church. Further introductions were made, and Ahmed's mother joined them.

'I remember you.' She beamed at David. 'We heard from Ahmed what a good friend you've been to him, as well as to Jess. And you must be Thomas? I'm Fatima. We've heard all about your holiday adventures. Didn't you take Ahmed and Jess to the Isles of Scilly with you? And you had cream teas on a different island every day?'

The chat continued, with Clare and David standing back as Fatima and some other women collected around the groom and best man, with young Tom in the centre. Clare noticed how quiet Harriet was, remaining on the fringe of the group and repeatedly looking back towards the car park as if waiting for someone. She seemed very different from her effervescent mother.

'It's Clare! Hello . . . Hello again, darling,' announced Celeste. 'Now, Harriet, there's a secret about Clare – she's a vicar! And her husband is a spy, but no one must know that either.'

Clare smiled, said she was not on duty today, and left Celeste to carry on with the conversation and greetings as the flow of guests swelled. Gradually, the group moved towards the church, with Fatima exclaiming at the beauty of the flowers festooning the arched doorway, and Celeste organising and posing for photos there.

Inside the porch, ushers had unboxed the orders of service and stood to greet them all. One was Rufus, the would-be special adviser. He welcomed Clare vigorously and made a point of name-checking David. Another usher was Martin, the bearded man she'd met in the garden who was multi-tasking today. Clare noticed how warmly he and Celeste's daughter Harriet greeted one another, and how his cheeks flushed as he spoke with her. Harriet seemed reserved, but she smiled at him and appeared to relax a little.

Once they were seated, with Tom occupied by a book extracted from her bag and saved especially for the occasion, Clare updated David on the dramas of the day thus far, and her concerns about Jess.

The nave was now filling up fast and Clare decided she'd better stop talking in case she was overheard. Music billowed from the organ, and Fiona, the vicar, gave the kneelers for the bride and groom a nudge with her foot to straighten them. A photographer bustled about rather officiously, Clare thought, relieved it was Fiona who would be corralling him, not her. She had too much experience of apparently biddable wedding photographers going rogue during the service and practically sticking their cameras up her nostrils or creeping up behind to lean on her shoulder and take a close-up of the couple during their vows. It's hard to look reverent when you're being used as a tripod.

Then there was Anna, visible in the church porch, her hand resting on Tinky's arm – who now appeared rather overawed by the occasion. Anna was calm, taking proceedings in her stride, catching her mother's eye and smiling. Tom turned to wave at his sister, then returned his attention to the dragons in his novel. Being allowed to read in church was a game changer and made for a much easier life with Tom. Clare had memories of her son's blood-curdling howls from beneath the pew in his earlier years, stretched full length and 'being a wolf'.

Susan made her entrance with her feathered purple hat in place. Clare had been right about the stylish headgear. She was escorted towards her seat by a strikingly tall and smiling young man, who had to be Fabian, the travel-writing brother. His curling blond hair gave him a leonine look as he scanned the congregation. She was surprised when Susan lingered at their pew, greeting David. And even more so when Susan smiled and leaned towards her.

'Clare, just a little request on the quiet. I do hope you don't mind.'

Tom's unerring instinct for anything of a covert nature kicked into action. He looked up and stared.

Fortunately, Susan did not notice. 'Athena mentioned you saw that tricky moment up at the house earlier and I just wanted to reassure you that everything's fine now. But, if you could keep an eye out for any difficulties, I'd be so grateful. Thank you, Clare.'

Susan moved on with a benign smile in place, kissing the pregnant woman a few rows in front.

'What difficulties, Mum?' asked Tom, all interest in his book gone. 'What happened up at the house? Is Anna in trouble?'

'No, I think there was a zip issue or something,' Clare improvised. 'And everyone's a bit nervous, I suppose. Super-mum to the rescue, if we face zippergate.'

Tom looked unconvinced, but perhaps realised he would

only be fobbed off further, as he shrugged and went back to his book.

'You've been put on high alert, then,' David murmured.

'So it seems, but I haven't a clue what for.'

Clare looked forward. Fabian was a handsome man, attentive to his mother and now kissing his aunt Celeste on each cheek, then stooping to envelop his cousin, Harriet, in a long bear hug. It was nice to see happy reunions.

A stillness came upon the church – the music stopped and the chatter calmed.

Then Fiona's clear clerical voice cut through the quiet, saying, 'Would you please stand.'

The procession began. Clare realised she was relieved, and slightly surprised, that Jess and her dad had entered the church. The wedding was on.

CHAPTER 5

A late arrival strolled from the car park towards the church. He could hear music coming from inside. Singing. All those cheerful voices, happy without him.

He didn't like any of them. Politicos. Out for themselves. Marriage — what a joke. Family — another joke, whatever people liked to pretend.

Why he had been invited to this sham baffled him. He knew he wasn't really welcome. Did they want to rub in how much he didn't belong, and never had?

Tristan had been in two minds about coming, but maybe a bit of light relief would be on offer: some family amusement, perhaps. He could always stir things up a bit. He toyed with the idea of entering the church, calling out an impediment or something. But he couldn't be arsed. Actually, if truth be told, he felt uneasy about messing with a church service. Messing with God. It was probably better to keep his options open there.

Looking around the churchyard, he noticed a grave with fresh flowers by the headstone — someone still remembered and honoured when they were thirty years gone. Tristan's gaze travelled along the row. He was surprised by the familiarity of some of the surnames and the simple tributes – *Remembered with love*. He wondered what might be on his dad's stone, or if he even had one. His dad's service had been at a crem. And Tristan hadn't gone. Why fake it? His dad was nothing to him.

Tristan noticed a group heading up the path. A stooped older man, some women and younger people: bell-ringers. He wanted to avoid them; he knew they would sit on the benches in the churchyard for a while before heading up in the tower to the ringing chamber, to ring out for the bride and groom. Martin's grandad had been a ringer, he remembered that. Tower captain. He'd offered to teach Tristan to ring. He was probably long gone, so he didn't need to worry about seeing him.

Tristan did not want to meet any of them. Was it shyness he felt, or contempt of small talk? Either way, being recognised did not appeal.

He headed off, threading through the graves to the far gate. He'd join the horses in the field beyond and sit by the river awhile. He'd done that as a kid.

The river curved invitingly through the meadow, green banked. A couple of horses methodically cropped the grass nearby, with a rhythmic soundtrack of tearing turf and crunching jaws. Two others stood beneath a spreading oak. They stood head to tail, flicking flies off one another periodically, with lowered heads.

It was getting warmer. Tristan took off his jacket and sat down. It was peaceful here by the water. He'd forgotten how much he liked this spot. He liked the clarity of the stream, the sight of reeds and stones on its bed and the patterns the current made on its surface. Harriet had once shown him sketches likening plaited hair to the flow of water. He'd been dismissive, told her how pretentious she was – but he remembered those drawings when sitting here. He'd been jealous of her talent, those intricate drawings sharp in his mind even to this day.

He used to sit in the church sometimes too, with no one else around. No one marking him out as the interloper. In the quietness of the old stones, he had felt most at home. Welcomed, even.

He'd had a heavy night. Maybe it was time to rest a bit. One of the horses moved across the grass to the others sheltering under the branches of the tree. There was a bit of a fracas, and it moved off again. It dipped its head and began to graze, tugging faster at the grass. He heard the hum of some distant traffic, some birdsong. He had some deals to clinch and scores to settle, but they could wait. He lay back on the sweet-smelling grass and closed his eyes against the sunlight.

CHAPTER 6

'Mum, someone's dead in the field.' Tom was pointing at the dark-haired figure lying supine on the grass.

After the service finished, Clare and Tom had made their way over to the meadow adjoining the churchyard. Tom wanted to explore, after being cooped up in church for the ceremony.

'Tom, get a grip. He's asleep or sunbathing. Don't disturb him.'

But the figure moved, rolled over and raised his tousled head to stare at her, then abruptly shut his eyes again.

Clare was greeted by a horse who strolled towards her, presenting his neck to be scratched. She gave it her full attention, wishing she had a carrot, or a Polo at least. It had been a while since she'd stroked a soft horse nose or ruffled a mane. She liked the smell and the huff of exhaled breath as the horse reached its head to nuzzle her.

She paused as Tom accosted the stranger.

'Hi. I thought you were dead,' Tom said to the man, who was now lying on his stomach, face averted.

'Not yet,' said the man, his face buried in the grass. 'Give it time.'

'What would you like on your gravestone?'

'Bastard. Sorry, probably shouldn't swear in front of a kid your age.'

Tom grinned. 'Mum wouldn't allow that word. The archdeacon would kill her. She swears sometimes too. But not if she thinks Anna or I can hear. And not in church. She works there – she's a vicar. Once, the stonemason brought the permission form for signing after he'd already cut the words on a gravestone. It didn't say a "B" word, but there was something else on it wrong. The archdeacon got very worked up about it. Do you like horses?'

'I like peace and quiet,' he said, decidedly.

'I do. In Cornwall, Anna, that's my sister, and I go riding every year. There's a pony called Jasper that fell down a tin mine and survived. I usually ride Nugget – he has to have suncream on his nose because it's pink and he could burn. Anna's eleven. She's too big for Nugget now, but I still ride him. I'm nine, but tall for my age. When I was little, I sat on Perran, but she went crazy. Mum lifted me off, and Perran galloped away across the field.' Tom spun round to look behind him, as if following the action.

'I rode ponies here, years ago,' the man countered. 'The girls didn't want me to, but I did.'

Clare came closer, worried Tom might be annoying the stranger. 'Hi. Sorry we disturbed your peace.' She paused a little distance away, looking down at him.

'That's OK. I should be getting going, anyway. Are you the vicar? For the wedding?'

'I'm Clare, Tom's mum. We're here for the wedding, but I'm not doing it – our parish is miles away, in Kent. We're just having a break during the photos.'

She sat and eased her feet from her shoes, pressing the grass down and enjoying the cool texture on her toes. Tom moved towards the stream, watching the flow of water and movement of the reeds. Spotting the twist of a fish, he rolled up his trousers to paddle.

'Your son asked what I wanted on my headstone. Cheerful kid.'

'I heard. He's spent too much time in churchyards – sorry. He thought you were dead, too, not dozing. His cousins have watched *Game of Thrones* and told him about it: Red Wedding deaths, and all that.'

The man sat up abruptly. 'Do you hear confessions, then, Vicar? There are plenty of people here with lots to tell you, if so.'

'That's not surprising. We all have things we regret; I know I do. Why do you ask? Is there something you want to talk about?' She hoped he'd feel free to do so.

'There's nothing to be said. But I like the church. The peace there. And by this river, too.'

While Tom waded and poked at the bank and water's depths with a stick, the two strangers sat together. At first they were quiet, but then Tristan began to talk. He told Clare something of his story: about feeling separate from his family but returning today; about not caring. He spoke about his father, now dead.

The horses moved closer from beneath the trees. One ventured towards Tom and stooped to drink from the stream.

While Clare listened, she was not afraid of this troubled man's words or the strength of his feelings. She wanted him to be able to talk – to feel safe to do so.

But then he stopped, just as suddenly as he had begun. He seemed unused to being so open. 'Thanks, Vic. See you later – I'm off, now.' He got to his feet and scooped up his jacket, briskly brushing down his trousers with his hands. 'Don't fall in,' he called to Tom.

Clare watched him go, then turned her attention to her son, relieved that there was a spare pair of trousers in the car for him. She prayed for the wounded young man, for his healing. He was ill at ease about returning to his family at Greenwood, that much was clear, and he was damaged – as well as being potentially damaging.

CHAPTER 7

Thinking that politeness required a return to the guests assembled in the churchyard, Clare made her way back there from the peaceful meadow, while Tom loitered some way behind her.

Coming through the gate, Clare saw Jess standing alone. The bride had pushed her veil back further, enjoying the sun on her face and a moment of relaxation after the service. Her white dress was an elegant sheath of draped silk, simple and close fitting, showing off her strong body. It cascaded behind her in layers of fabric, making up her train. She held her bouquet of golden and yellow flowers down by her side, at ease.

The ceremony was over, and all was well. Clare was glad to see Jess looking so serene, taking a moment away from the throng. The photographer was still busy organising more photos of various family members and other groups in front of the church doorway as the bells rang out in celebration. Clare didn't want to disturb the bride's moment of peace, so paused beside a yew tree, unnoticed.

Jess continued a little way further up the path while others were being summoned into position by the photographer. When she saw Tristan approaching, her demeanour changed:

her body tightened, her bouquet was no longer held loosely by her side, but was gripped in front of her, as if in defence.

'Why are you here? You weren't in the church.' She seemed shocked to see him and spoke accusingly. Tristan joined her in standing beside one of the nearby graves, while Ahmed chatted with his ushers and some guests near the church porch. Clare wanted to hear what Jess and Tristan were saying, but also didn't want to be caught eavesdropping.

'Charmed to see you, too, and in such finery, Jess.' Tristan seemed to be teasing her, at least at first. 'The bride amongst the corpses and headstones, like a gothic horror movie. Push the lids off their coffins, perhaps some skeletons will crawl out.' Clare winced at this. 'You look very lovely, Jess, and I'm only here to make sure our arrangement is still in place and to wish you a happy ever after and all that.' Jess stood stock still, glaring at him.

The photographer interrupted, calling for Jess to join the bridesmaids and some other guests who were waiting to pose in front of the floral archway and weathered stones. As she walked over, Ahmed took his opportunity, moving across to where his bride had been standing.

'Tristan, a word?' The groom smiled pleasantly, raising his hand in greeting to some other guests. 'Lovely to see you!' he called to the distant group. He then turned his face to Tristan's and leaned over, speaking in a low voice. 'I hope there won't be any problems today, Tristan. I want you to understand this: leave Jess alone. OK?' Clare had never heard Ahmed sound so serious.

'Oooooh, aren't you scary,' declared Tristan, all mock horror.

Ahmed reached for him and clutched his arm.

'Ahmed!' Susan called, cheerfully summoning her new son-in-law back to wedding mode, bright and breezy. 'More photos, please.'

Some of the guests were turning to look, half aware of something going on.

Ahmed stepped back. 'Sorry, I got distracted – on my way.'

Rufus, eager to please Susan, quickly took Ahmed's place beside Tristan. Clare moved nearer too, wanting to hear this conversation. Why had Ahmed been warning Tristan off, and what was the story behind those barbed comments Tristan made to Jess? Clare didn't envy young Rufus trying to smooth things over.

'Well, my old mate Woof-Woof,' Tristan declared, adjusting his jacket. 'Long time no see. Learned to say your *R*s yet, Woofy?'

It seemed that Tristan had found a welcome distraction. Then he noticed Tom standing hesitantly by the hedge and shouted to him, 'Tom, come here, kiddo. This is Rufus.'

Tom approached, curious, and Clare stepped forward to rejoin her son. She thought Tom would notice that Rufus looked uncomfortable, and that Tristan was no longer quite as friendly and funny as he had been in the field by the stream.

'Rufus and I had a great time at school, but shhh, don't tell anyone, will you? Not your mum, or anyone.' Tristan turned and nodded towards Clare, smiling. 'Just between us, mate.'

Tom was uncertain how to respond, then looked beyond Tristan to the man heading their way, relieved to see him. 'Hi, Dad.'

'Tom, you look like you've had a close encounter with the

stream. I think Mum put some spare clothes for you in the car.' In an unspoken agreement with Clare, her husband continued, 'Why don't you go with her to find them, get yourself dry.'

David turned to Rufus. 'I hear that you're interested in Home Office work.' He smiled pleasantly, then turned to Tristan. 'And I think you're another of Jess's family – Tristan, is it? Were you in the field with a stream?'

Clare was relieved that David was easing the tension in his courteous and calm way. Tristan shifted his pose from taunting troublemaker to a witty wedding guest with anecdotes to share. As Clare walked away, he was describing his encounter with Tom and how he'd been reminded of his visits to Greenwood years ago, when he had been about Tom's age or a bit older. Meanwhile, Rufus had gathered himself and stood taller. The flush in his cheeks subsided.

Clare paused to see where Anna was and to tell her where they were going, but her daughter was busy posing for yet more bridesmaid photos, so Clare simply shepherded Tom on towards the car park. Tristan had sauntered away from David and Rufus now too, calling out that he was going to explore some old haunts.

Jim, their host, was wheeling himself over to intercept his nephew before he reached another group of guests. Susan had obviously alerted her husband to Tristan's exchange with Ahmed, and the control operation was in place. Clare had sensed a ferocity in the father of the bride today, and wondered what he might say to his nephew to avert any problem developing.

Rufus was still determinedly engaging David in conversation, so she reckoned her husband would be subjected to a lengthy discussion of strategy in the effective use of special advisers, particularly in respect of any increase in Susan's team once she reached Cabinet level. Lucky him.

However the particular family or political dynamics might unfold, Clare was concerned about Tristan. He seemed like a troubled man and this was a family with complicated undercurrents. Several looked set to spill over before the festivities were finished.

Tom did not share her disquiet; he'd remembered the cheese-and-onion crisps that had been left in the car and asked if he could have some, or a chocolate biscuit from the secret stash in her overnight bag. Maybe not so secret.

CHAPTER 8

Sunlight reflected off glasses of Prosecco and silver trays as guests milled around on the lawns of the grand house, with drinks in hand. Brightly patterned frocks with coordinating hats and shoes were admired, the joyful occasion discussed and the happiness of the bride and groom remarked upon, together with the beauty of the service. The smiling and laughter as guests greeted one another were a celebration of love and life together, the community gladdened.

'You did so well, darling.' Clare was proud of her daughter's poise and maturity.

'Mum, did you see Athena lifting Tinky off the dress?'

'Yes, I think we all did. Well done for getting Trixie off her train, too.'

The image was a memorable one: Jess's head had suddenly been yanked backwards. In their enthusiasm, Tinky and Trixie had followed her too closely and pinned her long veil and dress to the floor with their feet. Both David and Tom had been stifling giggles. Clare had focused on smiling at her daughter as Anna's glance flicked over to her, anxious about the hiatus.

Anna could relax now, with the service over and photos

taken. She could also relinquish her role as Tinky and Trixie's supervisor, for a while at least – it was time for their harassed dad to take a turn.

Anna picked at her floral bouquet. Some of the marigolds needed rearranging. 'Mum, why was Jess crying earlier?' She sounded anxious.

'When was that?'

'After you left, when Susan was all stressy, Athena came back to our room and she and Susan went off together. I went to the loo and I could hear Jess crying. Now she looks happy, but she sounded awful.' Anna stood close enough to lean against her mother.

'I don't know why. People do get stressed on their wedding day.'

'Her dad got really angry. He was shouting at her mum later, too. Downstairs. Trixie and Tinky didn't hear, but the rest of us did.'

'That sounds grim. Were you OK?' Clare put her arm across her daughter's shoulders.

'I didn't want Trixie and Tinky to hear. Suki distracted them on purpose. Athena was back with Jess, I think. I feel sorry for Susan; Jim sounded scary.'

Clare hugged her daughter. 'Well done with it all. Sorry you had to listen to all that.'

'It's OK. Jess is fine now. She and Ahmed are happy, aren't they?'

They certainly looked so. Against a backdrop of yellow and blood-red roses and colourful banks of begonias, Ahmed stood next to his wife, his hand gently on her arm. Jess smiled at her husband and laughed at something Fatima said. Fatima seemed to be commenting on the bridal gown, or perhaps the veil, which was so finely embroidered and matched the exact length of the train.

'Did Tom really fall in a river?' Anna continued. 'He said he had to swim for his life.'

'I'm sorry to say it wasn't that exciting.'

'He said he met someone who spent ages talking to you. Tom said the man wanted to stop hating everyone so much.'

Once again, she marvelled at her children's capacity to overhear a conversation while seeming to be absorbed in something entirely different.

'Really? What else did Tom say?'

'He said that Ahmed was going to fight the man. But that Dad stopped them and sent Tom away.'

'Well, I don't think it was quite like that. I wish Tom hadn't heard about the Red Wedding. He's expecting all sorts of fights today, I think.'

'He's sitting with Tinky and Trixie and me at a separate table. There'll probably be a fight there.' Anna nodded, as one experienced in such things.

'Do you want a whistle? I think it will be OK. Jess has got goody bags for all the guests, and I think the ones for you guys have some great stuff in them. Tom will be busy with whatever is in his.'

'For about ten seconds. Who's the lady with the bright dress?'

'That's Celeste: she's Jess's aunt. She's fun. Come and meet her.'

They joined Celeste, whose chuckling laughter was audible across the crowded garden. Celeste immediately engaged

Anna in conversation, discussing the relative merits of various *Dr Who* actors.

'Don't you find some episodes quite scary?' Anna asked.

'Yes, darling, but I have a glass of sherry to give me
courage.'

Smiling at them, Clare turned to Harriet, who stood a little
apart, observing the clusters of guests. She was much quieter
than her mother. Perhaps she was used to Celeste making
enough noise for both of them.

'Anna's enjoying meeting your mother.' Clare liked Harriet's
subtle dolphin-shaped earrings.

'Yes, it's nice to see them having a good time.'

'I think I saw some of your work in the house: a sketch of
Jess sitting in a window?'

'Is that still inside?' Harriet's freckled face was alert. 'That
was years ago. Jess was about the age your Anna is now.'

'They change so fast – she's started at secondary school
already.'

'Yes, but characters stay the same,' Harriet said. 'Jess was
always fun, very sporty and kind. Your Anna would be a great
subject for a portrait, by the way.' She tilted her head towards
the young bridesmaid.

'She'd love that. What an amazing setting this is – it's so
beautiful.' Clare waved her hand towards the sloping stretch
of grass and staked-out marquees, encircled by trees and further walled gardens.

'An Eden,' Harriet replied, 'with the occasional serpent.
But, you're right, it's beautiful. Perfect, with the greens of the
trees and all the colours of everyone's clothes.'

Martin the gardener joined them. He was eager to engage

Harriet in conversation. They had shared childhood memories, Clare realised.

As the social groups interwove, Clare found David, who was being subjected to more of Rufus's self-promotion and still managed to look fascinated, which was deeply impressive. Her husband's reserves of patience were extraordinary. Athena was with them and she stemmed Rufus by greeting Clare and suggesting they stroll over and watch Tom and Trixie as they played giant Jenga, closer to the marquees. Fatima was there with one of Ahmed's aunts, offering the children encouragement.

'Your son has a steady hand,' Fatima said to Clare. 'Perhaps he'll make a surgeon one day, like Ahmed.'

'That would be good,' Clare replied. She noticed there was no sign of Tristan on the lawn, so the bride's provocative cousin couldn't vex her now. Her father looked relaxed, too. The tension that Clare had sensed earlier, and the anger that Anna had overheard, was no longer apparent as Jim laughed and chatted with Ahmed's family and other guests.

Fiona, the vicar, joined their group, having completed the formalities at church. Clare congratulated her on the service and the aplomb with which she had awaited Jess's arrival at the altar, despite her progress up the aisle being hampered by the bridesmaids.

'I'm just relieved nothing else untoward happened,' confided Fiona. 'No political protests.'

'Were you expecting some?'

'Well, I know Susan gets plenty of hate mail, and there have been some concerns about today. Her views on reforming education raised plenty of opposition, and the refugee policies are even worse. So, protests were possible.'

'That makes sense,' mused Clare. 'Jim seemed determined that everything should go smoothly.'

'Jim is certainly determined—' Fiona broke off as Fabian joined them.

'Two vicars together! Lovely to see you, Fiona – beautiful service.' He extended his hands in greeting as he congratulated her.

'Fabian, great to see you, too. I'm sorry Peter isn't able to be here. This young man goes here, there and everywhere, Clare, and is about to do a travel TV series, if I've heard correctly?' Fiona spoke in a similarly congratulatory tone.

Fabian raised his arms in mock amazement. He commented on the village's ever-impressive grapevine and explained that the series deal was not yet officially signed and sealed. As they talked about possible episodes and adventures, Fabian entertained them with stories of his travels in Nepal that year, near where Jess and David had first met, and the earthquake that had made his bed feel like a trampoline for several long unnerving minutes.

'I think I read your article about the Palio di Siena,' offered Clare. 'I loved it. You made everything about the race and experience so exciting. But, when I tried to find it again before we went on holiday to Siena, I couldn't track it down online.'

The urbane Fabian seemed wrong-footed, and then continued more smoothly, explaining that there had been some issues with the website.

'The Palio was amazing,' Clare continued. 'Do you know it, Fiona?' She described the early-morning practice event they had attended, the young horses skittish, ridden bareback around the dipping and curving campo at the centre of the

Italian city, in preparation for the race itself, a tradition from medieval times.

Anna had been horrified at the risk to the horses on the dangerous turns of the course and at the brutality of the jockeys – the crowd's fervour overriding concern for the animals' safety.

Different areas, or *contrade*, in Siena had fierce centuries-long rivalries and competed against one another with total passion. Clare's family had supported the *contrada* with a scallop shell as its symbol, simply because they had parked their car at a gateway in that section of the city and then walked through streets festooned with dark blue flags decorated with the shell insignia.

Clare recalled Fabian's writing giving a vivid sense of the communal experience of the Palio. He'd been embedded with a *contrada* throughout the process: the selection of horses by lottery; the jockeys employed by each area of the city; the prayers and shared meals on long tables in the streets; the wheeling and dealing, accusations, bitter enmities and alliances; the passionate recriminations and celebrations; and the crushing experience of defeat.

'Were you living with the dolphin *contrada*?' Clare asked. 'I think they are the big rivals of the shell one?'

'Yes – although, it was a while ago; I get them mixed up,' Fabian explained. He asked where else in Italy Clare and her family had explored, and whether they had made it to Assisi, or Spoleto, maybe.

'Which horse won when you were there?' Tom suddenly enquired from his side, having abandoned Jenga.

'Gosh, that's a question,' countered Fabian.

'I can check on Mum's phone, if you like,' Tom offered, helpfully. 'I think dolphin have the most victories; next is forest and the dragon.'

'Thanks, Tom – great offer. Maybe later,' Fabian murmured.

Clare was bemused by Fabian's attempts to deflect her son and came to his rescue. 'Tom, Fabian is planning a telly series of travel programmes. Where do you think he should go, if he can go anywhere?'

'The moon would be good. But you'd have to train as an astronaut to do that.' Tom was enthusiastic at the prospect.

'That might be fun,' said Fiona. 'I'd love to know what it's like up there.'

Fabian excused himself, saying he needed to check out the seating plan.

Clare thought it more likely that he was keen to avoid Tom's investigative skills. The bride's brother was not eager to have his Palio memories scrutinised by her son, that was certain. She wondered why he was so cagey about it.

CHAPTER 9

Jess, with her love of all kinds of sports, had remembered the children's enthusiasm for the Palio race in Siena. In the goody bags on their chairs were flags of the various *contrade*, along with other things to play with and do, including a stopwatch, sticker book and a disposable camera for each of them.

'I want Jess to organise my life for me,' Clare said to Fiona as they took their seats at an elegantly set circular table near to the smaller one where the children were gathered. She welcomed the opportunity to sit down.

Across their table, Clare was pleased to see that David's seat would be a little closer to the young ones than hers, and that he would also have Celeste next to him, knowing he would enjoy her company. Harriet, the artist, would be with them too; her place was next to Clare's.

The atmosphere in the marquee was convivial. Clare was glad to be sitting quietly with Fiona. The other vicar was easy company. Both clergywomen were content to leave conversational courtesies for a while and watch some of the livelier guests in their glamorous outfits. Anna and Tom were now cheerfully occupied using their disposable cameras. Clare hoped the flashes wouldn't annoy anyone.

She loved weddings, and it was so relaxing not to be the officiant today. Clare had enjoyed her own marriage service so much, too, despite wondering sometimes about the wedding she never had. Best not to dwell on that; even years later, those memories could still be surprisingly painful.

She had returned her first wedding dress to the shop, unworn. Actually, her mother had taken it back on her behalf; the prospect of revisiting the bridal shop and receiving sympathy from the kind women there had felt unbearable.

She had been naïve during that first engagement, and heartbroken at being betrayed. Her trust in her fiancé was shattered, her joyful expectations of their future together exposed as nothing more than wishful idealism. She thanked God for David's integrity and steadfastness; she had been so fortunate to meet him, and to be loved by him.

Her first fiancé had been all promises and show; he was the popular and extroverted ordinand studying alongside her at theological college, their match a marriage made in heaven, apparently. Less heavenly was the discovery that he had fallen for the overly sweet and softly spoken theology student who sat beside him in doctrine lectures, and who had gradually eclipsed Clare's charms. While her fiancé dallied with this other woman, Clare had been oblivious. She'd been busy with her New Testament dissertation, their wedding preparations well underway, along with discussions with the diocese about their curacies in adjoining parishes.

The break-up, when it finally came, had been agony. But she had recovered, and she had thrived. And, eventually, she had met David.

She watched as her husband finished a conversation with the

genial Fabian and made his way over to the table. Susan and Jim were lavish in their hospitality. Bottles of wine encircled a tower of flowers and foliage on each table, and cooled bottles of water glistened with condensation.

Harriet's company required some effort. She was stiff-backed as she found her place beside Clare. Only gradually did she warm to Clare's attempts at gentle conversation. She had been to Italy many times and could remember discovering Venice as a child and loving it.

'My parents were still together then,' Harriet eventually volunteered. After checking across the table to see that her mother was engrossed in conversation with David, her voice became animated: 'Venice's magic felt like a fairytale, prelapsarian experience. We counted the lions – the statues, on doorbells, crockery, flags – and our total reached several hundred. We visited Torcello and played football with another family there. I loved it, seeing the glass-blowers in Murano, too. Dad bought me a glass horse. Later, it got broken. Well . . . someone deliberately broke it, actually.' She bit her lower lip and shook her head, as if to dismiss that destruction from her mind, returning to the subject of the islands in the Venetian lagoon.

Italian memories lifted the atmosphere between the women, as well as talk of crime novels set there.

'I have quite a crush on Brunetti,' said Clare. 'Do you know him – from Donna Leon's series?'

'Of course.' Harriet smiled. 'I want to be Paola, despite all the cooking.' She leaned across to her mother, interrupting Celeste's flow of conversation with David. 'Mum, Clare reads Donna Leon, too.'

'Of course, darling,' Celeste replied. 'Clare has excellent taste in detectives. I suspect her husband is one, or a spy – but he isn't telling. I shall continue to interrogate him.'

Harriet turned back to Clare. 'Sorry, I think your husband is getting the full onslaught of my mother.'

The best man invited everyone to stand and welcome the bride and groom. This was followed by applause from every table and cheers from more enthusiastic guests, a shuffle of chairs, and benign smiles as Jess and Ahmed navigated their way to their seats.

'I think David is having a great time next to your mother and he'll love hearing about her travels. Your family contains several globetrotters, what with Fabian's adventures too.'

Harriet took another mouthful of wine before replying. 'Yes, but let's not dwell too much on Fabian's Italian escapades.'

Clare wanted to discuss nothing else, but made herself change the topic back to Harriet's experience of Italy and art.

It was Harriet herself who returned to the topic of Fabian. 'I think art must be truthful, whether it's a portrait or a TV series. But we make mistakes, don't we? And does that then corrupt all our later work?'

'What sort of mistakes?' Clare asked.

'Well, supposing a writer like Fabian exaggerated a story, or even fabricated it, to meet a deadline, or whatever. Should that undermine all his future work?'

The conversation was interrupted by a solicitous waiter checking that Harriet was happy with her vegetarian option. Clare had realised that ecological issues mattered to her neighbour – Harriet and Anna were kindred spirits about those. Fiona leaned over to ask Harriet about her current work. She wondered whether she would undertake commissions to paint politicians, and whether a portrait of Susan might be an idea.

'Uncle Jim would kill me if I got it wrong or did something he didn't like.'

'What, like Clementine Churchill burning that portrait of her husband?'

'Exactly, or maybe Jim would take it out on me, not the picture.' She smiled wryly, and the other women did too, sharing in the acknowledgement of Jim's capacity for fury.

'Is it that we don't want to see how others see us?' Fiona continued. 'As a portrait artist, you are reframing us, or the self-image which we curate, perhaps.'

There was a loud crash. Conversation halted, and all eyes turned to a figure standing and holding a microphone aloft.

'Sorry, guys,' announced Tristan. 'There's a problem with the speaker. Sound systems, eh? Before the official speeches, I want to congratulate Susan and Jim for a spiffing party.' He bowed in their direction.

Jim looked venomously at Tristan, while other guests looked on indulgently, with slight confusion at this interruption to their meal.

'I would like to say,' Tristan continued, 'congratulations, one and all.' He swigged dramatically from a wine bottle in his other hand, while still gripping the microphone. 'Congratulations one and all on this happy occasion. On great careers, too. Full marks there, Jess, Ahmed — and you too, Rufus. Who'd have thought it? You're doing well for yourself.'

A feeling of unease grew as everyone sat watching Tristan

gesticulate with the bottle in his hand, pointing it at Athena's boyfriend, the would-be special adviser.

'And Aunt Susan, of course,' he turned with a flourish towards her, 'our political star. What a fabulous day. Our great families. Hi, sis, long time no see. Hope you don't mind that I'm here.' He gestured towards Harriet, who sat immobile and slightly hunched forward, as if to stomach a blow. 'Happy families. Isn't it marvellous?'

David moved to stand beside Tristan. He smiled at him, touching his arm gently.

'Oh, hello,' announced Tristan. 'A bouncer. Sorry, everyone . . . Fabian, great to see you back here, from wherever you've been. OK, I'll stop. Bye for now.'

Tristan surrendered the microphone to David and was steered from the marquee. There was an exhalation of breath as people turned to their neighbours. Conversations, for the most part, were politely resumed, like water covering a stone lobbed into a pond, resettling as if nothing had happened. A few conversations were now focused on who that inebriated young man might be, or what that was all about.

'What a piece of work he is,' said Harriet, her hands splayed on the table in front of her, as if to steady her nerves.

'That was awkward,' countered Clare. 'Difficult issues, and wine never helps.'

'It helps me,' Harriet muttered as she picked up her glass.

'Sorry, yes, you're right. And all families have issues. Mine can be a bit of a soap opera.'

'I know you're trying to help, but some families are more like soap operas than others,' said Harriet, fiercely. 'Tristan is my half-brother. We don't see each other often.'

'Mum, is he OK?' Tom had appeared. 'Anna says he's pissed.'

'Accurate, I think, although I would probably say "tipsy" rather than "pissed".'

'You said Dad was pissed,' said Tom triumphantly, 'and you said that you were, too, after all that Pimm's in the garden.'

'Thanks. Very helpful reminders, Tom. This is Harriet — she likes Italy, too.'

'Mum's trying to change the subject,' Tom commented to Anna, who had joined them.

'Why did you leave me with the monsters?' Anna said, in a tone of accusation. 'Mum, Tom keeps leaving me with T and T while he goes off to take photos.'

'T and T?'

'Trouble and Tosser. Or Truculent.'

'Great word, truculent, but perhaps not kind to name-call?'

'Entirely appropriate, from what I've seen,' offered Harriet.

'I see more food heading for your table, guys,' Clare announced, also relieved to see her husband making his way back to his seat.

Celeste greeted him like a returning hero.

'No trouble,' David said dismissively. 'Tristan has gone for a walk to clear his head a bit.'

'He needs more than a walk to achieve that — maybe a custodial sentence might help,' Celeste exclaimed. 'You were magnificent, David, in a situation fraught with danger.' She then continued to itemise Tristan's shortcomings and probable criminal tendencies.

Harriet spoke more quietly to Clare. 'My half-brother isn't a monster, whatever my mum says. Difficult, unpredictable, and he can be a bully, but he's not a monster. My mum hasn't forgiven him for existing. Sometimes, I'm not sure I have either.'

Clare thought this might all relate to the 'difficult time' which Celeste had spoken about with such passion earlier in the day. Perhaps Tristan was the potential guest whose presence she had feared – it seemed likely.

'It was an awkward speech,' Clare replied. 'I had a more pleasant chat with Tristan earlier, by the river.'

'Where he and Martin nearly killed each other as kids?' Harriet spoke crisply, her eyes bright.

'Oh, well, I'm not sure about that. But it's a lovely spot, with beautiful horses in the field. Tom paddled while the photos were being taken.'

'Your two get on OK, don't they?'

'So far, so good . . . today.'

'Families. Well, if that's the most disruption Tristan causes, we'll have escaped quite lightly.' Harriet took another long drink from her wine glass. 'It was an embarrassing moment, sure – but we'll get over it. Mum rather enjoyed it, I think. Jim won't be happy, though. He still looks furious, but Aunt Susan continues to glow, as politicians must. The show must go on, and we all want a good day for Jess and Ahmed.'

'Of course. And, apart from the odd blip, we're on course for that.'

Clare wondered where Tristan might have gone and who would keep an eye on him, as the reception continued without his presence. Hungry guests tucked into the late lunch of minted lamb or mushroom risotto. She hoped he would sober up enough to rejoin the gathering and be able to enjoy being included in the day in some way. And she would like to talk to him again, if she had the chance.

Clare caught David's eye. He raised his eyebrows at her before turning to give his full attention back to Celeste and her ongoing tales of awkward moments at weddings. These were clearly numerous.

Harriet was now politely directing questions to the man seated on her right. He had a pattern of broken veins across his nose that were interspersed with blotches and pimples. Clare thought the artist might be wishing she had some charcoal to hand for a quick sketch.

Across the marquee, Clare noticed the bobbing feathers on Susan's purple hat, tilted towards her neighbour, Ahmed's uncle. They looked like senior versions of the bride and groom, having reached the pinnacles of their respective careers. Although didn't Susan have further to climb? Into the Cabinet, no less, if she could continue to impress the PM sufficiently.

Fabian stood behind his mother, then leaned his blond head forward to say something discreetly to her. Clare had noticed Fabian was solicitous towards Harriet, and hoped his good-humoured kindness might alleviate some of the pain from Tristan's barbs. Further down the table, Jim was watching his wife and son intently, grim-faced – it was best that Tristan kept well clear of his uncle.

CHAPTER 10

Later in the afternoon, Clare headed up to the house to retrieve a cardigan that Anna had left there. The grass on the lawn felt springy beneath her feet, and the air outside the marquee was cooler. As she crossed the paving stones of the terrace, she saw Susan and Athena huddled together inside – some crisis at hand.

Athena nodded, in agreement or submission to her boss, and moved off, stabbing at her phone. The minister's special adviser must have secreted her mobile in her bridesmaid's dress somewhere. Clare was intrigued. Did her underwear include a mobile-phone holder?

Guests had handed in their phones to ensure no unsuitable photos or posts could be made during the ceremony or reception, but David and Susan's team had been exempted from the phone prohibition. Clare had kept hers too; she wouldn't take photos or post anything, but she wanted to be able to check for updates about a parishioner who was gravely ill.

When Susan noticed Clare approaching, a smile immediately spread across her features. 'Clare, how can I help?'

'Sorry to interrupt you, Susan. I'm just on my way to collect Anna's cardigan.'

'Your daughter's a star; she's been a darling with the little ones today.'

'She's thoroughly enjoying herself.' Clare was relieved that Anna had done so well, but she judged it wiser not to allude to her daughter's entertaining nicknames for Tinky and Trixie.

'I'm sorry the children witnessed my nephew's performance earlier. Athena is dealing with it,' Susan said.

'Tristan?'

'Thank God your David walked him out of the marquee. Everyone needs a David, and an Athena. And a Martin. He's gone to walk with Tristan until reinforcements arrive.' Susan abruptly sat on one of the patterned sofas, removed a shoe and bent forward to massage her foot. 'Let's take a moment, Clare. Just a quick sit-down. If you're with me – that's allowed for the host, isn't it? Attending to a guest?'

Clare sat too and said nothing, inclining her head towards Susan.

'My husband will be angry,' Susan continued. 'Somehow, it will be all my fault. I only wanted peace in the family. You understand that, of course. We thought it was an opportunity to include Tristan, especially now that his father is gone. He was Jim's brother.'

'Weddings can be intense, with family difficulties bubbling up, but how nice Tristan was included,' said Clare, sympathising with her weary host. Susan might seem to have everything sorted, but things could still be difficult, even for her.

'I just can't afford to have a loose cannon shooting his mouth off like that. Poor Jess. All that sarcasm from him about happy families. Athena will have to head off any press sniffing for skeletons in my closet.'

'I don't think Tristan said anything specific,' Clare commented. 'He just seemed a bit the worse for wear.'

'That's naïve, Clare. Phones will start buzzing – messages heading out of here, with sharks sniffing blood in the water and searching for more.'

'Your rivals . . . or scandalmongers?'

'Both. Some bright spark with a nose for a story will be stalking Tristan right now, and others will be sniffing for dirt. We've tried to limit it, but if they can find a photo of me or Jess looking dishevelled and secretive, so much the better. I'm sorry, Clare, I don't mean to burden you with this.' Susan removed her hat and ran her fingers through her gleaming hair. 'Perhaps I'm the worse for wear, too.'

'No problem, Susan. It sounds tough.'

'Well, I'm tough too.' Susan put her shoes back on and arched her back. 'Athena is tackling the story, Martin is tracking Tristan and we carry on. That's it.'

Audience over, Susan stood and sallied forth, towards the celebrations.

Clare was relieved to have a pause in the confidences and conversations. She took her time finding Anna's cardigan and wandered through the quiet rooms, taking the opportunity to look around the house and half wondering where the cat might be.

She envied the enormous kitchen and adjoining boot room containing racks of muddied wellies and baskets piled high with hats, scarves and gloves. There was also a separate utility room with plenty of space for gardening clothes and straw hats to be hung. There were some fine panamas. A traditional Sussex trug containing secateurs and gardening gloves was on the sideboard, next to a metal toolbox. There was even a separate walk-in larder. Clare loved her rectory, but Greenwood House was something else.

Another whole room seemed to be a storage place for sporting equipment: on the floor was an unzipped holdall spilling over with shin pads, padded goalie gloves and a half-deflated football. Badminton netting and rackets lay on top of the wooden croquet box, while shelves around the room held rosettes, riding hats and a collection of sporting trophies. Clearly the family's leisure pursuits were varied.

The downstairs loo was larger than the rectory's family bathroom, and contained a shower unit too. There was a choice of Baylis and Harding handwash options; Clare chose the sea kelp and peppermint, having sniffed and rejected the sweet mandarin and grapefruit option, as well as the dark amber and fig. These soaps would cover your five a day.

She wasn't going to venture into the other bedrooms – that would be too nosy, even for her – but she checked the rooms where the bridesmaids had dressed. There was no sign of the cat, but Anna's cardigan was neatly folded up on the window seat.

As she made her way across the landing, Clare was discomfited by a photo on the bookcase at the top of the stairs, which she hadn't noticed before. Jess and a group of young friends were pictured in front of a London skyline. David featured amongst them and had his arm around a short girl with golden hair. Clare knew exactly who that was: a former girlfriend, from years ago. She hoped Anna hadn't seen this.

The lovely Jackie was now a police officer, apparently, and a rising star of the force no doubt, not that Clare cared. Well, not much. She'd never even met her. David had seen her at some conference recently and declined her offer of dinner. Clare would rather her daughter didn't ask about this other woman, or why her dad had his arm so easily draped around her. Cow.

Clare found she wanted to leave the house and rejoin the party. That invitation to dinner still troubled her; surely it was clear that David was off limits?

Heading back towards the sails of the marquee, she saw the two youngest bridesmaids wielding croquet mallets, playing intently with Suki and a taller woman with braided hair. Seeing those energetic sisters with mallets in hand, she was relieved that, given Jess and Ahmed were both doctors, several medics would be available to tend to any injuries.

Other guests had also left the tent and were strolling across the grass. Some were watching as band members arrived carrying their instruments. Tom was with the friendly Labrador, who seemed to wander at will. Two young men were looking up, pointing.

'Look, Mum!' Tom appeared beside her, his arm outstretched.

The word *Congratulations* was printed on a banner trailing across the sky, pulled along behind a light aircraft, now circling above them in broad loops. Then, on the other side of the banner, was emblazoned *Refugees have families, too.*

Fabian was with Tom. Looking skyward, he muttered to Clare, 'My dad is going to want to shoot that plane down.'

A new banner unfurled: *Remember the Dover Four.*

'Dad will want to nuke it, now.' He walked away.

'Who are the Dover Four?' queried Tom, his brow furrowed.

'They were four young adults who were deported by the government,' Clare explained, 'and now they've gone missing.'

'What has that got to do with today?'

'Susan's disgusting government policies, that's what,' Anna announced, joining them. 'And Dad couldn't stop her, could he, Mum?'

'That's right,' said Clare, 'but it's also grim for Jess and Ahmed to have this stunt pulled at their wedding.'

'But what about the Dover Four, Mum?' Anna asked, her voice getting louder. 'Don't you wonder what "missing" really means?'

Clare felt proud of her daughter's passion for justice, while simultaneously hoping she wasn't being overheard.

Before Clare could answer, Rufus accosted her. 'I'm looking for your husband. We need to deal with this. We were warned something like this might happen.'

'Who warned you?' asked Tom. But he was ignored by Rufus, who was now brimming with self-importance.

Rufus moved off abruptly, dissatisfied by Clare's silence and her lack of indignant fury, perhaps.

'Let's go inside and get some cake,' Clare suggested. 'I think they may be cutting it soon.'

'I'm not going anywhere, thanks, Marie Antoinette,' said Anna. 'I'm watching the plane. Don't worry, Mum, I won't cheer for it. But we should do.'

Clare handed her daughter the errant cardigan. Was she eleven or fifteen? What might lie ahead if Anna already had this kind of capacity for sniffing out injustice and hypocrisy?

'I want to watch it, too.' Tom's jaw was as firmly set as his sister's. As he spoke, the plane circled twice more, then headed off, its trailing banners fluttering as they shrank into the distance.

As she joined the groups of guests returning to the tent, Clare spotted Harriet in conversation with Tristan. They were standing between the canvas awning and the flowering border edging the lawn, where the marquee team had tucked away some unused coils of rope and a stack of wooden pegs. She hoped that things were going well between the half-siblings; she thought Tristan probably yearned for better relationships with his family, and perhaps Harriet did, too.

The other guests were taking final glances up before drifting back inside, towards their tables, but Harriet and Tristan seemed unaware of the ripples of questions and explanations, the fingers pointing skywards and mutterings of concern.

It was indeed time to cut the cake. The photographer was at the ready, but the groom had gone missing. Jess stood holding a large knife, with her mother beside her. Clearly their agreed approach to the plane stunt was to ignore it completely – or maybe Jess didn't even know it had happened.

The cake was iced in scarlet and purple; swirls of colour dripped artfully from layer to layer. Ushers had been dispatched to search for the groom, and Rufus, presumably, was searching for a rocket launcher to bring the plane down. Clare spotted Anna making her way back into the marquee, excitement over the plane having dwindled, but Tom was nowhere to be seen. Perhaps he'd found David, unless Rufus had already got her husband involved in Operation Planegate.

Suki seemed to be reassuring her mother that Ahmed would

rejoin them soon. Clare noticed Suki's elegant earrings, their sparkle matching the beads on her dress. Fatima held her patterned shawl around herself in the cooling air. She kept glancing over to Susan and Jim, taking the measure of their seemingly patient veneer.

Clare made a comment to Fatima about the cake and its elaborate decoration, and Suki joined in the chat with enthusiasm. The show would go on.

Anna marvelled at the intricate icing – tiny stethoscopes and scalpels entwined with foliage decorated the base of each layer – and she and Clare mused over what symbols others might choose for their own cakes. Suki suggested her mother would have a briefcase, a rack of dry cleaning and a computer garlanded with marigolds. She said her father's choice would have been a model railway and cookbooks. Anna thought her mother would have a Bible alongside a pot of red nail varnish and maybe a horse. Clare thought about suggesting chocolate and a vibrator, but mentioned neither.

Where had Ahmed got to? Hopefully he and Tristan had not crossed paths. And where was Tom? It wasn't like him to miss cake.

CHAPTER 11

DCI Jackie Carter had known the call would come one day. A blast from the past – that kind voice warmly saying her name. She just hadn't anticipated it being because of a political protest, slogans waving over a wedding.

'David. Good to hear from you. We were aware of the wedding and the VIPs in attendance. There were some mutterings about possible protests, but we hadn't got wind of anything concrete.' Jackie smoothed the lapels of her grey jacket, then took notes as David updated her.

There was little time for chit-chat, and, anyway, she had kept herself informed of his life – cosy vicarage, children and all. Smug vicar, too, swanning about with David in tow. She hadn't expected David to fall for one of those religious types.

Jackie's day had begun early, as usual. As soon as she woke, she'd checked her phone for any updates on her open cases, had a brisk shower, and then she was good to go. It was useful that her golden hair was kept cropped short. She liked a streamlined look and it was so much easier to maintain. She didn't have much time to think about clothes, so she had a uniform of sorts, though she rarely needed to don her official one these days. She always wore a sharp jacket, trousers and a decent pair of trainers or boots, depending on the season.

She enjoyed the drive to work along the bypass. She loved her car, a BMW, which she had spent years of her savings on. She slowed to navigate the streets, pausing at the usual junctions and preparing herself for the day ahead. She preferred to get in before the rest of her team, or most of them anyway. Everyone knew she was not to be messed with. She was fair, and she got results.

She'd left her partner slumbering; his own shift patterns were complex and he was easy-going about her intense schedule. They had been together for five years. There wasn't an earth-shattering passion between them, but it was an efficient arrangement: a shared home, utilities and food bills. They lived congenially enough alongside one another, and they both prioritised cleanliness and lack of clutter. Their kitchen, with its empty white surfaces and easy-wipe fittings, had the air of an operating theatre, which was exactly how she liked it.

Sometimes Jackie wondered whether an aversion to mess was a sound basis for a long-term relationship, whether enthusiasm for cleanliness equalled compatibility. But fastidiousness was not all that they shared; every so often they enjoyed partaking in drama-series binges, sex and expensive holidays. It was all good. It worked for them both.

She often thought about David. She'd wonder what he was doing, whether he would like her car, what he thought of a new TV programme – and if he was watching it too. She'd loved him and had been able to be completely herself around him. It had been hard to let him go and she didn't realise what she'd lost until it was gone – isn't that how the saying goes?

Anyway, after a long day of managing targets and reviews at the station, she was now liaising with him about the protest. She'd send someone over to the likeliest airfield to interview the pilot on landing. Obliging the local MP and Home Office minister was all part of the job. Maybe she would go herself to report to David and the minister in person. She patted her neat hair and almost smiled in satisfaction that her old flame would see her, sleek and smart as ever. If she saw Susan Zetland, there might even be an opportunity to mention those amendments to the policing bill – who knew?

She remembered that David had been friendly with the minister's daughter. Jackie had even met her, years back. David had always been more sociable than her; being with him had involved meeting lots of people, all over the place. They'd done Glastonbury together, and a trip around the Greek islands. They'd also planned to do the Turkish coast one day, but that never happened. David was the one who got away.

She wondered if he'd aged much – it was hard to tell from photos. A memory surfaced of the feel of her hand on his stomach and the dark line of hair going down from his navel. She had seen him a few years back at a counter-terrorism conference. He'd been guarded, but friendly enough, though he'd turned down her invite to dinner. The vicar clearly had him on a leash – dog-collared, no doubt. It was only dinner, so what was his problem? Not that she was bitter.

DCI Carter summoned her sidekick and headed for the door.

CHAPTER 12

Clare sat as the other guests milled around, waiting for Ahmed to return. The tables had been cleared of crockery and cutlery. Only the scattered menus, place cards and glasses remained, haphazardly arranged around the floral centrepieces. She was without company as Fiona and her military husband had headed home after the meal and Anna had also left the tent.

Clare had liked sitting with Harriet, prickly as the younger woman was. This family was a complex mix of personality, privilege and pain: Jim's forcefulness, Susan's political challenges and distress at her husband's wrath, not to mention Fabian's professional vulnerabilities – he'd certainly been uncomfortable about that disappearing article.

It wasn't surprising that Harriet was on edge, being back here with her cousins again, with her unpredictable brother, or half-brother, here too. But perhaps the relationship between Harriet and Tristan could improve. Their conversation outside the marquee had seemed promising.

As Clare looked around, she was bidding blessings upon them all, in this tangle of fractured relationships and tension. Blessings on the family, on the guests, the unhappy Tristan, the protestors and those impacted by the government's cruel refugee policy – everyone. On Jess and Ahmed, too.

Fatima exclaimed in relief as her son reappeared, arms aloft, ready to join Jess in cutting the cake, accompanied by a triumphant Rufus.

'Found him!' Rufus hurrahed. 'Here's the missing groom!'

Ahmed moved to Jess and kissed her, quickly taking the cake knife and brandishing it with panache. 'Ready to dismember our cake?'

Clare rejoined Fatima and the others crowding around the couple, as the chatter swelled again. Together, the newly-weds plunged the knife into the top layer, prompting a surge of applause from the circle around them. Athena held her phone up to capture the moment, but Clare's was still in her bag, left on her chair.

Anna reappeared, trailed by Trixie, who was whimpering half-heartedly. 'Mum, Trixie tripped on a croquet hoop.'

'Ouch, that sounds sore,' Clare sympathised. 'Let's take a look.'

She took Trixie to sit down for a rest and some pampering. A drink of water, a little bit of attention and some cake soon revived her. Leading Anna by the hand, the girl trotted back for another croquet game, the lawn now illuminated by light from the marquee.

'I rang the police about the plane,' David said, sitting himself down beside Clare. She smiled at him; he always knew what should be done and did it. 'Jackie Carter is the regional officer here nowadays: small world.'

Clare's smile became an artifice, as she attempted to give a measured response to this news. 'Lovely,' was her clipped reply. She knew David had loved that woman and wondered what feelings might remain.

'But there's no need to do anything more on that front today,' David reassured her, obviously glad to have managed that territory OK.

There was always an awkwardness around the subject of Jackie, and Clare avoided telling him why. She was embarrassed by the lingering impact of her own broken engagement, and the way she was so unsettled by any thought of David being with someone else, even if that had been before he'd even met her.

'If you'd married Jackie, you'd have had better wine at your wedding, maybe a marquee like this: the whole hog.' She couldn't stop herself.

'Better wine. Wrong wife. No contest.' At least he was trying to get it right. But he wasn't succeeding.

'Who said there was a contest?' Clare bristled. 'Life's not a competition.'

'Clearly—'

David's reply was interrupted as Celeste plumped herself down beside him, offering plates laden with cake and lumps of icing.

'I insist on a dance later. But, before that – cake.' She puffed out a breath, noisily.

'Cake and dancing . . . Fabulous.' Clare's smile widened. 'How are you doing, Celeste?'

'Well, darling, weddings make me teary.' She leaned across David towards Clare. 'I was betrayed by my husband, you see. Jim's brother, Max. You never know what's beneath the surface, do you? Well, you're OK, Clare, you've got the gorgeous

David, who would never betray you. But my husband excelled himself there.'

'I'm sorry. Harriet mentioned something about it.' Now wasn't the time to bring up her own experience of heartbreak, before she met David. Clare listened carefully.

'It was traumatic for her. Tristan was twelve. For all those years, her cunning father had been living a double life. Playing at being Mr Happy Family with Harriet and me, and all the while sneaking off to his other woman, and Tristan, too. It still shocks me that it ever could have happened.'

Celeste's voice faltered. Two sympathetic listeners and the whole occasion were bringing her anger and sorrow to the surface.

'We never came here to Greenwood as a family again. Susan and Jim were kind, but so shocked. Jim was furious with his brother. Harriet came back sometimes on visits with her dad, and she met the ghastly Tristan. What a shameful performance with that impromptu speech today. More fool Susan for inviting him, or maybe it was Jim playing happy families, or trying to. What Jim wants, Jim gets. He's abrasive, but he can be loyal, too. I've not visited here for years, but he's been good to me, and to Harriet.'

Celeste poured more wine into the glass nearest to her, as Clare and David sat attentive and still.

'Tristan leaves a trail of slime wherever he goes. Harriet has some sympathy for him – a poor, unwanted boy, unacknowledged and hidden away – but that's all crap. Excuse my language.' She pursed her lips.

'How was he hidden?' David asked.

Celeste steamed on: 'When his mother inconveniently died,

my errant husband had to come clean, presenting me with his homeless twelve-year-old son to accommodate. Or not. Poor, faithless Max: he'd got away with it for twelve years, then all hell broke loose.'

'It sounds incredibly difficult.' Clare refilled her own glass.

Celeste gestured towards Jess and Ahmed, who were now on the dance floor. 'I just hope their future is a happy one. Jess was always kind to Harriet. Fabian, too. None of them liked Tristan.'

That boy, grieving for his mother . . . for his lost home: Clare's heart went out to him across the years. The interloper, disliked and unwelcome. His father's life splintered by the news of his existence; his father's happiness lost because of Tristan's presence, despite the attempts to conceal that stark fact.

There'd been no room for Tristan in the nest. That much was obvious, as Celeste continued to unburden herself.

Tristan was dispatched to boarding school, coming back only for holidays in the city flat that his father had rented after Celeste threw him out, or for brief stays at Greenwood with Jim and Susan and their children, who loathed him. Harriet was sometimes there too – hating him, pitying him and perhaps fearing him.

Celeste had not been the only one wounded in all this. As Clare listened to the chronicling of events, she wondered how Tristan's day was going and where he was now, as the wedding celebrations continued without him.

CHAPTER 13

Ahmed's long arms encircled his wife as the newly-weds rotated to the music. They were ringed by smiling family and friends, the day a joyful success.

The band struck up a fresh tune and, when the drums kicked in for Queen's 'Don't Stop Me Now', the seated guests surged to join those already beginning to twist and twirl on the dance floor, their arms up and voices raised to join the singers.

Clare saw Anna jigging with Fabian, as Celeste and David joined the throng. She would have a boogie with Tom, if she could see him. Perhaps he was off with the dog somewhere. Suki and Fatima were dancing in a trio with Susan, then Athena and Rufus joined them. Rufus was keeping an eye on how his rhythms were being observed, as he made jerking stabs in the air.

As Clare watched, she caught Jim's eye. He manoeuvred himself to her side as she shifted her seat slightly to accommodate his wheelchair. He nodded at the dancers: a buxom woman laughing as a young man strutted body-popping moves beside her.

'They're having a good time, I think?' Jim half shouted.

'It's been a great day – thank you, Jim.' She could tell their host needed to hear that.

'I'm trying not to think about the plane nonsense. Jess wasn't bothered about it, and that's what matters.' He turned to address Harriet as she eased herself back beside Clare, leaving Fabian and the others behind on the dance floor. 'How are you enjoying yourself?'

Harriet duly obliged her uncle with a brief, polite response, which was difficult to hear with the volume of the pounding music.

Jim continued, more loudly, 'Tristan was making some nonsense, but David smoothed everything over. And Tristan is family, after all. I'm sorry your dad is no longer with us, Harriet. I'm missing him today.' He wiped his mouth with the back of his hand.

Clare watched Harriet struggling to find another appropriate answer, so chimed in herself: 'Did you and Harriet's dad grow up locally, Jim?'

'Not at all. We were city kids, from Bristol. The country life was all Susan. Her parents had a big place near Bridport.'

'I wonder if Jess and Ahmed will head down this way to live, too?'

'I'd like that. Susan's in London so much of the time, though, and I'm there too for work sometimes, so we'll see lots of them either way. Harriet,' he leaned across Clare towards her, 'I wanted to ask you about a portrait of Susan, if you could fit that commission in?'

'Thanks, Uncle Jim. I'll think about it,' Harriet said, fiddling with an earring.

'We can fix dates, now that the wedding is over.'

'I imagine you get lots of requests, Harriet,' commented Clare, noticing Harriet's discomfort. 'Have you got many projects underway?'

'I'm doing a series of mother–daughter portraits. I liked the way you and Anna stood together after the service. I wish I'd taken a photo; it would have been a good fit for the series.'

'Sorted, then.' Jim lifted a glass. 'Jess and Susan together, the medic and the Cabinet minister. Soon to be, anyway.'

There was a rumpus on the dance floor. A body on the ground. Some dancers halted, startled, while others bounced on unaware. An enthusiastic guest had slipped and was being helped to a nearby table, attended by Susan and others. Ice was procured, wrapped in a tea towel.

Ahmed was summoned from the dance floor. He crouched down and talked calmly to the woman, who was looking pale, her arm floppy and misshapen. Ahmed counselled a trip to A & E, and a sober friend was identified as a willing driver and escort.

Jim said approvingly to Clare, 'Ahmed knows what he's doing. I know I'm not the easiest husband. I'm glad Jess has landed a good one.'

The music's volume increased, and Clare was content to nod in his direction and smile. No sensible answer could be yelled over the noise. Even Celeste did not attempt conversation as she returned to the table, fanning herself with a menu card and seating herself next to Jim.

Clare noticed with relief that Tom had returned to the tent and replaced Celeste as his dad's dance partner. She was feeling wearied by the wedding family's dynamics and moved to join her husband and son, flinging herself into the dance in a way that made David smile and Tom goggle his eyes at her, but with a grin. She'd had enough of smoothing over other people's family issues for a little while; it was time to have some fun with her lot.

The dance floor pulsed, circles formed and spun, and energy ebbed and flowed. Every so often, people took a rest at various tables – removed their tight shoes, commandeered fresh glasses and attempted half-heard conversations – before returning to the throng. Some left the tent to watch the stars beginning to glisten in the darkening sky, while others lit cigarettes that glowed more brightly as the evening deepened.

Groups giggled en route to the loos, or to explore the tennis courts or the magnificent tree house festooned with fairy lights, while some people rested silently on the cool grass beneath spreading trees.

Tinky and Trixie went homeward – marshalled to their car. Their mouths were sticky with cake, and their dresses chronicled the day's adventures – grass rolling, nail-varnish experiments and all. Tom was content to dance on, with interludes of playing a game on his dad's phone. He went outside with the dog again, too, whose name, he informed his mum, was Monty. Clare was pleased to see the stocky Labrador at his side as he left the marquee.

Eventually, Clare decided to track Anna down. Her daughter had disappeared for a while, and soon it would be time to head off to their hotel. Darkness had thickened outside the marquee and the children would be tired tomorrow. They had all been having a great time as the party got going. What a wedding to remember, and a fine hotel breakfast lay ahead in the morning, too. There was no morning service for her to take, so perhaps a Sunday morning lie-in would be possible. But first, she had to gather up the children so they could say their farewells.

Clare headed for the lawns, dispatching Tom back to his father to wait inside the tent and then searching on for Anna. There was no sign of her in the queue for the loos. Perhaps she'd headed up to the house. Skirting the back of the kitchen tent, Clare remembered the tree house, which they had marvelled at earlier in the warmth of the afternoon. Maybe Anna had joined some other people returning there. Harriet had spoken of it and the whole place with great affection.

As Clare approached the trees, she thought she could make out Harriet illuminated ahead, climbing up the steep stairs into the lit playhouse above. Then her phone beeped, so she extracted it from the depths of her bag and checked the message, but there was no more news from the family of the parishioner who was so unwell. Hopefully he'd have a peaceful night. She'd visit on Monday. Now, she needed to find Anna; was she in the tree house?

'Harriet?' Clare called, as she mounted the twisting steps encircling the tree trunk. 'I'm looking for Anna. Have you got her hidden away up there?' She clambered on up, wheezing slightly, breathless from a night's dancing. 'Amazing place, this. Brilliant, isn't it? Let's all build a tree house or move in here and refuse to leave.'

CHAPTER 14

Clare stopped at the entrance. What was she seeing? The dark-haired man was slumped on the floor. Harriet knelt beside him, her face stricken. She was holding something that was protruding from him.

'It's Trist-Tristan,' Harriet stuttered. 'My brother. My half-brother. God, he's . . . he's . . .' A sudden rush of vomit, of shock and grief, followed.

Clare moved across to crouch beside Harriet and hold her. Her face was clammy and her body was shaking. Gently, Clare eased Harriet's arm away from Tristan's body and embraced her.

'There . . . OK, OK . . . It's OK,' said Clare, wanting to help and comfort. But it wasn't OK. It was anything but.

As Harriet leaned into her, Clare was looking over at the stilled man, the body – Tristan. She could see the knife embedded in him, now that Harriet had let go of it. She could see the blood. She knew the smell of it. He lay twisted, turned away from the women, very still. Very dead. His dark hair was across his face. It looked damp, unkempt – but what did that matter now?

'Harriet, here, I've got you.' Keep calm, keep calm – we need help. Where's Anna? Where's David?

She stroked Harriet as if she was an infant, holding herself as steady as all her training and experience had taught her. Hold steady; be rooted in love in all the craziness, whatever comes.

It wasn't easy when she wanted to shriek too. Clare felt her own fear and nausea, but her voice shook only a little when she spoke: 'Harriet, I'm going to call David on my phone. He'll get us some help. It's OK.'

Thank God for the sounds of the band masking Harriet's sobs, as she curled herself against Clare, childlike in grief. Clare's fingers were none too steady as she reached for her phone and jabbed at her husband's number.

'David. It's an emergency. I'm up in the tree house . . . behind the marquee. Harriet is here – the artist from our table. She's in shock. David, there's a body here – and he's been stabbed. I don't want to leave. Where's Anna?'

As David responded, the urgency of the situation hit Clare; when she spoke again, her voice was more insistent. He had to find Anna and Tom and keep them away from here. 'Yes, call the police. And make sure you find Tom and Anna.' She would wait here with Harriet, but he must keep their children away and safe. They mustn't see this.

Harriet sat up and began to rub at her soiled dress. She ran her fingers through her hair and wiped her face with her arm.

'Tristan,' Harriet said. 'I hadn't seen him for years until today. What a mess. You've heard the story. Everyone has. I can't believe it. Why was he here? He was always trouble. But now he's dead, Clare. Someone has killed my brother.'

CHAPTER 15

Harriet couldn't stop shaking. Clare held her steady, looking at the marks in the planks that made up the tree-house floor: swirls and thinly striped lines, like contours on a map. For now, her place was here, with inarticulate prayers for help, for peace for this murdered man, for Harriet, for all of them. Her focus was on those swirling lines, those patterns, and how to help Harriet, while thinking about how to shield Anna and Tom from this horror.

All must be brought to light: Celeste's fear of her husband's son; Jess's tension and rage; Ahmed's skirmish with Tristan; the things Tristan had said to her after the ceremony when they met in the field, with Tom there too – which felt like decades ago. What was David telling Tom? Where was Anna now? Her thoughts were spiralling – this must be the shock.

'I hated him.' Harriet spoke in a monotone. 'He was vile. Cruel to me. To Jess. To Fabian too, sometimes. To Martin. All of us kids.'

'Kids can be very cruel.' Clare sat still, wanting to encourage Harriet to talk.

'He was hurt, too. He lost his home . . . his mum.' Harriet stared at her brother's corpse and spoke slowly, as if discovering her feelings for the first time. 'Dad loved me better. I know Tristan knew that.'

'It sounds complicated.'

'It was actually very simple: I hated him. But sometimes I've felt sorry for him. And we talked today, just a bit.'

'You felt sorry for him sometimes?'

'He hadn't got anyone. Not really. Not after Dad died, and not even before then.'

'Maybe that was why Jim and Susan invited him today?' Clare kept her voice low.

'That was about the money, I think.'

'The money?'

'Jim and Susan are the executors of Dad's will: trustees. They're sorting the money until Tristan and I inherit. It's all set out.'

'I see.'

'Tristan gets nothing now.' Harriet was still, not trembling anymore. 'I get it all.'

Clare shifted her legs slightly. They were stiffening, and she loosened her hold on Harriet. 'You inherit everything?'

'Mum will be pleased. She hated him too, you know. We all did. Everyone was allowed to hate Tristan. He seemed to encourage it.' Harriet fell silent and stillness settled over them, the women as immobile as the corpse.

Beyond the tree-house cocoon, the music had hushed and some voices were raised. Noises of the movement of guests, disruption and disturbance, followed by the beginnings of order and organisation. Was that Rufus barking an instruction? Or Jim? It sounded as if Susan was speaking into a phone somewhere beneath them, or maybe it was to Athena.

Then David was calling up to her. 'Clare, it's me. Jackie is on her way.'

Jackie, thought Clare. I thought I prayed for help.

'Who's Jackie?' Harriet asked, turning towards Clare, whey-faced.

'She's a police officer David knows.' Clare put her mother-voice on. 'She's great. She'll look after all this, don't worry.'

The two women sat with the darkness spooling a thickening web beyond the lighted tree house. And with Tristan's body cooling beside them.

CHAPTER 16

Brisk – that was the word. *Professional*, perhaps. *Bitch* was another possibility.

Jackie had certainly arrived.

Harriet and Clare were ushered away separately. Jackie had been there, scarcely deigning to engage with either woman. Instructions were being carried out by her under-lings, while she, very much the officer in charge, looked on, appraising the two dishevelled women as they emerged from the tree house.

DCI Carter's tone helped Clare stiffen her backbone. She eased into extreme graciousness mode, being sure to refer to Jackie by her correct title, slightly inclining her head to the shorter woman. David would recognise that as the weaponry it was. Beware Clare when she was ultra-deferential.

For some reason, Clare was prevented from having more than the briefest word with David, ascertaining that the chil-dren were already collected and gone. His star of a sister, Gill, had arrived to take them.

Jackie and her acolytes had established a base for them-selves inside the house, documenting guests' details before dispatching them. At least Anna and Tom had escaped with their aunt, and Tinky and Trixie had left even earlier, thank God.

Clare was waiting in the large sitting room, as instructed. It felt like a lifetime ago she had sat in here with Susan, commenting on Tristan's drunken ramblings.

Susan was here now, crumpled, quiet and dazed. Jess and Ahmed were side by side on the sofa, looking devastated. Suki sat with them, her head against the wall, her eyes closed. She had a cardigan draped over her beaded dress and had removed her shoes; Clare noticed the darkened marks on her feet where her sandals had been strapped too tight. There were some magazines on the coffee table, with a discarded patterned shawl lying across them.

Clare was more concerned about Harriet than about Jackie's appearance on the scene. A larger inheritance, no longer to be split, seemed like a big fat motive to her. Where was Harriet now? Clare hoped someone was making her a hot drink and tending to her. She was obviously deeply shocked by the discovery of Tristan's body – Clare didn't feel too good herself.

Harriet had a financial motive, and she had been holding the knife. Had that been an instinctive reaction, an attempt to save her brother? Clare would have to tell Jackie and her crew about it; she didn't have a choice. But how could she explain her instinct that Harriet hadn't done this? Maybe it was more of a hope. She'd have to be honest about what she'd seen. But she didn't like the prospect of revealing something so incriminating.

Rufus seemed to have had some of his pomposity deflated. A meeker man than before, he asked if he could get Clare some tea, or something stronger. Grateful, she accepted the offer of coffee. She wanted to be warmed, to have her wits about her. She had cleaned herself up as best as she could.

Rufus and Athena were ferrying drinks to those in the sitting room and elsewhere in the big house. Most of the guests were being processed there, Rufus told her, or in the main marquee by a satellite group of officers: contact details recorded, any immediate observations taken down. He was happy to share what he knew with her, and with a surprising capacity to lower the volume of his commentary in the hushed room.

She thought David was perhaps with the team still in the marquee, or more likely liaising with Home Office colleagues. A murder at a junior minister's house was enough to rouse the press office, private office, every office. At least Clare's church services tomorrow were already being covered, but she would need to contact the churchwardens, to assure them that she and the family were all fine, before news of this leaked out and the parish drums began to beat in alarm.

Was she fine? No, of course not, but how she was doing did not feel particularly relevant, at this point. A young man was dead. She felt sick at heart, her chest ached. A young man who'd been chatting with Tom earlier. A young man who had watched the horses in the field with her. Abrasive, self-deprecating – wounded. His relationships unresolved, his sense of himself out of kilter – and now his life was extinguished. Destroyed. The evil of the killing, of someone actually pushing a knife into Tristan – forcing the blade in – overshadowed her. What sickness, what horror made such a grotesque action possible?

Clare was no stranger to wickedness, but the depth and

impact of this stunned her. Jess and Ahmed's joyful day had been smashed by grief and trauma.

She remembered to sip her coffee carefully, the liquid hot on her lips. Others were keeping their distance, she noticed. Perhaps no one wanted to know what she had seen. Perhaps they had been told not to talk. Everyone seemed remote. But maybe that was the shock.

She was detached, almost as if observing herself, sitting self-contained and cupping the mug of coffee with slightly tremulous hands. Fabian was next to his mother. There was no sign of Jim, nor of Harriet's mother, Celeste. Clare noticed Fatima was sitting on the window seat, her eyes fixed on her son. Ahmed's arm was around Jess's shoulders. Jess had changed her outfit. No more bridal gown.

Everything was different now. The day had changed from celebration to brutality. Clare felt grateful for the subdued stillness of the room, but became more perplexed by David's absence. What was going on? This was a murder enquiry. Where was the grit of V. I. Warshawski when you needed it? Or Kinsey Millhone? In her everyday life, she sometimes thought of them and their feistiness and drive. Now, she was in their world and needed their resolve.

Come on, Clare. Time to step up, say your prayers and do whatever needs to be done.

She noticed the police officer sitting unobtrusively beside the door to the hall. His presence perhaps accounted for the lack of conversation in the room, and also Rufus's lowered voice when he told her where other people were.

'Excuse me, I need the loo,' Clare said to no one in particular, and it was almost true.

Crossing the hallway to the cloakroom, she could hear Jim's voice from behind one of the closed doors – low and controlled. Celeste said something sharp and loud, but Clare could not hear the actual words, only the dismay. Then the library door opened, and Jim propelled himself out with a face of thunder. Celeste was continuing to remonstrate or protest at whoever was in the room with her. Jim moved fast across the hall, without acknowledging Clare, entering the sitting room which she had just left. Celeste emerged, escorted by David, who was leaning towards her but not touching her, even as she wept.

'Clare!' she cried. 'They've taken her away! She's gone.'

'What? Who?'

David's face was a picture of reassurance and calm, while Celeste's was smeared with grief and despair.

'Harriet. They've taken Harriet.' Celeste shuddered.

'It's simply procedure,' David interjected. 'They'll be looking after Harriet and going through some questions. And with you, too, Clare – with all of us. You've had such a shock, Celeste. Try not to worry.'

While her husband spoke, Clare embraced the older woman, absorbing her tears of rage and fear.

'Tristan has done this,' Celeste seethed. 'Even dead, he's destroying Harriet's life.'

Suddenly Clare was aware of the open door behind her. The police officer in there would presumably be memorising Celeste's words or noting them down.

'Celeste, I'm so sorry,' she said. 'Come, let's find you a seat.' She moved as if to steer Celeste back towards the privacy of the library, only to find David blocking the way.

'Let's go into the sitting room,' he said quietly.

So, this is how it is, Clare thought. Everything is different and this new world is full of hazards. Someone has murdered Tristan and it's Jackie's job to find out who that is and bring them to justice. We'll be watched, assessed and made accountable.

And David is on Jackie's team. He's part of the apparatus of officialdom as a Home Office senior civil servant.

Surreal as the day had been, surreal as the night was, Clare realised that things would only become more so. She dipped her head to avoid her husband's eye and guided Celeste to the sitting room, as directed.

Fatima was tearful but trying to conceal it, brushing the moisture from her face surreptitiously. Everyone was reacting in their own way to the craziness of tonight. Some dozed, others simply sat, silent. Fatima left the window seat and quietly asked Clare to step out onto the terrace with her for some air. That seemed to be allowed; most of them had given their initial interviews, now.

It was her interview that Fatima wanted to talk about. She thought Clare could advise her.

'I'm worried, Clare. And frightened.' Fatima was trembling as she spoke.

Clare sought to reassure her, asking how she could help and what the problem was.

Fatima composed herself, lowering her voice as she continued: 'When I spoke to the police officer, I was confused, and there are things I didn't tell them, things I kept quiet. What shall I do, Clare? If I change my story, they'll suspect me of something worse. It'll make me seem guilty.'

Clare did her best, saying that everyone understood the effects of shock and that the police would be used to people needing to clarify their statements. 'My memories feel unreliable too, in a way,' she said. 'I'm sure the police will understand that you need to correct or explain things a bit more, with whatever it is you want to tell them, and I'm sure it's best to do that.'

Clare itched to ask for more detail. But, as Fatima now seemed calmer and resolute, it wasn't fair to jeopardise that by probing unnecessarily.

The women were interrupted. The police officer opened the door to the terrace and invited them to rejoin the group inside.

'Of course.' Clare was all compliance. 'Sorry. We were just getting some air.' She might have added that she did realise there was air inside the house too, and she knew that this well-worn excuse for leaving the room was rather feeble. Instead, she smiled and thanked the officer for holding the door for them.

CHAPTER 17

Athena and Rufus continued as Susan's lieutenants, offering refreshment and attending to everyone's needs.

It was Athena who was mindful of Clare's grubby clothing and who thoughtfully suggested she might like to borrow something from Jess. Jess agreed and Athena went upstairs to find something suitable.

Clare donned the wrap dress in the downstairs loo and looked at herself in the mirror. She'd lathered her hands with the posh soap, but she'd need more than a whiff of sea kelp to clear her head of that night's memories.

She asked for help – prayed for clarity of mind and openness of heart in whatever else lay ahead for her. She tried to ground herself, taking some deep breaths while holding on to the basin with both hands, and repeated the prayer of her namesake, Clare of Assisi: 'May the Lord be with you always, and, wherever you are, may you always be with him.' Be with me. Help me. Keep me aware of what matters.

She splashed water on her face and patted herself dry, then took the smeared dress along to the utility room. Things had been rearranged in there; a bag of football gear was on the floor beside the washing machine, which had a heap of fencing gear lying across the top of it. She left her dress on the side, not wanting to disturb anything.

Further along the long corridor, Athena and Rufus were huddled together in what Clare remembered was the boot room. Athena had lost some of her composure; she was leaning against the doorway, then moved forward towards Rufus with some intensity. Clare wished she could hear what was being said. Whatever their conversation, it seemed to have shaken Athena.

She hesitated, then heard Suki approaching from the hallway, in search of her.

'Clare, thanks so much for helping my mum – you've put her mind at rest.'

'We're all questioning our memory of events. I know there are things I'd like to forget.' Flashbacks of Tristan's twisted body were all too vivid.

'I still can't believe that something like this happened at their wedding.' Suki shook her head. 'Poor Ahmed, and poor Jess. What a start to their marriage. We all wanted this day to feel so special for them, and Mum tried so hard to fit in with whatever they wanted.'

'In what way? I imagine some things were difficult.' Clare was sympathetic, but she also wanted to know what Suki's take on events was.

Suki grimaced. 'Let's just say my political views don't coincide with Susan's – I suspect that's no surprise to you. But we've not rocked the boat. We respect Ahmed's choices and support him. But what has he got himself into, joining this family, Clare? Sorry, I'm speaking out of turn, when all I wanted to do was thank you for your kindness to Mum.'

Suki moved to one side as Athena hastened along the corridor, passing them quickly with her face averted. Clare wanted to intercept her but was hesitant. Something had happened between the special adviser and her ambitious boyfriend, and Clare wanted to know what it was. What had Rufus told her? And why were the two of them loitering in that part of the house?

CHAPTER 18

Jackie was sure-footed. Things looked clear-cut. The half-sister. Financial gain. No love lost between them, to say the least. She was discovered with her hand on the knife. Motive and means sorted. Jackie could trust her team, on this one, to get the job done.

The sooner the case was wrapped up, the better. The Home Secretary's lot had been in touch, explaining that, of course, he could not interfere in any way, but that he had full confidence in them to execute a speedy investigation. No pressure, but a quick resolution would be welcome, of course. Yep, she'd got the message OK.

Jackie would interview Harriet herself, she decided. It was time to get on with it. David had been efficient and deferential, while she, as SIO, moved things forward. He had outlined a brief who's who, giving her a head start by telling her about the family and the key players. So, his friendship with Jess had survived – why not his relationship with her?

Susan had been cooperative, just as David had anticipated she would be, unlike her husband, who had glowered in a discomforting fashion. Jackie might have had him in the frame, if Harriet was not such an obvious prime suspect.

The interview at the station did not go well.

Harriet was obstinate and obstructive. 'Why are you asking me this? What are you assuming about me?'

Perhaps the short-cut option was not going to work; there seemed to be no prospect of a quick confession. Jackie opted for a more conciliatory approach, offering Harriet coffee and trying a reassuring tone.

'Harriet, this is a difficult time for you. We appreciate your cooperation. Can you tell me about your relationship with Tristan?' She leaned forward slightly, trying to build rapport with Harriet, who sat opposite her across the table.

'Why?' Harriet's face was impassive. She clutched her hands together on her lap.

'We want to have a fuller picture of the victim and his relationships.'

'I don't know much about his relationships.'

'Did you see Tristan at the wedding?'

'Everyone saw him. He made a speech.' Harriet faltered, remembering.

'Tell me about that.' It was like getting blood from a stone.

'Anyone can tell you about that. He said stuff about con-gratulating Jess and Ahmed. Thanking Susan and Jim. Stuff about happy families. It was awful.'

'Is your family a happy one?'

'One of us has just been murdered. I'm not wildly happy.' She looked as if she might cry. Jackie noted how she bit her lip, perhaps to try to stop herself doing so.

'Did you often meet up with Tristan?' She was going to try a different tack.

'No. Not at all. He kept separate from me and my mum.' Harriet lifted a hand and twisted one of her earrings.

'And from your cousin, Jess, and her parents?'

'I thought so. I was surprised he was invited to the wedding.'

'Why was he invited?'

'I think Jim and Susan wanted to improve things, maybe.'

'Why was that?' Jackie's voice was interested, without being unduly pressurising.

'I think they were in touch because of the will. My dad's will.'

Jackie was careful not to lean forward or demonstrate any quickening of interest. 'Your dad's will?'

Harriet looked directly at Jackie. Perhaps she realised that Jackie already knew this information. She spoke slowly, with emphasis: 'Uncle Jim and Aunt Susan are executors. Tristan and I are the beneficiaries.'

'And if one of you predeceases the other?'

'Yes, I inherit the lot – if that is what you're asking?'

'Thanks for clarifying that.' Jackie looked down, before continuing, 'Now, tell me about your movements. When did you go into the tree house?'

'Well, the first time, I took Anna up there – one of the bridesmaids – earlier in the afternoon. She wanted to see it, and we found her brother already up there with Fabian and Ahmed. I think lots of people were exploring the grounds. When we came out, others were waiting to climb up the stairs.'

'And the second time?'

'I wanted to get away from everyone and have a break. The

music was loud and I didn't feel brilliant.' Her brow furrowed. 'I thought I'd be alone up there . . . but, as I climbed up, there was a sort of scrabbling noise.' As Harriet began to describe that moment, her face paled.

Jackie was relentless. 'A scrabbling noise?'

'Yes, I'm not sure. A sort of scuffle, maybe.'

'And what did you see?'

'I stopped on the steps – they're quite narrow. I didn't really want to go up anymore. But then it was so quiet, I thought maybe no one was there and I'd been mistaken.'

'And then?'

Harriet paused. The table in the interview room had been wiped clean, with only the faint trace of the ring of a mug next to her own mug of cooled coffee.

'Everything went into slow motion. Walking in and seeing Tristan there. He was twisted away from me, on the floor. His foot was at a funny angle.' She stopped.

'What did you do?'

'Nothing. Well, not at first. It didn't make any sense. Then I went over to him, and Clare came.'

'Yes. How do you know Clare?' Jackie was interested in the answer to this question for many reasons, but her demeanour betrayed no particular curiosity.

'I don't. Well, I didn't before today. She's Anna's mother. The bridesmaid. Her husband works with my aunt, Susan, and he's been friends with Jess for years. I'd not met them before today.'

'What did you do when Clare arrived?'

'I'm not sure. I think I was sick. She was kind to me.'

'Did you argue with Tristan, Harriet?'

'No.'

'Not at all? Were you glad to see him at the wedding?' The tempo of questions increased, and Jackie felt she was getting more out of Harriet now.

'No. I felt uncomfortable around him. He could be cruel.'

'In what way? Was he cruel to you?'

'Yes, when we were younger. He was unhappy, I realise that now, and he took it out on all of us.'

'"All of us"?'

'Everyone. Tristan wasn't an easy person to be around. But I can't believe this. Can't believe it. Do I have to talk to you now?'

'No, this is just to help us get a picture of events. Your cooperation is appreciated.'

'Can I go?'

'Of course. Remember, we'll be talking to other people to put together exactly what happened.' Jackie's professional tone sounded almost threatening. 'Tristan is dead. Our job is to establish who killed him.'

Jackie was surprised to find David waiting for her at the end of the corridor outside the interview room. He explained he was at the station to liaise with Susan and her team as necessary, and to update the Home Secretary if appropriate. He asked whether there was anything else he could do to assist her.

Jackie could think of plenty of things she would enjoy doing with David. But instead she thanked him with professional politeness. Having David around complicated things. This was a high-profile case. She wanted to excel, with no distractions.

'We'll be talking to everyone in the morning. Nothing else needs to happen tonight.' She paused. 'Everything you've told us has been helpful. Maybe you can give me a bit more of an idea of the family dynamics before we sign off for the day? Off the record. Let's get a coffee.'

David nodded and followed. She took him to another interview room, not to her office; she wanted to keep this impersonal. She asked for coffees to be brought to them, and they sat on grey, plastic chairs in the austere setting. David seemed at ease and was unexpectedly friendly.

'How are things for you here, Jackie?' He seemed genuinely interested, looking her in the eye. 'We talked about the family, but I didn't ask about you.'

'I'm fine, and glad to be on the case, thanks. It looks fairly straightforward, but I don't want to make any assumptions. However open and shut things may prove to be, we must examine all options. Your boss has been helpful, but her husband was less so. Do you have any thoughts on that? What was his relationship with his nephew like?'

David paused before responding, thoughtful as ever. 'I didn't see them interact, but my impression was that Jim was wary of him, and displeased when Tristan spoke to everyone at the reception. Jim wanted a good day for everyone, with no disruption. Clare mentioned there was some tension in the house earlier and that Jim was on edge, perhaps about the possibility of political protests.'

'Was Tristan involved in the plane stunt?'

'Not to my knowledge.' David looked disappointed not to have more information on that, shaking his head apologetically.

'What was your impression of Harriet?'

'Clare spoke to her more than I did. She seemed nervous, but relaxed more during the meal. Chatted quite a bit. Clare liked her.'

Jackie simply nodded at this and refrained from mentioning that Clare's approval did not disqualify someone from being guilty of murder. It was still early in the investigation, there was a way to go yet. It was good to be with David again, to establish a new friendship. But he was off-limits – those boundaries were clear.

They talked about Susan's work, what exactly Athena's role was as a special adviser, and what David had gleaned about Jess and Fabian's relationship with their murdered cousin. Jackie had work to do in investigating all the angles, but Harriet was squarely in the frame, whatever the vicar's view of her might be.

CHAPTER 19

Clare was sitting in the lobby of the hotel, with her book open but unread in her lap. It was very late. She had dozed off several times, her head falling forward and then snapping up when she woke.

She heard the police car draw up. All the hotel lights were still on, the front door unlocked and ajar. As she walked inside, her footsteps echoing on the stone floor, Harriet seemed surprised to see Clare. The lobby was otherwise empty.

'Hi.' Clare indicated at the glass on the table. 'There's a gin and tonic here, if you fancy one. Sorry . . . the ice has melted.'

'Thanks. Why did you stay up?'

'Didn't think I'd sleep. And I wanted to see how you were doing.'

'OK. It wasn't too bad. Well, actually, it was.' Harriet let her bag drop to the floor as she settled on the sofa opposite Clare. 'How are Jess and Ahmed? Is my mum OK?'

Clare decided not to mention the second exchange she had witnessed between Celeste and Jim.

'You're trying to justify the unjustifiable,' she had hissed downwards at her erstwhile brother-in-law. 'Wanting to play happy families. For what? Susan's career? Max's legacy? Well, your brother's legacy is a murdered son, and God only knows what's happening to our daughter right now.'

Jim had been surprisingly conciliatory — attending to Celeste, listening, apologising and offering her a room in the house if she preferred to stay there. It was nice to see him being so kind to her. Perhaps he was wary of her coinciding with any of the press pack who might be heading for the hotel bar to pick up leads on the story. The plane protest would be old news now; the murder offered fresh blood.

Clare explained how people had remained in the house for a while after Harriet had left, everyone stunned and taciturn. Finally, they'd headed for the hotel. Jess and Ahmed, too. It was so close to the house: only a couple of minutes' walk down the drive, if that. The newly-weds had apparently booked a room for the night anyway, before their planned departure for a honeymoon in the Lake District.

The hotel sofa was deep, with squashy brocaded cushions. Harriet sank back into them. 'This feels surreal, Clare. We both saw him, but I still don't believe it. He'd actually been civil to me earlier.'

'You don't believe Tristan was killed?'

'That level of hatred. Of violence . . .' Harriet tilted her head from side to side, slowly. 'People did hate him, though. My mum did. I did too, often. He made enemies all over. But to be killed?'

'I know. It's unthinkable. What did he say when you spoke to him?'

'It wasn't so bad. He wasn't vicious or anything. We talked about easier subjects. He asked about my painting and how that's going. I think he was glad to have missed the service, but said he'd liked the sound of the bells afterwards. We both managed to avoid anything too difficult. Well, he wasn't exactly complimentary about the family, but he wasn't horrible. Now this means I get all Dad's money. The police were on to that.' She edged forward and picked up the drink which Clare had kept for her, sipping it cautiously, then leaned back into the soft cushions again.

'I guess they'll be gathering lots of information.' Clare moved her book from her lap.

'Yes, and who cares about money? Actually, Tristan did. He tried to get some from me once, you know.'

'That sounds awkward.' Clare thought Harriet seemed very trusting, confiding in her so freely. Perhaps it was because of exhaustion, or the gin.

'He called me – I don't know how he got my number – said he knew stuff about my mum and that he'd go public unless I paid up. I told him to get stuffed and that, if he bothered my mum, he'd regret it.' Harriet sat up straight and looked at Clare. 'Why am I telling you all this?'

'Maybe it's the shock. And it can be a relief to talk.'

'But this stuff's so private, it feels wrong to say it out loud. I'm just so scared. Now I'm the only one inheriting, I know they'll think I did it.'

Clare sat still, showing no sign that, as she gleaned further information from Harriet, she was wondering whether they might be right.

CHAPTER 20

Next morning, the hotel staff had laid out a buffet breakfast and grouped the wedding party together in a conservatory area, well distanced from the other guests. The hot food was kept warm in large metal dishes with hinged lids, beside a tray of pastries and baskets containing miniature pots of jam and individually packaged rectangles of butter.

'Come and join the suspects!' Rufus hailed Clare cheerily, as she made her way towards those already eating and sipping their drinks.

Rufus had adopted his louder persona, while others had grown more tentative. His voice barrelled on with a running commentary on sausages, tomatoes and the delights of black pudding. Congealed blood was not so appealing to Clare right now, who headed for the cereals.

Celeste looked diminished, the scarlet and royal blue of her dress at odds with the pallor of her face. When Clare sat down beside her, instead of a spoken greeting, Celeste simply nodded. There was not much to say. Other than Rufus, people seemed overawed by the prospect of whatever the day ahead might hold.

Suki valiantly engaged Rufus in conversation about his

sporting interests, a subject he was content to explore for some time, while others sat chewing their meal, reflecting on more private concerns. Fatima was absorbed with her phone. There was no sign of the bride or groom.

Clare had already exchanged early-morning messages with her sister-in-law, who was happy to have Anna and Tom to stay and reported that they were well occupied with the household's new litter of Cavalier King Charles spaniels.

Athena was drinking from a large flask of coffee as she crossed the room to join Clare and Celeste. She was dressed for a day's work: no longer the attentive, lilac silk-clad brides-maid, but kitted out in a grey jacket and trousers. She smiled at them, professional but still friendly.

'Were you up early?' Clare enquired, Celeste remaining silent beside her. 'How are Susan and Jim doing?'

'Well, your David and the police are keeping the press at bay, but we needed to have statements to issue, and the plane incident received some coverage.'

'Of course . . . Susan's political career,' Celeste muttered. She spoke louder, directing her gaze at Athena with undis-guised hostility. 'Meanwhile, my daughter is under suspicion and her brother is dead.'

Without missing a beat, the special adviser looked calmly at Celeste and responded, 'It's a terrible situation and such a sad loss. I am sure the police will resolve things as soon as possible.'

Athena is quite an operator, Clare thought.

'By locking up my daughter? That seems to be the plan, so far.'

'I think we'll all be questioned,' offered Clare. 'This is such a tough situation, and so worrying for you, Celeste. Have you seen Harriet this morning?'

The room fell silent as Harriet entered. 'Talking about me?' she accosted Clare.

'Clare was telling me not to worry, darling.' Celeste looked flurried and spoke quickly. 'Come and sit – have something to eat. Weetabix? Some toast? I'm having a croissant.' She turned to Clare. 'Harriet's a vegetarian, you know.'

Harriet slid into a seat beside her mother. She apologised to Clare, saying she knew she was only trying to help. She murmured to her mother and Clare that worrying was inevitable. 'They'll think I did it because of the money.'

'Lots of people had reason to want Tristan gone, darling.' Celeste was resolute and raised her voice. 'He was trouble for lots of people. Wasn't he, Rufus? Tristan was a troublemaker, and I'm not afraid to say so.'

There was a clatter of metal as one of the serving spoons hit the floor. A scatter of mushrooms and globules of scrambled egg landed on the polished wood.

'Sorry.' Suki bent down to retrieve the spoon.

'Don't think I can be distracted,' Celeste continued in a lowered voice. 'Rufus . . . Jess . . . Ahmed – lots of people might have wanted Tristan gone. Fabian, his parents – the whole lot of them. I will not be silenced when my daughter is at risk.'

'Of course not, Celeste,' Clare said. But she noticed how successfully Celeste had avoided further discussion of her daughter's financial gain.

Harriet also answered her mother: 'Mum, you mean well, but now isn't the time for more drama. Please.'

'You don't know what's at stake.' Celeste's eyes flashed, the volume of her voice increasing again. 'You could be stitched up, and I'll not allow it. I will not.'

'Aunt Celeste.' The handsome Fabian had arrived at the hotel and approached his aunt as the rest of the room looked on, their breakfasts paused or abandoned. He was wearing dark jeans and a teal-coloured sweatshirt; with his sleeves rolled up and the slightly weather-beaten fabric, everything was pitched perfectly for an authentically casual look.

'Are you joining us, Fabian? Ready to tell us what Tristan had against you, too?' Celeste addressed her nephew loudly.

'I'm here to see you all, yes.' Fabian scanned the room, addressing the group confidently. 'Mum wants to know if anyone would like to come up to the house. She says every-one's welcome.'

'I think we'll all be interviewed today.' Athena's pleasant voice was businesslike. 'Perhaps the police will use a room here, at the hotel?'

'Keeping everything away from our boss and her precious political reputation, are we?' enquired Celeste. 'Heaven forbid that a young man's death impact on anyone's promotional prospects.'

'Mum, it's time to stop . . . to calm down,' Harriet said.

'And to be careful not to be sued for slander,' Rufus added, stepping into the fray. 'Athena is trying to do her job. No one is seeking a promotion, here; we all just want to see justice done.'

Clare liked the way Rufus had stepped up to help Athena as Celeste's tirade continued, but she found his insistence that promotion was an alien concept somewhat ironic. Threatening Celeste with a slander action was hardly the way to calm her down. Rufus was no diplomat.

By contrast, Fabian was a politician's son. 'Aunt Celeste, of course you're right. There are lots of possibilities, and of course no one thinks Harriet is culpable – that's crazy. Harriet, we love you. I'm so sorry this has happened, when you've come back to be with us again.'

Harriet looked astounded at this unequivocal support.

His words also had the effect of calming Celeste, who looked at her nephew with sudden affection. 'Fabian, you were always a warm-hearted boy. Gay men are so often lovely – you are a darling.'

Rufus and Athena eased away. Clare noticed Athena's hand giving Rufus a steer, as they returned to a far table by the window.

Celeste addressed Clare: 'What must you think of us all? What does your husband think, too? He was at the station with that nasty policewoman, I hear.'

'We're both so sorry this has happened.' Clare flexed her own diplomacy muscles. 'Such a horrible event impacts everyone in terrible ways. It's not surprising you're angry, Celeste – we're all shaken up by this.'

Fabian nodded in agreement with her as he seated himself opposite them.

'Well, there are things your husband and the police should know.' Celeste lowered her voice, leaning in close. 'Tristan exploited people.'

'Aunt Celeste, I don't think rumours are helpful.'

'Really? Well, Fabian, that makes me wonder what you've got to hide.' Celeste lifted a croissant from her plate and tore it in two.

'I think Clare knows that already, or am I wrong?'

'What are you thinking about, Fabian?' Clare asked.

'I think your son's middle name is probably Sherlock, and his Palio knowledge is encyclopaedic, unlike mine.'

'I did wonder.' Clare tried to look as if she had indeed vaguely wondered, rather than suspecting that Fabian's in-depth, supposedly eyewitness article had been fraudulent.

Fabian looked rueful. 'I had a collision of deadlines to meet. Peter, my partner, had been there, so I got him to tell me all about it.'

'Who cares about that?' said Harriet, grimacing.

'Well, I think Tristan talked to someone about it,' Fabian said. 'That's my guess, anyway.'

'Did he ask you for money?'

'No, not about that.' Fabian looked discomfited and shifted in his seat.

Clare wanted to know what they were not being told. Harriet had suggested that Tristan asked her for money not to reveal something involving her mother. What had Tristan known about Fabian, which Fabian might have paid to keep quiet?'

'You must tell the police all about it,' Celeste pronounced, clasping his arm across the table. 'We don't need to know any secrets, Fabian, but the police need to know what kind of man Tristan was. All the enemies he had.'

'How much did we really know him?' Harriet asked, with sudden ferocity. 'It's easy enough to scapegoat him, but what was it like for him, coming here? Knowing we hated him – hated his existence.'

'No need to be dramatic, Harriet,' her mother announced, dismissively.

'I think every person is so complex, aren't we?' said Clare. 'Perhaps there is always more to know about each of us.'

'No need to preach,' snapped Celeste.

'Mum, Clare was just saying—'

'I'm sorry, darling. Apologies, Clare. I'm so angry with Tristan. So typical that he ruins everything.'

'Mum, things are pretty bad for Tristan. He's dead.'

They all looked at the archway entrance to their dining room as DCI Carter and two uniformed officers arrived.

'Good morning,' the taller of the two sidekicks announced. 'We will be conducting further interviews with each of you today. If I could ask you to wait at the hotel for now, we will invite you to come up to the house or into the manager's office here to give your statements. Thank you.'

All conversation ceased. Breakfast continued.

CHAPTER 21

'I brought you some flowers from the garden to brighten up your room.' Martin stood in the hotel lobby, smiling shyly, and handed Harriet a bunch of delicate sweet peas. Their perfume was exquisite.

The gardener was smartly dressed and his beard was trimmed. He was still wearing his wedding shoes, not the heavy work boots Clare had seen him in the day before.

Harriet and Clare had just finished breakfast and were on their way out of the dining room. The lobby was busy. Two couples were standing with an assortment of bags, presumably waiting to check out. There was also a woman with a brown spaniel, its tawny eyes alert and its tongue lolling.

Harriet took the flowers tentatively; she seemed surprised to see him. 'Thanks, Martin, that's so kind of you. Did you meet Clare yesterday?'

He nodded and turned to look at Clare, as she said, 'Yes, we met just before the wedding. I meant to say, the garden looked so beautiful yesterday, with everything in bloom. Am I right in thinking your grandad was a gardener, too?'

She sensed the need to deflect the conversation away from Harriet and was content to roll on with garden talk for as long as necessary. She also felt some sympathy for Martin, who seemed like he didn't entirely belong with the family, but clearly wanted to. His care for Harriet was touching. This was such a complicated and painful bereavement for her, given her unhappy relationship with Tristan. Martin appeared to be sensitive to this.

'Yes, my grandad loved that garden. He's in a nursing home in Bridport, so I'm staying at his place in the grounds of Greenwood, for now, and taking care of the garden too. His cottage belongs to Jim and Susan, but it's been his home forever. I was there last night after the police let us go. Fabian said they took you away, Harriet. Are you OK? What happened?'

'I'm fine. Thanks for the flowers.' Harriet paused, her expression pained. 'Sorry, I'm finding it all very hard to talk about.'

'That's OK, I understand. I'm here for you, Harriet. Everyone is. If there's anything you want or need, just say.'

'How are *you* doing?' Clare asked, looking at Martin. 'This is grim for everyone.'

'I'm all right.' His tone was almost offhand. 'I hardly knew him. Hadn't seen him for years.'

'He was horrible to you, Martin. I remember.' Harriet lowered her head and sniffed at the flowers. 'It was nasty.'

'He didn't like me being friends with you, or Jess and Fabian.'

'He was jealous.'

Clare was interested. 'What happened?'

Martin shrugged and said, 'Nothing much,' as Harriet answered simultaneously, 'That fight in the river. I thought you'd drown each other – don't you remember?' She looked at Martin as if puzzled by his low-key response.

'Well, boys will be boys. I got wet that day, sure enough. But you were OK, that's the main thing.'

They stepped to the side as two of the departing guests wheeled their suitcases past them, followed by the glossy-coated spaniel. The dog seemed reluctant to leave and had to be tugged away from loitering and sniffing at Martin.

'Tristan met my son in the field by the church yesterday. Was that the river you scuffled in?' Clare asked, wanting to know more.

'He'd have drowned me if Fabian hadn't helped. And Jess.' Martin was less casual now, speaking more slowly, as if reliving the scene. 'They pulled him off me.'

'I thought they pulled you off each other. You were both so angry and strong. I remember trying to get between you.' Harriet looked troubled at the memory, and Clare wondered whether that was why Martin had wanted to downplay the incident.

'I was sent packing afterwards. Grandad kept me away for the rest of that summer. I *despised* Tristan after that.'

'Martin –' Harriet's eyes were wide with shock – 'don't say that.'

'Sorry.' Martin looked awkward. Then, after a pause, he gestured towards the flowers. 'Hope you like the sweet peas.'

'Yes, they're beautiful,' said Harriet.

'I love their scent,' Clare chimed in, trying to ease the tension. 'Do you know anything about today's interviews, Martin?'

'No, nothing to do with me.'

'They'll still need to talk to you, Martin,' said Harriet. 'They're talking to everyone.'

'Well, I've got nothing to tell them, and it's probably better if I don't say what I thought of him.'

'Perhaps anything we have to offer might be useful,' said Clare. She thought that the animosity between those boys and that fight in the river sounded fierce, however dismissive Martin was about it now. And that he was probably more impacted by Tristan's death than he was willing to acknowledge.

'Everyone knew what he was like,' said Martin. 'I can't see anything I have to say being particularly helpful. Harriet, do you want to go out for a walk or something, later? It might help take your mind off it all.' He gestured at the hotel door. 'We could take your mum, too, head for Charmouth, have a walk on the beach?'

'That sounds lovely, being somewhere else, beside the sea.' Harriet looked wistful. 'But I need to be here today; the police expect us to be available. And I feel so tired, I'm not sure I'm up to going anywhere.'

'Whatever you want.' Martin straightened his posture and practically clicked his heels together. 'I'll be around, tidying the garden, doing what's needed. Let me know if you want anything. Anything at all.'

As he left, Harriet turned to Clare. 'I always loved our trips to Charmouth.'

'He clearly cares about you.' It was nice to see this loyalty and support for Harriet in all the shock of her loss. There was something deferential in Martin's attitude towards her.

'We've known each other a long time; he's a friend. Martin

fought Tristan in the stream that day because he'd been bullying us all summer. But we weren't thinking enough about Tristan's own grief and rage. His mother's death destroyed his world. His boarding school was awful. He only came to Dad's for holidays, sometimes to Greenwood to spend some time with us. He knew no one wanted him, knew we all hated him.'

'It sounds traumatic.'

'And maybe it's all connected in some way. What happened then, and now. Or maybe it's completely random and some maniac followed him, or someone planning to burgle the house or something.'

'Burglary could be a strong motive. Thieves can be opportunistic around weddings,' announced Rufus, smoothing his red hair as he emerged from the dining room behind them. Clare wondered how long he'd been nearby, listening to their conversation. 'We need to consider every option. Have you seen Athena anywhere?'

'Sorry, no,' Harriet replied.

'I'm helping to process the press enquiries and strategise our response on Susan's behalf, as well as assisting the police investigation,' he continued, self-importantly.

'That's helpful of you,' Clare said. Perhaps Rufus might audition to be the next James Bond, too.

'Susan needs to be able to count on us all. No casual comments to the press or anyone else, please. Are your children on social media, Clare?' Before she could reply, Rufus caught sight of Athena through the doorway into the dining room, talking into her phone as she moved. 'Excuse me,' he said. And then he was gone.

Harriet looked at Clare. 'Does anyone care about Tristan's death? He was a person, not just a blip in Susan's career or an opportunity for Rufus to climb the greasy pole.'

'Perhaps everyone's in shock and it's coming out in peculiar ways.'

'Well, I'm in shock and furious with all of them. Mum has gone berserk, which is par for the course; Rufus is mush-rooming an ever-expanding ego – I don't know how Athena can stand it – and Martin thinks a day at the seaside will make everything OK, or a bunch of flowers.' Harriet shook the sweet peas in frustration. 'Thanks, Clare, but I'm off to see what Mum is up to, now – hopefully not accusing Fabian or anyone else of being a homicidal maniac. I feel so sorry for Jess and Ahmed – all they wanted was a wedding, and they got this.'

CHAPTER 22

DCI Jackie Carter sat in Greenwood's well-stocked library, the morning light cascading over the books and piano as she used this moment of calm to mull over the case before she started the next round of interviews. She was seeing some family members in here, while other guests were being interviewed at the hotel. She was well aware that it would take time for the fingertip search of the tree house and the processing of its contents to be completed, even though its only furnishings were a couple of wooden chairs. The tree house seemed to have fallen out of use since the children of the house had grown up and left home. It was nostalgia that had caused them to revisit it, and curiosity on the part of others attending the wedding.

Jackie didn't expect much that would be useful to the investigation to be revealed. So many guests had mounted the spiral steps twisting up the trunk and entered the treetop hideaway, there were bound to be physical traces of many of them up there. The gardens and marquees would need to be searched too, and that would take even longer.

Mercifully, the forensic testing on the murder weapon had already come back, though that didn't tell them much either.

The only clear prints on it were Harriet's, which, as far as Jackie was concerned, could either point to Harriet being the murderer, or simply to the fact that the murderer had been clever enough to wear gloves or had been meticulous in wiping away any prints.

What was most frustrating to Jackie was the fact that Tristan's phone had gone missing. Either the murderer had taken it or Tristan had simply lost it somewhere – though, that felt a little too convenient. The team would do everything they could to find it.

Jackie and her colleagues' step-by-step approach and professionalism were exemplary. She had always been exact and methodical, both at work and in her personal life. Things would be done properly on this case. They had to be, when it was this high profile.

Harriet was the obvious suspect, although Jackie must remain open to other possibilities. Tristan's half-sister had a significant financial motive, as well as long-standing antipathy towards the victim. An argument or threat could have tipped her over the edge, and Tristan seemed happy to goad people. Plenty of people had seen that for themselves at the reception and told her about it.

If Clare hadn't searched for Anna up in the tree house, Harriet could have slipped away undetected. She hadn't called for help on discovering the body – if indeed she had discovered it, rather than slaughtering her half-brother in their childhood playhouse. She was the one found with him, and the one holding the weapon. It was just possible that she had reached for it unthinkingly; Jackie knew that people did peculiar things in traumatic circumstances. But grabbing the knife was suspicious, however much Harriet protested that she did so to try to help the victim in some way.

Seeing David again was a bonus. He'd aged well. His take on the players was proving useful, too, and Jackie trusted his judgement. She also trusted him not to make too much of their former relationship, and to be discreet about it. She'd certainly played it down considerably when she'd told her boss. She didn't want anything to obstruct her taking the lead on this. The momentum was with her, so the boss had given her the go-ahead.

She was curious about David's family. Clare had a stronger personality than Jackie had imagined – the vicar was no pushover. There were plenty of big personalities in this case, and her job was to get to the heart of what had happened to Tristan, and why.

Her thoughts were interrupted by a knock on the door. Her detective constable was escorting Jess into the room.

'Please, take a seat.' DCI Carter was abrupt but professional. She was asking the questions, while her colleague looked after recording the interview and noting any points of particular interest.

Jess sat opposite the DCI on one of the comfortable padded chairs Jackie had placed in the centre of the room; the other officer sat slightly further back, nearer the door.

Faced with interrogation, Jess was shivering, despite the fleecy tracksuit she wore. The more she tried to stop herself and focus on the questions being put to her, the more obvious the trembling became. Her answers were almost monosyllabic, interrupted by gulps as she attempted to calm herself down with deep breaths.

'Did you have any contact with your cousin Tristan over the last few days?'

'I'm not sure. No. Nothing.' Jess flicked her eyes away from the DCI's gaze as she answered. 'No, I'm sure. There was no contact. I was surprised he was here. I didn't think he'd come.' She twisted her hands and then held them still.

'Why?'

'I don't know. We'd not really kept up. I think my parents were being polite, including him.'

As the interview continued, Jackie sensed Jess wasn't telling her everything. Her memory was patchy – perhaps plausibly so, given the events of the day. Yes, she remembered cutting the cake, chatting and dancing. No, she hadn't seen Tristan since he'd been escorted out of the marquee by David, after making that unwelcome speech. She'd been with Ahmed the whole time.

Both bride and groom maintained they were constantly together during the reception, but several guests recalled seeing them apart. Why the discrepancy? The problem with secrets in a murder case was identifying those that were relevant and those that were not.

Jackie leaned towards Jess and asked again, more firmly, 'After you cut the wedding cake, what exactly did you and your husband do with the knife?'

Jess held her breath for a moment and screwed up her face as if chasing a memory.

'We cut the cake together; lots of people were around us, clapping and taking photos. It's hard to remember exactly. I think we put it on the table beside the cake. Yes, we left it there. Why do you ask?'

'These details are relevant to the investigation. We are getting as full a picture of events as possible.'

Jackie was bland, but Jess was not duped. She looked horrified.

'Was that the weapon? Did our cake knife kill Tristan?'

'Sorry, I'm not able to comment on matters which are still under investigation.' Jackie was crisp, and used this moment to circle back to a previous area of questioning. 'Did your mother, or any of her team, have any contact with Tristan prior to the wedding, as far as you are aware?'

A hit. Jess blinked and let out a slight gasp. 'Why is this relevant?'

'*I'm* asking the questions in this interview. Was there any communication between them?'

'Nothing that I'm aware of. I don't think Tristan even replied to the invite. My mother's team are focused on her political work, so they had no reason to talk to Tristan.'

'It seems your cousin may have taken an interest in the political moves in the Home Office.' This was not a direct lie. Maybe he had done – who was to know? And Jackie wanted to dig a little.

'Did Athena tell you that?' It was like taking candy from a baby.

'I'm asking what you are aware of, in terms of any interest Tristan may have taken in your mother's political affairs.'

'I don't know anything about my mother's work, other than that she is a dedicated minister in the Home Office and a public servant.' Jess's voice was firmer; the medic, well-practised in handling difficult conversations, was coming to the fore. She wasn't shaking anymore.

Susan herself was more forthcoming. She and her husband were hospitable to the police, eager to be seen as cooperative and supportive. Jim, in particular, had changed his tune overnight – from Mr Obstructive to Mr Biddable. Quite a transformation.

Susan had discovered that Tristan had approached her team for information and comment on the refugee policy plan. He'd not mentioned the familial relationship, simply emailing her office and receiving a standard reply. Athena had produced this information and passed it to her boss that morning, who had told the investigative team. It seemed Tristan had been sniffing around for a story, or for leverage of some sort. No one seemed to think he might actually care about refugees.

Still, Jackie wondered, had he shown potential to cause problems for Susan's career trajectory? That would have given her, or Jim, cause to silence him. Or was inviting him to the wedding an olive branch, an attempt to restore the relationship? Susan and Jim had each declared that to be the case. Their replies were tailored and remarkably similar on that point.

Athena had been measured and professionally courteous during her interview, apparently forthcoming and explicit about Tristan's contact with the office team, but rather more vague about her impressions of the day, despite having been a bridesmaid. She described organisational aspects in precise detail but had little to say about the mood of participants or any undercurrents. In fact, she had nothing of interest to offer, only bland expressions of shock and calmly stated concern, volunteering herself to assist the investigation in any way she could, in her capacity as Susan's special adviser as well as a family friend. She was appalled at what had happened on the bride's special day.

Athena had become friendly with Jess at uni and had been very grateful to be offered work experience with Jess's mother in her constituency office. After graduating, she'd landed the role of parliamentary assistant and then become one of the special advisers in Susan's ministerial office, initially in the Department for Education and then moving with her to the Home Office. Jackie thought that Athena had done rather well out of her friendship with Jess and wondered at what point she had learned that her fellow student's mother was a successful MP with a likely ministerial career ahead. It had been a friendship worth cultivating.

The gardener, Martin, was dispassionate: involved, yet behaving as if things were of little relevance to him. He'd known the family all his life – known Tristan in childhood, too. He was stilted in reply to her questions. He'd seen nothing, noticed nothing.

The family had closed ranks, except for Fabian. In a welcome display of candour, he told her about Tristan's implied threat to his professional standing, but Jackie couldn't take the potential threat to a TV deal seriously as a motive for sticking a knife into someone. Yes, Tristan had made some reference to places where Fabian had or had not been – tenuous stuff at best. Fabian was a golden boy, basking in privilege. A lost TV series would be a temporary setback. Other opportunities would come his way, whatever professional embarrassment Tristan might cause. Entitlement – the gift that keeps on giving.

Had Tristan jeopardised Susan's career, or their family life in some other way? His death would not make any promotion to the Cabinet more likely – quite the reverse. The victim disturbed people. What deep waters might he have stirred that day? Who had resolved to silence him, or to exact revenge? Or was the artist after all of her father's money – simple as that?

Harriet was their prime suspect, and deservedly so – there were already the beginnings of a solid case being built against Tristan's sister. The evidence pointed towards her.

But the vicar woman – Reverend Clare – was championing Harriet, having only just met her. At interview, Clare emphasised Harriet's shock and distress in that tree house, and was reluctant to describe how she had actually been holding the knife when Clare discovered her with the body. Jackie didn't tell her team, but she was well aware of her own bias against Clare, formed over a long period. The woman irritated her. Possibly anyone who had married David would have done. What did he see in Miss Goody Two-Shoes? She was all politeness to the DCI, of course, but there was animosity there, Jackie knew it. She didn't trust her not to shield or protect the artist in some way. Clare would have her own agenda – Jackie was sure about that.

CHAPTER 23

The house was peopled, yet forlorn. Clare arrived in Greenwood looking for Jess, who had asked her to come over from the hotel. The atmosphere could hardly have been more different from that of the previous day. The upbeat music of the wedding preparations and celebration had been silenced. Piles of boxes that had contained layers of wedding cake and floral corsages were now stacked haphazardly in the hallway; a heap of discarded table linen lay in a corner of the kitchen; the sideboards held an assortment of serving dishes, a mix of washed and unwashed glasses, scrunched paper lists and abandoned Post-it notes.

There was little energy or will to sort and tidy; attempts to return to normality felt too hopeless. Faces were disconsolate, and conversations were held in regretful brevity. The cheery family photos on display now seemed a mockery, as if the artifice of a carefully curated façade had been exposed.

Susan and Jim were trying to carry on with things as best they could, but the cheerlessness of the house reflected their heavy-heartedness. There was much to be done, yet the listlessness of shock and mourning pervaded.

Jess had slipped upstairs after being interviewed, having

messaged to ask Clare and Athena to join her. Clare was slightly surprised by the summons, but, whatever support Jess wanted, she was eager to give.

Now, the three women were closeted in Jess's old room, the debris of yesterday's bridal preparations still littering it. Jess sat cross-legged on the sofa, Athena next to her. Clare perched on the bed, beside a heap of towels and dressing gowns.

'I just wanted to be back home, away from the hotel,' Jess murmured. Then, more surprisingly, she added, 'And away from Ahmed, too.'

Clare didn't want to draw any conclusions too hastily, but this seemed an odd thing for Jess to say the day after her wedding.

Jess now wore running shoes and had brushed out the intricate styling of her long hair, finding a scrunchie to tie it in a loose ponytail. 'I can't face anyone,' she explained. 'Even Ahmed. I just need some space. Tell me, what do you think happened?' She looked at Clare, her face contorted with worry.

'I think we're all at sea,' Clare improvised, not wanting to say too much.

'I heard it was the cake knife that was used to kill Tristan. Mum said the police were tracking where it was put, and I was asked about it. What do you think?'

Jess certainly seemed at sea, and with good reason. This was her wedding, and her cousin was dead. The image of Tristan's body was never far from Clare's mind, either.

'I think we need a drink.' Athena poured them each a glass from an opened bottle of wine left over from the previous day. 'And Tristan made trouble everywhere; lots of people probably wanted him gone.'

'Like Rufus?' Jess asked.

Clare was taken aback by her abruptness, and she noticed that Athena was jolted by it, too, having to catch her breath before replying.

'Rufus was uncomfortable about their schooldays, sure, but don't overstate it, Jess. We mustn't blow things out of proportion. We'll all go crazy if we start accusing each other.'

'I wasn't accusing Rufus. Although, he doesn't want any scandal if he's after a job with Mum. She'll be distancing herself from anything untoward even more zealously after this. Tristan used things he knew about us . . .' Jess paused, as if struggling to know what to say next. 'I'm also really worried about Ahmed.'

'Ahmed?' Clare hadn't anticipated this. She politely sipped the drink which Athena handed to her, then rested it on top of a stack of magazines on the bedside table.

'I don't know where he put the knife after we cut the cake. He carried it away with him.'

'That's ridiculous!' Athena spoke brusquely. 'He'd never hurt anyone. He was probably carrying it to the caterers, to chop up the slices. The two of you have a golden future together, Jess. Be grateful.'

There was quite a contrast between the two women's situations in life. Athena and Rufus didn't share Jess's privilege, nor her and Ahmed's job security and status. Clare thought this was probably very evident to Athena, but perhaps less so to Jess.

'I'm not feeling I have much to be grateful for right now.' Jess lifted up her drink. 'Mum needs you to smooth things,

Athena. Her Cabinet dreams look shot unless this is sorted soon. How do you think she is?'

'She's amazing, so resilient, and David and the office are pulling out all the stops for her. Actually – I'm sorry – I should probably get back to things. Sorry, Jess.' Athena seemed more relieved than sorry to be putting down her glass and leaving them.

'Of course. Mum needs you, and you must prioritise her. See you later.' Jess was distracted in her farewell, barely looking at her friend.

Athena closed the door quietly behind her.

There was regret there; Athena's political aspirations and commitment to Susan had obviously resulted in strains in the friendship with Jess. Maybe that was why Clare had been invited to join the two younger women in Jess's room, as additional support. Jess seemed isolated. And what had she meant about Tristan using things he'd known about all of them?

'Did Tristan trouble you much, Jess?' Clare asked. 'He was a bit edgy in the churchyard, but maybe he was trying to wish you well.'

'That's not really relevant and I don't want to talk about it, sorry.' Jess spoke quite sharply, as if irritated by the suggestion, then paused. 'I wish I could, Clare.' She lent her head back and closed her eyes, as if to shut out the memory of her cousin.

'Sure. I just wondered if he'd been in touch at all.' Clare was remembering that angry scene, when Jess had brandished her phone at Athena, before the wedding.

Jess made the connection for her. 'Are you thinking about that message I got? Athena thought you'd noticed how upset I was. That was something else, some idiot messing up our honeymoon bookings. I'd planned lots of surprises for Ahmed, and they had double-booked and got the dates wrong. I was furious. But it doesn't matter, now.' She looked down, rearranging a pile of hair ties on the table in front of her.

Clare couldn't help but feel that Jess's explanation was too long to be entirely truthful. It reminded her of the time a shame-faced Tom and his friend Freddie had given multiple reasons for Anna's rabbit scampering away, before confessing that they had taken it out of its chicken-wired enclosure and let it run around freely on the lawn.

Clare could not seriously consider this shocked and sad woman to be a suspect in Tristan's death – that image of a vengeful bride in a blood-stained dress belonged in the realm of gothic-horror fantasy, not a Dorset wedding. Yet Jess was definitely hiding something, but was it relevant to Tristan's murder?

'Thanks for the chat, Clare. I think I need to get some rest, now.'

'Sure. Take it gently, Jess. And please let me know how I can help with anything.'

As well as the shock and grief, Jess was carrying other burdens, too.

CHAPTER 24

Clare sat on a stilled swing seat beneath a huge oak tree in the hotel grounds. She had returned to the peaceful spot after her conversation with Jess and Athena at the big house, and it was a relief to be alone.

She completed her delayed morning prayers and scripture reading. She liked to begin the day with those, but everything was disrupted today – it was mid-morning already. It was strange to have a Sunday morning not in church, but it felt good to have time to pause now, especially given the tense atmosphere amongst the Zetland family and their entourage. Jackie and her team pulling in people for interviews had set everyone on edge.

Clare couldn't stop thinking about Tristan. She kept commending him to God's love in Christ and lamented the destruction of a life cut off so savagely. The waste. The loss. She prayed for the perpetrator, for everyone impacted by this horror, and for all who would be affected over the years to come. She wanted to do whatever she could to help resolve things.

Jess had been very tense at the mere sight of Tristan in the churchyard, and she was offering an unconvincing explanation for her rage on the morning of the wedding. What had really been going on? She said she wanted time away from Ahmed now, which seemed strange, and Clare thought Athena had been struck by that reaction, too.

Jess was troubled about Ahmed moving the knife which they had used to cut the cake, and which had been used as the murder weapon. The use of that knife was horrible, but her suspicion of Ahmed seemed disproportionate. Clare agreed with Athena that Ahmed could simply have been putting it out of harm's way or taking it to the caterers. Jess was anxious about Ahmed's role, but any of the other guests in the marquee could have got hold of it later.

There had been tension, this morning, between the two friends. It was tactless for Jess to say that Rufus might have wanted Tristan gone; no wonder Athena bridled at that. Jess was struggling with shock and grief, but everyone had been impacted by this murder – Athena, too.

Why had Tristan congratulated both Ahmed and Jess on their careers, in that strange, insinuating speech of his? Maybe Tristan had some inside knowledge. He'd mentioned Rufus's career success too, in passing. They had been at school together; had contact continued afterwards, maybe?

Clare wanted to know more. If Harriet was not to be the only suspect, others must be in the frame, and she would need to play her part in exploring alternatives. She felt remote from David, who seemed caught up in Jackie's investigation and its implications for the office.

She hoped Anna and Tom were doing OK, and she was glad of the puppies at her sister-in-law's home. The ponies, too. Thinking about that soothed her a bit, as did the rhythm of the words she read from Psalm 121: *Where does my help come from? My help comes from the Lord, the Maker of heaven and earth.*

The big tree was not as quiet as she had assumed. As she sat, she heard the rustling of its leaves and the occasional deeper note as it creaked in the breeze. Its roots were connected with those of the other trees in the garden, she thought, as she mulled over the connections in this community. David had a friendship as an adult with Jess – but the bride's childhood relationships predated that by many years. Was the cousins' childhood somehow the source of this eruption of violence? She needed to think clearly. Someone was guilty and she mustn't prejudge anything, or anyone.

Her envy of Jackie's time with David was unhealthy and she knew she should just let go. But the woman was so officious – so neat, too, with her pixie hair and pointy boots. It was hard to imagine David loving her, but he had. It was probably best not to imagine too much of that. She needed to get a grip. And be grateful for her marriage.

The family rifts here were obvious, with Tristan's arrival on the scene destroying Harriet's family unit. There were social differences, too. Susan and Jim were affluent and influential – her political future on track, even then. Martin was from a different social stratum, so how had Tristan's arrival impacted on him? He'd been sidelined. His devotion to Harriet and to Jess was still evident. What about that river fight, all those years ago?

Anna and Tom had their rifts. She supposed all siblings did. She had differences with her own siblings, but always with a sense of belonging – not this long-term enmity stemming from wounds of the past. Harriet and Tristan's father had been ruinously duplicitous, running his two families until circumstances eventually forced him to reveal the truth, with all its destructive consequences. Perhaps he'd been trying to protect the two households from pain until that became impossible, but what a mess he'd caused.

How was proximity to a murder going to impact on the young? What had Tinky and Trixie been told? Thank God they had left before the crime had been discovered. Perhaps it might be possible to avoid telling them anything at all, for now. That ship had sailed, as far as Tom and Anna were concerned. Better that they were away from all this aftermath, with the waiting, the questions, the unease and the suspicion.

But she wanted to talk to them about it, and also just be with them. She wanted to chill in front of the telly, play a board game, muck about a bit, with the dog joining in. Wanted to be with the people she loved, and who loved her.

Right on cue, there was David, walking towards her – he'd sought her out. She was happy and stood to meet him.

'How are things going with Jackie?' she asked, pleased with her own calm demeanour. She was trying, and asked God to help her. She threaded her arm through her husband's. 'Let's walk and talk.'

'Sorry, I've only got a minute – I just wanted to see you. I need to get back to Susan pretty quick and be on hand for the office – everything's crazy today. It's not like you to volunteer going for a walk, either. What's happened to you?' He smiled.

'Just because I'm not Jess, it doesn't mean I'm allergic to exercise,' she protested. 'I simply know my athletic limits, that's all.'

'Indeed. Your sporting limits are legendary.' He hugged

her. 'Any more news from Gill? I rang her earlier, but haven't heard any more since then.

'Anna and Tom weren't very chatty when I spoke to them, but Gill says they're OK, busy with Ruby's litter and the horses. How are you doing, with everything?'

'I'm fine, more concerned for you and the long-term effects of all this on Jess and Ahmed and everyone else. This investigation could take a long time and be horrible in all sorts of ways.' David frowned at the prospect.

'Why do you say that? Won't it be over soon?' Clare was hoping for a quick resolution.

'I want it over quickly just as much as everyone else does, even if that means that Harriet did it. But these things can't be rushed.'

There was comfort in embracing her husband, having that solidarity in the melee of awful possibilities. Clare outlined some of her thoughts about the case briefly, but her suspicions seemed so tenuous, and who knew what conclusions Jackie might draw from any comments David passed on to her.

'I had a strange conversation with Jess,' she told him, as they sat down together on the wooden swing seat. 'She's uneasy about Ahmed and she got Athena's back up by saying something about Rufus.'

'Everyone's uneasy, with how disorientating this is,' David replied. 'Poor Jess – it's not surprising she was tactless about Rufus. Who wouldn't be?'

Clare didn't pursue it. Responding to murder in their midst was unchartered territory for all of them. It felt strange not to share everything with David, though; usually, she could unload anything on him.

As David returned to the house, Clare strolled after him towards Greenwood's walled garden, remembering the vegetable patch with its ordered rows and the glasshouses there. Ahead of her she saw Martin, now in his work clothes, carrying something into a round building, followed by the dog.

A wheelbarrow with a rake protruding from it blocked the path. Clare shifted the barrow and looked through the doorway into which Martin had disappeared. The cool, darkened space had the lingering sweet scent of an old apple store, and the shelves circling the walls had been swept clean, ready for this year's crop. The tail-wagging dog welcomed her, and Martin put down some sacking and said it was nice to see her – not entirely convincingly.

Clare was in vicar mode. 'Hello again! How are things with you, Martin?' She was struck by how solitary he seemed, carrying out tasks with only the dog for company. She wondered what it was like for him, being alongside the family but not part of it.

'I just want to keep busy,' he said. 'There's always plenty to do, and I want to help as much as I can.'

'It was kind of you to bring Harriet those flowers. Was it difficult for you, seeing Tristan again? Sorry if I'm being nosy.' She wasn't sorry at all; she wanted to know.

He stooped to the dog before replying, perhaps trying to delay his answer. 'I've known them all for years; he seemed much the same as ever.' He had sidestepped her question.

'Do you have any thoughts about what happened?'

'I think Harriet deserves better than this from her family. Tristan never should have been asked back here – and it's no way to celebrate a wedding, inviting someone like him. It could've been anyone that killed him; Tristan was always a nasty piece of work – Celeste told you that. Who knows what trouble he'd got himself into. It could have been anything, with him.' Martin hoisted a dusty, heavy box from the floor and deposited it on a shelf, then brushed his hands free of the dirt.

'It was good of you to walk with him, after he did that speech. Susan mentioned how helpful you were,' Clare continued, conversationally.

'We do what we can. As I said, I've known the family for a long time.'

'What did Tristan talk to you about, if you don't mind me asking?' She wanted to learn all that she could.

'The police asked me that too, but I didn't have much to say. Tristan would never have confided in me, and he was quite far gone, even though it was still early in the day. He teased me a bit about old times, but no more than you'd expect. Then I think he went to find somewhere to sleep off the drink. It's strange that he was here again and now gone. Can't get my head round it, really.' The gardener shook his head slightly and patted the dog again.

'Yes, the whole thing feels unbelievable, you're right. I'm going to have a walk to clear my head a bit. Which way do you suggest I go?'

'Take the path through the big field, past the church, and you'll find lots of tracks to choose from in the woods beyond. I can show you the way, if you like?'

It was considerate of him, but Clare preferred to be alone, so she bid him farewell, thanking him for the offer. She thought he'd probably rather continue tending to the plants and doing other odd jobs, and hoped he found the dog's company a relief. Everyone was coping as best they could. She missed the children and hoped they were OK.

CHAPTER 25

Clare hadn't intended to eavesdrop, but nor had she made her presence known when she realised that the newly-weds were within earshot. She was curious to hear what they were saying.

'It would be better if we kept it quiet.' Jess moved so quickly that Ahmed had to stride out to keep pace with her.

'What? You want us to pretend we're still together, but split? Are you serious?' His voice was raised with emotion.

'Yes. For the time being.' She stopped and turned around, a wild look in her eyes. 'I can't go on with this.'

There was no way Clare could reveal she was nearby now. Awkward didn't even begin to cover it. She stood still, lurking behind a helpful copse of trees, hoping that, if she didn't move, she wouldn't be seen.

'With this? Do you mean our *marriage*? But our relationship is the best thing that has ever happened to me, Jess, and I know you feel the same.' Ahmed looked at her imploringly.

'Everything's different. I need to take a pause. I have to.'

'You sound as if someone else is making you do this. But we're married, Jess. This doesn't involve anyone else.'

'Do you think I can't make a decision for myself? Can you

hear yourself?' Jess's indignation flared up. 'You're patronising me.'

'Is this about Tristan? I love you, Jess, and you love me. Tristan's got nothing to do with it. We can face Tristan's murder and all its implications together.'

Jess walked on. Clare was unsure what to do, so she just stood there.

'I'm aware of where this is heading,' Jess said. 'I think Harriet will be facing a prison sentence. The police have their sights on her. There will be a trial and who knows what other kinds of hell. Things are different, now.'

'You're different, that's for sure. There are things you never told me, Jess. We need to be open with each other.' Ahmed's voice shook. It sounded as though his whole world was disintegrating.

Jess was relentless. 'I need to be open, do I? One of my cousins is about to be jailed for life, and the other is dead, and you think everything will be solved by me being more open?'

They were so close now that Clare had no option but to greet them. She began approaching from the shelter of the trees, skirting round a clump of nettles and trying to look unaware of the heated conversation she'd witnessed.

Ahmed was first to spot her and stopped abruptly. With the briefest of waves towards her, he turned back in the direction of the house. 'Look . . . I'll leave you to it, for now. Let's talk later, Jess.' And then he walked away.

Clare halted, facing Jess at the junction of the paths. 'Sorry to interrupt. Would you like some company, Jess, or shall I leave you be?'

'It's OK. I'm fine.' Jess looked anything but fine. 'Sorry,

Clare. Yes, I think I do need some time alone. I'm all over the place.'

'You've had a huge shock. We all have. Who knows how to deal with this?'

'Ahmed seems to think he knows what's best. He thinks we should all carry on as if nothing's happened.'

'Maybe he's trying to hold steady.'

'I wish he'd try being steady with the truth.' Jess's fierce words didn't match the forlorn expression on her face. She looked exhausted. 'Sorry, Clare, I really can't talk about it.'

'Sure, of course.' Clare watched as Jess walked past her, further into the woodland.

The horses were scattered across the field, cropping grass diligently. One lifted its head briefly but didn't otherwise move position as Clare followed in Ahmed's wake.

He was waiting for her by the gate. 'Sorry to rush off so rudely.' He removed his glasses and wiped them, seeming to catch his breath. Clare wondered if he'd been crying.

'Not at all. Why are we all apologising to each other so much today? The murder put us all on edge . . . at odds. I'm just sorry about all this awfulness for you and Jess.'

'She wouldn't talk to you? I feel like she's keeping us all at a distance.'

'Maybe that's her way of coping.'

'You and David face things together. I've seen how you back each other through thick and thin. Political stuff, parish stuff, family life . . .'

'Maybe you're right, but there are also distances between us sometimes, too.' She paused, not knowing whether she should snoop further. But she couldn't back out now. 'Ahmed, what's going on with you two?'

They walked in silence for a little while, their heads bowed as they made their way across the tussocky grass, trying to avoid the brambles.

'Jess is talking about separating. She won't really say why; she just says everything is different.' Ahmed sounded incredulous, as if unable to make any sense of what was happening.

'Everyone's had a big shock. We're all reeling.'

'She's treating me like a stranger.'

'Are you holding anything back from her?' Clare slowed her pace.

'What do you mean?' Ahmed shook his head in disbelief.

'Well, there was the altercation between you and Tristan yesterday. Have you explained about that?'

'I was no fan of Tristan's, that's for sure. He was trouble – for Jess and for others – and I wanted to make it clear he wasn't to cause her any hassle, of any kind. But my view of him, and that rather clumsy attempt to warn him off, has no bearing on this. It's Harriet who's under suspicion. That's another reason Jess is upset. They were once so close. Harriet said no to being a bridesmaid and wasn't even sure about attending the wedding at all – she was so uncertain about returning here, all because of Tristan.'

'It's good that she came, and that she and Jess are more in touch again.'

'Not so great if she ends up with a life sentence, is it?'

CHAPTER 26

That afternoon, Clare was sipping a cappuccino in the hotel's courtyard garden, enjoying the sun on her face. She had the place to herself, and the flowering wisteria made for a fragrant backdrop. She was busy tackling work emails and changing arrangements for Anna and Tom. She'd had to cancel their football courses this week, but they'd be happy at Gill's, spending time with their older cousins and with the horses. If you had to get caught up in a murder, the summer holidays were a better time to do it.

The puppies were a bonus, and the fact that they were already sold and paid for was even better. Gill had a waiting list, with several prospective owners very sad that Ruby had not produced a bigger litter. Clare was relieved, as life was busy enough without adding to the home menagerie. It was bad enough that Tom still wanted a parrot.

It felt strange to slip into the everyday again, however briefly: confirming details for this year's harvest supper, working out the collection rota for the food bank and making an appointment to meet with a bride and groom.

She hoped their wedding day would be tragedy free.

What a disaster Tristan's death had been for Jess and Ahmed.

Their relationship had been fractured, with Jess withdrawing for whatever reason and Ahmed floundering. She felt sure Ahmed wasn't telling her the whole truth about his contretemps with Tristan.

Rufus was approaching, his phone clamped to his ear, a folder tucked under an arm. His head was nodding repeatedly. 'OK, sure. I'm on it.'

As he finished his call, Clare looked at him and made space on the table for his things. Part of her wanted to make a swift exit, though that wouldn't be kind.

'How are you doing?' she asked. Then she remembered Joey from *Friends* using the same question as a pickup line and wanted to disappear even more.

'Me? Great. All good, thanks.' Rufus sat down, heavily.

A young woman appeared and took his coffee order – it was a complicated one, with precise instructions about varied milks and froth. Rufus then tapped his fingers at speed on his phone, while Clare moved her iPad further to the side of the wooden table.

He put down his phone abruptly and said, 'Actually, can I talk to you about something?' He paused, seeming unsure whether or not to continue. 'You see, the thing is, I'm in a bit of an awkward spot.'

'Of course, yes, I'll help however I can.' Clare's interest quickened.

Rufus's drink arrived. He moved a teaspoon and straightened a napkin, waiting until the waitress was at a safe distance before speaking. 'How public do you think this investigation will be?'

'I'm no expert, but I think the police will try to be as discreet as possible.'

'It's all very tricky.' Rufus lifted his coffee cup, then put it down without taking a sip. 'I was at school with Tristan, you know.' He pulled at the collar of his blue checked shirt. His discomfort was obvious, with his nervous movements and flushed cheeks.

'Right,' Clare said, encouragingly.

'It was a difficult time, and I'm worried the police will contact the school.'

'Is there something you'd rather was kept quiet?' Call me Miss Marple.

'No, no, I don't have anything to hide. Just something I'd rather keep private.'

Clare wondered what the difference was. She thought Rufus looked sheepish and young, more like one of Tom's friends than a budding political adviser.

'He was a strong character at school. A bit of a ringleader. He was expelled, you know.'

'Were you involved in some way?'

'Not with the blackmail. Well, not when he blackmailed the exams officer.'

'OK. So, what happened then?'

Here it came.

'Tristan knew this teacher was vulnerable. We all did. He was single in a school that stank of "family values" and he was ineffective in class – all the boys ran riot in his lessons.' Rufus tugged at his shirt collar again.

'Sounds tough.' She resisted the urge to ask more questions.

'Tristan got close to him and made the rest of us behave in

class. The teacher, Mr Lightfoot, used to make time to listen to Tristan, and Tristan pretended to confide in him. They had private conversations, then Tristan threatened to accuse him of assault unless he showed him the exam papers.'

'Wow, that's quite something.'

'We were *all* terrified of not doing well in those exams.' Rufus leaned forward, drank some coffee and spoke softly. 'The thing is . . . reputation matters.'

Rufus didn't need to spell it out for Clare to understand. He must've looked at the papers too. Though, she wondered if there was something more to this that he wasn't telling her. Surely just looking at the papers wasn't enough to make Rufus so worried.

'This all happened so long ago,' she said. 'I can't see how it would possibly matter anymore.'

'You're right, it was ages ago, but it still isn't a good look. I'm hoping your husband will understand. Maybe he could help smooth things over a bit.'

'He'll want to help, if he can.'

'But I don't want anything to come out publicly.'

'I'm sure the police are very experienced about this, Rufus,' she said, trying to mollify him.

'Yes, OK. Thanks. Righto.' Rufus gulped down his drink and looked around. 'Thanks, Clare. It was very helpful to talk.'

Left alone with her cooling coffee, Clare thought about Tristan. He'd certainly made people uneasy and exploited their vulnerabilities. She thought back to the intense discussion between Rufus and Athena that she'd witnessed in the boot room on the night of the murder. Could it all be related in some way?

Rufus was clearly worried about losing his reputation before he'd even established one. Tristan made him nervous – had some power over him. Clare had a tenuous connection with a retired chaplain of their school. Perhaps he might be able to shed some light on past events there.

CHAPTER 27

Madonna was a big horse; her midriff was a solid barrel, shimmering in the sunlight. Anna could put her whole weight into brushing her. Madonna would shake her head periodically, flicking away flies with her mane. Her hooves rang a metallic sound if she stamped away from the pressure of the grooming. There was a peacefulness in the rhythmic strokes and the scent of horse and hay.

Tom perched on the mounting block in their aunt's yard, watching his sister. The farrier was due later, and Tom was looking forward to that. He was thinking about the murder, though, and about the victim.

'He liked horses – Tristan.'

'How do you know?'

'He said so, in the field with Mum, after the service.'

'Those things he said were gross.' Anna's brushing raised puffs of dust skywards.

'Yes. He was drunk, though. When do you think Mum and Dad will pick us up?'

'I don't know. They want us out of the way. They probably think the puppies are keeping us happy.'

'Dad used to go out with the police officer.' Tom stretched a leg out in front of him.

'How do you know that?'

'I heard Auntie Gill say something about it on the phone.' He stretched both legs, while balancing himself on the mounting block.

'Weird.'

Madonna shifted her weight, then rested on a tilted hoof. Anna continued her steady work, sweeping strokes over the horse's hindquarters. She had borrowed clothes from her aunt, some oversized dungarees.

'Maybe we can help solve it, if we saw something important.' Tom sounded hopeful.

'Maybe. But I don't want to get anyone in trouble. We could say something we saw that was nothing to do with it.'

'Are you worried about saying something about Jess?'

'Why do you say that?' Anna turned towards her brother, brush in hand.

'You wouldn't want to get her in trouble.'

'She was really upset before the wedding. Furious. Mum saw it, too. But Mum doesn't know who made her so cross.'

'How come you do?'

'Jess told Athena. When they talked about it, they shifted into French so Tinky and Trixie wouldn't understand. Suki wasn't there and they forgot about me. Or thought I was deaf. All this "*Pas devant les enfants*" stuff.'

'Pathetic.' Tom didn't understand the words but got the gist of being excluded.

'It was something Jess didn't want Suki or Ahmed to know

about, that was obvious. When Suki got back, they started banging on about headdresses again. I was with the cat.'

'Maybe you should tell Mum or Dad.'

'Jess would never hurt anyone. She's a doctor.'

The mare shifted her weight again and tossed up her head.

'So's Ahmed,' Tom said, 'but he was ready to punch Tristan – I saw.'

'Maybe Ahmed knew what it was about?'

'Dad saw all of that, anyway. There's nothing new to tell him.' Not about that, anyway.

'OK.' Anna moved to Madonna's far side, opting not to tell her brother the other things she'd noticed.

Tom decided to keep his own counsel, too. He was watching his sister while chewing a piece of hay – it tasted good. He liked the smell of hay, too, even if the muck heap was gross. He wanted to watch the farrier, and to spend longer with Ruby and her litter. There were good things about being removed from the scene of the crime. But there was also lots to remember about it, and much to ponder. What to say – and what to keep quiet.

CHAPTER 28

'Good morning. Is this the correct number for Reverend Clare Brakespear, please?'

It was Monday morning, two days after the wedding, and Clare had returned to the hotel bedroom after breakfast. She had work to do to prepare for next Sunday's services. Surely they would be able to get back home long before then.

'Yes, this is Clare,' she answered quickly; she knew who she wanted this to be.

'Tim Cassidy, here.' Bingo. 'Former school chaplain at Glenavon College – although, that was some years ago, now.'

'Thank you so much for calling me back. I think Serena Barker explained something of the situation to you?'

The clerical grapevine had done its work. Serena, retired Archdeacon of Hackney, was a mentor to Clare and also a former diocesan colleague of Canon Tim Cassidy, who had previously been chaplain of the school attended by Tristan and Rufus. Clare wanted the lowdown on their schooldays, and now it seemed that she would get it.

'Indeed. Serena spoke very warmly of you. But I understand you've been caught up in a tragic situation.' His voice was sympathetic. 'I'm very sorry to hear the news of young

Tristan Zetland. Such a loss. What a charismatic boy he was.'

'I only met him briefly, but I enjoyed talking to him.'

'I'm sure he was always a lively conversationalist. I hope this is a convenient moment to talk.'

Clare was glad about the timing of the call. David had gone over to Greenwood House, but she was still in their room; she could be confident of the privacy of this conversation.

Tim gave her some background about the school, about Tristan's sudden arrival as a bereaved boy and the pastoral care which the school had tried to offer. 'Rather unsuccessfully, I'm afraid. The school community had a range of problems, and I fear Tristan's experience there was not a happy one.'

'Could you tell me more about that?'

'I gather you're aware of the exam-paper incident, and the pressure Tristan exerted on that unfortunate teacher to gain access to questions in advance? There was little option but to expel Tristan, after that – although, thankfully, the exam board were discreet, so it was possible to minimise any reputational damage to the school.'

Clare was unconvinced that the school's reputation should have been a priority, but decided not to comment.

'It's always a difficult balance, reputational damage and transparency. We all have our moments of folly as youngsters – and as elders, too.'

'Yes.' She didn't have a problem agreeing with that.

'Tristan was one for pushing boundaries. There were incidents of petty thieving and throwing his weight around, but he also had great potential as a leader. The head teacher had high hopes for him, if he could be steered in the right direction.'

'Do you know whether he had any influence over a contemporary, Rufus Winslade, at all?'

'Good at chess? Redhead, eager to please?'

'That's the one.'

'I wouldn't say this to anyone, obviously, but, between ourselves, young Rufus was easily led, and I believe he was party to a number of Tristan's enterprises, shall we say.'

'Enterprises?' She wanted clarity.

'Local shopkeepers raised concerns – that was not unusual. But it went further than that.'

'In what way?' Clare began taking notes; she'd have to pass this on to Jackie.

'It transpired that Tristan coordinated an operation that involved pupils placing orders for items to be shoplifted on their behalf, including multiple pieces of expensive clothing being procured on school visits overseas: skiing trips, school exchanges and the like.'

Skiing trips didn't feature on any curriculum Clare had experienced, but she got the idea.

'The organisation was quite sophisticated, I believe.' Was there a note of pride in the retired chaplain's voice? 'Tristan had quite a team of operatives at the height of things.'

So that explained Rufus's nervousness about reputational damage. Clare was right to have suspected there was more to the story.

'This is only hearsay, Clare, but, as it happens, I lunched with a retired colleague only a few weeks ago. He mentioned some updates on our old Glenavonians which would be best left out of the alumni bulletin. Although, some strange things *are* included there – former pupils telling us about the anti-snoring device they've invented, or that their DIY guide to curing chlamydia has been published.'

'Goodness. What did your colleague say?' Glenavon College was definitely not the school for her children.

'His niece had been involved with one of our former students until a couple of years ago. She extricated herself from the relationship when she realised that he was supplementing his salary by occasionally shoplifting items to order. Apparently, he claimed that everyone from their old school year did it, but not very often, so they could always argue their way out of trouble if apprehended.'

'Was Tristan's name mentioned? Or Rufus's?'

'Not specifically, but I'm telling you because the school year concerned was the same as theirs, so I think a connection is possible, or even likely. I also gather from another source that this ring, if you might call it that, had ceased operating over the last year or so. Perhaps it might be relevant.'

'I think it could well be. Thank you very much for taking the time to call, and for this information. I'll pass it on. I'm very grateful for your help.' No wonder Rufus was worried.

'Not at all. I'm very sorry that it's needed. Young Tristan, Rufus and all of you are in my prayers, of course. Keep in touch and let me know if I can be of any more use, won't you? Take care of yourself, too.'

Clare took down some contact details and thanked him again. After hanging up, she sat for a moment before completing her note taking. She felt sorry for Rufus, having something so incriminating hanging over him. Having someone as mercurial as Tristan perhaps threatening to discredit him must have been a nightmare. And, if the shoplifting story was true, was Athena aware of it, too?

Jackie and her team would be here today; Clare would pass this information on to her in person, despite her reluctance to engage with the DCI. If Harriet could be cleared, so be it. But there was no pleasure in strengthening the case against Rufus, only sadness and regret.

CHAPTER 29

Clare couldn't settle back to her sermon preparation after the phone call and opted to track her husband down at Greenwood. She found him on the terrace at the side of the big house, listening to Susan in full flow.

'Athena is on it, with the press. Thank God it's recess. But I ought to get into the office this week, show them that everything is on course – and catch up with the constituency caseload; I can't abandon people.' Susan fiddled with her chunky necklace, then saluted Clare with a brief gesture.

David was calm. 'This could take a while, Susan. The office will be fine.'

'But my profile won't be. The knives are out already, with people lining up to demonstrate their suitability for my portfolio "until things are resolved". Snakes.'

The door opened and Jim joined them from the house. 'Have you seen Jess?' he asked. 'She went out for a run some time ago. She headed for the woodland track.'

'She's a grown-up, darling,' pacified Susan, while raising her eyebrows quizzically at David.

'Would you like me to look for her?' David offered, sympathetic to parental concern, and Clare thought not especially eager to continue the conversation about Susan's career taking a nosedive.

'I wanted to check she was OK about everyone coming for lunch here,' Jim said. 'You know, to have a change from the hotel menu. Now, I'm wondering where she is, after everything.'

'You're right about lunch,' agreed Susan. 'I'll get Athena on to it. Jess won't mind. The pub in the village will make up some sandwiches for us. Jackie and her lot will be back later this afternoon, but they can fend for themselves. She was with Harriet again this morning.'

So, Clare would have to wait before passing on the information about the alleged shoplifting outfit.

'It's warm enough to be outside,' Jim indicated the terrace, 'but I'd like to be sure Jess is OK. That's a kind offer, David, I appreciate it. We value your help too, Clare.'

Clare was struck by the change in the older man; his latent belligerence had been tempered by events. His nephew, however troublesome, had been killed, and his daughter's wedding had been a disaster. While Susan steamed on with relentless resolve, Jim was less sanguine. He seemed more aware of the possibilities of ongoing risk to them all. His fatherly anxiety touched Clare.

She was relieved when a text from Gill arrived, letting her know about her own children's morning, and she walked further into the garden to reply to it, while David set off in search of his boss's daughter.

Jess still hadn't reappeared when the larger group joined Clare in the garden and assembled on Greenwood's sunny terrace to pick at an assortment of food laid out on platters.

Celeste's voice was brittle but bright, others were quieter. Everyone seemed relieved that the interviews were over – for now, anyway. Fabian mentioned that he hoped this might mean the crime was nearly solved. He suggested that perhaps, after all, it would prove to have been an interloper who had come across Tristan and robbed him – probably taking his phone. Or some political protestor misfit who had turned violent. As Fatima, Susan and others agreed with him, Clare thought that clutching at straws had its advantages for all of them, diverting attention from disturbing possibilities closer to home.

She noted Suki's yawn and Fatima's wearied expression, while Rufus munched his way through plate after plate of the buffet as one way to soothe his jagged nerves. Clare watched him closely, then tried to turn her attention back to the others, not wanting to look too beady-eyed. The sandwiches on offer were tasty; she was savouring the strong cheddar in hers. She knew David would appreciate the coronation chicken ones, and thought it was a pity that Tom wasn't here for those, too.

Ahmed was attentive to his mother. Clare liked the way he shielded her from an onslaught of conversation from Celeste, deflecting questions and soaking up her anecdotes and declarations of emotion. By tacit consent, conversation about Tristan and the police investigation dwindled while lunch was consumed. The heat of the afternoon was much discussed. People talk about the weather when they don't know what to say.

No one commented on Jess's absence until Fabian eventually asked Ahmed if he'd taken some food up to her room.

Then he was distracted by Susan changing the conversation. Clare knew that David had been out looking for Jess, and was worried when he returned alone. He'd shaken his head towards Jim and Susan, and then taken a seat beside Clare without comment. Harriet was missing too, perhaps preferring to be alone after another interview with Jackie.

People were taking mugs of tea and coffee and moving from the terrace on to the upper lawn, to sun themselves on benches or scattered chairs. Fatima had settled on a lounger and seemed to be dozing. Clare saw that Rufus was assiduous in following Susan's suggestion of offering refills, alert to her every hint or instruction. Clare sat beside Celeste, stroking Monty, the brown Labrador, who nestled his head on her lap. Celeste talked on, relentlessly.

Martin arrived, proffering a bowl of raspberries, which Suki offered to wash and prepare. Celeste and Athena set off with him to pick some more, Celeste's restlessness skilfully being put to use by Athena. Clare assumed the observant special adviser had noted Susan's glances of concern directed at her voluble sister-in-law, and the tightened muscles on Jim's face. Athena was proactive, anticipating her boss's wishes and dealing with things with a combination of subtlety and decisiveness. No wonder Susan depended on her.

Fabian proposed that others join him in looking for Jess. He looked slightly awkward about doing so and Clare wondered whether that was because *he* was making the suggestion, rather than Ahmed. Fabian had emerged from the house holding his sister's phone, which he'd found tucked away in the kitchen when he called her number. He, Rufus and Ahmed then set off in different directions to search for her, perhaps eager for some kind of activity. Clare wanted to stay near the house to await Jackie's return.

Gradually, the varied degrees of concern for Jess's whereabouts were shifting to anxiety. Harriet was taciturn when she rejoined those still on the lawn, simply saying she would take some lunch with her and join those looking for her cousin.

Jim withdrew inside, and Susan also retreated to make some calls.

Clare enjoyed the realisation that she and David were alone, apart from the sleeping Fatima – the other guests had scattered, and even the dog was now slumbering, with his head on her foot.

She looked at her husband's face as he leaned back in his sloping chair. 'No sign of Jess anywhere?' she said. 'Maybe she just needed time away from everyone – what a circus.'

'Yes, she needed time to herself yesterday, didn't she? We all did,' he murmured.

'What shall we do about getting home? Anna and Tom are OK with Gill for a couple of days, but I'll need to get back to the parish. How much longer do you think this will last?'

'Hard to say; it's full on for the police team.' David sounded weary.

His replies to the salvo of questions were too vague for her liking. Whose side was he on? Jackie had obviously been homing in on Harriet as suspect number one, and David was lukewarm in his response to the news of Clare's conversation with Rufus and to the hints she gave that there could be more to reveal there. In fact, he was platitudinous, non-committal about everything, and dismissive about political protestors being involved in the murder. At least Clare agreed with him there – surely that theory was too convenient to be taken seriously.

But she was frustrated David had no real insight to share – he'd only say that things would take time. Clare felt she was being civil-servanted and it set her teeth on edge. She didn't want to ask her husband more about what Jackie and her gang were doing. If he wasn't going to divulge things, why push him? She wasn't telling him all she'd heard about Rufus, either.

Perhaps realising he was only exasperating her, David returned inside to continue liaising with the office; some situation or other was brewing, as ever. Clare sat on, emulating Fatima in taking time to rest, not wanting to dislodge the dog. She found herself becoming more concerned about Jess. But plenty of people were searching for her, and Clare told herself there was no reason to panic. She was out of sorts: anxious about talking with Jackie, irritated with David and embarrassed that she had been snappy at him.

She closed her eyes.

Clare woke some time later to discover her canine companion was now enthusiastically welcoming Jess, who stood on the grass before her, breathing hard.

'Clare, you need to come with me,' she gasped, half bending over with the exertion of her sprinted return. 'Something terrible has happened.'

CHAPTER 30

The base of the quarry had plentiful bracken, and the fronds partially covered the form of the fallen man. Rufus lay still, with an arm flung out beside him, perhaps in an attempt to lessen the impact of the fall. His other arm lay beneath his crumpled torso.

Ahmed was first to reach him, sliding down the steep-sided quarry, avoiding rusty implements, broken furniture and other junk that had been launched into the pit over the years. He shouted for assistance as he tentatively turned Rufus onto his side, making initial assessments and then clearing his airways, beginning mouth to mouth.

Everywhere there was disruption. Those summoned from the house were running to offer help. Once Athena reached them and saw who it was that Ahmed was tending to, she frantically screamed her boyfriend's name. Jim had summoned an ambulance again, to what had once been their rural idyll. Fabian had come from the woods when the commotion reached his ears. Susan was white-faced, holding on to her daughter and stroking her back, as Jess craned forward to see what was happening beneath them.

Clare and David had both scrambled down the bank in

Ahmed's wake, Clare side-stepping David's half-attempt to make her pause at the lip of the drop. Her palms were grazed from clutching at roots and branches on the descent, her knees and backside muddied, but she was there to hold the hand of the injured man, and to speak gently to him.

'Well done . . . Well done, Rufus. Ahmed is here, helping you. Hold on – that's it. Well done. The ambulance is coming . . . You're OK, Rufus. Well done.'

He was alive, although his hand felt cold in hers. How had he fallen? Or *had* he fallen? Was this another crime? And, if so, what had happened and why? The questions were churning in her head, even as she tried to sound calm and reassuring for Rufus's sake.

Whatever had happened, the urgent need was to help Rufus, and Ahmed was doing all that he could, as Clare tried to give the wounded man strength and encouragement. Rufus coughed and groaned, twisting his head slightly, then became quiet again.

David was circling them, moving in to help Ahmed and Clare steady Rufus's weighty form and adjust his position, while calling up to the others not to come down but to be ready to guide the paramedics. Jess had moved from her mother's side to join Athena, attending to her stricken friend, who was sobbing above them, occasionally still calling Rufus's name. Jess managed to keep Athena above the quarry and away from her injured boyfriend, consoling her as best she could.

Clare could hear them, but kept her focus on Rufus, stroking his arm, responding to whatever Ahmed needed to do and quietly telling Rufus what was happening, that

Ahmed was helping him and that the ambulance was on its way. He seemed to clutch her hand, but then his grip slackened. Perhaps she was imagining it.

She didn't know how much time had passed, but relief washed over her when she saw that the paramedics had arrived and were coming towards them. The first thing they did was fit an oxygen mask to Rufus's face and administer some kind of injection. Clare continued to whisper to him as they worked. When it was time for him to be moved, she unpeeled her fingers from his and stepped back. A cheery tattooed medic took her place, giving a constant flow of chat and reassurance to the unresponsive man. They roped up a stretcher and half dragged, half lifted the unconscious Rufus out of the quarry. The ambulance was waiting on the track nearest the lane, and, once Rufus was loaded up, they took off to the hospital. The sirens blared.

After the immediate crisis, Fabian drove Athena to the hospital. Her seemingly inexhaustible reserves of competence and efficiency had run dry. Everyone else scattered, shaken by what they had witnessed, unsure what to do when there was nothing to be done.

Clare collected mugs and plates left across the terrace and upper lawn. The plates had been licked clean of crumbs by the assiduous Labrador. She was joined by Martin, who began folding the fabric-covered chairs, commenting that it looked like rain later. Clare realised he was right; clouds had thickened while she'd cleaned herself up, and the sun that had lulled her into sleep earlier in that long afternoon was now obscured by clustered grey shapes. Martin seemed to appreciate her willingness to work together with him to restore some order to the garden; he was at a loose end, too.

Under the greying sky, the day had chilled and the patterned seat cushions looked gaudily out of place.

'Harriet wouldn't hurt a fly,' Martin said, as he collected up a stray napkin that had been dropped beside a flower bed. 'You need to tell your husband that – the police won't listen to me.'

'I'm sure they'll investigate everything carefully,' Clare lied, suspicious that Jackie would now be reluctant to waste time investigating anyone other than her prime suspect. There would be an added urgency after Rufus's fall – no one wanted any more accidents.

'How come Ahmed was on the scene so quick?' Martin almost growled as he moved closer to Clare. She stood still as he jerked his head towards the house. 'Fabian was outside somewhere, too, and anyone could have done this, pushed him over.'

'Perhaps it was an accident, and let's hope he recovers.' Clare knew she was being overly optimistic, but she didn't know what else to say. 'How far was the fall?' she asked Martin.

'Twenty foot or more.'

'I wonder why he was by the quarry.'

'There's the den on that side of the quarry. Several of them. Maybe he was heading there. Meeting someone?'

'Maybe he stumbled and fell.'

'Yes, and maybe Tristan came back and tripped him. This was no accident, Clare.' Martin was solemn, insisting that she faced the implications of what had just happened.

She knew he was right, and perhaps Jackie was right, too, to focus on Harriet. Clare didn't want to assume Harriet was innocent too easily, but she didn't believe she was guilty. As far as Clare was concerned, others were suspects too. She hoped Jackie would keep other possibilities alive.

The very ground beneath their feet on the soft lawn felt unstable now. In this time of sudden violence and shocking death, any malevolence seemed possible. Anyone seemed capable of anything.

CHAPTER 31

Jess was hunched in the corner of a sofa, holding her knees up to her chin as if shielding herself from the memories, as if willing herself back into the refuge that the woodland hideaway had provided before this fresh disaster. On the coffee table in the sitting room, the floral arrangements from the wedding tables had begun to wither: the flowers were curling inward, the golden petals laced with brown lines.

Having tidied the garden with Martin, Clare had joined the family in the house, but set herself a little apart, sitting in a high-backed armchair against the far wall of the large room. Jess was a friend, but Clare's link with the wider family was more tenuous. Susan seemed to regard her as an extension of David, a professional adjunct with useful and reassuring links to the Almighty. In this crisis, her presence seemed to be valued, although she felt herself to be something of an interloper as the family came to terms with this latest shock.

'I was in the den . . . earlier.' Jess spoke slowly and deliberately to her father. 'I remembered it while I was out for my run and went there after. It's still cosy – hidden. I heard people calling for me. David . . . and later Fabian. I thought Fabian would come and look for me there, but he just called, he didn't come close. No one stooped down and came in, so I was safe.'

'You're safe now, sweetheart. No one's going to hurt you.' Jim moved closer to Jess, stopping beside the sofa. Clare had seen his concern for his daughter, but not heard such tenderness from him before.

'I've got nothing left to hurt, Dad. I heard him fall, but I didn't help.'

'You'll need to tell the police all about it.'

'What's there to say? I heard a sort of shout and crashing branches, but it was quite muffled at that distance. I didn't even move for a bit. It was a while before I went and checked, and looked over the edge.'

'You can tell them that. And you did help. You saw him and came and got us.'

'I didn't go down to him. Ahmed did. That delay may have killed him, Dad.'

Clare thought it was strange that Jess had not checked on him – she was a medic, after all.

Jim was more reassuring, perhaps rightly so, saying gently, 'He needed more help than you could give. He needed the paramedics and the hospital. They had to be called.'

'Do you think he chucked himself off? Do you think he meant to die?'

Susan walked into the room, stirring sugar into a steaming mug of tea, and answered her daughter: 'Who knows? The police will find out. You drink this, and I'm bringing you a hot-water bottle.' She put the mug down on a table beside Jess and stood there, as if to ensure that it was drunk.

'I'm OK, Mum.'

'Ahmed would want us to take care of you, darling. He's gone to check on Fatima. He saved Rufus, you know.'

'Saved him?' Jess turned her body to face her mother. 'How are you so sure? How come he was there so fast?'

'He was looking for you,' her father said. 'Everyone was. We were worried.'

'Yes, I'm sorry.' Jess subsided, her stiffened back now slumped against the sofa cushions. 'Sorry to have worried you. I needed to get away.'

There was silence in the room. Jess, with her eyes closed, was unaware of her parents' attentive gaze on her. Clare watched as they beheld their daughter, then exchanged glances with one another.

As if resulting from an unspoken agreement, Susan spoke quietly but firmly: 'I think we may have to prepare ourselves. Celeste has gone back to the hotel, but Harriet has been taken away by the police.' Jess groaned as her mother continued, 'Of course, the police may find that Rufus was responsible for his own fall. For whatever reason. But something is going on with Harriet. She was such a quiet girl, but she has had trauma. We've not really known her for years.'

'We need to keep an open mind. Not prejudge anything.' Jim sounded weary, with his voice apparently resigned to an unwelcome reality.

The parents seemed to be bracing themselves against Harriet, as if by doing so they were defending Jess in some way. Were they simply scapegoating their niece in order to deflect suspicion from Jess or another culprit? They must have realised there was enmity between their daughter and their errant nephew.

'Forgive my intrusion,' Clare heard herself say, shifting position in her chair as Susan and Jim turned to her in some surprise, 'but could we be jumping to conclusions, here? There may be suspicions about Harriet, but perhaps there are other possibilities?' She ploughed on, sitting more upright as she did so: 'David and I were wondering why Tristan was here.' She winced internally at using her husband in this way, but he'd back her up if it came to the crunch. 'We wondered whether others here might have had reason to silence him, and if you had any thoughts on that?'

'Thank you, Clare.' Susan spoke with sincerity, as if accepting a proffered gift rather than a suggestion that others might be implicated in her nephew's murder, or that there was anything unusual in the wedding invitation being extended to him. 'It's so helpful to have you here. You were wonderful with Rufus in the quarry, and you and David are such a support to us all. I have no doubt that the police will be thorough in every aspect of the investigation, and naturally will consider all avenues.'

Yep, she was an experienced politician.

'I'm just sorry that offering hospitality to Tristan has resulted in this tragedy.' Susan gave her husband no opportunity to speak, continuing seamlessly in her exploration of the uncertainty about Harriet, citing her special adviser: 'Athena didn't want to say anything, but she did mention earlier that both she and Rufus had noticed how ill at ease Harriet was yesterday. But that could mean anything, couldn't it?'

Susan seemed a little more open to different interpretations of Harriet's behaviour. Maybe it was a good thing that Clare had spoken up, uncomfortable as it had been to do so. Jim didn't seem to have minded; he just looked at her thoughtfully while his wife spoke.

'But we may have to face unpleasant possibilities.' Susan's voice grew firmer again. Back on track. 'Of course, we can't reach any definite conclusions. I'm simply suggesting that we recognise the very sad possibility that Harriet may be quite damaged, and the terrible consequences of that for her and for others.'

Jess, still curled tight, turned herself away from her parents, pushing her face into the back of the sofa and lying still.

Clare was silent. What was there to say?

CHAPTER 32

Unbelievable. Jackie had maintained her professional poise for the remainder of that long day. She'd interviewed Harriet at the station and others in situ at Greenwood, but the lack of clarity about exactly who had been where and when as Rufus fell was frustrating to say the least.

It was after dusk when the DCI eventually left the grand house; she put her headlights on as she drove slowly along the gravelled drive and then accelerated away.

Her team had established a timeline that excluded precisely no one from ambushing Rufus at the edge of the quarry and pushing him in. Harriet, their prime suspect, had certainly had the opportunity to attack him – but so had all the others.

An accidental fall seemed unlikely in the extreme.

The likeliest explanation was that Rufus had some information which threatened Tristan's murderer. And that he'd paid the price for not informing the police before someone took the opportunity to silence him.

Clare Brakespear had recounted some tale of shoplifting and shame. A somewhat belated piece of information. Rather vague, too, although it would be followed up. Everything would be. Methodical, painstaking work was the way forward; Jackie would tolerate no shortcuts.

Clare was obviously eager to head home and seemed shamefaced about not contacting the police immediately regarding the rumoured shoplifting operation. Jackie didn't think it would have made much difference, but had resisted saying so.

As the evening drew to a close, with the interviews and examination of the site concluded, there was no reason to detain the group further. It was time to let them go. Jackie was glad to be driving away herself, despite how inconclusive the day's investigation had been.

The initial phase of the enquiry was over, but the DCI and her team still had a murderer to catch. Possibly a double murderer, if Rufus didn't recover. The motley group of suspects could disperse, but they would be seeing her again.

CHAPTER 33

Life carried on as September began. The Brakespear family had returned home from Greenwood to their normal day-to-day lives. But what is normal life? Every week, Clare was with people in the parish for whom a diagnosis, an accident or a shattering disappointment had changed everything in a moment – their once ordinary day now anything but.

Her parish church remained in the heart of the village and was solid and sure through all things. Its squat tower had been there since the 1300s, present in all that the community went through, year by year. The wooden board beside the vestry listed incumbents and the dates they had been vicars from 1315 onwards. You could see who the parish priest was when Henry V fought the Battle of Agincourt; who'd been vicar during the years of the Great Plague, the Fire of London, the Civil War and the Blitz. At the bottom of the long list of names was Clare's own. Five years earlier, Anna had pointed it out to a friend and commented, 'Mum's the first girl.'

As parish and family life continued, sometimes it was almost as though the events of the wedding had never happened. Everything that was part of the rhythm of days carried on: the children catching the school bus, the dog slumped at

Clare's feet as she tackled relentless emails, the visits to people now facing the challenges of life and death. The curve of a new baby's ear, early-morning sunlight, laughter and mugs of tea – all part of a normal week, joy and grief and everyday life mashed together.

She loved the village, with its layers of community. Loved its people, with their idiosyncrasies. There was the woman who was strangely invested in the idea that Clare would make a complicated gingerbread house with her children, relentlessly asking about how things were going with the festive recipe she had passed on. (Christmas wasn't for another three months. Estimated preparation and decoration time: two and a half hours. Never going to happen.) There were those who cut the churchyard grass and checked the fire extinguishers, and those who busied themselves in attempts to improve Clare's personal grooming, providing helpful suggestions about face creams or recommending a hairdresser who would 'sort out your highlights properly'. Thanks.

That morning, David was walking the dog while Clare made breakfast with the children in the scruffy kitchen. She carried on with life – they all did – but on some level things were different since the events at Greenwood. Clare had sent a card to Rufus, a painting of the Houses of Parliament half hidden in a dawn mist. He was still unconscious and unmoving. She hoped he would one day be bustling about Whitehall again, tapping his phone with self-absorbed gusto.

Initially, after her boyfriend's fall, Athena had seldom left his side, but, after some days of his limbo state, she had returned to the office, brushing off expressions of sympathy or concern.

Harriet had been released, having been held to assist with enquiries. Susan had given statements of no comment, in contrast with Celeste's willingness to protest her daughter's innocence to any journalist who made themselves available to her.

Jess had gone into hiding, cutting herself off from contact with almost everyone. Ahmed had remained with her in their shared flat, but David thought things were strained between the newly married couple. Ahmed was also spending a lot of time with his mother and sister.

Tristan's body had not been released to his family. David believed this was in case of a challenge to the medical evidence about his death, but the unease of this added to the sense of suspended reality, of unfinished business. David was not party to Jackie's thinking. The case she was drawing up against Harriet was moving forward without information being shared.

'I liked Tristan,' Tom announced to his mother and sister while chewing his Saturday breakfast pancake and leaning back on a red kitchen chair. 'I wish Harriet hadn't murdered him. She didn't seem like a killer.'

'Who says she did kill him?' Anna countered, reaching for the chocolate spread. 'You're swallowing police bias. Dad says nothing is settled yet.'

David might have been surprised to be quoted so assertively, but he was out with the dog, and Clare kept quiet.

'Soon will be,' Tom muttered gloomily. 'And I'm not swallowing police bias. I think it's a miscarriage of justice. Lots of people were there. I heard Tristan ask Rufus to meet him in the tree house. Harriet isn't the only suspect. Why aren't you doing anything, Mum? Why can't Dad stop it?'

'It's hard to know what to do,' Clare replied. 'It's up to the police and the courts, now. But what you heard could be relevant, Tom. Let's think about it.' She moved a stack of paperwork off the kitchen table.

'Celeste hasn't given up.' Anna waved her phone at her mother. 'She's launching a petition about it. I've signed it already. You should too, Mum.'

'I'll need to look at it carefully,' Clare stalled.

'I thought we were supposed to *work* for justice, as well as pray for it.'

'Why don't you talk to Dad about it when he's back with Mia? They should be home soon, unless she found a deer to chase.' Clare retreated towards the stairs and a shower. She hoped Harriet would be cleared of suspicion, but taking sides so publicly seemed premature. It was up to the police to check every possibility, and that would include whatever Tom had overheard. 'And please get your football bags ready. It'll be time to head for practice soon.'

The siblings looked at one another. They knew an evasive tactic when they heard it.

The next day, there was no avoiding the new arrival who walked up the path as Clare was in the church's stone porch, bidding the congregation farewell after the Sunday morning service. The tall woman sported an orange and brown checked coat, and was carrying a large beige handbag.

'Celeste, good to see you.'

'I needed to track you down, darling. I hope you don't mind, but you have to help.'

'Of course. Come in and have some coffee. David is still here, and the children.' Clare gestured for her to come inside.

'Another time that would be lovely.'

Celeste held back as a family came out and exchanged greetings and farewells with Clare, the younger children holding sparkly artworks. Celeste also smiled at them warmly, then turned her gaze to Clare again, who moved out of the porch to stand with her.

'I've got Harriet in the car. Please come and talk to her, Clare. Perhaps you can get through to her. I can't.'

'In what way?'

'She's given up. Totally. Hardly speaks. Gives her solicitor nothing to work with. Zero. I'm at my wits' end.' There was desperation in Celeste's voice as she appealed for help.

Clare followed her back through the churchyard to the car park, feeling slightly self-conscious that she was still in her service robes.

'That's quite an outfit,' Harriet said by way of a greeting, as Clare stood by the car window. 'Sorry about this. Mum was relentless.'

'It sounds very difficult.'

'I don't feel much.'

'Would you like to come and look in the church, or walk in the churchyard, maybe? There's no need to talk, unless you want to.' Clare took in the unwashed hair and the dark, ringed eyes. Her voice was soft: 'Maybe we could just sit together for a while, leave your mum in the car – if that's OK with you, Celeste?'

Celeste bobbed her head and slid into the driver's seat, as Harriet silently acquiesced to the suggested stroll to a nearby bench. She followed Clare at some distance, walking slowly. It was a good place to sit. The solid bench had its back to the church wall and looked out over the churchyard to the patchworked countryside beyond. The women settled beside one another.

Harriet kept her gaze lowered, her expression dulled. 'You can't sort it, you know. Mum thinks there's a magic wand to be waved, but there isn't.'

Clare was shocked by the change in her. Harriet was in despair.

'Means, opportunity, motive for killing Tristan. Same goes for shoving Rufus into the quarry, apparently. I could have pushed him to stop him from incriminating me. That's the theory, anyway.'

'I suppose the important thing is whether or not it was you,' Clare said gently.

'Not terribly relevant, Vicar, if I'm the one heading for jail anyway. Might be some interesting portraits to be painted in my new community – if they don't see a paintbrush as too dangerous an implement to give me. A stick of charcoal is risky, too. Who knows what I might do with that?' Harriet's expression was bitter, as well as exhausted.

'It matters to your mother.'

'She'll cope. Susan and Jim will help. They're helping with my legal fees. Fatima's also very good to her – they've been in touch – and she has plenty of other friends. They all know the likely outcome of the trial, it's clear.'

'My Tom doesn't think you're a killer, nor does Anna, for what it's worth. They have a nose for these things.'

'Shame they're not jurors. When I was their age, I believed

in people, too. Not anymore. Thanks for the chat, Clare —
sorry to bother you, but Mum insisted.'

Harriet spoke as if she was ending the conversation, but
didn't move. Nor did Clare. A bird landed on the damp grass
in front of them and pecked at the ground. Another joined
it, slightly further away, beyond the nearest grassed grave.

'It feels like karma. How Tristan was treated, how his life
was, and now this.'

'I think bad things just happen, not because we deserve
them. Innocent people shouldn't be in jail.' Clare's voice was
level.

'Thanks, Clare. I know you want to be kind, but there's
no point.'

'Come on, Harriet, is there more we can do? There must be
other possibilities. Other people were targeted by Tristan, so
what about them?' Clare became more animated in response
to Harriet's limp passivity.

Harriet's voice continued in monotone: 'I don't want to
start hoping. Or stirring up muck and suspicion amongst
people I care about, when nothing good will come of it. I just
want it over. To be left alone.'

'Is there something you're keeping to yourself? It's not a
time for secrets or heroics.'

'I'm not heroic. Tristan made life difficult for people. That
doesn't mean they killed him.'

'Someone did.' Clare vividly remembered Jess's fury on the
wedding morning. 'Did he threaten Jess or Ahmed in some
way? Is that it?'

'I don't know. Maybe. Maybe Susan, too — it's possible.
But there's nothing definite and no reason to implicate them.

Fabian has already explained about the Italy stuff – that was bad enough.'

'A cancelled TV series hardly matches a prison sentence.'

'There was the picture issue, too.' At last, Harriet offered something.

Clare kept her tone steady. 'Right. What happened about that?'

'It was stupid. Fabian had a financial issue, a debt.' Harriet was beginning to open up. 'I only knew about it because he once asked me about copied art. Turned out he used someone I know, so I pieced it together.'

'Someone copied a painting, for Fabian?'

'Crazy, really. It was a Stubbs. It's in the hallway. Two horses grazing. One has its head lifted, looking out at you.'

'I saw it.' Clare remembered it clearly; it was a gem.

'Fabian got a copy made and I think Tristan knew about it. Maybe Fabian asked him for contacts, someone to sell a dodgy painting on the quiet. Fabian isn't the brightest. Asking Tristan for help – not a good move.'

'Maybe he was paying him.' Clare's mind was racing with possibilities.

'Probably. Anyway, the paintings weren't swapped. It's still the original there.'

'What happened to the fake?'

'I don't know.'

'It's worth pursuing. It could be a motive for someone else.' Clare's commitment to investigating the options grew. If Harriet was innocent, they needed to uncover the real culprit – even if it involved some unwelcome disclosures.

'Fabian wouldn't hurt a fly. He chickened out of the whole picture-swap thing.'

'Sure, Harriet, but maybe someone else planned to take over where he left off? Maybe Tristan offered the painting to someone else? Or planned to use it to make the substitution? It would be worth a lot.'

Harriet raised her head, sloping her body backwards, looking at the top of the beech trees and the open sky. Some birds flew over. 'Maybe, but that doesn't change things, and wishful thinking doesn't help. Mum means well, but I can't cope with her feelings. At least Susan and Jim don't say much.'

'Have you heard from Jess?' Clare asked.

'She and Ahmed almost split, you know. Another triumph for Tristan. She texted; I haven't replied. What would I even say? I've cut everyone off. It's not easy for people, adjusting to me being a killer, obviously.'

'It sounds as if you feel everyone's sure about that.'

'Well, not Martin, maybe. He's driven over a couple of times. But I've not seen him. He brought us a box of veg. He texts too, but I don't read them all. I'm not even sure why I'm telling you all this. I don't really know you.'

'Maybe that makes it easier.' Another bird landed on the ground in front of them – a magpie, this time. It looked quizzically at them before pecking at a patch of earth near Clare's feet and then hopping further away.

'It feels like I'm living in a Sunday-night drama series; we could be in shot now.'

'Who would you like to play you?' Clare wanted to keep Harriet talking.

'Someone with decent hair. But they'd make her a scruffy

artist. Maybe give her a dog, probably a sorry rescue. You'd be a plump vicar with no make-up. Maybe a troubled past. You'd probably drink.'

'Thanks. Sounds glam.' Clare was glad of the increased energy in Harriet's voice, and the hard-edged humour.

'They could make a true-crime number out of this; pity Tristan isn't here to milk it. He'd have loved it. Susan wouldn't, though. Uncle Jim would get lawyers on to it, try and stop it. Expensive. But it's irresistible, isn't it? Bet they'd want Jess to find the body in a dramatised version – a bride with blood spattered on her frock. That's box office.'

'I can see it now.'

'All the politicos will be suited: Athena in a sharp jacket, jewel-coloured; Susan glossy, with a manicure and hair tossing all round.'

'Bridesmaids frolicking.'

'No problems in the rural idyll. All the men chiselled and chinned. Ahmed may be a bit anguished, when not looking sinister. Fabian's already so good-looking, there's nothing to be improved upon there. Bet they give Martin a West Country burr; the setting is Hardy country, after all. Maybe he can chew a straw and channel his inner Gabriel Oak.'

'Tristan as villain?'

'Sure. Me as Tess, obviously, sticking in the knife.'

Harriet's tightened face had eased slightly, the lapse into fantasy providing some release. She was engaging, albeit with world-weary bitterness.

They sat quietly for a moment before Harriet asked, 'Do you know how Rufus is doing?'

'Early days. They say it will be a long haul.'

'Mum wants to know. She lit a candle for him in the cathedral.'

'It's lovely that people are thinking of him.'

'I hardly met him. Fabian told me he was after a job with Susan, if he could get one, when she gets a Cabinet post. Though, that seems a lot less likely now that her house is murder city. Unless she can play the "law and order" card, send all of us convicts to an overseas holding centre, perhaps? Will you come and visit? Get a vicar's pass?'

'I'll visit you wherever — I'd rather it was in an artist's studio with a good pub nearby, though.'

'How sweet does ordinary seem now?'

'Yes, the joys of a typical, dull day at home.'

The women sat on, companionably. There was comfort in being together, the church wall solid behind them, the countryside in full view.

CHAPTER 34

Some choir members left the church and headed towards the car park. They chose to walk on the pathway past Harriet and Clare, who were still seated on their bench. One older man looked curiously at Harriet, and another was trying to catch Clare's eye, with a query to raise about the evening service perhaps.

Clare nodded her inability to talk and kept her focus on Harriet, so the women were left uninterrupted, just receiving general mumbled greetings as the group passed by.

Once they were out of earshot, Harriet picked up the conversation, sounding resolute. 'Clare, I don't want to make this more awkward than it needs to be. I'm probably heading for prison. I feel numb, like it's an out-of-body experience.'

'It feels surreal to me, so I can't imagine how much more so it is for you.'

Harriet looked at the ground, scraping her foot to and fro, scuffing up dust. 'Anna and Tom are right: I didn't do it. But it's pointless to say so. And it's difficult for people, not knowing whether to pretend to believe me or not. I don't think my solicitor does.'

'I believe you.' Clare realised that she meant it.

'You have to say that – you're a vicar.'

'No, I don't. I say it because I want to, and it's true. But I'm not sure what's to be done – other than pray, of course.'

'Well, that's not done me a lot of good so far. Let's hope Mum's candle does the magic for Rufus. She was very upset after he was hurt. That seems to have got to her more than anything.'

'She's worried for you. Bringing you here is part of that, maybe.'

'I can't talk with her about it. I don't want to talk to anyone.' Harriet's voice was expressionless again.

'Well, we may need to discuss things, to plan a way forward. We need to investigate the picture-forgery angle, for a start.' Clare wanted to stimulate Harriet into action and to encourage her out of this.

The conversation paused. An elderly couple had gone over to one of the more recent graves and they stood there together for some moments before walking slowly away. The churchyard was now deserted after the last attendees at morning service had left.

'Images of Tristan lying there keep coming back to me. Do you see them too?' Harriet asked.

'Sometimes.'

'I wonder if he'll haunt me. Or haunt whoever did it. Or the tree house. Do prayers work to stop hauntings?'

'Yes.'

'Did you pray in the tree house for him?'

'Yes.'

'And for me?'

'Of course.'

Harriet turned to look more directly at Clare. 'Do you pray for the person who did this, too?'

'Yes, for everyone.'

'I went to a crime-fiction festival with Mum — years ago, up north. One of the writers said the perpetrator is not always the worst person in her novels.'

'Makes sense. How we judge one another seems very inaccurate to me. I don't think we can rank each other on a guilty scale. It's clear that sticking a knife into someone is wrong — sick and brutal — but there are reasons for doing things. Not justifications, but reasons.'

'I think I'd rather have it all over with. Go off to prison, get it done.'

'Does the investigation itself worry you?'

'There are things it would be better people didn't know, that's for sure.'

'Yes, but sometimes things lose some of their power by being brought into the open, maybe? And finding out the truth is the only way of getting the police off your back.' Clare ignored the sense of satisfaction she felt at the prospect of thwarting any intention Jackie might have of convicting Harriet. There was nothing personal in this, she told herself. Or tried to. And she could use her connections with the Zetland family to pursue the case. She could visit Greenwood again, for a start.

Then Harriet surprised her: 'Mum has a secret. I'm not sure what it is, but it's a big one. For all her openness and apparent candour — she has something hidden. And I think that somehow Tristan knew about it.'

'What makes you say that?'

'The level of Mum's fear of him. Tristan hinted about something to me once and I told him where to go. Mum disliked him, sure, and there were plenty of reasons for that. His existence was a nightmare for her. The discovery of it, all the angst with my dad, how Tristan was – all of it.'

'Have you asked her about anything she might be keeping hidden?'

'It's part of the reason I've closed down. Whatever her secret is, perhaps it should stay that way.'

'It sounds very difficult for you, as if you're pulled in different directions, with conflicting feelings.'

'It's exhausting. I want the truth about Tristan's killer to come out. But I'm scared of the mess that will be brought up in the process. If I'm heading for jail anyway, what's the point?'

'No wonder you're exhausted. But solving the case is not your responsibility. Others are working on it – DCI Carter and a whole team. But you can help them, and so can I. We're not just bystanders. We can explore possibilities together. The forgery angle, and also talking with your mother.' Clare felt rather pleased about this approach. Clearly there was no question of her competing with Jackie in any way.

'Help away, then. But be careful, Clare,' Harriet warned. 'Someone pushed Rufus into the quarry. It wasn't me, but somebody did, and I don't want anything to happen to you.'

CHAPTER 35

It was two days before Clare had the opportunity to head to Dorset again. When she reached Greenwood's imposing entrance, Jim was surprised to see her and tentative in his welcome, apologising that Susan was busy with Athena, but ushering her inside to come and see Jess. He didn't seem keen to spend time with Clare himself. She proffered reasons for the impromptu call, citing a visit to her sister-in-law Gill, who lived nearby, as her excuse for dropping in. She'd calculated that arriving unannounced was the best way to secure entrance to Greenwood again – and, judging from Jim's lack of enthusiasm, she'd been right.

Jim shouted for his daughter to come and join them, explaining that she quite often came to visit and that Ahmed was on call today, so had stayed in town.

Clare mentioned that David was pleased to see Athena back at work, and she asked if there was any more news of Rufus.

'No. His parents are there permanently, now, I understand.' Jim looked down at the hallway's chequered floor as he said this, as if not wanting to engage with her directly, nor with the pain of the situation.

'This uncertainty must be such a nightmare for them.'

'This is not easy for anyone, is it? What brings you here, Clare?' His sudden question held more challenge than enquiry; he raised his eyebrows at her and his directness was discomforting.

'Clare, brilliant to see you!' Jess was all smiles as she hastened down the stairs to join them, holding what looked like a bundle of laundry in a heap of floral fabric. 'Dad, where's Mum?'

'Making plans with Athena,' Jim replied. 'Fending off more press interest, probably. Trying to get on with work priorities without anyone stirring.'

Clare could take a hint. Reminders of Tristan and the wedding fiasco were unwelcome.

'I don't want to stay long,' she said hastily. 'Just looked in to say hello before heading on to see Gill.' This sounded lame, even to her. 'Sorry to just turn up.'

'No problem,' Jess said brightly. 'I've been sorting through stuff in my old room. It's good to take a break.' She put the pile of clothing on a sideboard and hugged Clare. 'Let's catch up. Any chance of a coffee, Dad?'

Jim grunted in assent and took himself off into the kitchen, while Jess led Clare towards the library. On the way, Clare noted that the Stubbs painting of the horses was still in situ in the hall.

'Whenever I come in here, it reminds me of being interviewed by that policewoman,' Jess confided. 'That Debussy music is still open on the piano – I haven't touched it since. I kept looking at it while she went on and on.' She curled herself up in one of the large chairs and gestured at Clare to make herself comfortable in another one. They could hear the radio from the kitchen, which Jim had presumably switched on, and some disturbance from outside – the weather had turned blustery and there was an unexpected splatter of rain against the window.

Clare reminded herself that she was here to check on the painting and gauge how the family were, however awkward that might feel. She felt traitorous, though her care for Jess was genuine as she asked how she was doing.

'Hard to say,' Jess replied eventually. 'Numb, maybe. I wish there was more we could actually do; this waiting is horrible. I think Ahmed was right about us skipping the honeymoon and getting back to work. People know about all this, thanks to the press noise. It was best to get the return over, and all the sympathy. The tilted heads.'

Jim had wheeled himself into the room. 'I wish your brother had your work ethic,' he said, manoeuvring towards them.

'You're too tough on him, Dad. It makes him nervous around you.' Jess stood abruptly and closed the music on the piano, reaching up to replace it on the shelf behind.

'What do you mean?' Jim's face reddened alarmingly.

Jess had ignored an unwritten rule of the household, not to challenge her father's version of reality. Clare knew they were all a little wary of the prickly Jim – with good reason. His moods changed so disconcertingly.

'Nothing,' Jess answered, sitting down again. 'Well, yes, maybe I do mean something, Dad. Be kinder to Fabian.'

Clare thought she was brave. Perhaps the new world after Tristan's murder had room for more reality in their family dynamics.

Jim didn't share this view. 'I think you can leave me to

manage my own life, thank you. I've left your coffees on the kitchen table.'

'Maybe one of the positive outcomes of this nightmare will be to talk about some things that need to be addressed.' Jess stood, reaching out an arm towards her father.

Clare hadn't anticipated this level of disclosure. Perhaps her presence gave Jess confidence.

'Like your relationship with Ahmed? Or is it only other people you want to improve?' Jim snapped back. Ouch.

Jess seemed unintimidated. 'Ahmed and I have our issues, sure. Perhaps everyone does. In our family, we all have to cope with Mum's work and those political pressures. We keep quiet about it. I realise Suki was tactful about the education stuff.'

'We're loyal and we get on with it.' Jim turned as if to leave the room, dismissing his daughter.

'But the refugee issue is a different level. Not just the usual press stuff, or Mum voting for rubbish policies, or attending endless constituency events. This is her bag, and it really matters. People are dying, and I don't want to be complicit in it.'

Jim paused to answer his daughter. His jaw was set, and a raised vein was now noticeable on his temple. 'I don't remember you standing for election, Jess, or did I miss something? Your mother has achieved an enormous amount for her constituents and for this country, with courage and conviction. Her political choices are nothing to do with you – or with me, for that matter.'

'That plane flew across our wedding reception, Dad. Those four people are still missing. Mum is part of that.' Jess was not backing down, despite her father's anger.

'There's no need for hysterics.' The two were like prize-fighters squaring up.

'No need for denial, Dad. Fabian has his own way of coping – he goes away. I focus on my work, and on my life with Ahmed. But I feel ashamed about what Mum is involved in now. Athena, too. She's my friend, but her hands are dirty with this. It impacts all of us. Suki never mentions the school or other stuff, but I know how people feel. How I feel.'

'While you give me the benefit of the view from your high horse, you might like to reflect on who paid for the marquees, the dinner, the dresses and indeed this home, which you have enjoyed for thirty years.'

Clare's stomach clenched. She'd rather not be party to this; it was too much.

'You're right. I am grateful. I'm just telling you how I feel about it.'

'It would be more helpful if, instead of complaining, you supported your mother and me in trying to get this mess resolved as speedily and quietly as possible.'

'Dad, I think you're an amazing support to Mum, and to all of us – Harriet and Celeste, too – but maybe we can be a bit more honest with each other? Not have to be marvellous all the time?' Jess took a deep breath; Clare thought she was trying to compose herself, preparing to continue without resorting to aggression. 'Let's drop it. I'm sorry, Clare – you don't need this. Sorry, Dad – I don't want to make things more difficult. I think I'd better head back home. If that's OK with you and Mum? I don't want to abandon you, but let's not argue, either.'

'I'm sure your mother and I will cope. More normality is

probably the best way forward. This investigation will be with us for a while longer.'

'Dad, there may be things coming out into the open that are unwelcome.' As Jess spoke, Clare noticed a wariness in Jim's eyes. His gaze took in both women. His annoyance was gone.

He answered Jess slowly: 'I know, darling, I know. That's what I'm worried about.'

The rain had stopped as Clare made her exit, and the atmosphere in the house had calmed. She supposed flare-ups of emotion were unsurprising with all that the family were dealing with. Jess seemed to have become emboldened, and some of the family's polished equilibrium had dissipated. Was Jim's hostility simply a manifestation of his concern for his wife and family, or were there things he wanted to ensure remained hidden, which might be relevant to Tristan's murder? Both father and daughter had acknowledged the possibility of unwelcome disclosures.

Jim had been happy enough to acquiesce to Clare's request to revisit the garden before she left, seeming relieved to bid her farewell. Jess excused herself from joining her, and Clare was content to be alone in the grounds again.

The grass was wet from the earlier shower, and she was glad of her sturdy boots. The lawn was littered with autumn leaves, soggy underfoot, and cobwebs glistened with moisture amongst the foliage in the dampened flower beds. The beauty of the garden was wistful in its autumnal appearance, very different from its sunny wedding splendour.

Clare made her way to the tree house. It had an abandoned air: the grassed area around the trunk was muddy, the steps upwards discoloured with wet clumps of soil and patterned with crushed leaves. It wasn't easy to climb those steps again.

Inside was stillness, and a place to pray for Tristan, for Harriet and for all. For resolution and justice. Prayers again for whoever had stabbed Tristan here, and for wisdom in establishing what had happened, and why.

How had the knife been brought here, unobserved? Or left secreted inside? How had the killer been unseen? Had they somehow dropped themselves down from the tree house, without using the stairs?

Clare rested her hand on the balustrade. Could someone have stood on it and hauled themselves upward into the higher branches? It was possible. She leaned out and looked up. They could have climbed up further, manoeuvred themselves around the trunk, then dropped down on the far side of the huge tree, out of sight of her or anyone else approaching. It would have taken agility and courage – or desperation.

Jackie and her team would be aware of this, and also of the political and family issues which Clare was exploring. Clare was sure that Tristan had known things which could discredit this family, whether about Jess or others.

Had Jess engineered the dispute with her father this morning in order to distract Clare from returning to questions about her extreme tension on the morning of the wedding? And was Jim only concerned to defend their reputation and his wife's career, or were other concerns at play? The family's veneer had cracked, but Clare was certain there was more to be learned.

Coming back here reminded Clare of her own family's response to events. Their views on tree houses, in particular. She and David were coping with Tom's determined campaign to have a tree house built in the rectory garden. It felt gruesome, but maybe it was his way of processing what had happened, and Anna was staunch in her support. Clare could ask for help in building the thing. She knew the parish's farming family would be brilliant, and Bill, the stalwart churchwarden, too. But Clare was in no hurry to embark on that project. She had her own grief to process, and building a tree house was no help to her. It was sad enough to be back in this one.

CHAPTER 36

Harriet had told Clare, when they liaised about this visit on the phone, exactly where Martin was staying on the Greenwood estate. Clare decided to call by, and now stood in the somewhat basic living room inside what had once been his grandfather's home. Martin welcomed her into the modest space with considerably more warmth than Jim had been able to summon on her arrival at the big house.

She looked out into the cottage's garden – at the solitary, solid tree there, its roots bubbling up in lumps beneath the disrupted grass. On the dusty windowsill was a curled postcard picturing aquamarine seas at Kynance Cove. Some words were faded on its back, in a childish hand: *Wish you were here, love H x*. It had been written years ago. It was touching that it had been kept.

'Sorry to be nosy,' she said, replacing it as Martin returned from the kitchen to ask whether she'd like sugar in her tea. 'I love Cornwall. Harriet mentioned she went there as a child. We often go – Anna and Tom love it. Childhood times at Greenwood must have been idyllic, too.'

'They were.' Martin had been washing his hands and he dried them as he reminisced. 'The four of us were together every summer, as well as the Easter holidays and May half-term. Fabian and Jess had ponies, and Harriet and I got to ride them too. We used to play all sorts of games, everywhere across the estate. Fabian came up with different ideas every day, and sometimes we'd make up plays and perform them. Jess was always a fast runner, but Harriet was brilliant at hiding, and Fabian could mimic anyone.'

Martin smiled as he relived the memories. Clare had never heard him so talkative.

'I've always loved it here,' he continued. 'Everyone was happy – even Harriet's mum and dad. We couldn't believe it when the split came, and when Tristan came on the scene. Everything changed, then. It was crazy. Harriet's happiness was finished, that's for sure.' He shook his head and was silent.

Clare remembered something Anna had shown her online: a photo of Martin on a London march supporting refugee rights. Could that have caused problems between him and the Zetland family? Might he have been involved with the plane stunt?

It was easy enough to ask him about it, and Martin was unperturbed, answering as he fetched their drinks from the kitchen, bringing them through on a metal tray.

'No, that kind of caper's not for me. I think Susan probably heard about my views; a couple of papers carried that picture. Athena said something about it – she wanted to make sure I wouldn't cause any embarrassment for Susan. It was no big deal. I told her there was no way I'd mess things up here, however strongly I felt. After all, I want to keep living here.'

He volunteered that the postcard from Harriet had been

sent before she knew of Tristan's existence. What a shock that had been. And now the shock of the murder.

'It's still hard to believe that he's gone.' He shrugged.

'And Rufus injured, too. There was some tension between him and Tristan, I think.' Clare was circumspect; there was no need to spill everything she knew, however helpful Martin was.

'Rufus was another one out for himself. Wanted a job with Susan, I heard – just like Athena. Maybe Tristan knew some-thing about that.'

'He seemed to like being informed about things. You don't suppose he saw that photo of you in the paper, maybe?' She was thinking aloud.

'Maybe he did, and told Susan or Jim – who knows? But it was Athena who spoke to me about it. She's quite something.'

There was a brisk knock on the door, and Martin went to open it. 'Speak of the devil,' he muttered, looking at the visitor's outline through the dimpled glass. Then he opened the door and said, 'Athena, good morning.'

Athena looked beyond him into the cottage and, seeing Clare, acknowledged them both with a dip of her head. She spoke crisply: 'Sorry not to have messaged you, Martin, and to just turn up. But Susan and Jim wanted me to reiterate the importance of complete discretion with regard to all the press interest, and to mention that they will need to discuss tenancy issues with you at some point. I know you're probably well aware already; this is just a courtesy call and a reminder, really.'

'Sure.' Martin nodded.

'I'm so sorry about what happened to Rufus,' Clare offered.

'He's fine.' Athena's usually friendly face was stiff, almost expressionless. 'Well, not fine, but I'm doing OK. Thank you, Clare. I'm keeping David and the office updated.'

Martin gestured at the room and offered Athena tea.

She declined, saying she must be on her way; she had various errands to tick off her list. 'It's better to keep busy.' She spoke rapidly. 'Susan's here, but heading back to Whitehall again tomorrow. The show must go on.'

'Of course.' Martin's voice was considerate. 'But, if you need more time out, you should take it.'

'I'm fine . . . I will be fine.'

Clare watched as Athena took a step back with each staccato word, and Martin said goodbye.

Closing the door, he said, 'I feel sorry for her, and I need another drink. More tea?'

'Thanks.'

As he busied himself with refills from the ancient kettle, Clare looked around at the cracked lino floor and spartan room.

'How long did your grandfather live here, Martin? I heard he was tower captain – was that for some years?'

'Yes – he taught me to ring, and Fabian learned for a bit, too. You'll know about ringing – it takes a bit of skill.' Martin smiled again as they returned to the living room; he seemed to enjoy chatting about his past. 'Grandad lived here from when he was a kid – his dad worked for the family here, years back, long before the Zetlands came. The cottage was Grandad's private territory, not for the big-house family.' He became more sombre. 'I never invited Harriet or the others here.'

'Why not?' Clare queried.

'Class, I suppose. And money.' Martin's voice had a grittier edge. 'Grandad wanted some privacy; he might not have owned this place, but it was his home.'

'Will he be able to return here, or will he always need residential care?' Clare realised this was a difficult time for Martin, for many reasons.

'He'll stay in the nursing home, but he doesn't realise it yet. It's hard for him.'

'It's a big adjustment. Is he pleased you're here?'

'Yes, he likes to hear about everything. He's loyal to the family and to Greenwood, and I am, too.'

Clare wondered whether the family appreciated that steadfast loyalty and if they realised the significance of this cottage to Martin. It was his home now, as it had been his grandfather's before him. Athena had referred to tenancy issues – hopefully Martin would be able to stay.

Clare thought Athena was driving herself too hard, distracting herself with a demanding workload to avoid dealing with the distress of Rufus's injuries and the uncertainty about the timing of his recovery. If indeed he did recover. The possibility that he might not had to be faced. How might any future career be impacted by his injuries? He and Athena had a hard road to travel. No wonder the proficient special adviser was keeping a tight lid on her feelings and remaining detached from others' sympathy. It was one way to cope.

CHAPTER 37

Clare was happy to be back on home territory again after yesterday's trip to Greenwood, or at least on her local high street.

This week's sermon was percolating as she sat in the café, stirring her coffee: it was on the feeding of the five thousand. 'You give them something to eat,' those disciples had been told. Sharing what we have, using the resources we've been given. Generosity. Gladly receiving all that we are given, day by day, and sharing it. Maybe she would invite the primary-school choir to sing, if it wasn't too late to ask, and include them in sorting the gifts brought along for the food bank, too.

Harriet arrived, looking around the café nervously until she saw Clare's wave.

'Sorry I'm late,' she said, pulling off her beret and unwrapping a blue woollen scarf from her neck as she sat down.

'It's fine. I had a meeting here, and since then I've been people watching and doing a spot of work.'

'Am I part of your work?'

'Murder has a way of sneaking up the priority list.'

Clare updated Harriet about Tom's enthusiasm for building a tree house, and her visits to Greenwood and Martin's cottage. She described revisiting the tree house, and her ideas about the possibility of someone climbing up into the higher branches of the tree before finding another route to clamber down, circumventing the steps. It was frustrating that physical evidence was limited. Not that she'd have had any access to it.

'So many of us went into the tree house during the afternoon,' Clare remarked, 'the forensics will have traces of everyone there, not just you and me.'

'Maybe the vicar did it? You bobbed up there, did the deed, then returned to discover me, was that it?'

'Obviously . . . Just don't tell the bishop.'

'Martin went up there at some point, and, from what Tom told you, it sounds as if Tristan invited Rufus to meet him there. What was that about?' Harriet was fully engaged in their pooling of ideas.

'It's easy to assume Tristan was malevolent. But perhaps not. Perhaps he wanted to apologise to Rufus . . . to put things right. Or indeed to Fabian . . . about that picture stuff.' Clare hoped so. When he talked to her before the wedding reception got underway, Tristan had wanted things to be better. But had he wanted it enough to act upon it, or had he simply followed his old patterns of disturbance and disruption? Provoking people instead of peacemaking?

'You're very charitable.' Harriet's tone was sceptical. 'It's more likely that Tristan was going to get some more cash out of people, if he had leverage.'

'Maybe. Perhaps Athena will know more about the Rufus angle. Can you talk to your mother about whatever she might have feared about Tristan? Or is that too difficult to ask her?'

Harriet shook her head. 'She's unlikely to tell me, if this is a secret she's kept from me for years. But maybe she'd talk to you. It's worth a try, if you're willing?'

They were interrupted when Clare was greeted by two mothers with their babies, ready to be admired. Both infants sported novelty hats: one, a knitted strawberry helmet; the other, a tiger. Both were regulars at the village toddler group held in the church hall. One mother updated Clare about diocesan safeguarding training dates; the other mentioned a neighbour's hospital admission.

Harriet listened and watched the babies, who were both focused on the conversation, turning their heads from speaker to speaker like spectators at a tennis match. One stretched out a raised fist, then seemed to enjoy unfolding and refolding its fingers. Alerted to this fresh entertainment, the other baby copied, and both giggled. They were still busily doing so as their mothers left the café.

Clare continued listing actions to take, as if in a committee meeting. 'I need to ask Tom some more questions, and there's Fabian to follow up with, and anything which could disrupt Susan's political prospects gives her and Jim a motive. He defends her so fiercely – even against Jess.'

'This is horrible; we're talking about my family. And yours, if Tom has other things to tell you.' Harriet rubbed her hands across her face as if to massage the contents of her teeming brain. 'I'm scared and I don't want to go to prison, Clare. Please help.'

'You can help yourself, too. What is it that you're not telling me?'

Harriet dabbed at some coffee spillage on her saucer, letting it seep into the napkin. Her silver seahorse earrings caught the light as she spoke. 'I think Jim knows something – something that Mum knows, too. They've kept in touch through the years.' She paused, and Clare gave her time. 'Maybe it was financial. Things were tight for Mum. She trusted him. Jim was furious at the whole double-life thing that Dad pulled. He and Susan tried to help Mum, and kept inviting me and Dad to stay, along with Tristan. Then, after Dad died, Mum got invited to the wedding. For whatever reason.'

'You think Jim was behind the invitation?'

'Maybe it was Susan, wanting to reconnect our families now that Dad has gone. Wanting Tristan and me to relate to one another, as the two beneficiaries of the will. Whatever.'

'Was it all about the money?' Clare tapped the table, thoughtfully.

'I think it was more personal than that. This might sound crazy, but I think Jim and Mum had a connection. It sounds ridiculous – I can't believe I'm saying it – but it feels better to have told you.'

As she voiced them to Clare, it was as if Harriet was at last able to acknowledge her own suspicions.

'Once or twice, Mum stopped her phone conversation when I came into the room, or used a fake "super, right" voice to say I was there.' Harriet spoke more quickly as she unburdened herself. 'I think it was easier not to think about – it was all so awkward. Once, when I answered the landline, years ago, it was Uncle Jim calling. I was surprised it was him, and he was obviously surprised to hear me, too, and said he didn't need to leave a message. At first, I assumed it was nothing, but now I wonder about that – and Mum's refusal of all Susan and Jim's invitations to Greenwood after she and Dad split.

Perhaps Jim gave us money and Mum was embarrassed about that. Whatever the reason was, could Tristan have known something about it?'

'We'll have to ask your mother,' Clare said, decisively. 'It's the simplest approach. She may not tell us anything, or she might be able to put your mind at rest.'

'OK – she likes you – let's see her together, and also follow up on some other leads. We can ask Fabian about the picture. I'm not sure about the refugee-policy protest stuff – can David help about that?'

'Maybe, but it's difficult for him. I'd do better to get Anna on to it. She can find out all sorts on that phone of hers.'

'We need to find out whatever we can, for Tristan's sake.'

'Yes – and do you think he'd want you to be shut away for years for something you haven't done?' Clare believed there had been the beginnings of a better relationship between the siblings, however fragile.

'No, I don't. Because, beneath it all – the split, the anger – we were connected. That's what Martin didn't like.'

'People say blood runs thicker than water.' Ouch. Clare wished she hadn't mentioned blood. Nil points for tact.

CHAPTER 38

Before she could follow up on Harriet's suspicions about Celeste and Jim, Clare had some more pressing family concerns to deal with. She had decided to accompany David, who was taking Tom off for a chat with Jackie. She'd wanted to keep the whole thing low key, but Anna had not been easily fooled. Her daughter always knew when she was tense, however convincingly Clare imagined she was playing it.

'You'll be OK, Mum,' she said as she hugged her goodbye. 'There's nothing to worry about.'

Great, I thought I was the grown-up here.

Tom was animated in the car, discussing police tactics and weaponry, but was silent once they entered the interview suite with its easy-wipe mauve sofas and pile of pre-school picture books. Clare wished she could make this easier for him.

She had gone for a smart-casual look and was wearing trousers with a pink striped shirt. She attempted to quell her mean inner voice, which was eager to make snarky remarks about Jackie's suit – that jacket was actually quite creased.

She made herself focus. She was determined to be pleasant and demonstrate to Tom that there was nothing to fear from this encounter. Her voice went croaky when they exchanged greetings, and she felt embarrassingly flustered about where exactly she was supposed to sit – on one of the seats near the table, or on one of the chairs set further back. Jackie was unperturbed, of course, at ease in her own territory. David was supposed to be taking the lead – why couldn't he sort this stuff out?

Finally, they were seated in a semicircle, Tom with a parent on either side of him, and Jackie facing them all, a coffee table between them. Beneath it was a box containing plastic bricks and some Lego figures.

David stepped up to give Tom encouragement to recount the conversation he'd heard between Tristan and Rufus.

'Tell Jackie what you remember about it, Tom. Mum and I are pleased you're doing this. Take your time, and just say if you're not sure about something – that's fine.'

Their son had been in the garden, lying beside a pile of logs on the edge of the lawn with the dog, Monty. To her credit, Jackie was a good listener, clarifying some points but allowing Tom time to tell things in his own way.

'Tristan called him Woofy, and Rufus didn't like that.'

'Right, I see. What else did Tristan say?' Jackie spoke slowly and calmly, looking interested.

'I didn't hear it all because they were whispering. Rufus wasn't happy; Tristan sort of laughed at him. And he called Harriet a name, too.' Tom shuffled his feet.

'OK. Tell us what you remember about that.'

'It was when the gardener came up to them and Tristan was saying things about him smoking. That Harriet wouldn't like smoke on the planet or something.'

'Right. Did he say anything else?'

'He said she was vegan or veggie or rabbity or something. Anna is a vegetarian, but I don't call her names.'

Clare wasn't thrilled that 'rabbity' had been added to the potential repertoire of names that Tom could call Anna, but there were more important things to think about right now.

Then Tom continued, 'Tristan called the other man Marty, I remember.'

'I see. What did Tristan say to Marty?'

'Something about having a fag – that's a cigarette – in the den, I think.'

'I see. Anything else?'

'Athena – she was a bridesmaid with my sister – she said something about refugees to the gardener man, when she came. After Tristan had gone. The plane had upset her and Susan, I think. The one that had the banners behind it. The man told Athena not to put the thumbscrews on. You use them to torture people with. They have them in the Tower of London.'

'Right.'

'She said loyalty was important and that it was good to chat.'

Listening to her son, Clare realised it didn't amount to much. There had been some teasing, perhaps some animosity between the former school fellows, but Tom had heard nothing incriminating. And Athena had presumably been making it clear to Martin that he was not to ruffle any feathers that day, about refugees or anything else. Millions of people were appalled by the government's policies; there was nothing exceptional in Martin supporting a protest, nor in Athena's desire to keep a lid on anything which might embarrass her boss.

Tom was more forthcoming about the skirmish between Ahmed and Tristan, in the churchyard.

'I was a bit wet, from the stream, but Mum was OK about it.' Now it was Clare's turn to smile encouragingly, as her son continued, 'Tristan wasn't very nice to the man who got hurt later, Rufus. But Ahmed wasn't very nice to Tristan, either. He was a bit rough.' Tom looked round the room at the adults and faltered, as if reluctant to criticise the groom, his friend. This episode had unsettled him more than Clare had realised, and she felt bad about not thinking of that. He was unused to adults grabbing at one another, and this had been different from playground scuffles or mock wrestling with his dad.

Jackie reassured him, and Tom continued with his account of events. He had seen Ahmed's sister and mum strolling in the garden, and Tristan had asked someone else about his own sister and where she was, but he wasn't sure who. Clare was surprised that Tom had overheard some reference to a painting being valuable, but he was vague about who had mentioned this – he thought maybe it was Tristan, and Jackie didn't push him.

Instead, she thanked him for telling her everything he remembered and said how helpful he had been. She was quite convincing. Clare was sure David would think she had been very nice. Tom, too. Clare wasn't quite ready to admit it, though. She simply didn't like Jackie, that was the nub of it.

So, they'd done their duty, bringing Tom in to tell the police what he knew, and he'd gained confidence during the interview. Clare was proud of his careful accuracy and of his politeness. It was always a relief when her children's good manners made an appearance. She knew it was ridiculous, but it mattered to her that Jackie thought well of Tom.

The interview was over quite quickly, although it hadn't felt rushed. Another policewoman came to show them out, chatting with Tom pleasantly and happy to answer his enquiries about handcuffs and tasers as he left the room, followed by David. Clare was mystified by her son's expertise in weaponry of any kind; there wasn't a mean bone in his body.

Before Clare could follow the others, Jackie called her back, asking if she wouldn't mind having a quick word while David and Tom went to the car. The women remained standing; it was understood that this would only take a moment.

It was nice to hear that Jackie was grateful to them for bringing Tom in. She also expressed a hope that the experience had not been upsetting for him in any way. Clare was only mildly defensive – Tom wouldn't be upset; her son was very resilient.

When Jackie asked if there was anything else Clare had noticed or remembered which could be useful for the team to know, Clare realised that a suggestion from David might be behind this conversation. She tried not to look surprised that her opinion would be welcome to the DCI.

'Thank you,' she said. 'I guess there are complicated relationships here, aren't there?' Well, she wouldn't win any prizes for that observation, and Jackie just stood in the doorway and looked at her, waiting for more. Clare found it hard to know what to say. 'There were family tensions, and tensions in the school relationship between Tristan and Rufus and beyond – but you know about that.'

'Yes, the background you provided on that was helpful,

thank you.' There was something perfunctory in Jackie's crisp response, but Clare thought she was probably trying to sound appreciative, though she missed the mark.

'I think old relationships or rivalries can fester, can't they, and resurface in unexpected ways,' Clare offered, while suspecting that this generalisation wouldn't cut much ice with Jackie either. The DCI wanted something more concrete.

Clare was suddenly aware that she'd rather avoid talking about old relationships with her husband's former partner, so continued hurriedly, 'Martin was a bit left out by the family and isn't a fan of the government's policies, and of course Athena is very loyal to Susan, and it was widely known that Rufus hoped to get a job in the team, too.'

Why was she telling Jackie things that she already knew? Jackie was just standing there, not showing any particular reaction. It was unnerving and Clare could feel herself blustering.

'I think Harriet only clutched that knife because she was in shock. I wondered if someone could have climbed upwards out of the tree house and got away like that, or used a rope?'

Jackie simply nodded, saying nothing and showing no particular enthusiasm for this theory.

'I do think the possibility of a forged copy of the painting is something else to explore; pictures by George Stubbs are worth a fortune, aren't they?'

'Right, yes,' Jackie said, nodding yet again. 'Thanks very much for this, Clare.'

Clare felt like she'd failed an exam paper she didn't know she was taking, but perhaps Jackie was always one to keep her own counsel. With her nodding and her silence, the

detective made inscrutability into an art form. Clare felt like
an overenthusiastic amateur, faced with Jackie's resolutely
non-committal expression.

'You're probably already looking into the family background, the work relationships and everything else,' Clare
added. 'And thanks for your kindness to Tom today.'

'Thank you for accompanying him, and for all your support in the investigation,' Jackie responded, neutrally. After a
slight pause, she stood back to allow Clare to leave the room
ahead of her; the conversation was obviously at an end.

Before heading their separate ways, the women performed
a ritual exchange of civilities as they bade one another a good
day, standing to one side as a group of officers hurried past
them along the corridor.

It had only been a quick conversation and Clare had tried
to help. But, as she left the station, she thought that little
would shake Harriet's position as Jackie's prime suspect, and
mentioning the forgery issue or other possibilities wouldn't
make much difference to that. Tom had done well – perhaps
a treat was in order on the way home. Preferably something
that didn't involve armaments. Maybe an ice cream.

CHAPTER 39

Jackie and her sidekick, a new addition to the team, walked into the shop. The bell jangled as they opened the door. Canvases were propped against the walls, which were filled with prints, painting and etchings. Charcoal forms, swooping birds, massive leaves and Turneresque sunsets meant there was plenty to look at.

The young woman who sat in the glass-fronted inner office in a tangerine jacket was uninterested in the arrivals and, though she looked up for a moment, continued her phone call. Jackie checked her own phone as they waited. There was no update from any of her team, and nothing more from David either. It was thanks to him that she was following up this forgery story, though she doubted anything would come of it. She was pretty sure Harriet was her woman.

The gallery employee emerged from the office and addressed them warily. Maybe she thought they were about to offer her a sales pitch of some kind. Her eyes brightened with interest as Jackie introduced herself, showed her credentials and asked to see Mr Simmons. This was clearly out of the ordinary.

Mr Simmons was apparently in the studio upstairs, but could be fetched. Much to the disappointment of the curious young woman, Jackie suggested she could find him herself. She wanted to see exactly what he was doing up there and give him less time to prepare his answers.

She and her accompanying officer made their way up the narrow stairway, where still more paintings jostled against framed posters advertising exhibitions from years ago.

The upstairs studio had windows on three sides and was crammed full. There was an assortment of sculptures, chairs piled high with books, and a couple of sofas with colourful fabrics heaped on them. There was an easel which bore an unfinished sketch of a fruit bowl. The real fruit bowl was set on a round table in the centre of the room – its contents now more shrivelled than in the sketches.

Chris Simmons was seated at a wooden desk that was almost obscured by magazines, paint tubes and an assortment of tools. He was tapping on a laptop set amongst the towers of papers. He looked up in irritation as Jackie and her sergeant walked in.

'Chris Simmons?' Jackie flashed her card as he rose.

'Yes. What is this about?' He looked beyond the police officers as if to berate his orange-jacketed colleague, but she wasn't there. Jackie was sure the young woman would be getting an earful later.

'I want to ask you about some horses.'

CHAPTER 40

Clare had brought her dog with her to visit Celeste and Harriet. Mia the golden retriever was always useful, either for providing a distraction when situations felt awkward or for bringing happiness into a room with a swish of her feathered tail.

'She's so friendly, darling,' Celeste cooed, as Mia nuzzled at her. 'Do let her be free.'

Clare kept the buoyant animal on the lead, despite Celeste's request. She still shuddered at the memory of her dog's ebullience amongst the churchwarden's collection of Toby jugs. He had sought to reassure her that a certain type of super glue would be both effective and almost invisible when it came to making the necessary repairs. Clare suspected this was for her benefit rather than being strictly accurate.

Celeste's large metal sculptures stood in the hallway, but her sitting room contained numerous intricate ceramics at tail-swiping height. Clare was glad she'd been cautious.

She held Mia's lead tight while admiring a wall display of Venetian masks. A gilded sun was nestled cheek to cheek with a silver crescent-moon, the sun's rays flaring outwards extravagantly. Lace-and-feathered eye masks were hung as if ready for an evening masquerade; there were leather ones with a cat-like design, a burnished golden lion mask and a traditional carnival-style jester mask. Harriet had reminisced at the wedding about childhood holidays with both of her parents in Venice, and here were the mementos of those happy times.

The three women talked about the display while Mia was fussed over by an affectionate Celeste. The dog was less interested in standing by the masks than in a full reconnaissance of the rest of Celeste's home. In the studio, she was particularly interested in the heavy-duty welding equipment, sniffing the gauntlets and protective clothing which Celeste donned for metalwork.

As a compromise, they agreed to have their drinks in the garden as the day was so mild, allowing Mia to explore outside without restraint. After an initial roaming of the flower beds, she settled close to them, with her head on Celeste's knee. She was a tactful creature.

Harriet had tied her hair back. She wore a green dress and a black jacket, looking more formal than usual. She had clean hair, and her freckled face looked resolute. She was clearly ready for the conversation ahead.

While her mother petted the dog, Harriet explained why she had asked Clare to join them. 'I think there are some difficult questions for us to think about, Mum, and having Clare here will help us to do that.'

'You sound positively alarming, darling,' Celeste exclaimed, and then addressed Mia, ruffling her ears: 'Having you with us is a treat, isn't it, Mia? You're a lovely dog, aren't you?'

'I don't want to intrude,' Clare offered, 'but perhaps there are things it would be helpful to talk about, to untangle who really killed Tristan.'

'Fire away. Let's put our heads together. We'll get this sorted, Harriet. We'll fight for your freedom.' She lifted her chin.

'There's no need for armed combat, Mum. But there are secrets I think Tristan knew about, which may need to come out into the open if we're going to catch his murderer.'

'Tristan had a nose for trouble,' Celeste replied, looking downwards.

Now that mother and daughter had begun talking, Clare sat listening, letting Mia absorb Celeste's nervous movements, providing her with canine reassurance.

'Mum, what did he know?'

'Some things are private, Harriet. I don't need to tell you everything. And it's painful to talk about.' Celeste bent over the dog, her face turned away. When she continued, her voice was shaky with emotion. 'I've always wanted what is best for you, darling. And you've done brilliantly. Your art is wonderful . . . your career, everything.'

'I'm my own person now, Mum. You don't have to protect me from anything.'

'Goodness me!' Celeste looked at Clare. 'One day, your children will be all grown up, Clare. It takes a bit of getting used to.'

Clare smiled but didn't speak; Celeste was an expert at steering the conversation off into more congenial tangents and Clare wasn't going to assist her.

Harriet pressed on: 'Is it possible that Uncle Jim knows something about it too?'

Celeste placed her hand on the top of Mia's head, as the dog leaned against her. 'This is difficult, darling, and you have enough to cope with right now. I don't see how unearthing everything will help. You've suffered enough, thanks to your father and this whole Tristan business.'

'It was dire, Mum, but we got through. You've always supported me – taking me to exhibitions, putting up with my moods. I know I haven't been easy to be around, the last few weeks.'

Clare could see their bond was strong, even if there were some areas that were sensitive.

'Well, thank you, darling. I've tried. It isn't always easy to know what's best for your children. Your uncle Jim has helped us in many ways, but quietly. I'm not even sure he told Susan about it.' She looked at Clare with distress in her eyes. 'It's hard to know what the right decision is sometimes, isn't it?'

'Yes, life can be very complicated,' soothed Clare, wanting to keep the space open and to welcome whatever Celeste was about to say. She had a small inkling of where this conversation was going.

'The thing is, darling, Tristan isn't your only brother.'

Whatever Harriet had expected, it wasn't this. She was open-mouthed, and Clare could see she was trying to fathom what her mother had said.

Celeste continued: 'You see, sometimes there are reasons for keeping things quiet. I knew it would be traumatic for you.'

Harriet gathered herself, and stuttered, 'It's . . . It's not about me, Mum.'

Clare sat motionless; she'd envisaged various possibilities and was relieved that this reality had now been acknowledged, however difficult it might prove for Celeste and Harriet. Harriet embraced her mother, and the two of them were hushed for a few moments.

'Whatever happened, I'm so sorry you had this secret, Mum. It must have been so hard.'

'It seemed the only option, at the time. After discovering Tristan's existence, I went a little wild.' Celeste smoothed her skirt with both hands.

Harriet stumbled back into her seat. 'What? You had a baby *after* you and Dad split?' Her voice was high pitched and incredulous. 'I don't believe it.'

'Exactly. I knew it would be too much – for you, and for me. I wasn't sure what to do. I left things late . . .'

'When did this happen? You were pregnant, and no one noticed?' Harriet was wide-eyed as she began to absorb the import of her mother's declaration. Clare was unable to help her, but at least mother and daughter were talking and listening to one another.

'I denied it myself, and then I had help.' Celeste spoke with resolution. 'It was that summer after your father left, when you had that long stay with Jim and Susan, and then stayed on and did the start of the autumn term at school with Jess.'

'When you were ill?' Harriet frowned, seeming to search her memories.

'Well, not ill, but confused – and increasing in size. I needed to be away from you. I couldn't imagine what you'd have felt. You were in such shock about your father. This would have been yet another betrayal.'

'Betrayal? It might have felt so to me then, but not now.

I can't believe you went through all this, Mum, and I never knew.' Harriet spoke more evenly now.

'I'm a survivor, darling. Jim knew, and he helped with the practicalities and lent me some money.'

Clare felt the puzzle pieces fall into place. She had some idea of why Jim had been so supportive and helped Celeste keep her secret. She also remembered Celeste's anger at him for inviting Tristan to the wedding. Perhaps there were other, deeper reasons for her rage against him, too.

'What happened?' Harriet was focused on her mother.

'It was surprisingly easy to conceal a pregnancy from friends. No one expected it, and – with careful clothing, large handbags and lots of scarves – it's amazing what people don't notice.' Celeste half laughed at the memory. 'Then I started talking to people on the phone, rather than meeting up. My vicar knew – he and his wife were very kind.'

'And Uncle Jim?'

'Yes, he was appalled at what your father had done. Horrified. He was very supportive, and he wanted to help you, too.' Celeste tilted her body towards her daughter, consolingly.

Harriet was tentative. 'Mum . . . Uncle Jim wasn't . . . You and he weren't . . .'

'Goodness me – no, darling. The child's father was someone quite different.'

Clare could recognise a lie when she heard one, but merely looked sympathetic as Celeste drew herself upright and continued, 'A fling, after the news of your father's double life. I had a few of those, I now regret to say. Well, I don't completely regret them; there were some great moments, but ultimately it didn't help.'

'And you got pregnant.' Harriet patted Mia, distractedly, and the dog raised her head.

'Yes. I was a little careless.'

'So was he, by the sound of it.'

'Times were different, then. And he was married – I'm not proud of that.' Celeste clasped her hands together.

'Did he know about the baby?'

'Of course not. There was no need for him to be involved and I didn't want his wife to find out. I was ashamed of being "the other woman" after experiencing such betrayal from your father. I wish I hadn't done that to someone else. The vicar was very understanding – just as you would be, Clare.'

'I hope so. It sounds like it was such a difficult time for you.' To say the least.

'I knew what I had to do. I decided not to tell anyone, and to give the baby up.' Celeste folded her arms.

'The baby was adopted?' Clare asked.

'From birth. Jim helped with that, too. Little Harry was adopted by a lovely family.'

Clare was surprised by the name, but Harriet didn't seem to have registered its similarity to her own; she was more preoccupied with the child's adoptive family.

'How do you know they were lovely?' Harriet sounded accusatory, as if she'd appointed herself the child's advocate.

'Jim checked it all out. He helped me with the agency and the costs of the clinic too. I went private and stayed there for a while. It was a peaceful place, on the coast. Norfolk.'

'Norfolk?'

Of all the surprises, Clare was unsure why Harriet found this one so extraordinary.

'Yes, Norfolk. Far away from you, and from everyone I knew.'

'It sounds very lonely,' Clare said.

'The social worker was professional – kind, too. Harry was a plump little baby. I had a day with him, then it was time to say goodbye.'

There was a pause while Celeste took in a deep, shuddering breath and gave them a tentative smile. There was something poignant about her restraint in talking about her infant son, especially as she was usually so loquacious. She seemed physically frailer, too. Clare saw how taut Celeste's neck muscles were, next to the chunky beaded necklace which now seemed too weighty to suit her.

Harriet reached over and stroked her mother's arm. 'I'm so sorry, Mum.'

'You had enough to deal with. Your father's behaviour, and the appearance of Tristan. I didn't want there to be any more shocks.' Celeste spoke more briskly: 'And I knew he was going to a happy home.'

'You sound so sure.'

'I was sure. He went to a very good home, and you had a steady home here with me, and with your father gone.'

Clare felt how brave Celeste was, glossing over the pain of this, for Harriet's sake.

'Did Dad know?' There was a hint of sharpness in Harriet's question.

'Absolutely not. I knew I could trust Jim not to say anything.'

I bet you could, thought Clare.

'Did you ever hear more about the baby?' Harriet asked.

'No. But perhaps it's a good thing that you know now. Once he's eighteen, he could seek me out. People do.'

'Would you like that?'

'I'm not sure. I was worried about it, before you knew.'

Neither woman seemed to know what to say next, but Harriet appeared to accept Celeste's story and gave her mother an encouraging smile. Clare was sad for her, discovering another huge deception like this. Both women were trying to help one another, but this was heavy.

The secret child explained Harriet's intuition about her mother's fears, and the phone calls between Celeste and Jim that she'd overheard. Clare wondered if there was a possibility that Tristan had somehow found out about this. He'd told Harriet he knew something about her mother and he'd even wanted payment to keep quiet. Could that have been about the baby? Surely, if Jim hadn't told Susan the whole story, he'd have been careful about leaving any records lying around. But maybe Tristan had found some correspondence that summer, or perhaps Jim had let something slip.

Harriet seemed to have put the whole situation about her murdered sibling to one side with this sudden news of another half-sibling's existence, but, as mother and daughter began talking again, Clare wondered about the possible implications.

If Tristan had implied to Celeste that he knew about her son, what might she have done to keep this secret from her daughter, or from others? Or maybe he'd even tried to blackmail Jim, believing, as Clare did, that Jim was the baby's father.

Or had Tristan told Harriet at the wedding and precipitated a murderous rage? But Clare had just witnessed Harriet's shock at her mother's revelation. That was genuine; no one could feign that.

This was all wild speculation, Clare told herself as she went indoors, followed by a docile Mia, to use the bathroom and give the mother and daughter some privacy. But, for Clare, Celeste's revelations opened up numerous possibilities. What had Tristan known – or surmised? Who might he have threatened or angered?

The masks on the wall looked down on her. At least Harriet and Celeste could now be open with one another about this adopted child. Hopefully he was being raised in a loving and happy home, without secrets and shame.

CHAPTER 41

'I'm sorry, dear – I thought you were all in the garden.' The short woman bustled past Clare in the hallway, then bent down to caress Mia, who was ever ready to make a new friend. 'I didn't want to disturb Celeste; I just popped by to drop in her ironing. I'm Celeste's cleaner, Stella. And you must be the vicar lady she's told me so much about. It's lovely to meet you.'

'That's right. My name's Clare, hello.'

The woman left off fussing at the excited dog and held out her hand to Clare. As she did so, Mia reached her head up to sniff happily at this interesting person and to thwack her tail against Clare in the process.

'Aren't you friendly?' she crooned, returning her attention to the dog, who accepted such admiration as nothing more than her due. 'Celeste has told me about how good you've been to Harriet.'

Presumably the woman was referring to her, thought Clare, though she was still staring intently at Mia. 'It's been a pleasure to get to know her,' she said. 'And Celeste. She's been very welcoming. This is Mia.' Mia had now stretched herself out at Stella's feet, offering herself up for a belly rub, which Stella duly obliged her with.

'How old is she?' Stella asked, as Mia lolled her head from side to side, mouth wide open.

'Just three, but still quite puppyish at times.'

'They never grow up, do they? My Skip is fifteen, but you wouldn't know it. He's just like he was as a puppy.'

Clare doubted whether he was quite as skippy as he had been fourteen years ago, but she agreed that dogs were always full of personality.

'Harriet was young when Skip was a pup. They were friends. I've still got the drawings she did of him. She's so clever.'

'Yes, isn't she.'

'People take advantage of her, in my view, and of Celeste. But I don't want to speak out of turn.'

'Of course not,' said Clare, very much hoping that she would.

'It's happened to me and my husband, too. Our son's marriage ended and he's brought his three to live with us. They don't want to be with their mum and her new man in their old place, but it's a squash at home now, and the youngest is allergic, so poor Skip can't go in the living room or kitchen anymore.'

'How awful. Poor Skip.'

'Celeste is the same – although she has got more room, of course. She had to have Harriet live here again, after what happened. Terrible. You're precious, aren't you?' Stella continued to scratch the dog, while Clare willed her to carry on talking. 'You'll know all about it – the money and that awful debt.'

Clare had no idea what she was talking about, but made an indeterminate sound, crouching down to stroke Mia too.

'I'd best say no more. But it was a lot of money and there was bailiffs and threats and all sorts.'

'Terrible.' Clare was shocked and unsure what to say.

'Well, I mustn't keep you. Celeste didn't want me disturbing you today. I only popped back with the ironing, in case she needed it. I must get going.'

'It's been nice to meet you, and lovely for Mia, too.' She wanted to hear more, but the woman was already heading out to the kitchen, asking Clare to let Celeste know that her ironing was back and saying hurried farewells over her shoulder as she left. The dog lumbered to her feet, now that the belly scratching had finished.

So, Harriet was in serious debt; she had become homeless and financially dependent on her mother. Clare had been told none of this by Harriet or Celeste, and the fact they'd tried to keep Stella away during Clare's visit suggested that they were actively concealing this from her.

This was unwelcome news, as it strengthened the case against Harriet – she had even more of a financial motive, now. But what felt worse to Clare was the realisation that Harriet had been hiding things from her, that she'd been content to work with Clare to expose others' secrets while keeping her own. Was she trying to divert suspicion elsewhere, perhaps?

There was a lot to think about. Clare tugged at Mia's lead, encouraging her to rejoin Harriet and Celeste outside. She gathered herself, determined to look cheerful and interested in wherever their conversation had led them. Perhaps DCI Carter had good cause to be treating Harriet with suspicion. Clare worried that she might be wise to do the same.

CHAPTER 42

The next day, Clare still felt hurt and unsettled by Harriet's secrecy. She had thought they were seeking the truth about Tristan's murder together, but Harriet had deliberately kept her in the dark about the dire financial situation she was in.

Harriet had Celeste's shocking revelation to digest now, and Clare wondered how things were going between mother and daughter after all that had been disclosed yesterday. After Harriet's initial shock, there would be further repercussions – both in coming to terms with her mother's sustained dissembling over so many years and also concerning the father of the adopted child.

Clare was somewhat relieved to have a day of straightforward pastoral visits, and was hopeful of no further revelations. After taking home communion to two elderly parishioners and calling in on the village toddler group, she headed off to the hospital, but not her local one. This pastoral care was related to the Greenwood wedding, and all that had happened there. She was going to see Rufus.

As Clare walked into Rufus's ward, she was pleased to see his mother and father by his side. They had messaged asking her to visit, saying that her card had meant a lot and that she would be very welcome. The room had a large window, shaded with blinds against the autumn sunlight. Cards and photos were displayed on top of a chest of drawers, alongside a tray of cups and saucers, some puzzle books and pens.

Rufus was still, his red hair bright against the pillow, his face pale. His mother's hand rested on his.

'Thank you for coming.' Rufus's father stood and greeted Clare, shaking her hand. His face was an older version of his son's, his hair a more faded hue. 'And thanks for your card.'

'I'm very sorry to be meeting you in these circumstances, with Rufus unwell.'

'We appreciate your support.' Rufus's mother was dignified as she met Clare's gaze, without moving from her place.

Clare greeted Rufus too, unsure whether he might be able to hear her. He showed no sign of doing so. Then she sat across the bed from his parents and asked them about their son. They told her about his childhood – his cross-country running and his passion for chess and gaming, his cheeky humour as a boy – and his stillness here in the hospital, through the long days and nights they'd spent beside him. There had been no significant change in his condition; he'd stabilised but had remained unresponsive since the day he fell. Clare noticed that they did not mention Athena.

Rufus had not always found friendships easy, his father explained. He'd been restless with life at home, eager to go to uni and to get a job in London afterwards – keen to get on. Even as a boy, he had wanted to progress, to move forward.

'We'd love him whatever he did or didn't do,' his father said, as his wife reached out to smooth their son's perfectly arranged hair. 'We just never expected this.'

'You think we don't know about half of what you've done, don't you?' she said, addressing Rufus. 'But you've always been easy to read.'

'I'm glad we've had this time with him,' her husband commented. 'We've been able to say how proud we are of him.'

'You can feel the love in this room,' Clare said, looking round at the cards and photos.

'I hope he can hear us,' Rufus's father said wistfully.

'Of course he can,' his wife replied. 'He relaxes at the sound of your voice – I've seen it. Not like when some others are here . . .'

'Let's leave that for now.' Her husband looked troubled and patted the back of her hand.

'Yes, sorry, I shouldn't have said anything.' Rufus's mother turned towards Clare and, looking for a change of subject, said, 'It's nice to talk about him. Thank you so much for coming.'

'It's good to be here with you – thanks for inviting me.'

'We're not very religious, but we appreciate it, all the same.'

The stillness of the room settled more deeply as they listened to Rufus breathing and watched his chest moving up and down. Rufus's father asked for prayers for their son, and Clare prayed with thanksgiving for Rufus and all the love surrounding him, as well as the skill and care of the medical team. She prayed for peace in the love of God for him and for recovery and healing.

The quietness was underpinned by gentleness as the two parents sat with their bodies bowed over Rufus, who seemed at ease, breathing slowly and rhythmically.

A nurse wheeling a rattling trolley of equipment arrived to check on him, and Clare took her leave.

Rufus's father walked a little way down the corridor with her and gripped her arm in farewell. 'They must find who did this,' he said, vehemently. 'They must. People were jealous of him, you know; I wonder if that was it. Or if he knew something about Tristan's death. They were friends, after all.'

'Yes, I'd heard that.' Clare schooled herself not to prompt for further information. This wasn't the time.

It came anyway. 'They were all friends. It was Tristan who introduced Rufus to that girlfriend of his, Athena. But Rufus didn't want us to say anything about that. He was loyal to Tristan, despite the bad history there.' His mouth twisted into a rueful half-smile.

'Rufus had lots of interests at school – and after, I think,' Clare offered.

'Yes, until this happened. He was going places, that's for sure. Athena, too. My wife isn't sure about her.'

Again, the reticence about Athena. People react so differently to crises involving loved ones – to injuries, hospital stays and the precariousness of life. Perhaps Athena felt she had to stay away, now, leaving space for Rufus's parents. Clare reiterated her sympathy and offered any further help that might be useful.

'Thank you. Thanks for everything.' He shook her hand again.

Clare moved away from Rufus's father slowly, resisting the urge to speedwalk when she saw the clock in the corridor. She should just about have enough time to make it home before school finished.

As she continued to her car, she wondered how Athena was managing, and about the misgivings Rufus's parents had about her. It was a surprise to hear that Tristan had brought Athena and Rufus together. What was the connection between Tristan and Athena? And why had Rufus wanted to keep that quiet?

It could be innocent – a coincidence. Plenty of people feel the need for privacy. Athena was friends with Jess, so perhaps she'd wanted to be discreet about any links with the bad boy cousin? Tristan certainly wasn't a favourite with Athena's boss, Susan. Perhaps that was it. Or perhaps not.

She would look for an opportunity to ask Athena about it. And tomorrow she would follow up on the copy of the Stubbs painting which hung in the hall at Greenwood House. Asking questions about a copied painting would surely be easier than some other aspects of this investigation.

CHAPTER 43

Fabian and Peter's home was in the old Arsenal stadium at Highbury. It had been transformed, but reminders of the glory days were not completely obliterated. The crowds of passionate fans, chanting and jeering, their faces painted in red and white, might no longer be roaring there, but a sense of them lingered and some of the stadium features remained.

Clare crossed the former pitch, now divided up by artfully placed hedges and benches to form separate garden areas on this site of hallowed memories. Art deco crowd stands had been converted into smart apartments, their balconies decorated with the garden tables, chairs and potted plants of their affluent occupants.

Fabian greeted her at the security-gate entrance to the South Stand apartments, seeming delighted to see her.

Inside the streamlined flat was a high-tech music system, plus a rack of shiny guitars. On the wall was a photo of a fencer, presumably Fabian, at a match. He was wearing a protective white jacket and breeches, meshed mask and gauntlets, and pointing his foil at an opponent, poised for their contest.

Long grey sofas stretched across the living space, below brightly coloured canvases of abstract shapes.

Clare was here to discuss a different artwork: the forged copy of the Stubbs picture of two horses. Harriet believed Fabian had commissioned it and that Tristan had known about it.

But Clare was in no hurry to embark on difficult questions just yet. It was nice to be with the genial Fabian and to discover this part of London. The journey had also provided a welcome distraction from her misgivings about Harriet, and from the new information regarding Athena and Tristan's prior relationship, too.

Clare and her host talked generalities: the local area, the pottery studio, the Bookbar café and the corner greengrocer's with enormous pineapples. She'd lingered on her walk from Finsbury Park station, savouring the anonymity offered by the city streets.

Fabian thanked her for the help she was giving his parents and sister, and for helping Harriet, too. He rested his arms along the back of one of the large sofas as he confided in her.

'You heard about the TV series, I guess? Thanks to Tristan, it came out that I filched Peter's memories of his Italy trip and used them for that article. It's undermined my journalistic credibility somewhat. So, I decided it was best to retreat from the TV deal before getting the chop.'

'Sorry. That sounds disappointing.'

'Actually, it's a relief to have the Palio nonsense spiked. I'm rubbish at pretence. You rumbled me easily enough at the wedding, I think. So did your son. There are no flies on him.'

Fabian seemed remarkably relaxed about the episode, shrugging off any embarrassment with surprising ease.

Peter emerged from his study and explained how sorry he was to have missed the Greenwood wedding. He'd been touring with his band and also fulfilling a photography commission in Nashville, Tennessee. He'd heard about Clare and the events of that day. He had the distracted air of someone disturbed during their work – his hair was dishevelled and his glasses were pushed up above his forehead.

While Fabian made their drinks, Peter entertained Clare with descriptions of Nashville's bars and music venues. His photos of brunch at the Ruby Sunshine diner had her salivating; she could taste that brioche with peaches and cream. He'd been photographing a wedding in the city and showed her pictures of the two handsome grooms. It had been a beautiful service at a Presbyterian church, followed by a reception with poker tables, cigars aplenty and a relaxed vibe. Clare guessed there'd been no murdered guests to spoil the ambiance.

Fabian joined them in looking at the pictures. Each group of guests had been photographed beneath the grooms' names in lights at the reception, as if at the Oscars or Met Gala.

'When it's our turn, can we have poker tables and a neon sign?' asked Peter.

'You can have anything you want, as long as we don't get married at my parents' place or go anywhere near that tree house on our wedding day. I suppose at least Tristan can't cause any trouble now, when our turn comes,' Fabian added.

Maybe the gallows humour seemed OK to him, but Clare felt a bit sickened. She was still struggling to cope with Tom's enthusiasm for a tree house of their own. Fabian hadn't seen Tristan's corpse lying murdered in their childhood haunt. Nor, thank God, had Tom.

She steeled herself to ask what needed to be asked. 'There was something I wanted to talk to you about.'

Fabian smiled, looking easy-going and friendly. 'Fire away.'

'The Stubbs painting.'

His blue eyes widened. 'Of the horses? What about it? It's in the hall at Mum and Dad's.'

'Sure. But Harriet wondered what happened to the copy you commissioned, Fabian. Tristan mentioned it the day he died.' Clare was relieved to have got the awkward part of the conversation underway, though she felt suddenly nervous, reaching for her bag to give herself something to do and pulling out an unnecessary hanky.

'Was he still peddling that tale? It was just an idea I had, but nothing came of it.' Fabian was now less genial, and Peter was quiet.

'Was the copy painted?'

'Clare, some things are better left undiscussed. I'd rather not be cross-examined, either.' He smiled, but his handsome face was taut. 'There's nothing of concern here, just Tristan stirring.'

'Was he blackmailing you? Someone mentioned that possibility.' Maybe this was too direct, but she needed to push him a bit.

'This is ridiculous. Why are you asking such absurd questions, Clare?' His eyes narrowed. 'Harriet's obviously put you up to this. It's bad enough having our family mixed up in a murder, without us making crackpot suggestions about one another.' Fabian stood up, walked over to the bookcase and moved a photo of himself and Peter to one side, as if to calm himself.

'I suppose it's a matter of trying to look at all the possibilities, that's all.' She blew her nose, although she had no particular reason to do so.

'Well, you two behaving like you're Cagney and Lacey is

only going to get people's backs up, Clare. The Stubbs mischief-making isn't any of your business and is completely irrelevant.' Fabian looked like his father: stubborn and pugnacious.

'Sorry. You obviously don't want to talk about it.' She replaced the handkerchief in her bag.

'You bet I don't. And I'm sorry if that's why you came here. Or why Harriet sent you – to poke about.'

'Excuse me – I have some calls to make.' Peter could hardly leave the room quick enough. Clare couldn't blame him.

Fabian sat down again, heavily. 'OK, so I thought of getting a copy of the Stubbs painted. The purpose of that is entirely my business and nothing to do with you, the family or anyone else. As you say, the original painting is safe and sound at Greenwood House. Tristan had no reason to trouble me with anything about that picture, and I'm surprised at you, Clare, and at Harriet, for implying otherwise. There's nothing further to discuss.'

Clare backed off with another vague apology, suggesting that, instead, they put their heads together about any ideas they had of what Tristan might have been up to, and who he'd antagonised. It was unsurprising that Fabian objected to her questioning, but he was angrier than she'd anticipated – defensively so.

Seemingly mollified, Fabian suggested they look at the political angle further. Why might Rufus have been targeted, if not for some political reason?

Then he shook his head. 'I can't do this. It seems so absurd, looking for reasons for this to have happened. There is no plausible reason. Sure, Tristan could be ghastly, we've known that for years – Jess, Harriet, Martin and me – even if the adults were slow to admit it. But for someone to kill him? It makes no sense. And to try and get rid of Rufus, too . . . Do you think Rufus saw something?'

'Who knows? Harriet feels she is under suspicion, whatever happened. Of course you want to keep stuff private, Fabian, but perhaps things need to come out into the open.'

'It's horrible. I'm sorry not to be more help, Clare.' He looked genuinely regretful, his earlier hostility evaporating.

Apart from generalised suggestions about political rivalries, Fabian had nothing to offer. Was his reticence about the faked painting simply a desire to hide a shameful episode, or something more sinister?

In the narrow hallway were some large rectangular parcels stacked against the wall, ready for posting. Clare wondered if they might contain forged art, and, as if reading her mind, Fabian commented that Peter had some framed photographs due to be dispatched to clients.

Clare was not brazen enough to check their address labels, nor quick enough to find a reason to be left alone to do so, as Fabian ushered her to the door.

She bade him farewell with unease at being stonewalled; he was hiding something. But Clare hadn't been completely frank with him either. She presumed Fabian knew nothing about Celeste's son, or the child's paternity.

As she headed out of the stadium and down the terraced street to Arsenal tube station, she pondered what Fabian might do next. They had parted on good terms, but she had raised something which he wanted to keep quiet. How would he respond?

CHAPTER 44

Later that day, Clare was back home at the rectory again when she heard Tom answer the landline. He seemed glad to talk with Ahmed, despite the interruption to the film he and Anna were watching after school. Legolas and Gimli were in battle against hordes of orcs. The body count was rising, orcs slaughtering and being slaughtered, the fantasy rather different from the impact of an actual killing.

Clare was pleased to hear their relaxed chat, but when she took the phone from Tom, Ahmed's tone became urgent as he summoned her to London. He had heard from Jess, who wanted them to get together straight away.

It was unusual for Clare to head into town twice in one day, or to join David there at such short notice, but the children seemed happy enough to continue watching the film with Jo, a friend and neighbour, who came to sit with them for the remainder of the evening. Clare could set off for the train to Charing Cross easy in her mind about things at home, even if she was unsure what the sudden rendezvous might entail.

Hopefully, it meant things were moving forward in some way. It wasn't only about clearing Harriet now; it was about getting to the truth, whatever that might be.

Clare was more circumspect about Harriet, but still hadn't told David or anyone else what Celeste's cleaner had said about the debt. She didn't want to strengthen others' suspicions against her fellow sleuth. Clare told herself that what she had learned was only hearsay. But why hadn't Harriet said anything about the financial pressure she was under? Was she afraid of losing Clare's trust? It was keeping quiet that had eroded it.

Clare had tried to learn more about Harriet's financial situation by googling her. It seemed that a portrait by Harriet would not come cheap, but Clare did not have the know-how or the resources to find out about any debts she might have. Presumably Jackie would be able to access that information.

It was uncomfortable to keep this from David, but Clare didn't want him to pass it on to the police. She wanted to help prove Harriet's innocence for many reasons, and if doing so also involved besting the lovely Jackie, she wasn't averse to that – despite feeling ashamed of that motivation. She tried to tell herself that maybe the police already knew about the money, anyway.

She felt more uneasy knowing that Jim had been involved with Celeste, while the rest of his family remained unaware. Or was Susan already apprised of her husband's secret?

Clare threaded her way speedily through the mixture of meandering tourists and more purposeful commuters heading for home, and arrived at the Prezzo beside Trafalgar Square. Jess was already there. She'd picked a secluded table towards the back, with some benched seats against the wall. A young couple seated nearest to them were leaning close across their food to hear one another above the restaurant's hubbub of chatter, scraping dishes and background music. There was minimal risk of any conversation being overheard.

Jess explained that she'd met her mother here, at the same table, earlier in the evening. 'She summoned me here, but I met Athena on the way, in Waterstones. Mum said not to tell anyone about our meeting, so I pretended to be browsing the cards and choosing books for Tinky and Trixie. I feel bad for not having been more in touch with Athena, or with anybody. I just wanted to shut myself away, do my job and watch trashy TV to keep going.'

'That makes sense. A few episodes of *Say Yes to the Dress* and I'm ready for anything. How's Athena coping?' Clare concentrated her attention on Jess, putting her elbows on the table and resting her chin on her clasped hands.

'Immaculate. Cream trouser suit, hair with new highlights. She's working late this evening; there's a meeting with interest groups who want to lobby Mum. Rufus's parents are doing the bulk of the vigil with him – she said they appreciated your visit.'

'It was good to see them, and Rufus.'

'It was a bit awkward with Athena. I cut her off, went down those spiral steps to the basement and hid out in the children's section until it was safe to come back up and find Mum in here.' Jess tucked her loose hair behind her ears and looked around the restaurant, as if expecting to see Susan arrive in there again.

'How was that?' Clare sat back.

'She looked awful, like she was trying not to cry. Mum never cries. She said Fabian was in trouble. I thought she meant about that Palio article, but apparently Athena had heard from Fabian because he couldn't get through to Mum, and he told her Harriet was accusing him of forging one of Mum and Dad's paintings.'

'Right.' It seemed Clare's best option was just to listen. Especially given she was in no rush to acknowledge her role in all this. As yet, Jess seemed unaware who had visited Fabian and asked him questions earlier that day.

'I tried to explain that Harriet loves Fabian and would never accuse him of something without good reason. Mum seems to think Harriet is setting him up, to take the heat off herself.'

This filled Clare with dread. Was Harriet trying to use Fabian as a scapegoat? And was Clare now complicit?

'Mum believes whatever Athena says, and Athena's suggesting Harriet is guilty. If I question Athena and her influence on Mum, I'm told I'm unreasonable or upset. Whereas Athena is professional and dependable – despite all that she's suffered as a consequence of attending my wedding.'

'Wow – your mum said that?' Clare felt she was caught up in something more and more difficult to keep a grip on.

'Yes, my wedding was the problem. Seriously, that's how Mum sees it. That plane stunt was all because of Mum's policies, and it overshadowed Ahmed's and my day, even before the murder. Her job constantly dominates our family, and even my friendship with Athena is intertwined with Mum's career. But my wedding was the problem.' Jess seemed torn between indignation and hurt at her mother's attitude.

Clare grimaced in sympathy, recognising the long-term grievances emerging. 'I'm sorry, Jess. This sounds so painful.'

'I'm to sort everything out with Fabian about this forgery

stuff, without Mum being involved. No one's to tell Dad. Mum wants all this to go away – to be covered up, if necessary. Her poker face was in place pretty quick. She looked like Hillary Clinton, but I've got more trust in Clinton's political priorities. Sorry to dump this on you, Clare; I needed to say it out loud and I can't tell Mum how I really feel.' Jess shook her head, as if to relieve the tension she felt.

'It's complex. And I agree with you, it's better to have things out in the open.' Clare braced herself to tell her own story of her visit to Fabian, but she was interrupted by Ahmed arriving, followed almost immediately by David.

Her confession would have to wait. And she wasn't sorry.

CHAPTER 45

'It's good to see you both.' David's tone was warm as he greeted Ahmed and Jess. 'How have things been?'

Ahmed was non-committal as he sat beside his wife, shuffling himself along the benched seat. 'Where to start? We've been carrying on. I'm not sure what else we can do.'

Jess gave her husband a nervous look before she launched into conversation, leaning across the table towards David and Clare. 'I asked Ahmed to get hold of you both because there are things we need to talk about. I'm sorry that you're involved in this mess.'

'It's fine; we're friends,' Clare said, while wondering where on earth this friendship would be taking them next. She needed a gin and tonic.

'You're kind. But there's a lot to tell. I'm sorry, Ahmed, but there is stuff I've never told you, either. I thought having Clare and David here would help.'

'OK.' Ahmed's face was impassive.

'I wanted to tell you earlier this evening, but Mum summoned me here because of some stuff Athena had told her about Fabian.'

Their waiter arrived to take their order, delaying Jess as

choices of pizza and pasta dishes were made. They were hungry, so garlic bread was added to the mix.

Clare leaned back in her seat as Jess recounted the forgery story, not wanting to reveal how much she and Harriet had been collaborating on that front already. She thought she was being convincing until she noticed David's sidelong glance at her. He wasn't fooled. Perhaps he already knew about her visit to Fabian's flat today – from Jackie, maybe? That was absurd. It was more likely to be from Susan or Athena. Jackie wasn't telepathic.

Jess recounted her mother's concerns about Fabian, saying, 'Maybe Tristan did have some hold on him.' She swallowed nervously before adding, 'He had something on me, too.'

'I knew it.' Ahmed suddenly looked ready to sweep the contents of the table to the floor and tear the place to pieces.

'It seems lots of people were caught up in Tristan's web.' David kept his focus on Jess.

'Yes, that's true.' Jess directed her attention to Clare.

As Jess began to explain the dire professional implications of any relationship between a health-service worker and a patient, everything fell into place – Jess's tension on the wedding morning, and her fury presumably directed at her cousin, because of course it was him who'd messaged her. Jess was compromised, and Tristan knew about it. A bridal secret, along with the other undercurrents of that day.

'He was an out-patient, and we shared a table at that café where all the Australians work, right opposite the exit by orthopaedics. He'd had a skiing accident; I'd seen him in clinic. He was friendly. It was so easy to cross that professional boundary.'

Jess didn't falter; it was as if she was recounting a medical history. But she twisted an empty glass in her hands, as though it was revolving with her relentless thoughts.

'This was years ago, when I was on rotation. We bumped into each other again – I was coming back from a run and he was there. We had another coffee and there was a film that we both wanted to see, so we went together. It was all very low key.' She put down the glass and rubbed her face with her hands. She didn't look at her listeners, but simply continued recounting the sequence of events.

Next was the note from him, marked *Personal* and left for her at work, saying that he wanted to meet again. Then another came and she panicked and cut off all contact. He had a knee injury, nothing psychiatric. Nothing prepared her for the news of his death, and how he had died. It was suicide – a deliberate overdose. He'd left a note, a message of apology and love for his family.

Jess ploughed on, addressing the table and not looking up. Clare felt sick, listening and watching.

'I was so ashamed – I still am. And I'm afraid. Tristan contacted me after the death and said this guy had been his flatmate. So, I don't know if he devised it all from the beginning, or whether he took advantage of the situation in front of him. It was devastating.' Jess gulped at the memory, obviously close to tears, but she didn't stop telling the story.

'Tristan wanted help covering the rent, said he'd be homeless if it wasn't paid straight away, that he was in trouble because his flatmate had died so suddenly. He told me about the note, about how he'd died. Said he hadn't told anyone else about my involvement, or his flatmate's obsession and grief about losing me. It was such a shock. I couldn't believe it.'

So, Jess had helped pay the rent for months. Tristan had never said anything that was a direct threat of exposure, but she wasn't going to risk not paying up; they'd both known what he could reveal, and what that would mean for her.

Everyone was silent, absorbing her account. David nodded as she spoke, and Ahmed's hand rested on hers. Ironically, now that Jess was revealing this tragic episode and its implications, including giving her a motive to silence Tristan, Clare felt even more sure of her innocence.

Steady-voiced, Jess continued, 'This happened years ago, and I wanted to leave it behind. Forget it ever happened. I'd had no contact with Tristan for years. He'd got a new flatmate – I thought it was over.' She looked at her husband, who sat with his head bowed, still unspeaking. 'Then I realised that this could impact on you too, if Tristan ever went to the press. He sent a horrible message to me on the morning of our wedding, saying that I could rely on his discretion and that he wished us both every happiness in our professional and personal lives. But it was obviously a threat, and I could tell he meant exactly the opposite. Finishing off my career quietly or otherwise would be bad enough, but this could've been terrible for you – and Mum – if it ever got out.'

'Why didn't you tell me? Do you not trust me?' Ahmed looked sad rather than surprised, finally looking up at his wife and shaking his head.

Clare wondered if Tristan had meant what he said, and whether Jess could have trusted her cousin. Perhaps he did wish her well. But Jess had been sure that he meant her harm.

'Anything that matters to you, matters to me,' Ahmed continued, now with tears in his eyes. He removed his glasses and rubbed his face with the back of his hand.

'I'm sorry for not telling you sooner. I realised yesterday I had to tell you, but you were back so late. Then, today, Mum messaged me and sounded desperate. But now you know. You all do, and I can't go back.'

'Thank you.' Clare was relieved that Jess had finally freed herself of this desperate isolation. 'It sounds so difficult. I hope it helps . . . to have shared it.'

'In a way, it's a relief. But I hate that it happened at all. The way Tristan used this – it's relevant, isn't it? It gives me a motive to want to get rid of him, for a start. But, also, there could have been others he targeted. Perhaps this will help to take the pressure off Harriet, once the police know.'

'Are you OK to make a statement?' David asked. 'It would be the simplest way forward, to contact the police and do that.'

'They'll need to talk to Fabian, too.' Jess was resolute. 'It's no good Mum or others trying to shield him. Can you talk to Jackie, David? I don't want to shop my brother, but there was something going on there with that painting, whether Mum likes it or not.'

'I could talk with Jackie, but it would be better coming from you. I don't have anything to offer – you're the one with the information on this, Jess.'

Clare admired Jess's courage in outlining the grim history of this young man's distress and death. She noticed the way he'd remained nameless. Was that an instance of professional discretion, or evidence of Jess dehumanising him, distancing herself from his suffering? And why exactly was Jess telling them about her mother's concerns about Fabian?

Susan's attempts to involve Jess in covering for her brother were unsavoury – it seemed as if everyone was either shielding someone or deflecting blame onto them to avoid suspicion themselves.

Politicians and their teams and families got into every kind of mess, as people do – it was the cover-ups, the fabrication and the collusion with deceit that became the bigger problem. Those lies undermine trust and corrode decency.

CHAPTER 46

'Hi, everyone! Fancy seeing you all here!' Athena's voice half sang her greetings.

Clare jumped, and noticed Jess looked stricken, as if caught red-handed.

'Athena . . . Hi.' David's tone was upbeat. 'I thought you'd still be beavering away with the policy group. I'm glad you've escaped.'

'I thought I'd be there all night, but I've done a runner. I often come here for some food before going home. You should've said you were heading here, Jess. Did you get the books you wanted?' Athena stood beside their table, exuding confidence in her smart cream jacket and trousers.

'Books?' Jess looked mystified, then caught up with herself. 'You mean from Waterstones, earlier? No, actually – I got called away.'

'Did you meet up with your mum OK? I haven't seen her since she left the office, but I assume you've had a chance to chat?'

Clare picked up the accusatory edge. Jess was either unaware of it, which seemed unlikely, or was impressively pretending to be quite at ease.

'Yes, thanks so much, Athena. Why don't you join us?'

Ahmed was already looking around for a spare chair to add to their table, and Clare began to shift glasses and cutlery to make space. But Athena held up her hands, as if to say, *Hold it.*

'No, it's OK, thanks. It's great to see you all, but I don't really feel like company this evening – sorry. Actually, I may call in at the hospital and see how Rufus has been doing today.'

'Any news?' Ahmed asked.

'No change. There never is.'

Jess stood to hug Athena and asked her to let them know how Rufus was doing. Her earlier antipathy seemed to have gone. 'Take care of yourself, Athena,' she said, a sympathetic hand lingering on her friend's arm as Athena began to retreat. 'You're working so hard for Mum, together with this awful worry about Rufus.'

Clare stood and added her own murmurs of concern for Athena's well-being, as David and Ahmed looked on. Since Clare had last seen her, Athena looked more fragile; she had lost weight, her face was thinner and her eyes were more prominent on her narrowed face. Her hand seemed bird-like, clamping her bag, almost clawed.

Emboldened by the revelations of the day, Clare quickly mentioned what Rufus's parents had said about Tristan introducing Rufus and Athena to one another. She tried to make it sound casual, as if she had just remembered and wanted to raise it in passing before Athena left them.

Athena dismissed that news cheerily. 'Yes, that's right. I used to drink in the same pub as Tristan sometimes, in Clapham. I met Rufus there and then we got together. It wasn't really anything to do with Tristan – I'd almost forgotten about that first meeting – but maybe that's what Rufus told his parents.' She spoke hastily and was clearly eager to be gone. What she said could've been true, or perhaps a convenient version of the truth.

As the quartet at the table settled again after her departure, Jess sighed. 'That was awkward. I didn't tell her I was meeting Mum – I didn't realise she knew.'

'You needed to be discreet,' Ahmed said, trying to soothe her. 'Your mum specifically asked you to tell no one. And Athena certainly kept it quiet about having met Tristan in that pub. That was a shocker.'

'Well, I understand that.' Jess was loyal to her friend. 'And at least I've been honest with you all now. Do you think Athena will realise I've told you about Tristan threatening me and tell Mum? She knew about that before I told any of you.'

'It's no problem if she does.' David was calm. 'You're addressing something very difficult.'

Clare thought he was right, and it was kind of him to support Jess.

'It's better to have it all out in the open,' Ahmed said, loyally. 'I hate the thought of you carrying the weight of that alone.'

'But what about the implications for your career, if this comes out?' Jess asked, her face screwed up with worry.

'This has no bearing on my work. Your career's the priority, here, and I'm sure we can explain the situation and make it right. What I can't get over is the way Tristan made use of someone's death to exert control over you. It's sick.'

Ahmed and David were practical about steps forward, telling Jess to contact Jackie, to ask for advice from her union, and to ask for an urgent meeting with her manager.

'No one at your work will want to go public on this, Jess.' Ahmed was all reassurance. 'Coming clean about the whole thing will mean it can be addressed, and whatever the consequences are, we can face them and then move forward.'

'Losing my job sometimes feels like quite an attractive prospect.' Jess shrugged. 'I could just curl up at home and never leave.'

'You'll be doing all sorts of amazing things for people, in whatever job, in no time,' said David, ever the staunch friend.

Clare felt a rush of affection for her husband. She was proud she'd married such a warm-hearted man.

'First, I want to do what I can to help Harriet,' Jess replied. 'And I think you feel the same, Clare.'

'Sure. I want to help Harriet. And you too, Jess. Both of you.' She gestured at Jess and Ahmed. 'But murder is messy. Messier than in crime novels, anyway. We all may have difficult questions to face.'

Clare tried to find the right words. She wanted to help reveal the culprit, whoever it was, and the way to do that was to expose the whole web of diseased relationships around Tristan. Not only to bring them in her prayers to a merciful God, but to reveal them to people with their own agendas and secrets, to police officers like Jackie, with their procedures and limitations. This was far from easy. How candid should she be with the DCI, and with David? She thought she'd been hiding too much already.

She wondered whether her husband had also noticed Ahmed's lack of surprise at Jess's revelations. She remembered the bridegroom confronting Tristan at the wedding, and David downplaying the incident. Ahmed had avoided answering her questions about it when they had walked together the next morning. Had Ahmed already been aware of the threat Tristan posed to Jess's happiness and professional reputation, and potentially to his own?

Perhaps Clare was going to upset her friends, but she pushed ahead anyway. She had to. 'Ahmed, forgive me for being so direct, but I keep coming back to the clash you had with Tristan in the churchyard at the wedding. I wonder, did you have any idea that he was hassling Jess?'

Clare was right. David looked surprised and ill at ease at this questioning of his friend. But not as shocked as Ahmed, whose gaze faltered.

'That certainly is direct, Clare.' Ahmed paused.

This time, the question came from his wife: 'Well?'

Perhaps in male solidarity, it was David who eventually spoke, as Ahmed seemed to be lost for words. 'That's quite a question, but it's probably best to talk about it, mate.'

Mate? Clare thought. Since when had David called anyone that? Male friendships were a mystery to her.

Bizarrely, the chumminess seemed to release Ahmed's tongue. 'OK, so I didn't know the details, but I was aware that something was going on.'

Jess looked astonished. 'What? You knew something? I've been going through hell trying to protect you from this stuff, and now you admit you knew the whole time?' Her earlier relief transformed into rage at her husband.

Ahmed's indignation matched that of his wife. 'This is crazy. Now *I'm* the one at fault for trying to keep things quiet for you, for trying to shut Tristan up? I knew he was bad news and had something serious on you, but I didn't know exactly what it was. And now you're blaming me for trying to help you? I can't believe you.'

'You could have told me.' The ferocity on Jess's face made her look like Jim.

'Priceless.' Ahmed's anger expanded as he spoke. '*I* could have told *you*, could I? Well, you could've told me, too.'

'I tried to tell you.' Jess gripped her fork and held it up vertically, as if on guard. 'I was going to tell you this evening. I did tell you.'

Ahmed lowered his voice and spoke deliberately. 'Jess, I knew that, whatever trouble you'd been in, Tristan would try to use your sense of integrity against you. I wanted to make sure nothing stopped you having the happiest wedding day, without Tristan causing you any harm. That's all.'

'And what exactly did you do to stop him?'

'What are you accusing me of?' Ahmed's head jerked upwards.

'I'm not accusing you of anything. But, knowing you have hidden things from me, that people saw you accost him in the churchyard – it makes me wonder what else went on between you.'

'Listen to yourself, Jess. Next, are you going to ask if I murdered him? Is that the way this is going?'

Jess didn't notice the beep of her phone, but Clare was aware of it – and of David scanning a message that had reached his screen.

Her husband put his hand on her arm and raised his phone to quieten the enraged couple. 'Look, something important has happened. Your mum has messaged, Jess.' His gravity silenced them. 'I'm sorry, but the news is bad. Rufus has deteriorated and his condition is critical now. He's not expected to survive the night.'

'Does she say whether Athena is there?' Clare asked, while Ahmed and Jess both stared at them, open-mouthed in dismay.

'She doesn't say. I think she's contacted you, Jess.'

Jess scrabbled in her bag, then rose from her seat while she read her phone. 'I must go. Sorry, everyone. I have to be with Athena now.'

'Of course. I'll go home. Call me if there is anything you need.' Ahmed spoke as if their fierce exchanges had never happened. 'I'll make up the sofa bed for Athena, in case she wants to stay with us later.'

David was apologetic and said this news meant he should get to the office urgently. He suggested Clare join him there, so they could travel home together later.

As the others scattered, Clare summoned the bill, visited the loo, then checked the news alerts on her phone – there was no mention yet of this development. Poor Rufus, his parents, Athena . . . everyone. She pondered the conversation that had unfolded, the way Ahmed and Jess had traded accusations and hurt.

Now, she wanted to be at home, to be sure her children were tucked up safe and sleeping, not accessing any news stories. If Rufus died, she would have to tell them in the morning. Another senseless death. How could she explain it to Anna and Tom?

She couldn't explain it – that was the point. Violence unleashed was continuing to bear its brutal fruits of pain and discord. It felt as if more horrors emerged with each attempt to unpick the truth of what had happened and why. What else might lie in wait for them all before any resolution was reached?

CHAPTER 47

Susan's Home Office team were used to emergencies – they were part of the daily routine, or the hourly routine sometimes – but they weren't so used to murder in their midst. The minister's nephew's death had caused a stir, but nevertheless her private office had steamed on, with Susan setting the tone of 'business as usual'. Susan's boss had made consolatory noises, while checking that the press remained broadly sympathetic to Susan and her family. Civil servants had prepared briefing notes to give to any new minister should Susan be removed from her post, but so far these had remained unused.

Rufus's serious injuries had been another shock, but, after a couple of days, Athena had returned with a zealous energy only heightened, it seemed, by the crisis enveloping her. David had told Clare that she discouraged discussion of her boyfriend's condition or of the police investigation, and referred any queries to the department's press office, who were adept at sounding helpful and saying nothing.

But now the prospect of Rufus's death would surely change things. Other Londoners were still unaware of the story which would no doubt be featured in tomorrow's news bulletins. A bus lumbered past as Clare descended the steps to the Home

Office building, and she thought that, by tomorrow evening, Rufus's face would be familiar to its passengers. The press would want photos of his sad parents, too.

As David hastened down the stairway to sign her in, he was hailed by Susan, who had just arrived at the entrance. She was wearing a cobalt-blue coat with a double row of gold buttons, and her matching handbag had a golden chain. Seeing Clare, Susan greeted her too and swept her up to come straight to her office along with David.

'It is lovely that you're here, Clare – your help is so valuable,' she enthused.

Startled, there was nothing for Clare to do but acquiesce and follow in the minister's wake. They walked through the open-plan outer office, its deserted chairs askew and lights dimmed. Susan's team were already busy in her office, but this was a deepening crisis for the minister and they were quiet as Susan issued a stream of comment and instruction.

Clare seated herself as discreetly as possible on a green leather sofa in a corner of the room, away from the desk by the window around which Susan and her team were standing. Susan's office was large and there was plenty of room for Clare to retreat.

David cut straight to the point: 'Is the Home Secretary aware?'

'Not yet, but we should warn his office so they're prepared for any further news. Athena will contact me directly when anything happens. This is all so sad for her.' Susan turned to a young woman who appeared to have taken on Athena's usual role. 'Seema, see if the Home Secretary has any availability for a face-to-face tomorrow morning, please. His private secretary may be able to make space. Let's keep my afternoon appointments in the diary, for now.'

Did nothing faze this woman? Susan had shed her coat and now rattled off further directions. 'David, you'll need to draft a note to go to our colleagues, reminding everyone it's "no comment" and to direct any enquiries to the press office.' She tapped her desk with a pen, as if beating a rhythm of tasks needing to be undertaken. 'And contact DCI Carter about any progress she's made – I need to be up to speed when I meet with the Home Secretary. Number Ten will take his views into account.'

Clare thought Susan's focus was quite something. She didn't know whether to admire it or be slightly appalled. Seema was red-eyed, perhaps grieving at the news of Athena's impending loss. Clare hoped that meant Athena had other friends to support her through this, especially while her relationship with Jess was complicated.

Susan clearly had no intention of stepping back from her role, even temporarily, and was readying herself to fight for it. Had Susan known about her husband's affair with Celeste? And, if so, to what lengths might she have gone to conceal it and protect herself from scandal?

Clare pushed these thoughts out of her mind and instead prayed for Rufus's recovery. Perhaps he might rally; sometimes situations changed. It was possible.

David had said that Susan was fortunate the PM set great store on appearing to be loyal, steadfastness being one way to disguise a lack of flexibility and a limited mindset. Her current job might be safe for a few days, but surely the anticipated promotion was no longer achievable.

If Susan lost her ministerial post, Athena's job would also end. Susan's successor would have their own coterie. Given the need to distance themselves from their predecessor's troubles, any new incumbent would jettison Athena, no question. David's job would be safe. His responsibility would be to welcome and brief the new minister, integrate them into the Home Office team and get them up to speed on policies and priorities.

Clare wondered how Athena would cope with so much loss if Rufus died: her partner, her work and her career hopes. And how would Susan and Jim manage the ongoing revelations and pressures in their family?

Susan stopped issuing instructions, and Clare realised that the crisis meeting had finished. Plans seemed to be all set for the morning. David would be busy. Clare was proud of his efficiency and good judgement; ministers and colleagues could rely on him. She wanted to back him up too and help him to do all that must be done.

CHAPTER 48

The news about Rufus deteriorating was a shock for everyone. Harriet had dropped all her plans for the following morning once she heard. She'd left her latest portrait sketches at Celeste's place and joined Clare at the rectory instead, saying that she wanted to talk about how Rufus was doing and to review things together.

Clare was touched that she wanted to meet up. They were a team – or were supposed to be. Should she simply ask Harriet about her money problems? Perhaps it was better to wait; she didn't want Harriet to feel she was accusing her of anything underhand. Between them, they were unearthing significant information and there seemed to be no sense in disrupting that.

The two women had put on boots – the grass was wet from rain the night before – and crossed the field behind the house. Mia sped ahead, then paused at the entrance to the woods, her golden fur outlined against the coppery tones of the autumn bracken. She was alert for signs of deer or the rustle of a squirrel heading for safety up a tree. She regarded it as her duty to clear the area of interlopers. She had already rid the pond of ducks, who flapped and quacked skyward as she barked at them.

As they walked, Harriet told Clare about the phone conversation she'd had with Jim. They'd discussed her newly discovered half-brother, and Harriet had now reached the same conclusion as Clare about the paternity of her mother's child.

'I'm sure Jim is the father. If he was never involved with my mum, or wasn't this baby's dad, he could simply have said so. But he avoided the question completely. I asked him outright in the end, and he carried on as if he hadn't heard, just talking about his priority having been to support my mum through a challenging period and to respect her privacy.'

Clare had wondered how long it might take Harriet to realise and was impressed at how resilient she seemed. She had so much to cope with.

'How do you feel about that?' Clare asked, thinking that Harriet looked healthier today, her freckled cheeks flushed in the morning air.

'Weirdly, I feel very little,' Harriet said. 'I'm glad to have contacted Jim and talked about it, and I think about all that sorrow for Mum and how hard she worked to keep things steady for me. And I feel sorry for my dad. He dealt with all those years of disapproval about his secret life and child, but he wasn't the only one. I don't think concern for me was the only reason Mum kept it quiet. No one wants to be called a hypocrite.'

'There's a lot to think about.'

'I feel more concerned for Jess and Fabian. Aunt Susan is so strong, she'll weather anything, but I remember how I felt about Dad when I learned about Tristan. It was unbearable, like being split in two.'

Clare shared that concern for Jim's family. Susan was robust, but this was a devastating betrayal, however resilient Harriet thought her aunt would be.

She tried to reassure Harriet about the impact on Jess and Fabian. 'It will be painful. But they are older than you were. They have their own lives – their own homes and partners to anchor them.'

Mia appeared from the undergrowth in front of them, proffering a sodden tennis ball that she had unearthed from the depths of the woodland.

Stooping to pat and congratulate her, Harriet said, 'Life's joyful for dogs. And so straightforward.'

'There are fewer family dynamics. But Mia is good at reading us.'

As if on cue, Mia increased her attentiveness to Harriet, picking up the dropped ball and offering it to her.

'You're ravishing,' Harriet complimented her. 'If I ever paint you, Clare, Mia will have to be in the picture too. And you should wear that red scarf.'

They carried on through the mosaic of fallen leaves, the path weaving between tall silver birch and broad oak trees. Clare slowed her pace when Harriet spoke.

'We seem to keep uncovering more background information about my family, but it feels like none of it brings any resolution to the case.'

'I agree. Everything seems increasingly complex – Fabian's possible forgery, the whole political angle, and now your mother's bombshell and Jim's part in concealing it.' Clare pushed some bracken to one side to clear their way through the woodland.

'There's Jess and Ahmed, too,' Harriet said. 'We love them, but now we know they both had motives and opportunity.'

'I know – we can't discount them, as much as I want to. We need to see whoever killed Tristan convicted, and whoever attacked Rufus, too.'

'Are you saying they're not the same person?' Harriet edged round the brambles protruding over the path.

'It's possible,' Clare answered, cautiously.

'Two murderous acts of violence in two days – it would be a bit too much of a coincidence if they weren't connected.' Harriet's voice was sceptical.

'Connected, sure, but they don't have to have the same culprit.'

'What a suspicious mind you have – and you a vicar.'

'Maybe being a vicar helps me see the potential within all of us to behave badly at times, given sufficient pressures.' Including you and me, thought Clare, conscious of her reservations about Harriet, and well aware of the possible harm she was causing by not telling Jackie everything she knew.

'Surely the likeliest thing is that Rufus saw something that would incriminate Tristan's killer?' Harriet suggested.

'Or maybe Rufus and Tristan were each a threat to the same person, and so were attacked by whoever that is.'

The two women paused as the path emerged from thicker woodland to follow the line of the hedge above the railway tracks. Mia led them with her tail up and head raised – proud to be carrying the tennis ball. There were some blackberry bushes in the hedgerow. Clare tried one of the darker berries and offered another to Harriet. They tasted sharp, but good all the same.

After a long pause, Harriet began speaking again. 'I wish things had been different between me and Tristan. We did have some good times, though. It's funny how those memories have started to come back, now that he's gone. We had a wild water fight once. Susan let us have washing-up bowls, all sorts. We rampaged around the garden, filling up from the paddling pool and outside taps, chasing one another and getting drenched. Then Martin turned up. He was fully dressed, and Tristan and Jess soaked him and things got ugly. He and Tristan were never friendly with each other.'

'Your mum was very warm towards Martin at the wedding. He seems like a very kind man.' Clare picked another blackberry and ate it. The dark juice stained her fingers.

'Yes, he's always been good to me. He looks different, now. He's got that beard. He's at odds with Susan's politics big time. I don't agree with her, but I don't want to antagonise her.'

'She's got a political tightrope to walk.'

'Being wrapped up in an unsolved murder is not a good look.'

They heard barking, and a flash of pale fur streaked through the trees. Mia was in pursuit of a deer that was bouncing and leaping over bracken. A second deer joined it, both weaving and jumping through the woods, chased by the dog.

'Don't worry, she never catches them,' Clare said.

'I don't want to tell the police about Mum,' Harriet said, almost under her breath.

'Jess didn't want to speak about Tristan's blackmail either. But not everything can be kept under wraps.'

Mia rejoined them, panting from the exertion of the chase

and eager for praise. They congratulated her on her triumph and headed towards home.

'I think you'd be wise to tell the police about the child,' Clare said. 'Or ask your mother to. Everything could be relevant, perhaps in ways we can't see. There's a whole web of connections, relationships and motives. Rufus's parents told me it was Tristan who introduced him to Athena. I didn't realise Athena knew Tristan that well.'

Despite her declarations about the need for candour, Clare didn't disclose her reservations about Athena. They were too vague. But she couldn't shake from her mind what Rufus's parents had said about their son tensing in her presence.

Clare also didn't ask Harriet about the money. She decided it was better to keep going and investigate other options, without alienating her. She hoped she was right, and not unwittingly assisting a murderer. But surely Harriet was innocent. No one could have faked that reaction in the tree house. Clare was certain of that. Almost.

CHAPTER 49

After the intensity of the previous couple of days, Clare had longed for a family weekend with less drama. David managed to keep work calls to a minimum; the updates he received described how Rufus was hanging on, and Clare continued to hope for his recovery. She and David decided to hold back on saying anything to the children about Rufus's decline – there was no need to pre-empt anything.

On Sunday afternoon, they called in on their neighbours to meet their newly arrived charges: four chickens recovering from life as battery hens. Anna and Tom helped feed them and checked for eggs, while Mia sniffed through the fencing of their pen and barked a couple of times, uncertainly. It was fun to hear about the chickens' different personalities, as they clucked and pecked, seeming delighted with their new freedom.

Clare loved their names: Cher, Tina, Suzi and Bonnie – the quartet of rock chicks. The children were less impressed by their parents' rendition of various hits, although Clare was rather pleased when they joined in with 'Total Eclipse of the Heart'. They knew some culture, anyway, even if they begged her to stop belting out 'Fernando'. The chickens were unfazed.

Monday morning was refreshingly ordinary, too. David

had left for work very early; Clare admired her husband's commitment, and his compassion for Susan. He could see that it took courage for her to attend the gossip and mutual admiration sessions with political colleagues in the Westminster corridors, wanting to make it clear to the Home Secretary and PM that she was a popular junior minister and not easily expendable. She worked hard for policies she believed in, and to fight for her constituents too.

The PM might put on his caring face for the cameras and express his 'full support and concern for her', but that wouldn't necessarily translate into her keeping that ministerial post. Susan needed positive headlines, preferably ones which reflected well on the PM. Clare hoped that she would do something more positive for refugees. Perhaps Susan's family troubles would make her more sympathetic to people in desperate circumstances.

As Clare planned her own week ahead, she knew she would be meeting with Jim to prepare for Tristan's funeral. His body had finally been released; his next of kin could proceed with arrangements. When Jim rang and asked her to conduct the service, Clare had agreed at once. There was no need for him to know of her reluctance or uncertainty. Of course she would officiate; it would be a privilege.

Jim was grateful, unaware of the personal cost of taking this service. Clare knew she was called to do it, knew she would be strengthened to do so. And meeting with the family, learning more about Tristan, might help with uncovering what had really happened to him that day.

When Clare returned home after having delivered Anna's forgotten PE kit to school, she found a car she didn't recognise in the rectory driveway, with no sign of a driver. The vehicle was fully packed, the back seat and boot piled high with bags and what looked like bedding.

A man stepped out from the side of the house, his hands in his pockets. His coat was tweedy and his shape paunchy, his chin stubbled and flecked with grey.

As Clare emerged from her car, he stood, waiting.

'Good morning. Can I help you?' she enquired, masking her irritation that he had been on the pathway that led round the side of the house and into the garden.

'I'm looking for the vicar.'

'Yes.' She'd speak with him out here. She wasn't inviting a stranger inside when no one else was home. 'How can I help?'

'My parents used to live here in the village. Me, too.'

'How lovely, you're a local. What's your name? I'm Clare Brakespear, the vicar.'

'Yes, I've heard about you. My cousin still lives here. My parents are in the churchyard. I want to book a slot there, too – for me.'

'Right. I'm heading to church now to meet one of the churchwardens there. Shall we walk down together and talk?'

'Thanks. You probably should know I've got a few problems.' His gaze was open and confiding.

'Right.'

'And I've nowhere to stay.'

'That sounds difficult.'

'But I wanted to get this sorted. To manage my final resting place, anyway.'

The morning had just got busier.

CHAPTER 50

The journey westwards to Greenwood had taken longer because of the fog, but Clare had left early, determined to be punctual. It had meant driving through darkness for an hour or more before encountering more reduced visibility in the Dorset lanes, as wisps of silvery moisture wrapped around everything in sight: the hedgerows, the looming outlines of homes, barns and signposts. She'd suggested meeting at the start of the day as she wanted to be back in good time for school pickup. She was relieved that she would just about avoid being late.

She parked in the grand driveway. The house looked some-what mysterious, cloaked in mist as if set designers had puffed dry ice around to spook it up. It was a while since she'd seen *The Rocky Horror Picture Show* and she knew that Jim was not about to burst into a raunchy song, much to her relief, but this still had aspects of a haunted-house scenario.

Jim's attitude on the phone had been different when she rang to arrange the visit. He sounded appreciative that she was taking the time to come and see him to talk about Tristan and the preparations for his funeral service. She felt honoured that she had been asked.

Jim was courteous in his welcome, but the hall was chilly as she entered. There was the Stubbs painting of the horses, but she noticed some of the photos around it had been rearranged.

He saw her looking and mentioned that he and Susan had decided it would be good to have a photo of Tristan in the house. They'd chosen a picture of him on a beach, flanked by Jess and Fabian. The trio stood near to one another, yet untouching, staring at the camera as if tolerating the moment. It smacked of being a command performance.

Clare wondered if this was the best photo available, but perhaps few had been taken of Tristan with his cousins. The one which included Harriet and her sketch pad had been demoted.

As Clare and Jim discussed the outline of the funeral service in the comfort of the living room, Clare concluded that Jim had been unsettled by the level of his own grief. Used to being in control, he had nonetheless been unable to subdue all of his feelings at the death of his nephew. Perhaps the occasionally wavering voice which he attempted to disguise by clearing his throat betrayed his distress at the death of Tristan's father, too.

Clare knew that the brothers' relationship had been complicated and wondered what Jim had felt about concealing the relationship he'd had with Celeste, his brother's wife. Max had always been presented as the errant brother, the duplicitous husband – and Jim would have been well aware that things were not as straightforward as that. Now, he also had to deal with Harriet's knowledge about the adopted child.

'Sorry,' Jim said, as he answered her queries about choice of readings and music, 'I'm finding it hard to concentrate. Thanks for your patience, Clare.'

When they'd met before the wedding, Jim had been intense and authoritative, with a bonhomie that seemed forced. Now, he was almost deferential. Clare's expertise was of use to him, perhaps that was it? But there was a new humility about him. The intimidating father of the bride was less sure of himself when it came to planning a funeral.

She risked a more searching question as they completed the outline of the service: 'Jim, do you have any thoughts about what happened to Tristan?'

'I think it's up to the police to establish the facts, Clare.' His voice was gruff. 'Conjecture is unhelpful.' Well, that was her told. 'I think we're done here; thank you for your time.' Now her host was terse. Anything relating to the murderous events of that day was clearly off limits.

They sat in an awkward silence. After a few moments, Clare gathered up her papers and started to pack her bag.

Jim was resolutely looking out the window, avoiding eye contact with her. But then he started: 'Who's that? It looks like Max, but it can't be,' he croaked.

A figure was approaching through the mist which still hung over the lawn. They both watched as the man emerged from the haze.

'Oh, it's Martin,' Jim breathed, in relief, 'wearing some old clothes – left at his grandfather's, probably. Things that belonged to Max. My brother. It's his old Barbour and hat.' He was suddenly garrulous. 'Apologies, Clare. I don't know what came over me.'

Clare suspected his discomfort might involve a degree of guilt. Jim was uneasy about his relationship with his late brother, that much was obvious.

Jim wheeled himself to open the door to the terrace, leaving Clare in the draughty room behind him.

Martin drew near, stick in hand. 'I've come about the house,' he said, without any preamble.

'Yes. Would you like a coffee? Come into the warm. Clare is here. Come on in; we've just finished.' Jim's welcoming manner had returned.

'Coffee? I got the lawyer's letter this morning.' He sounded abrupt and hostile.

'I hope it wasn't too fierce. There's no real rush, you know, but to make it legal we had to give written notice.' Jim waved an arm as if to minimise any distress caused.

'The letter was brutal. I'm not happy about it, Jim. Notice to quit, kicking me out now that Grandad is of no more use to you. I knew this was coming, but it's still shocking.'

'Sorry about that, Martin. Solicitors can be so formal. You've been a good friend to us all. Let's have a coffee.'

Was this return to solicitude an act for Clare's benefit? Something felt performative about it.

Martin removed his boots before following Jim inside. Monty had joined him, snuffling a welcome, with his tail slapping against the gardener's legs.

But then Jim checked his phone, wrong-footing Martin and surprising Clare as well, as he said, 'There's some news here from Susan. You'll be pleased to know she's planning to say the refugee plan will be under review, due to pressing human-rights concerns, and that she and the government are determined not to separate children from families or to undermine marriages with lengthy periods apart. Quite a policy shift. Or a move towards one.'

'I'll believe it when I see it, Jim. I don't trust speeches – it's action we need,' Martin retorted. 'And I'm soon to be another addition to the homelessness statistics, whatever happens with Susan's policy review.' He was not to be appeased, shaking his head dismissively at Jim's words.

'Well, politics is Susan's game, not mine, and I'm sure we can sort something out. Come to the kitchen, both of you. Excuse me putting the telly on while I brew – we can turn the sound down. I'd like to see the announcement, and you can too.' Jim continued to be conciliatory as he found milk and fresh mugs while the kettle boiled.

Martin and Clare stood and watched the newsreader mouthing headlines, then images of commuters looking disconsolately at railway departure boards. Then words travelled along the television screen, much as rolling digital announcements appeared in train carriages announcing the stops ahead. But this announcement was less expected.

Breaking news: Home Office minister Susan Zetland resigns in order to support her family.

Jim hadn't noticed, and Clare was unsure what to say. Martin half coughed and pointed at the screen as Jim looked round, alerted by his noise and manner.

'Ah.' A pause, as Jim read the words. 'Not what she'd hoped for.'

'Nor those who had been led to believe that a change in refugee policy was imminent,' Martin snapped.

Clare was less surprised. David had still thought this outcome was probable, even if postponed. Susan's profile had been badly damaged.

'OK, Martin. I get that you're not happy about that. But this is my wife's life-long career of public service.'

'Sure. Who cares about abhorrent human-rights abuses perpetuated by this government, and a complete disregard for people's well-being or any form of justice, when your wife has lost a ministerial salary?'

'It's probably best that we skip the coffee, Martin.' Jim grasped the arms of his wheelchair, restraining himself. 'I want to speak with Susan and message Jess and Fabian. I don't want to lose my temper or chuck coffee, and right now I feel close to doing both. Please let yourself out. And leave the dog inside.'

'Sure. Dismissed. Bye, Clare.' Martin padded from the room in his socks, shutting the door behind him, not letting Monty escape.

That was that. Or was it? Jim was hot-headed, fair enough. He was probably embarrassed to have been so wrong about the day's events. It must've been a huge disappointment for him, and for Susan. Martin was angry – at the use of refugees as political accessories in parliamentary party manoeuvres, and about his housing. It sounded very harsh that he was given notice like that. But, with Susan out of the Home Office, maybe he and the family would not be so much at daggers drawn? He was a thorn in their side with his political activism. Perhaps things would be calmer on that front with Susan no longer a minister.

Clare knew David would be late home tonight; he would have a new boss to brief.

She made her farewells to Jim, who was evidently shocked by the news. Perhaps he and Susan were less of a team than he'd realised; he'd clearly been blindsided by this. Could this be Susan's way of repaying him for keeping her in the dark about Celeste's hidden child?

As she drove away, Clare wondered whether Athena had been told yet. Perhaps she was cushioned from political upheavals since she had finally taken a leave of absence from work when Rufus's situation had become critical. David would contact her; no doubt her phone would soon be choked with messages of concern. Or, in some cases, there might be revelry in the drama, cloaked as concern.

Poor Athena. Her job; the buzz of being alongside Susan in that upward trajectory – the issues, the rivalries, the success; the prospect of life alongside Rufus as they moved on towards life as a power couple: all gone. Clare would ask David to send her best wishes, too.

CHAPTER 51

It would be a small, low-key service at the crematorium chapel. Hopefully, low-key enough for the press to be unaware of it, or at least kept at bay. The family would use a different name for the booking. Susan, now simply an MP and former minister, would be able to attend without facing a barrage of questions or clicking cameras as she emerged from the car and made her way into the building.

Clare had not anticipated Tom's request to attend, nor his vehement campaign about it, supported by Anna.

'I liked him.' Tom was in K.C. mode. 'Lots of people didn't. But I did. And I was one of the last people to have a proper conversation with him, as well as you, Mum. I want to be there.'

'He's right,' Anna chimed in. 'And if he's going, so am I. We'll be OK, Mum, and it's something we want to do.' She knew her mother so well – she knew exactly which buttons to push. 'It's part of the grieving process, Mum, remembering him and offering him to God, together. There's no need to keep us away, as if death is taboo for the young. Don't exclude us.'

Tom also demonstrated that he had listened to pastoral

conversations over the years and was similarly adept at using them against his mother. 'Yes, we'll only feel left out and imagine dreadful things if we're not allowed to be there with everyone.'

What effective barristers or lobbyists each of them would make – skilful and relentless. David would be attending, Jess and Ahmed, too, with Harriet, Celeste and others from the family. The children could sit with their dad, and it mattered to them to be there. Perhaps they represented something important: Tristan's capacity to connect and befriend. He had relaxed with Tom, without seeking advantage. He had spoken to Clare with a humility that no one else seemed to be mentioning, and with some regret at what he had become, or at his way of relating with others. He had spoken of his childhood, too, and perhaps Anna and Tom offered a link with that part of his life.

They travelled in separate cars. Clare needed to get there early to check the layout of an unfamiliar crem chapel, to meet the team there and check the music choices and other practicalities – the position of the lectern and the switch to close the curtains around the coffin as the service ended.

To keep things discreet, Jim had arranged to book the preceding service time and slot, too, as Clare had suggested. Tristan's was the last before the lunch break for the crem staff. That meant there was no prospect of attendees for the subsequent service arriving and spotting the mourners for Tristan and getting their phones out for a photo or social-media comment. Clare prided herself on careful planning.

Harriet had written some words about her brother, in addition to Jim's notes. Clare had spoken with Fabian and Jess, but neither had memories they wanted to share, and Susan had remained similarly distant from the preparations. Celeste had suggested using Psalm 23, and Jim had agreed.

"'The Lord is my shepherd,'" Fabian read with careful solemnity. "'He makes me lie down in green pastures, he leads me beside still waters.'"

Clare remembered Tristan's drowsy state in the meadow as the horses cropped the grass, and his yearning for happier times there. Had God travelled with him through death? Was there mercy, healing and rest for him? She believed so and was glad to entrust him to God.

"'You prepare a table before me in the presence of my enemies.'"

Tristan had had plenty of those. One of them had killed him.

As the service continued, Clare had the sense of Tristan there with them, smiling wryly at the occasion, approving of Tom's presence and his choice of trainers. The faces of the congregation were varied: Jim, with his jaw clenched and tears on his cheeks; Susan's gaze fixed on the service book in her lap; Anna looking directly at her mother, while holding her father's hand; Tom leaning his whole body against David's other side, forming one shape together. Sitting at the back were Jackie and two colleagues, smartly suited but not in uniform.

Clare was grateful for the measured rhythm and familiar words of the liturgy, which she added to with more personal words of welcome and reference to the trauma and shock of Tristan's death. It felt right to say that, in their situation of not knowing, or indeed understanding, what had happened to Tristan and why, God knows all.

Clare said, addressing God, "'To whom all hearts are open, all desires known, and from whom no secrets are hidden.'"

Jackie seemed startled by Clare's directness. Surely she was used to how funerals were taken, these days? It was much better to refer to challenges and pain, to acknowledge disappointments and regrets, rather than pretend that all was well, when it wasn't. Jackie also looked up when the police were included in the prayers. Perhaps that was unexpected, too.

Harriet's head was bowed when Clare briefly glanced at her. She was pleased to meet Tom's eyes as he sat up, connecting with her words. He had seen the goodness in Tristan.

She was surprised to see Martin there, but less surprised that he was near Harriet and Celeste, seated just behind them. They were next to a couple whom Clare did not recognise – wider family, perhaps? There were a scattering of young men and women, one of whom was crying.

'We'll each have our own memories of Tristan: perhaps good memories of his humour and friendship; other memories that may be more painful and troubled. Maybe we have very mixed emotions as we meet today – sorrow and other feelings, too. We can bring ourselves just as we are to God, with whatever is in our minds and in our hearts. Perhaps with anger, or with a sense of unfinished business. We come in respect of Tristan and to commend him to God, to the God who is love, shown in the love of Christ. As we give Tristan to God's keeping, we can do so with confidence in God's wisdom and mercy. God knows us completely, better than we know ourselves, or one another.'

Clare's eyes searched those of the people seated in front of her. All of them were known by God – every layer of them – nothing was hidden.

She'd said enough. It was time to invite everyone to stand together, if they were able, as she prayed the formal words of commendation, entrusting Tristan to God, merciful redeemer and judge. Then she said the words of committal, releasing Tristan's body to be cremated, dust to dust, ashes to ashes, in sure and certain hope of the resurrection.

Praying the final blessing over the congregation, Clare sensed the familiar shift in herself. Her resentment of Jackie had become compassion for her in the relentless challenge of her work. Her distrust of Jim was now entwined with a deeper warmth towards him, in whatever his struggles might be. She was not surprised by Athena's absence, but was struck by how separate she now seemed to be from the lives of Jess and Susan, having once been so involved in them. Blessings on them all.

After the service, Clare stood at the chapel exit to shake hands with the departing congregation. The warmth of Celeste's greeting was as anticipated; the sincerity with which Jim grasped her hand and thanked her for the 'incredible' service was more of a surprise. Susan was remote, smiling at the handshake, but with an averted gaze. Jess hugged her, barely suppressing sobs, and Harriet touched her arm, wordless. Fabian and Peter were similarly quiet, but smiled with relief that the service was done, and that Fabian had played his part, doing the reading on behalf of the family. Jackie thanked her quite formally for the service as they shook hands, and Clare thought that maybe the DCI had softened towards her.

In the courtyard outside, there was space to mingle. A fish pond and a fountain gave everyone something to look at when there was nothing to be said. Funeral flowers were laid out on wooden stands, and the wreath that had been on Tristan's coffin was brought out by the undertaker's crew and laid beside them. People had stilted conversations, lingering a little longer because no other gathering had been planned. Jackie and her colleagues stood slightly separately, until David and the children joined them. Clare was slightly surprised to find that she didn't mind.

Amongst the wreaths was one shaped with interwoven basketry, some fabric braided between the greenery and flowers – it was no surprise that this one, so carefully crafted, was from Harriet and her mother. The large yellow display of tulips and carnations was from Susan and Jim, on behalf of all their family, and a smaller arrangement held a dedication card with words of condolence sent from Rufus and Athena. Clare wondered whether Tom would notice and query how Rufus could send a card when he was unconscious, but decided David could deal with that one, if so. Anna and Tom had helped to choose and pick some garden flowers that morning to bring to the service, tied with ribbons from various bouquets received at the rectory over the years. Tom had added some grass from the field behind their home.

Anna was now at Susan's side. Clare fervently hoped she wouldn't ask about the refugee policy. Tom and David were with Harriet and Martin. Clare silently urged Tom not to get too close to the pond; she hadn't brought any spare clothes for him today. Celeste had moved across to speak with the police, who still hung back after David and the children moved on from them.

That's friendly and generous of Celeste, Clare thought,

seeing the older woman engage Jackie in genial conversation. There was unfinished business for Jackie and for all of them in addressing Tristan's death, but today was a closure. In the funeral, there was a shared recognition of his death, and a marking of his life. A life stolen from him.

Greetings exchanged, the clusters of people were breaking up as individuals began making their way to their vehicles, preparing to rejoin ordinary life. Clare was on her way to find the crem team and thank the manager when Jess caught up with her.

'Sorry, I couldn't speak properly to thank you, Clare. But that was just as it should be. It was sad, but just as it should be. Thanks for the service, and for . . . everything. It's good you know about things; you and David make Ahmed and me feel less alone.' She looked over towards the car park, where Ahmed was waiting, standing with Celeste and Harriet. 'All our relationships have changed, and suspicion hangs over all of us.' Jess frowned at the thought. 'I guess that's why Jackie was here – to watch us.'

'I think it was also about paying her respects.' Clare was surprised at her willingness to defend Jackie.

Jess grimaced at this; she seemed unpersuaded. 'Maybe. But we're being watched, I feel it. The press are after any story about Mum's downfall.' She paused. 'David has always been a good friend to me, Clare. Maybe I haven't appreciated him, or you, enough. Things around Tristan are so complicated.' She turned her back to the car park and everyone who had gathered there, lowering her voice confidingly: 'I've been demented. It sounds mad now, but I even wondered about Ahmed, at one point. You see, I saw him take the cake knife.'

'Have you asked him about that?' Clare touched Jess's arm; she wanted to support her, but was also on high alert. What had happened to the weapon? And how had it ended up in the tree house?

'Yes. He said he just put it down on one of the tables.'

So, they were no further forward. Someone else must have taken it from there. Clare tried not to reveal her disappointment, simply saying, 'The police need to have an open mind, however difficult. But, like you, I trust Ahmed completely. I realise I trust Harriet, too. I don't believe she's guilty.' I only wonder occasionally, and that's different, she reassured herself.

'Me, too – and thanks again, Clare. Let's catch up later. It was great to see the children today. They were so sweet to me. I had a big hug from both of them.'

'They care about you. Tom liked Tristan, too – they had quite a chat by the river. I like to think of Tristan in the field with Tom, chatting and laughing.'

'It's a good image.' Jess smiled. 'I hope he is at peace now – or in my better moments I do. Sometimes I'm just so angry at him – for getting himself murdered, and at our wedding. As if it's all his fault. Such a waste. His life gone, and Rufus in that state. I want it over, and for DCI Carter to do her stuff.'

'I feel the same.'

'I'd better go. Take care.' Jess kissed her in farewell and headed to the car park.

After watching Jess walk away, Clare went to the office to thank the crem manager, who had lingered and seemed disappointed that no press had made an appearance. He'd been eager to repel any who attempted to encroach, assuring Clare of his own discretion many times, and now seemed keen to discuss the attendance of the police officers and his view of any suspects in the case.

'I thought they were all very tense. Very on edge. Being a murder, it makes people nervous. No idea who did it, then?'

'It's a difficult time for them. Thank you for your help.' Clare used her professional vicar voice to discourage his speculation.

'Yes. What did you think of that bloke, bringing his children along? Suspicious, I thought. Maybe he was using the kids as camouflage.'

'Who knows? Thanks again.' She would enjoy telling David that he was someone's chief suspect.

CHAPTER 52

Clare shook out her robes and put the cassock and surplice on a hanger, ready to take everything to the car. She mulled over the service, and those there, and the crem manager's suspicions. Anna and Tom would be delighted to hear that their presence had made their dad a likely villain in someone's eyes.

There was a knock on the vestry door. The crem manager with more sleuthing? He stood there, jerking his head behind him, explaining that there had been a late arrival. It was Athena, the ever-capable Athena, who had mistimed her journey. She was dressed in solemn navy, holding a large handbag in front of her body.

'I'm so sorry, Clare,' she said. 'This gentleman explained you were still here. I've missed everything, haven't I? Everyone's left.'

'It was generous of you to come, with everything you're coping with. How are you doing, and how is Rufus?'

'I'm OK. And Rufus has stabilised. You've been good to his parents; it means a lot to them.'

The crem manager stood by the door, showing no inclination to leave for his belated lunch break.

Clare gestured at the vestry. 'It's a bit small in here. Why don't you come with me, Athena? We can put my things in the car and walk in the grounds a bit.'

The manager half bowed and left them to it, recognising his dismissal.

Clare gathered up her books, bag and robes, and, with Athena beside her, walked in silence. It was unlike Athena to have so little to say. The car park had emptied. There were no early arrivals yet for the first service after lunch. Clare handed Athena an order of service, with the photo of a young Tristan on the front, smiling and wearing a trilby hat at a rakish angle.

Athena took a step back, clutching it. 'I think it's better I was late. I can't do this.' She pushed the order of service back at Clare. 'I'm not sure I could face Susan yet. Or Jess. You know I've been hung out to dry, Clare? Susan's dropped me. Her career has had a setback, and mine has disappeared. Even if they'd offered me support about Rufus, I might have told them where to stick it.'

'You're going through such a lot. I'm sorry.'

'Sorry?' Athena was shaking, her hands clenched. 'That doesn't really cut it, Clare. Everyone is sorry. But no one can do anything. Tristan and the rest of that family destroyed Rufus. They've ruined everything. I might have caused a scene at the funeral, told some home truths about Tristan.'

Clare wondered why Athena had come if she only wanted to vent her rage, rather than be with others and pay her respects. Maybe this seething anger was a surprise to her, too, and being with Clare had released it. She waited, and Athena continued.

'I hadn't realised how furious I am – with Tristan, Susan, Jess. All of them. Even your David. Everyone is carrying on in the office without me. Jess and Ahmed are rolling on into their sunny future together, and Susan will soon be queening it at constituency events. Eyes still on the Cabinet prize, even if it's postponed for a while.'

Athena carried on; the floodgates had opened. 'I can't bear them, and Rufus's parents are almost as bad with their questions and disapproval. You know they're hoping you'll take his funeral, Clare, if he dies after all? And he still might – there's a long way to go yet. They'd expect me to be there. But I couldn't do it. I couldn't even do today, and his would be worse – far worse. It's no accident I was late. I nearly didn't come at all, but I thought I'd better put in an appearance.'

'It's good to see you, Athena.' And it was good she was expressing this tumult of feelings.

'There's nothing good about it. I'm in hell. Just how Tristan liked people to be. It's what he did to Rufus, and now he's doing it to me.'

'What did Tristan do to Rufus?' Clare knew this mattered.

'He threatened Rufus. Tristan said he'd tell people about their time at school together. But he also knew about some dodgy deals Rufus had done and threatened to expose those too. Rufus only told me about them after Tristan was gone. He couldn't hide his relief that Tristan couldn't tell on him anymore.'

'It sounds like Rufus was very afraid of what Tristan might do.'

'Maybe it wasn't so bad.' Athena collected herself, adjusting her bag on her shoulder. 'I'm probably exaggerating. There wasn't any love lost between them, that's all. Forget it.' So, Athena was backtracking for all she was worth. 'Anyway, can you let David know I came? Ask him to say the right things to Susan – that I'm sorry I was late, blah-di-blah, all condolences offered, blah-di-blah – to Jess, too?'

'Of course.'

'I think I'll take a stroll here and then head off. Thanks, Clare.'

'Would you like to meet up a bit later? Maybe get something to eat?'

'Eating is not high on my priority list.'

'Sure. I'm wondering about support for you in all of this, Athena. Have you any family or friends around?'

'I'm fine. My mum calls by. My sister came too – I hadn't seen her for a while. I'm better alone, for now. I'll be OK. There's no need for a vicar check-up.' Athena's ironic laugh was hollow.

'It's good your family are around. Perhaps your GP or others need to be aware of what you're going through?'

'I've seen the doctor. But there's no need for anyone to know that. I'll be fine. Bye, Clare.' She rocked a little.

Was she drunk? Clare worried she wasn't safe to drive. She watched as Athena began to walk away, grieving and angry, but coherent, with no sign of immediate risk of self-harm. At least she had some family support and was under the care of her GP.

Cars had begun arriving in the car park now, with one or two passengers stepping out gingerly, uncomfortable at being there and wearing new or unfamiliar dark clothes. A suited man lit a cigarette, cupping his hands to do so, glancing across at the dog-collared cleric and the departing special adviser, or former special adviser.

'How are Anna and Tom?' Athena had turned back and startled Clare with her question. 'School and everything OK?'

'Sure. They're sad, of course. About Tristan. They came to the service.'

'Really? Why?'

'They wanted to. They were part of the day, I suppose. Feel an involvement.'

'Who else was here? Did Martin come? Harriet? I thought she'd be arrested, by now.'

'They were here. Susan . . . Jim . . . Celeste.'

'Did Celeste have lipstick on her teeth again? Sorry, that's rude. I'm more of an outsider now, like Tristan was. Maybe I'll be the new disrupter. Spill some beans about Susan or Jess.'

'That would be one approach.'

'Don't worry. I can't be bothered. I'm tired of it all. Tired of talking, too. I'll get out of your hair.'

That was it. Off Athena went into her low-slung, open-topped car, closing the door with a slam.

Clare watched as she drove away. As bidden, Clare would pass on messages of condolence via David, but that wasn't all she would be telling him. The turbulence within Athena was understandable. But the resentment and animosity of her words were troubling. Clare felt infected by her bitterness. She wanted to snap her irritation at the bystanders now staring at her, probably wondering if she was taking the next service. She was angry with the nosy crem manager, fed up that she was hungry and now needed to get to her next appointment quickly, with no time to eat.

Typical.

It was time to get going, to shake it all off. Maybe she

could grab a sandwich from a garage on the way to her care-home visit and eat it at the traffic lights. She would choose the filling carefully – egg mayonnaise down her front was not a good look. David had taken the children home. They would all be fine.

CHAPTER 53

When Clare paid a pastoral visit to Greenwood a couple of days after the funeral, she was so early, she parked her car by the church and tapped out some emails on her phone. She decided to walk from there up to the house. It was a fine day, and the autumnal colours were glorious in the sunshine. The bright sky and rustling, coppery leaves lifted her spirits.

She hadn't expected to come across Martin, big stick in hand, the brown Labrador at his side. She called out a greeting as he approached her down the lane.

'Martin, good to see you!'

She didn't want to ask immediately how much longer he would be staying, although she was curious. They exchanged comments about the beautiful day, and then it was Martin who broached the subject, seeming unruffled about it, now.

'You know I was asked to leave the cottage? Well, I think it's time to go. Jim's been decent enough, says there is no rush to get me out, now. I guess my politics are no longer a problem. I'm not sure what Susan thinks, but she's not been around much. And I'm useful with all the jobs to be done around the place.' He tapped at his boot with the stick he was carrying.

'Well, there are big changes ahead for everyone,' Clare offered.

'Yes, but none of this changes anything for the Dover Four, does it? Or for the others. The plane protest achieved nothing. It doesn't feel like there's any point.' He looked defeated, rather than angry.

'There are various ways to express our views, and it's important to do so.'

'Maybe. But I'm heading off. I might walk the coast or get another gardening job. I can be a barista, too. Could go anywhere.'

'Lots of options.' But rather lonely ones, she thought. Martin's beard was no longer so well kept, and he seemed despondent. 'Will you keep in touch with anyone?' She wanted to probe a little.

'With Harriet. And I'll miss Monty. Maybe I'll get a pup myself. I think Harriet would like that. Maybe she'd do a picture.' He looked more cheerful at the thought.

'I'm hoping she'll draw our golden retriever. She's in demand.'

'Celeste said you'd been good to Harriet.'

'I want to do what I can. It was good to see you at the funeral. I'm here to visit Jim and Susan. I hope things work out well for you in your new job, or wherever you're headed, Martin.'

Perhaps she'd been too strong in her concern; the gardener seemed embarrassed, and ended the conversation quickly, walking past her with the dog, muttering his thanks and goodbyes without any eye contact.

She continued up to the house, wondering how the family

would be. Perhaps Tristan's funeral had enabled some degree of consolation about his death, but so much remained unresolved.

Jess had messaged to say that she was hopeful her job might be open to her again after the due processes and a suspension period had been served, so some things were moving forward. It was a surprise to find her at Greenwood, chattering with her parents about a trip to Italy. It sounded like a welcome break for Susan, who must have been exhausted by all that had happened. Jim mentioned how Jess coming down and suggesting the trip had cheered his wife today.

'Jess wouldn't take no for an answer.' Susan smiled. 'Insisted I stopped moping, threw me into a shower, put on some Bruce Springsteen and started looking at holiday options for us all. Maybe Fabian and Peter will come too, and Ahmed. This will be your Anna, one day, Clare, sorting you and David out.'

Clare couldn't work out whether Susan's good humour was genuine, or a convincing veneer.

'I think time in the land of gelato and cappuccino is just what Mum needs,' Jess added. 'I'm a doctor and I prescribe Montepulchiano, Pienza and maybe Siena.'

'Not Siena – too many Palio memories there for Fabian, or lack of them,' Jim quipped.

This family was resurgent, and now joking about Fabian's career embarrassment. Clare presumed Susan and Jim were as yet unaware of the work disciplinary which Jess was facing, or the reasons for it. Surely a patient who'd died by suicide wasn't cause for merriment. The Zetlands' capacity to reset themselves after any setback was impressive, but seemed somehow dislocated from reality.

Clare saw that the large kitchen showed signs of the pressures that the family had been under. Fewer traces of the wedding remained, with no photos or leftover orders of service visible, but there was a messy stack of empty cereal boxes and other packets awaiting recycling, together with discarded magazines and envelopes holding charitable appeals. Unwashed dishes were piled on the sideboard. Perhaps there had been a deeper need for Jess's intervention than Jim or Susan cared to acknowledge.

As if prompted by Clare's unspoken thought, Jess stood to clear the table of dirty mugs and went to the sink to find a cloth to wipe it clean. She tipped the shrivelled grapes from the fruit bowl into the compost bin.

Clare asked after Fabian and was told somewhat glibly that he and Peter were well and had found the funeral very helpful as part of the process of moving on.

That was good to hear, but the sense of the family's privilege nudged at her, too. The contrast with Martin and with Harriet struck her. They were both outsiders, as Tristan had been. Athena, too. Would this family simply shrug them off and move on?

She was being harsh. This was painful for all of them. No one was unscathed. Any signs of healing were a blessing. But the ease with which this family moved forward gave her pause. Had one of them achieved their objective, in silencing Tristan and escaping blame?

CHAPTER 54

Jackie was not impressed. Lost career, stolen or not, Susan should not be swanning off to Italy with her family before the case was closed. There was no point trying to prevent them. Susan's ministerial job might be finished, but her power and connections still remained. David was pacifying on the phone – he'd clearly spent too much time around the vicar. Jackie would've kept them all within fifty miles, if she could, and locked up if necessary.

Martin was clearing off, too, and she had insisted he keep her apprised of his whereabouts. His vague plan of walking the South West Coast Path was as feeble as it came. He needed to get out of this protest stuff, get a job and get his life out of neutral, in her view. He reminded her of her younger brother, who thought an occasional shift at the leisure centre equalled a challenging career.

Perhaps it was better for Martin that he was heading off west to ramble along the seashore, away from Harriet. It was obvious she was giving him the brush-off. Jackie had wondered if Martin had the makings of a stalker – she had sniffed it on him, with his intensity about Harriet and his unease around others. But she was probably being overly suspicious.

Harriet remained her number-one suspect, but things had stalled. Since Susan's resignation, the burst of press interest had subsided, although Fabian's career was on the ascendant. His coffee-table book of travel essays and artful photos had been published in haste. No Palio references, however.

Jackie had other cases to pursue, with evidence to present in a separate trial and multiple staff reports to conclude. The data collection for the latest slew of targets was almost complete.

It was time to stir the pot on this enquiry. Should she call Harriet in again, for further questioning? Or have another go at some of the others? She wondered what David was doing today. Perhaps it was time to give him another update. She'd be circumspect; he'd probably tell Clare anything she said. But perhaps he might have something useful to share. It could be that Clare had relevant information, too. She was around the Zetland family a good deal, and Jackie had realised the vicar was no fool.

The information Clare had unearthed about Rufus and his connections with Tristan beyond their schooldays had been useful. Clare was right, too, that a rope could have been used to get down from the tree house, although evidence for that theory was inconclusive. Jackie had followed up on the art-forgery angle, thanks to Clare's prompting. But the vicar was too soft about Harriet. Another perpetrator wearing gloves was a possibility, but Jackie couldn't get past the fact that Harriet had been found in situ, holding the weapon and with a major financial motive.

She was willing to consider alternatives. Susan's family seemed to have resigned themselves to the likelihood of Harriet's guilt; they were markedly less vehement in the artist's defence than Clare had been. That caused Jackie a degree of disquiet. She wondered if implicating Harriet was convenient for others.

The valuable painting of horses still hung in the hall at Greenwood. Chris Simmons had recently remembered that, some time ago, Fabian had commissioned a copy of it, after all. Mr Simmons had conveniently forgotten about this when he'd first been interviewed. The work had never been completed, nor paid for. Or so the story went. The gallery owner had been guilty of no offence; it's not a crime to copy a picture.

But what had Fabian's intentions been? Presumably to profit from selling the copy, passing it off as an original. Or, more likely, to sell the original and substitute it with the forged copy at Greenwood.

If that was the plan, how desperate would Fabian have been to conceal this criminal enterprise from his parents? Was the privileged young man so used to things going smoothly for him, and so unable to bear the prospect of exposure on this scale, that he might have taken violent action to stop that from happening? It was time to call Fabian in for a chat about forged art.

In the bleak interview room, Jackie wanted to shake Fabian up a bit and ruffle his smooth assurance, but this was proving difficult. Despite being summoned to the station, Fabian looked relaxed, with his handsome face and tousled hair untroubled by any pressure Jackie could exert.

'Your dad asked you to source a copy?' Her face was a cartoon of scepticism.

'Yes.'

'And he has only now remembered this fact – rather convenient for you, isn't it?'?'

'Convenient or not, that's what happened. It was supposed to be a surprise gift for my sister. She loves horses.' He ran his fingers through his blonde fringe, moving it to the side.

'Things tend to be convenient for you, Fabian, don't they? Convenient that your book came out just as your family was in the news. Are sales good, after your cousin's murder?'

'I don't know.'

'Well, I know things have been a bit tight for you financially. Losing the TV series must have been a blow.'

'Commissions come and go. It's a fluctuating industry.' Fabian spoke as if this explained everything.

'But you can count on your dad to stump up for you. Protect you. Your mum, too. Unless they weren't impressed by the forgery plan – however much your dad is covering for you now. That would have been a worry. And Tristan knew that, didn't he?'

'There was no forgery plan.' His expression was slightly puzzled, as if unsure why anyone could have supposed there was.

'So you say . . . But Tristan had a habit of knowing things. Uncomfortable things.'

'I'm not sure what you're implying.' Fabian continued to look quizzical.

'I'm wondering what you would do to keep uncomfortable things hidden – family secrets.'

'Every family has things they prefer to keep private. That doesn't mean we kill each other to keep a lid on things.' Fabian leaned back in his chair and crossed one leg over the other.

Perhaps he was buying time or simply keeping up the show of nonchalance.

'What was Tristan keeping quiet about in your family, Fabian?'

Jackie had no real expectation that he'd reveal anything, but she knew his parents wouldn't like him being brought in. David wouldn't be happy either; he'd realise she was on a fishing expedition. But what else was going to stir the waters? If she kept going, maybe she would land something. So far, Fabian was holding his own, offering apparent cooperation, but saying nothing. He was quite the politician. Susan would be proud.

'I don't know what to say. Nothing comes to mind. I'm sorry not to be of more help.' Fabian's sincerity would have convinced her if she'd been less experienced. 'We all want this over and done with. Thank you so much for all your hard work.'

Perhaps he wanted her to doff a cap at him, or curtsey. Patronising git. Whatever her thoughts, Jackie kept her manner entirely professional.

'Just tell me, Fabian, what did Tristan say to you about the painting?'

'There's nothing to tell. Tristan may have mentioned it – I think perhaps he did. The copy was meant to be a surprise gift for my sister, and that's all I can tell you. Sorry.'

It was pointless. The investigation had stalled, again.

CHAPTER 55

Clare had arranged to see Harriet again in London. Since the funeral, they had been in contact sporadically, and now wanted to talk face to face again and consider their next steps. They'd agreed to meet at the National Gallery on Trafalgar Square, a place they both loved. Clare had arrived slightly early, so was making the most of the opportunity to enjoy time with a familiar picture.

She had stood in front of this painting in the National Gallery as a dungaree-wearing teenager, and many times since then, looking at it and feeling the life in it – like instress from a Hopkins' poem. The slapped-on sludges of paint were golden and yellow. Some of the sunflowers were wilting in the vase, but nonetheless the whole canvas was shouting at her, *Live! Live! This is life! Live it!*

The café had become more expensive, but they could still get a coffee, then take in a picture or two. The Corot set of four, perhaps: *The Four Times of Day*, or maybe the Renoir, with that young, blue-hatted girl at the theatre, leaning forwards into new experience.

Clare turned away from the sunflowers and saw a familiar

figure in front of the Renoir, considering the girl in the painting. It was Athena, absorbed in what she saw.

Clare paused, then stepped towards her. She didn't want to miss the opportunity to talk. 'Athena?'

Startled, Athena clutched her smart designer bag to herself and moved away from Clare's voice. Then she seemed to realise who it was and collected herself. 'Hello, Clare! It's a surprise to see you here.'

'Yes, but it's less surprising to find a special adviser near Whitehall.' Oh no, that was tactless; Clare cursed herself for not thinking before she spoke.

'Well, I'm not one anymore, although I am going to the office later. I've got my pass to hand in and my gym bag to collect. Not that I used it much – I was too busy, then.' Athena sounded bitter.

Clare took in the sour look on her face and thought it was unsurprising that she was resentful. Athena had worked so hard, and what had the payback been? She tried to be welcoming: 'I'm meeting Harriet for a coffee, if you've got time to join us?'

'Thanks, but I don't think I do. I might get one in the office with David. Sorry, I just don't want to be late.'

Clare knew when she was being given the brush-off, but she couldn't resist trying one more time. 'Well, we'll be in the café here for a while. Find us later, if you fancy it. We'll take a stroll in the galleries, too.'

'I didn't know you two were friends.'

'We only met at the wedding. But everything that happened, it's shaken us all up, hasn't it? And I know it's been especially hard for you.'

'Thanks,' Athena said briskly, her eyes fixed on her feet.

Clare immediately felt like she was saying all the wrong things, but battled on. 'I'm just so sorry about your job, and Rufus.'

'Thanks. But work isn't everything.' Athena paused. She looked like she wanted to say something further but couldn't quite find the words. When she spoke again, it was more slowly, heavily, as if this was a matter of great importance: 'There are things people might want to be aware of about Rufus.' She was looking to one side of Clare, not quite meeting her eye.

The gallery was becoming increasingly crowded. Clare stepped to the side to avoid a trio of girls posing for selfies in front of a Monet and evaded the group looking at a painting of a circus performer, moving closer to Athena.

'What do you mean?' Clare asked tentatively. Was Athena going to confide in her about the shoplifting ring? Or maybe she was going to explain the intense exchange which Clare had witnessed her having with her boyfriend that night at Greenwood, after Tristan's murder?

'Nothing in particular. Only that there was a lot more to the relationship between him and Tristan than people realised.'

'Right. In what way?' Clare wanted more.

'Nothing . . . There's nothing to say.' Athena shook her head slightly, as though clearing the thought away. 'Sorry . . . I've got to go to the office. Please give my best to Harriet. It was lovely to see you.'

Athena quickly turned away, manoeuvring herself through the clumps of visitors, threading between a couple absorbed in their audio-guide headsets, on past a child's buggy and out to the tiled stairwell. It was so frustrating. Athena had seemed on the brink of confiding something significant about Rufus and Tristan, then had clammed up and fled.

Clare headed to the café, where she found Harriet sitting at a table, waiting for her. She told Harriet about her strange exchange with Athena.

Harriet was initially confused. 'Wait, was she implying that Rufus did it? Or that there was something shifty going on?'

'I don't know. She was being odd and sort of conspiratorial. She said nothing concrete, and then suddenly rushed away. I'll message David. Maybe he can check up on her, and perhaps she might tell him what's on her mind. This weird behaviour could just be the shock and grief coming out in strange ways.'

'Maybe Rufus flipped. Maybe—' Harriet broke off, looking over Clare's shoulder.

'Hi. I thought I'd find you both here.' Athena was at their table, a false smile plastered across her face.

'Athena! Take a seat!'

'No, thanks – I just wanted to apologise for being a bit abrupt in the gallery, Clare. It took me by surprise, seeing you there.'

'No problem.' Clare smiled, worrying about how much Athena had just overheard.

Athena carried on explaining. 'Then I realised I couldn't face the office, and thought that maybe I could give some things to you instead – for you to hand on to David? Please tell him to chuck any stuff of mine; nothing there matters, anyway.'

'Sure.'

'I'm just tying up loose ends. You know how it is. Here's

my pass and some keys, all present and correct.' She reached down and placed a lumpy brown envelope on the table in front of Clare.

'Of course,' Clare said. 'The team will miss you – and Susan.' Clare didn't know if this would soothe Athena or result in an outburst.

'The engines of state will roar on without me, I've no doubt about that. What's that line? All things come to dust, every player struts on the stage – you know the Shakespeare quote . . .'

'Well, we'll be strutting for a bit longer,' said Clare. 'Even though Tristan's left us.'

'He didn't choose to go, did he? Rufus certainly didn't choose to fall, either.' Athena was suddenly agitated. 'Just as I didn't choose to leave Susan's ghastly job. There . . . that's everything.' She indicated the envelope, which lay on the table. 'When you give that to David, please thank him. He was decent to me.'

'Sure. Thanks, Athena.'

'I must get out. Good to see you both. Bye.'

The two women didn't speak and just looked at one another. Harriet's eyebrows were raised so high, Clare thought they'd disappear. After a moment, and presumably when Harriet felt it was safe to talk, she said, 'I don't know Athena well, but even I can tell she's acting strangely.'

'Yep.' Clare cast a look over her shoulder towards the door to the street.

'She had no reason to dislike Tristan, did she? Or none that we know about.'

'No. I have some alarms sounding about her well-being.'

'Do you think she might be planning to harm herself?' Harriet's face was full of concern at this possibility.

'Not necessarily, but she does seem very up and down. I think I'll head after her and come back and find you later, if that's OK? I want to check on her.'

Harriet nodded fiercely. 'Sure, go. I'll commune with medieval art in the Sainsbury Wing.'

Clare hurried off, with her bag, envelope and jacket in hand, not certain which way Athena would have headed. Then, there she was, standing outside on the pavement, as if unsure where to go.

As Clare approached, Athena looked disconcerted and irritated to see her. 'Clare?'

'Hi. Sorry to follow you out – but there was something on my mind.'

'What?' Hostility was etched into Athena's face.

'I know how tough things are and I wondered if you might want some company. Maybe I could walk with you for a bit, we could head to St James's Park?' She sounded implausible, even to herself.

'I don't need nannying, thank you, Clare. I just want to be left alone. I know you and Harriet think I'm guilty. So don't stand here pretending to be my friend.'

'Why would we think that, Athena?' That was some leap. But a revealing one.

'I don't want to talk about it.' Athena looked furious.

Clare could see the conversation was over. 'Sure . . . I'm sorry to have hassled you. I'm not suggesting you're guilty of anything, I just wanted to see if you were OK.'

'I don't need an intervention, Clare. Did you think I would

finish myself off, top myself or something? I don't have the energy. And I don't want to be interrogated. Just leave me alone.' Exasperation rippled from her.

With nothing more to be said, Clare bobbed her head at Athena's tight face and turned back towards the café.

She found Harriet still at their table, looking at her phone with her forehead furrowed. 'It's the police,' she said. 'Jackie is calling me back in. They're coming to pick me up here.'

Clare's own phone buzzed with a message from David. Jackie had rung him at the office this morning. *Had a call from Jackie, things are moving again. Take care and speak soon.*

So, Jackie had called him yet again, had she? And she was homing in on Harriet, too. David was giving her the heads up – he knew she was meeting Harriet today. He'd wanted her to distance herself from Harriet, but wouldn't come out and say so; Clare just felt it. She'd like more distance between him and Jackie, but she wasn't going to say anything about that, either.

Instead, she responded to Harriet: 'I'm so sorry. How awful. Can I come with you?'

'There's no point, but thanks anyway. Could you call Mum in a bit? Just to let her know and to warn her I may be back later than expected. She's been so good to me. In more ways than you know.'

An older woman at an adjoining table lifted her head from her book, alert to their conversation. Clare hoped *she* wasn't as obvious when she was eavesdropping.

Harriet dropped her voice. 'I wish I'd told you ages ago. I . . . I regret that I didn't. It's a long story, but there was a time when I was completely broke and deep in debt. Mum knew I was skint and she let me come home when I couldn't afford to live on my own anymore.'

'These things are personal,' Clare said quietly, now sympathising with Harriet and immediately feeling a renewed trust in her and in her innocence.

'I was stupid to keep anything from you. I'm really sorry. Jackie has known for a while – that's probably why she's calling me in again.'

'Thank you for telling me, and it's OK. It really is.' Well, it is now. 'I'll ring your mum. Harriet, I also think it's worth telling Jackie about our meeting with Athena today. About how strange she seems.'

'I'm not sure they're interested in me offering up alternative suspects, Clare.' Harriet's voice was sharper than usual as she said this.

Clare knew she was probably pushing too hard, but she needed to make her point. 'There's Athena being strange, the whole forgery fiasco with Fabian, and Martin – involved in those protests, and being evicted now, too.'

'Anyone with a heart or a brain opposes my aunt Susan and her policies. But I get money from Tristan's death, Clare. Jackie won't see anything beyond that.'

'What about Jim and your mum? Does Jackie know about that?'

'I'm not suggesting Mum as an alternative. The notion of her being involved is absurd.'

'I know. But, if Jackie can have an awareness of all the other things going on, at least that widens the field.'

'Widening it to include Mum? Or my uncle? No way.'

'OK. But there are others.'

'Why don't you pay for our drinks so we're not arrested for that, and I'll go outside and wait for the police car. Thanks for phoning Mum, and maybe avoid telling her about your suggestion that she did it.'

'Anything else I can do?' Clare asked, despite feeling suddenly tired of being the object of everyone's anger.

The woman at the neighbouring table watched them again, intrigued.

'Solve this mess, establish world peace and get government policy changed on refugees while you're at it.' Harriet stood and reached to clasp Clare, then drew away, rallying herself. 'Sorry, Clare, I know I'm being a cow. Thanks for doing so much for me.'

The sunflowers of the painting had spoken of life, had called Clare to live. A few of the flowers in the earthenware pot were broken-stemmed and fading. Some were dying. The painting spoke of the reality of life and death – and the call to live, to relish each moment and every breath. Clare watched Harriet lift her chin and walk out through the heavy doors to meet the police car.

CHAPTER 56

Clare's call to Celeste was informative for both women. Ringing from outside the gallery, she had to shout over traffic noise to let Celeste know that Harriet would be home later than anticipated, and then moved to a quieter side road to continue the conversation as she tried to calm Celeste's fears for her daughter. Celeste commented that no one realised how kind Harriet was, prompting Clare to say that Harriet had mentioned how generous Celeste had been, providing her with a home when she'd been in terrible debt. She hoped Celeste might tell her more – and she was in luck.

'She didn't want anyone to know how she lost her money. So typical of her, trying to keep things under wraps.'

'I'm sure you're proud of her,' said Clare, thankful that she could now at least hear Celeste clearly.

'She is very loyal, and some of her friends get into an awful mess. Well, we all do – you have been very understanding about my difficulties, Clare, and so has Harriet.'

'Life can be complicated for all of us, can't it, Celeste? You mentioned Harriet's friends?'

Clare was rewarded for her persistence as Celeste continued, 'Yes, one of the artists from Harriet's shared studio, years back, was very foolish; she got herself into debt and then borrowed from one of those awful loan sharks to try to keep afloat, but of course things only got worse – much, much worse. Those people are wicked, Clare. Utterly heartless.'

'Yes,' Clare agreed, but Celeste was well into her stride and needed no further encouragement.

'Skylark – that's not her real name, darling, but you know what some young artists are like – well, she ended up with bailiffs coming round and threatening her, terrifying her children too, and Skylark didn't even have enough money to feed them, and her car got repossessed as well. They were all about to be made homeless, and the threats those bailiffs made – it was horrific. So, when she heard what was going on, my Harriet bailed her out. Paid every penny, everything that was owed – everything. It was a fortune.'

Clare was dismayed. Harriet had helped her friend and kept it quiet, and all the while Clare had assumed the worst of her. Celeste carried on with the story, divulging how Harriet had covered the costs of her friend's rehab and counselling support for the children – had helped get her back on her feet and into recovery.

Jackie might know about Harriet's dire financial circumstances, but did she know the whole story? Clare felt ashamed that she had ever doubted her generous friend, that she had misjudged her. Harriet was innocent, and Clare was unequivocal about that now. But how could she convince Jackie?

CHAPTER 57

Before this case, the Home Secretary's office had been in contact with Jackie and her team on occasion, but now they were calling almost daily – asking about progress and time-scales, always with the explicit assurance that no pressure was intended, and that they were simply requesting an update. Dream on. If Jackie didn't succeed in resolving the enquiry, and speedily, this would have a significant impact on her career. There was no question about that.

Pressure was a constant for her. The sheer workload of everyday policing and their crazy shift patterns meant that her team were permanently overstretched. They faced demands to meet ever-changing targets, along with instructions to document every breath taken, every paper clip issued, every word spoken. Although there were some complications for her in having David involved in this high-profile case, at least he was sympathetic whenever it was his turn to call her directly, and sometimes he had information to offer too. Like today.

He'd wanted to let her know he had just heard from Clare, who had been with Harriet when the team had gone to pick her up for some further questioning. Jackie was sufficiently open-minded to follow up on new suggestions, especially when they came from him. She wasn't so blinkered in her search for evidence of Harriet's guilt as others might think. It had been important to follow up on the forgery angle. She wanted to make progress and to show she was doing everything she could to solve the case.

Jackie had rung Clare directly. Their conversation was brief and matter of fact. Jackie thought Clare seemed slightly wary of her – perhaps she hadn't expected her call – but she was professional all the same. They both were.

'Thanks for this, Clare.' Jackie was polite. 'Your input is very helpful.'

'I'm concerned about Athena's state of mind, and I gathered from Rufus's parents that it was Tristan who introduced Rufus and Athena. It's complicated; I wasn't aware of that connection. Athena also mentioned that Rufus was very relieved after Tristan's death. But then she sort of tried to take it back. She was erratic after Tristan's funeral, but she's in a much worse state today.'

'And you believe that she might be at risk of self-harm?'

'Possibly.' Clare explained what she'd observed, answering Jackie's questions, and then raised another issue. 'I think you should know about something else. About Harriet.'

This time, Jackie said nothing, so Clare continued: 'She may have kept her financial situation secret to protect someone else. My understanding is that she bailed out a friend who was in debt and in desperate need of help – that's why Harriet's own finances are in such a dire state.'

'Thank you. I want to be clear that we apprise ourselves of all circumstances.' Jackie knew that this was a slightly annoying answer.

'Thank you for listening to me, and for everything that you're doing. There's so much to untangle in all this.' It seemed that Clare was becoming more aware of the responsibilities Jackie carried, and there was a new warmth in her appreciation. Was that a note of respect in her voice? Jackie was surprised to hear it.

'Indeed. Thanks for your assistance, Clare.' Jackie put down the phone. Perhaps the vicar wasn't so bad.

After this, Jackie had rung Athena, who said that she was walking along the Embankment. Jackie could hear background traffic noise and snippets of other people's conversations as Athena passed them.

She had anticipated a quick chat that wouldn't tell her much. In past encounters, Athena had been cooperative and professional, with little useful to say. But, today, Jackie had found Athena obstructive and antagonistic, both defensive and accusatory, casting aspersions on Harriet, and even at one point on Rufus, announcing, 'Rufus had a motive too, and so did plenty of other people, that is blindingly obvious, so why don't you leave me alone and get on with catching the real killer, detective? I can't keep getting dragged into this; this is unacceptable police harassment, and I have nothing further to say.'

Yet she continued to say a good deal, with an aggression that hissed in each word. Jackie decided to delay Harriet's interview. Athena had jumped the queue, and a police car would be heading her way too.

Once she was at the station, Athena appeared to be enjoying herself. Perhaps she missed the drama of political life. She played to the audience in the interview room, striding in and announcing it was time to reveal the truth and come clean.

'I was terrified,' she gasped, as she recounted her version of events. 'Rufus told me he did this for me. For us. And for our future. He said Tristan was going to ruin him. That he'd never be able to get a decent job in politics, or anything else, ever again. He said he'd had no choice: he had to do it to silence him.'

Athena scarcely paused for breath, seeming shocked by her own story.

'He actually thought I would comfort him. Help him, even. He was distraught about what had happened and what he had done, but he was more distraught about the idea of being caught. He thought I'd be willing to cover for him. He was sure of it.'

'What did Rufus want you to do?'

'Be complicit. Be his Lady Macbeth. He was panicking. He'd held it together talking with you, and with Clare, he said, but he'd been desperate to tell someone what happened.'

'What had happened?'

'Tristan had taunted him and threatened him – or so he said. About more than the school incidents. But I wondered if it was just a stupid wind-up and Rufus had flipped, really lost it. His eyes were different, like he'd taken something. He looked so hard and relentless. I was terrified. He said that we would rise together as planned and he'd let nothing stop us.'

Jackie thought it was Athena who was oddly relentless now, completely fixed on venting her emotions and explaining what had happened, speaking fast and glaring slightly wildly at her interviewers as she did so.

'Where were you when he told you this?' Jackie asked, keeping her face impassive.

'Looking for Jess. She'd been gone for ages. Rufus must have caught up with me. I thought he'd headed away into the woods, but there he was, telling me all this, looking ferocious – feral.'

'Feral?' It was difficult for Jackie not to raise an eyebrow at this. She asked for more clarity. 'And he showed no sign of this the previous evening? He'd behaved normally?'

'He was quiet and hardly said anything. That wasn't like him. I thought he was in shock. We all were. But, also, we didn't see each other much because I was looking after everyone after Tristan was discovered, helping Susan and Jim. It was only there in the woods the next day that he came out with it all.'

Jackie nodded. Athena was being recorded, so they would be able to go over things again. Many times. This version differed from the hints Athena had made to Clare about Rufus's state the night Tristan had died and about his relief immediately following Tristan's death. Perhaps Athena realised it would seem odd that she had kept quiet about it when she'd been interviewed earlier that morning, before he fell. Jackie could sense something was off.

'What was your response?'

'I couldn't speak. It was too shocking. But he saw me recoil. Saw me shrink away from him. He saw something of the horror I felt . . .' She faltered.

'Then what happened?'

'He grabbed at me with both hands.' Athena gripped her hands together tightly. 'I tried to twist away from him and

314

back away. I think I was whimpering. I was so scared.' She lowered her chin and swivelled her head, as if echoing her movements of that day.

'Where were you?'

'Right by the quarry. On the lip. I knew he saw me as a threat – an enemy. Is that crazy?' She raised her head and fixed her intense gaze on Jackie again. 'He told me all this was for us, and then he went for me. He was going to silence me, as he'd silenced Tristan.'

'Why did you think that?'

'My memory of it feels confused. It was traumatic. I was frightened; I thought I'd be sick or wet myself. He was grabbing at me. I think I stumbled as I was scrabbling away. It's hard to remember every detail. I was trying to get to my feet, and he was coming towards me.' She stopped speaking and bit her lower lip. Then she said, more slowly, 'He was going to hurt me, push me over the edge.'

'What did you do?' Jackie asked quietly.

'I think I was crying. Maybe I said "no", or "please" – I think I was trying to reach out to him, but it was as if he was a different person, not himself.'

'What was Rufus doing?'

'I don't know; my head was turned away from him. I was twisting myself to get away. And then I heard him fall.'

'What exactly did you hear?'

'He made a grunting sound, and then I heard the noise as he landed.' Athena turned and vomited, retching over the floor between her chair and the detectives. Some splashed onto Jackie's shoes and navy trousers.

Great, these trousers are dry-clean only.

Jackie asked her colleague to stop the tape – the interview was suspended.

Once Athena had been escorted from the room, the two detectives discussed this new development.

'Athena pushed him, boss. No doubt in my mind. She's lying. Every word.'

'Maybe . . . But she's quite convincing. In parts, anyway.' Jackie was more circumspect. She'd wiped her clothes and shoes and didn't want to rush to conclusions. Athena's story of the attack and Rufus's fall could be true, even if embellished to dramatic effect.

'She's our perpetrator,' said her colleague. 'Athena stabs Tristan to keep him quiet. Rufus is horrified when he realises, so she kills him before he tells anyone.'

'Why does she want to keep Tristan quiet? He's got no dirt on her – or nothing that we know about.' Jackie wanted more. 'She might have done it, but that's not enough. We've got no motive. We have to let her go. We must play this by the book.'

'Because she has powerful friends?'

'Because, if she did it, we want to get a conviction.'

CHAPTER 58

Clare texted Harriet suggesting they meet up as soon as she was finished with the police. Harriet eventually replied, saying she'd had to wait at the station for ages and was then only interviewed in a perfunctory manner, and not by DCI Carter.

They met at Jess and Ahmed's flat; Harriet had arranged to stay with her cousin, rather than travelling back to Celeste's place in Winchester, so it was a good opportunity to pool together what they knew with Jess and try to find a path forward.

What they knew was not much – only that Harriet was possibly no longer the prime suspect, which was a relief. Clare and Harriet both thought Athena had become the focus of the investigation today. The police had issued a statement saying a thirty-two-year-old woman was helping with their enquiries. It had to be her.

Jim had rung Jess, in taking-charge mode. She put him on speaker, so Harriet and Clare could hear, as they sat together in Jess's cosy living room.

'The press may be at your door already, Jess. Make sure you say nothing.'

'There's no sign of anyone, but thanks for the heads up. How's Mum doing?' Jess kept her tone light.

'I'm here too,' Susan interjected. 'Dad has you on speaker. I'm all right, just sorry about Athena's ordeal. She's been a dedicated colleague, and such a loyal friend to all of us.'

'I think we might need to be a little more circumspect about that, Mum,' Jess said. 'Remember you've been her golden goose, and with the potential to deliver a job for Rufus, too. I know it's been an awful time for her, I'm not denying that. But perhaps there's been a degree of self-interest in her friendship with me, and all of us.'

'I'm very sorry to hear you speak about your friend like this.' Jim sounded both disappointed and deeply patronising, and Susan was similarly dismissive of their daughter's concerns.

Clare was frustrated with both of them; how could they be so unaware of their daughter's feelings? She saw Jess swallow down her irritation, simply moving on and asking her parents if they had spoken to Fabian. Her self-control was admirable.

'Yes, Fabian rang,' Jim replied. 'He's fine, but surprised by this, as we all are. Everyone's worked out who that statement was about. Martin even came up to the house to talk about it, and to ask whether it means Harriet's in the clear.'

'Harriet's here with me now,' Jess said, hurriedly, presumably wanting to pre-empt any unfortunate comment about her cousin being made.

Susan was quick to respond: 'Lovely – and, in any case, the important thing to remember is that we're all in this together. All in it together – and we all need to maintain confidentiality about absolutely everything.'

'Yes, Mum.' Jess rolled her eyes in response to her mother's sloganising, but her voice betrayed no sign of it. 'We *are* in this together. And now it's up to DCI Carter and her crew to sort this.'

'Yes, I know that. Good to talk. Please give my love to Harriet.' Susan was clearly dismissing her daughter.

'Will do. She's sending her love to you, too.'

Harriet looked surprised to hear this, but gave a thumbs up, as Jess said goodbye and ended the call.

Jess put down her phone and hugged her cousin impulsively. 'Being closer to you again is the one good thing to have come out of all this.'

Clare saw how the two were increasingly at ease with one another, their childhood connection gradually being restored.

'And discovering a new cousin, as well, maybe,' Jess added.

Harriet tensed slightly. 'Thanks, Jess, and for being so supportive about that. To lose a half-brother to murder and discover a new one in a matter of weeks has been way too much for me.'

Jess must have been told of the birth of the child that Celeste had put up for adoption, Clare realised, and clearly was aware that Clare also knew about him. Presumably others in the Zetland family now knew about the boy, too. Maybe that was why Susan was continuing to impress upon Jess the need for vigilance in keeping family confidentiality? But perhaps Susan remained unaware. The subject was still raw, and Clare didn't want to assume anything. She kept quiet.

'No need to thank me; it is better to know, and I admire your mum,' Jess said. 'But my dad was an idiot not to have told my mum; she could have helped Celeste, too – she certainly knows all about discretion.'

So, Jess apparently hadn't questioned who'd fathered Celeste's child. Clare thought she'd have worked it out, but maybe not. And Harriet was obviously not going to enlighten her.

'Your dad was amazing,' Harriet said. 'Maybe he felt ashamed of my dad's behaviour with all the Tristan mess and wanted to make up for it in some way by helping my mum.'

'Will she want to contact him? This new half-brother?'

'Who knows? I think it's a matter of waiting until he's older, seeing if he initiates anything. He may not even know he's adopted. It's complicated.'

'Surely his parents will have told him?'

'Hopefully. Hopefully he'll know he was chosen and wanted. I think Tristan suffered from being treated as a shameful secret, being foisted on Dad and all of us like that.'

Clare thought how sad it was that Tristan's uncle and sister had only begun to reach this more charitable view of him after his death. But Jess was unimpressed.

'Tristan was a nightmare. Sorry, guys, but that's how I see him. He caused hell.' Jess moved into the kitchen as if to avoid the turn the conversation was taking. She put the radio on and called out that she was making toast for them all.

Harriet leaned towards Clare, confidingly. 'He wasn't exactly the ideal wedding guest, fair enough. But I've wanted to tell you, I've been thinking about him a lot, and sketching him sometimes. You pray for him, don't you? Maybe this is my way of doing that. It feels like no time since we were with him in the tree house. But like years ago, too.'

'Yes, I feel the same. I dream about it sometimes.' Clare had only told David that.

'Me too. Sometimes I dream that I'm by his body, and you're not there – I'm alone with him. Then he sits up, laughs and pulls that knife out of himself, and says he was only joking. Then I wake up and remember it's true, and feel fooled all over again. I wake up . . . and it's real.' Harriet's face was sorrowful. How could Clare ever have suspected her?

But suspecting Athena felt only slightly less difficult. Memories of Tristan's murdered body still felt surreal. Clare still found it almost impossible to believe that someone had done this to him.

CHAPTER 59

Clare was munching the toast and Marmite which Jess had prepared when Anna called about the press release; she had alerts set up on her phone. She and Tom were now heading to friends' houses after school for hastily arranged sleepovers. Anna was alarmed at the news, initially thinking Harriet was under suspicion, until Clare assured her that Harriet was not in custody and was older than thirty-two anyway. On hearing that it was possibly Athena who was helping with enquiries, Anna piped up about a conversation they'd had after the murder.

'Mum, Athena asked me if there was anything I was worried about, after Tristan died.'

'She did?' Clare put down her toast.

'Yes – and Tom. Before we left. She was a bit pushy about it. But being chief bridesmaid didn't make her in charge of everything.'

'No. Maybe she was anxious.'

'We didn't tell her anything. I *had* seen her, though.'

'What?'

'Her and Rufus – being strange. But everyone was – Jess and Ahmed had a row too, didn't they? After we'd gone. I'm glad they got back together.'

'Tell me about Rufus and Athena.'

'I can't remember much.'

'Tell me.' Clare closed her eyes briefly as she spoke, trying to stay calm.

'OK, Mum, don't stress.'

'I'm not stressing, but I'd like you to tell me. It might be something the investigating officer needs to know.'

'Jackie?'

'Yes, Jackie.'

'Do you like her?'

'Anna, please just tell me.'

'Athena was with Rufus at the hotel. We were waiting for Auntie Gill to pick us up – it was late. Athena swore at Rufus, quite a lot. I didn't hear what he said, but it was definitely him. Athena said something like, "Just say nothing. And do nothing. OK?" It was like when those cows were following us in that field, and you told me to stand still. You were fierce, and so was she. You scared those cows away.'

'What happened then?' Clare was not to be distracted by talk of dispersing a crowd of heifers.

'Tom called me, so I had to go.'

'Did Athena notice you?'

'I don't know. He called quite loudly, so she probably heard. Maybe she noticed me then, but I don't know.'

'Right. And later Athena spoke to you and Tom?'

'Yes, and Tom didn't tell her anything either.'

'Thanks, Anna, that's very helpful.' Better late than never. 'I can ask Tom about it. Don't talk to anyone else about it, OK? Just me or Dad.'

'Are you OK, Mum? Where's Dad?'

'I'm fine. I'm here at Jess and Ahmed's, with Harriet. Dad has to work late, but we'll be home later tonight. Are you OK to borrow anything you need from Hannah?'

'Yeah, her mum's going to give me a lift so I can collect things for school tomorrow. Freddie's mum got Tom's stuff for him when she collected Mia. She said there was a man outside the house. Maybe the same one who told me he had seen Athena the other day.'

'I hadn't heard about that.'

'Sorry, I forgot.'

Really? As if. And this was worrying. 'What happened?'

'He was at the house, waiting for you. I didn't talk to him. Well, not much. I went inside, and then he left. I think he didn't want to bother me. But he said that, earlier, a woman in an open-topped car had turned up, but she didn't stay. He said she had a Chanel bag – that's how I knew it was Athena.'

'A Chanel bag?'

'Yes, it wasn't even a fake. I saw it at Jess's when we were getting ready. Trixie and Tinky liked the two Cs, but said they'd have preferred it to be Ts.'

Clare was reeling, but kept Anna talking. So, Anna had overheard something, and Athena knew and had then checked out Anna and Tom, and later gone to their home, at about the time Anna would be getting home from school. This could all be a coincidence and mean nothing. But it didn't feel that way.

Athena had asked after Anna and Tom after the cremation, at the end of that unsettling conversation. If that woman went near her children or threatened them in any way, Clare would kill her – and explain it to the bishop afterwards. Alarm bells were ringing, big time.

Clare grabbed her things while explaining to Jess and Harriet that she needed to head home immediately. Harriet suggested that Athena might have wanted to ask Clare for help in some way, and Jess agreed.

Clare was unconvinced. Athena hadn't wanted her help today. There was no way Anna or Tom was sleeping anywhere but within sight and sound of her tonight, with Mia on guard. Not that Mia would be much protection – she'd tail-wag a welcome to any homicidal maniac who crossed her path. But her presence would be a comfort. Clare wanted David to come home too. It was time for everyone to be under one roof and to put up the barricades.

CHAPTER 60

David said he'd checked that all the doors were locked, but Clare wanted to watch him check again, once they were all safely back in the rectory. The children were sleeping, and Mia had had her final turn around the garden before settling down on her squashy dog bed in the hall. It was good to be home, and together.

David told Clare that Jackie had investigated the forgery issue, and Clare had heard about that from Harriet, too. Fabian might not be squeaky clean, but that didn't mean he was a cold-blooded murderer.

Fabian wasn't a convincing suspect, in Clare's eyes. He seemed too languid to stir himself to commit a violent crime. He was tall, though, which might have helped him clamber down from the tree house. That scuffle which Harriet had heard – could that have been someone letting themselves down from the tree house another way? Or even hauling themselves up into the branches above and then clambering down?

Jess was athletic – she could do something like that – but surely scrabbling about in a bridal gown and then remaining undetected was impossible. Both a wedding dress and a beaded bridesmaid's outfit would show the marks and dishevelment of such acrobatics all too unmistakably.

This was ridiculous. Once Jess had finally come clean about Tristan's hold over her, Clare had dismissed her as a suspect. Don't go back there, she told herself.

Why was she asking all these questions about someone climbing up into the branches? Keep it simple, Clare. There would have been time for someone to come down the tree-house steps without being seen by Harriet, if they'd moved fast. The scuffle she'd heard could have been the noise Tristan's body made as the last moments of life left him. Grim thought.

David thought she was on to something about the different descents, and it was good to finally be able to talk about it. He was circumspect about Athena, but willing to at least entertain the possibility of her guilt – even if any motive still felt vague. Knowing that she and Tristan had a history opened up possibilities.

David was less hasty than Clare to omit Harriet from the list of suspects. The financial motive weighed heavily on him, even if Clare was convinced that Harriet was a generous person, rather than a greedy one.

It was getting late and it had been a full day; Clare stifled a yawn. She was relieved to have liaised with Jackie about Athena, and was beginning to feel more neutral towards the DCI too. Her previous animosity seemed absurd now. It all stemmed from her own experience of being betrayed and jilted, years ago.

David and Jackie had been together at one time – so what? Clare was now snuggled up with him on the sofa, in their home, together. Their family was safe, their priorities together clear. He was her steady, clever man and she was his sparky vicar. She could be frank with him about her suspicions and her investigation, and she could be kind to Jackie.

She was disturbed from her thoughts by a call from Harriet, hoping to find Clare still awake. She had a bizarre tale. She'd stayed on at Jess and Ahmed's, although the couple had gone to see Fatima and Suki that evening.

'I was half asleep when the bell went, and it was Athena, demanding to see Jess and very unhappy to find me there. She asked what I'd done with Jess, as if I was hiding her or something. She shoved past me so hard I fell against the radiator and onto that metal shoe rack. It hurt like hell. She was rampaging around, turning on lights, shouting Jess's name.'

'It sounds crazy,' Clare said. 'And frightening. What did you do?'

'I was sitting up, then Athena literally snatched at my hair. I don't know what she was playing at. Next thing I know, someone else cannons through the open doorway, flattening me and rugby-tackling Athena.'

'Who was it? Are you OK? What about Athena?' Clare was horrified.

'It was Martin, doing some kind of Superman number. Making out that he's rescuing me. Athena was doing her nut, threatening him with an assault charge.'

'It sounds horrendous.' Clare was making appalled faces at David, who merely widened his eyes at her.

Harriet continued, 'Martin said he was there because he saw Athena arrive and attack me. She was beside herself, saying I'd fallen, she hadn't touched me, and that he was a psycho, assaulting her. It was madness.'

'Sounds it. What did you do?'

'I wanted caffeine, and needed to calm everyone down, so I made some tea. Athena sulked a bit, then said something nasty, and they both started up again. It was vile. Martin says he was watching and saw it all when she pushed me over – as if that's supposed to make me feel better. I guess he was looking out for me, and when I asked why he was there, he didn't say anything, just stared at his tea. Athena kept saying she was there to see Jess, and she said she wants what's due to her.'

'What might that be?' David asked, speaking for the first time.

'That's what Martin said, but meaner. He asked if she wanted a round of applause, or a holiday in the Caribbean, or maybe a flight to a refugee holding centre. He said that she was keen on people being dispatched there, like Susan is. Then his phone rang, and he said he had to leave – something needed sorting. He checked I was OK being left with her, which was a bit over the top, but nice of him. He came on all heavy with Athena – said if she harmed me, he'd hunt her down! You couldn't make it up.'

'What did she say to that?' Clare wondered if it would wind Athena up even more.

'She told him she knew his sort and he didn't scare her – he could piss off. He just looked at her as she carried on, saying he was violent and obsessive and I should be careful around him. He didn't answer – just took his mug to the kitchen, washed his hands in there and stuff, then came back into the living room, looked at her again and left. I told Athena I'd had enough and went to bed in Jess and Ahmed's room. I just left her to it. I heard her leave eventually, so I thought I'd see if you were awake.'

'What a night,' Clare said. 'Will you be able to sleep, after all that?'

'I'm glad I got to talk to you about it, and at least things are quiet now. The calm after a storm. Before the next one. It seems to never stop.'

Clare and David urged her to get a decent night's sleep and to be in touch if she was concerned about anything else.

Then the two of them talked long into the night: Clare finally told David about Celeste and Jim's possible motive for murder – to keep their relationship, as well as the adopted child, secret – and the way this implicated others in the Zetland family, too. David was convinced that Ahmed was only interested in preventing Tristan from upsetting Jess at the wedding, and that there was nothing more sinister between the two men, but Clare was less sure about that. She also wondered aloud whether everyone underestimated the pressure on Fabian to succeed in his career, and his potential for ruthlessness in pursuing wealth and status to match that of others in the family? That apartment he and Peter shared wasn't cheap – she questioned how much Peter earned as a photographer and in the music business, and how they could afford it. Besides the Stubbs issue, how else might Fabian have been supplementing their income, and how much might Tristan have known, or guessed, about that?

Had Tristan liaised with Athena about the family to uncover secrets together, or had Athena simply been loyal to Susan, with no awareness of what Rufus and others had been getting up to as part of Tristan's schemes?

They exhausted themselves in analysing all the options, until it was time to call it a day. Clare took a final look into each of the children's rooms, managing not to trip over Tom's discarded clothing or Anna's shin pads, before getting herself ready for bed and curling up against her husband, who was already stretched out and sleeping. Clare wasn't ready to doze off. She had too many thoughts whirling around in her head – and images of Tristan's murdered body, too.

She turned over and rearranged her pillow. The moon had risen and a sliver of light shone through a gap in the curtains and across the bed.

She was thinking about the Zetlands and how the roots of enmity ran deep in the patterns of that family and their circle. No wonder Harriet was tense when she attended the wedding.

David was breathing deeply as he slept. Clare lay herself closer alongside him, enjoying the warmth and steadiness of his presence. He had confidence in Jackie, and Clare was impressed that the DCI had called Athena into the station. Interviewing her meant that the police investigation wasn't so focused on Harriet any longer, which was a relief.

She wanted life to be ordinary again, her children to be carefree and this whole horrible business over. She'd done her best to help resolve things; now, she just wanted it done. She snuggled closer to her husband and tried to get some sleep.

CHAPTER 61

Clare's phone was charging beside the bed. Its screen lit up as a text arrived from Harriet. Then another. Then a missed call.

Clare was drowsy when she eventually reached for the phone to see what was going on, but she was soon wide awake, listening to her voicemail.

Jess and Ahmed had returned to find Harriet, like Goldilocks, sleeping on their bed.

Clare listened to Harriet's message with increasing incredulity as David slept on, the shape of his body silhouetted in the shaft of moonlight coming through the chink between the curtains. Harriet's voice was breathless, and she spoke fast.

'There's stuff you must hear, Clare. Fatima turned up — she'd followed Ahmed and Jess home; she'd decided to tell them something. She moved the knife, Clare. And never said. She said she was too scared, but she'd moved it after Ahmed put it down on one of the side tables. She was worried one of the children could reach it, so she'd wiped off the icing and had meant to put it somewhere safe. Jess asked her, and Fatima said no one noticed and she ended up putting her shawl over it and carrying it. Once she hadn't told the police about it, she was too scared to admit it later, because it sounded so suspicious.'

As Clare listened, she remembered Fatima's distress after her police interview. Why on earth hadn't she asked Fatima more about it and tried harder to find out what she'd omitted to tell them?

Harriet said Ahmed had extracted more details from his mother.

'She told him she tucked the knife under her shawl and left the marquee with it. He asked who was near, and she remembered there was quite a crowd – she mentioned Fabian was nearby, and Martin, although she called him the gardener, and Susan. She said no one looked at her, and Suki was with the other bridesmaids. Then she thought she saw Suki amongst the trees, but she realised it couldn't have been – because Suki told her later she'd been with the younger ones.

'I'm so angry with her, Clare. Someone got hold of it to kill Tristan. Anyway, she ended up talking with my mum outside, still holding the shawl with the knife in it. Then, she put it high up in a tree, out of reach so a child couldn't get hold of it. It's unbelievable. Ahmed sort of squawked at her when she said that, but then he and Jess got hold of themselves and told Fatima she had to tell the police.'

Harriet said she wanted to tell Clare all this, so was leaving the message, and she also wanted to ask where Athena was now – and Martin? She said that Jess and Ahmed might be all cosiness, embracing Fatima and comforting her, but her uneasiness was growing. What else could they do? Should they do? Apart from tell Jackie in the morning?

Clare asked herself the same questions, while forcing herself to consider the implication of Fatima's words. Taken at face value, this meant that Tristan's killer could have accessed the weapon from outside the marquee. Why had Fatima not come clean earlier? Clare was frustrated – why hadn't she asked Fatima more? This meant that who had been inside the marquee after the cake cutting was no longer relevant. Someone Clare had discounted because they had stayed outside, and who had generally been below her radar, was now uppermost in her mind. It was time to wake David; she wanted to talk this through.

CHAPTER 62

It was a beautiful night, with a bright moon and still air. Anna had left the back door ajar. She wasn't sure what had compelled her to step outside, after she'd sat up in bed, drawn her curtain aside and seen the garden magically illumined in silvery light.

Mia hadn't stirred as Anna slid downstairs, through the kitchen and out onto the cold grass. Anna could feel its damp chill though her slippers. She had just wanted to get to the garden, see the moonlight and be part of the scene. Make her own choice about doing so.

She tied her dressing gown tightly and headed for the apple tree, thinking she would pull herself up to sit in the cradle of its hospitable branches, as she and Tom often did. The platform of their tree house had been constructed in response to her brother's campaign, but its walls weren't built yet.

She half wished Tom was out here, clambering up with her, but the delicious mystery of moonlit time was best savoured alone.

Or maybe not so alone.

A figure was visible amongst the shadows as it approached, saying Anna's name quietly. Anna stiffened, unsure. Her night

adventure had become unsettling, and her feeling of being
ethereal, part of the night garden's mystique, changed into
feeling vulnerable and chilly. Her hands gripped the rough
tree bark as she adjusted her body to balance herself and avoid
falling.

'Hello, Anna,' the voice spoke again. 'What a night! So
beautiful out here!'

Out from the kitchen bounded Mia, barking twice to welcome the visitor, with her tail wagging. She bounced towards
Athena, then turned to station herself beside the apple tree,
head turned up towards Anna, delighted to have located her
and to be part of this unusual night excursion.

'Why are you here?' Anna asked Athena, emboldened by
the dog's presence.

'Why are you out so late? Or so early? I wanted to talk with
your mum. I've been trying to speak with her. And I need to
talk to your dad.'

'About work? You don't work for Susan anymore.'

'You're well informed.' Athena sounded nonplussed. She
reached into her bag and clicked open a cigarette lighter,
holding it up in front of Anna, close to her feet. 'Do you
mind if I smoke? Not a good influence, of course, but we're
outside, so no damage from passive smoking. I'm no threat
to you, Anna.'

'Of course not,' said Anna, stoutly. 'Mia wouldn't be so
friendly if she thought you were.'

'Dogs know, but people misjudge me. Can you understand
that?'

'Sure.' Anna thought the best thing to do in these peculiar
circumstances was to carry on as if everything was fine, and

just imagine how she would re-enact events for Tom's benefit later. She might prefer not to mention this episode to her parents, when they had been so antsy about sticking together, away from some unnamed threat.

'I want your dad's help. I need to get the record straight, get myself a new job – and he can help with that.'

'Right.' Anna might be young, but she knew that people didn't generally seek career advice by turning up at someone's house or lurking in their garden at three or four in the morning. She also remembered the argument between Athena and Rufus which she and Tom had overheard the night that Tristan died. She knew that Athena remembered them being there, too. Was that the real reason this woman was here?

Athena lit a cigarette and coughed a little as she smoked, as if unused to the experience. Mia circled the tree a few times beneath Anna, then meandered to the tall eucalyptus, standing sentinel at the corner of a flower bed.

'Tristan's death was so shocking,' Athena said. 'And horrible for everyone.'

'Yes.' Anna wondered why people felt the need to state the obvious quite so often. 'And it was sad about Rufus.' Now she was doing it, too. But it seemed rude not to mention him. 'Do you like smoking?'

Anna was curious. Why do something so smelly, and which made you cough – as Athena was now doing, even as she tried to smother her half-choked gasps – something which also, ever so gradually, killed you?

'Not really. I'm just fed up with doing the right thing. My bit of rebellion, I guess.'

'Not pushing Rufus into the quarry?'

'Who told you that?'

'No one. It's just what I thought probably happened.'

'Great. I've been wondering what you and your brother thought.'

'It's complicated.' Anna thought she'd better be vague. 'I don't think you hurt Tristan.'

Athena turned as if she'd heard someone. Mia had moved towards the side of the house, purposefully.

'Not again.' Athena sounded exasperated as she saw Martin walking across the lawn towards them. She muttered to Anna, 'He keeps turning up. Be careful.'

Then all hell broke loose.

As Martin approached Athena, David ran from the house, shouting – and, with some incongruity, brandishing a frying pan. Mia seemed to think some new game was afoot and barked again enthusiastically, circling Martin and jumping up at the tree where Anna was perched, and into which Athena was now also scrambling. Clare stood in the kitchen doorway, calling across the garden and restraining Tom, who was eager to join the fray. Panic was almost choking her, but she made herself stay calm while Tom yelled proudly, 'I called 999, Anna! I saw Athena in the garden with you!'

Anna was distracted by the challenge of retaining her place in the tree into which Athena had also launched herself to get away from Martin. Clare could see her daughter in danger and she knew she couldn't get to her before the murderer did. She knew who it was now; everything had fallen into place as she listened to Harriet's message, and then Tom had come into their room and she and David had hurtled down the stairs and into the garden.

There was bedlam in front of her as Martin was now being tugged and jumped at by a delirious Mia, while David stood by, frying pan ineffectual by his side. Anna held her place and steadied Athena, who'd dropped her cigarette below them, coral-tipped amongst the grass and fallen leaves. Curls of smoke rose.

'OK, everyone, that's enough!' Clare spoke firmly, as if she was calling a bunch of children in for tea. She gripped the doorframe as she looked out at the nightmarish scene. She was careful not to show any sign of the terror she felt at standing across the garden from her daughter – her child under threat. 'David, can you get Mia before she causes an injury? Martin, please stand still and stay where you are – it'll be better that way.'

'Yes . . . easy, Mia, good girl,' David said, although exactly what was good about the golden retriever's continued leaping and prancing was unclear. But she settled enough for David to stick a hand in her collar, and Martin stepped further back from the moonlit tree and reached down to her.

'Athena is a threat to Anna and to all of us,' he said. 'She attacked Harriet earlier tonight.'

Clare let go of Tom, who nevertheless kept to his spot, knowing that remaining unnoticed was key to being able to stay and see what happened.

'It's not as simple as that,' Clare commented as she approached, walking with slow deliberation. She must keep things as steady as possible, without any sudden movement.

'No, you realised I saw your capacity for violence, didn't you, Martin?' Athena spoke with a new calmness, looking down on the gardener. 'I came here to ask Clare for help – David, too. You came to silence me, admit it.'

Mia barked sharply up at her twice, while still being restrained by David and patted by Martin.

'You're deranged and dangerous,' Martin retorted. 'I'm protecting Anna from you.'

Clare could see that Anna was content to stay beside Athena in the old apple tree. Martin was the aggressor, here. The memory of him stowing something in the apple store at Greenwood had come to her, clarifying everything. She spoke as peacefully as she could manage: 'Martin, Anna is safe, and so are you. We can take this step by step. Everything can be sorted out.'

'Yes, that's right,' David said. He reached his arm up, half lifting Anna from the apple tree and half catching her as she dropped herself down.

Athena stood higher up amongst the branches, holding herself against the trunk. She was partly obscured by foliage, but Clare could see she was rigid with fear.

'Keep him away from me!' she urged, as Martin moved closer, across the grass.

Clare saw the knife, saw Martin go towards the tree again, and called, 'Stop! Stop it. It's over, now.'

Something in her voice delayed him, and David pulled him away.

Martin's expression was all indignation. 'It's Athena you need to stop,' he gasped. 'That woman was about to attack Anna.'

Anna faced him, one arm now around her mother and the other holding her brother. Tom had left his post by the kitchen door and clasped his sister with both arms gripped tight around her waist.

'All Athena did was blow smoke at me. You were the one with the weapon.'

Clare watched the knife drop. Martin let it fall at his feet.

'I brought it in case I needed to defend anyone against you, Athena.'

'No one touch that knife.' Clare's voice was a command. 'Tom, Anna – into the house, please. Take Mia with you and close the door. Turn the key, Anna, please. Dad and I will be inside with you soon.'

'You and I will wait out here,' David said to Martin, walking him away from the knife, and further from Athena.

Mia, now biddable, responded to Clare's summons and was content to be taken into the house by Tom and Anna. Perhaps she was aware that the children needed her.

Once they were all inside, Clare stepped towards Athena and stationed herself below the tree to provide another buffer between her and Martin, whom David led further away. The two men sat on the bench on the furthest side of the lawn. Martin slumped, turning himself away from David, and curled in on himself.

'I don't understand,' Athena said quietly to Clare.

'The police will sort it out. Tom called them; he saw you and Anna from the window and told us.'

'I saw the violence in him. He knew I was a threat to him, didn't he?'

'Harriet said so. He brought a knife.' It lay in the grass, not far from Clare's feet.

'I wanted to talk with you again, and with Anna, but it was difficult.'

'Difficult?'

'I thought she knew what Rufus had done.'

'To Tristan?'

'Yes, to Tristan.' Athena made a strange keening sound, still above Clare, still holding on to the support of the tree, encircled by its branches. 'Rufus—'

'You thought Rufus murdered Tristan?'

'I did, but now I'm not so sure.'

Clare waited.

Eventually, Athena continued: 'I thought Rufus had killed Tristan, and then he came for me. But was it Martin, all along? I thought Rufus was a killer.' Athena half sobbed again as she leaned her head against the tree. 'The way he was that night. The way he was so relieved Tristan was dead. He said he was free of him, at last. It was terrifying, how he reacted. I thought Anna heard him, too. I couldn't shut him up.'

Clare reached up her arm. 'Come down, Athena.'

'Nothing makes any sense.'

'I'm with you on that. Things will be clearer in the morning . . . maybe. Things usually are.' And there's a lot to tell Jackie, she thought.

'It's morning already . . . almost.' Athena lowered herself to half sit, half crouch on the tree-house platform, then leaned forward to grasp Clare before jumping down. 'It's been a while since I've climbed a tree,' she said, then checked herself. 'Why was I a target for Martin? What was going on?'

'Who knows what was going on in his mind, or in anyone's,' said Clare, thinking of Rufus lying still on his hospital bed and the anguished faces of his parents.

She had a strong suspicion about who had harmed Rufus, and why. Perhaps Athena had been afraid of him, but Clare thought it more likely that she'd wanted to silence him and to make sure nothing came out about his dealings with Tristan.

The women stood together until they heard the approaching sound of a siren. Soon, blue lights flashed across at them as a police car turned noisily into the driveway. David and Martin remained still. Clare felt her legs might not carry her, but somehow got herself round to the side of the house and returned with two uniformed officers. It was going to be a long night. Or morning.

'Jackie will be on her way,' called David, as if that would resolve everything.

CHAPTER 63

It would take time for any semblance of normality to return. It was a week after the events of that surreal night, and Harriet had joined the Brakespear family at the rectory. The adults sat in the steamer chairs in the garden, with Mia rolling on the fallen leaves on the grass, and Anna and Tom made do with the wooden bench on the lawn. Clare and Harriet wanted to talk face to face, and Clare wanted to stay at home with the children as much as possible in the aftermath of Martin's arrest and the events of that night.

Anna was missing Saturday training in order to be with her family for this debrief.

'What will happen to Martin?' she asked.

'He'll have been having lots of interviews,' David said. 'It's good that he decided to confess; it means the trial will be much more straightforward.'

'Can we go?' Tom asked.

'It'll probably be on a school day.' Clare could see David was relieved to have a neutral reason for the prohibition.

'I don't want to go, anyway. I never want to see Martin again,' Anna said. 'It's sick. Why did you visit him, Mum?'

'Because he asked.'

'How is he?' Harriet asked tentatively.

'Different. He seems to regret what he did, but isn't fully acknowledging it either, or not accepting how wrong he was. But he's definitely regretting the consequences.'

'Why did he want to see you?' Anna persisted.

'Who knows? Maybe he's bored, or lonely. Perhaps he's confused about what has happened, or regretful and just wants to talk. The prison chaplaincy team are visiting each day while he's on remand because he's at risk of self-harm.'

'Why did he do it?'

For a while, no one attempted to answer Tom's question. Perhaps there was no answer, or no adequate one.

'I don't know, Tom. It's impossible to say why he allowed himself to be so violent,' Clare eventually offered.

Clare knew she would never forget the conversation; her memories were vivid. Martin had been beardless when he entered the visiting room, which smelled of disinfectant. He looked younger and pale, a diminished version of himself. He'd asked to see her, and seemed to have plenty to say.

'I'm sorry for disturbing you at home that night, Clare,' he'd begun. 'I think you know I wanted to protect you all from Athena. I knew she was dangerous; I had to keep Harriet safe from her, too.' He seemed to believe what he was saying, seeing himself as some kind of defender of the innocent, and believing Clare sympathised with that view.

Clare wasn't fooled by the rambling speech of self-justification, but didn't interrupt him. It seemed that the wedding had brought on some kind of crisis: an awareness that he would never belong in that community or family, whereas Tristan was welcomed back into the fold despite all the pain he'd inflicted on Harriet and others. And Martin was expendable.

'I saw them together,' Martin said. 'Tristan and Harriet, talking. After the plane protest. No one even really noticed that, and I could see Tristan was worming his way back into the family again – no one was willing to keep Harriet safe from him.'

Clare thought it more likely that Martin feared Harriet's attitude to her brother becoming more positive, and that he'd been fiercely jealous when he saw them speaking together. She remembered noticing the conversation too, and hoping the siblings might become reconciled in some way. Martin's reaction had been very different.

'I understood then that I'd never belong,' Martin continued, bitterly. 'I'll always be the outsider, disposable. I can be evicted, chucked out from Greenwood, but Tristan was welcome – he's family.'

And Clare could well imagine how Tristan might have goaded the angry, resentful man. How he'd casually reignited old rivalries and memories of humiliation – and paid a terrible price for that careless malice.

Martin said he'd become angry – and he was angry again as he told her about it. 'I'm nothing to them, the Zetlands – nothing. Tristan said that, and other things.' He paused. It seemed there were things too painful to be repeated. 'They don't care about Harriet either, never have. No one protected her from Tristan. Except me. I had to protect her against Athena, too. That was why I had that knife with me in your garden, to make sure Athena couldn't hurt anyone. They're all the same. Out for themselves. And they get away with it. Whatever they do. The plane stunt achieved nothing. Nothing was going to disturb that perfect wedding. Nothing. Well, not until Tristan's death.'

Martin seemed to see himself as some kind of avenging hero, but his long-winded explanations and self-justifications were confused, punctuated by diatribes against the justice system, the political processes which benefitted Susan 'and her kind', and railing against Athena and anyone who displeased him.

'I'm not sorry,' he'd said. 'It had to be done. The man had to be dealt with.' He seemed convinced, and it sickened her. There was no glimmer of self-doubt – or not yet, anyway.

Clare didn't want to repeat the murderer's words and justifications to her family. Nor did she want to dwell on his gleam of pride as he described the ease with which he had swung himself out from the tree house and down to the ground by way of the branches at the far side of the tree. He'd worn gardening gloves and had taken a weapon with him as he went to meet Tristan in the tree house. But he hadn't needed it. Instead, he'd taken advantage of seeing Fatima stowing the wedding-cake knife and had used that instead. He seemed proud of that adaptability, too.

He'd kept the gloves concealed in the turned earth of a vegetable patch, then moved them the following morning. She'd been told by Jackie that the police had discovered Tristan's phone buried in one of the beds of the walled garden, too – but Martin made no mention of that. He said that he thought Clare might have realised he was hiding something when she met him in the round outhouse where the apples were stored. He was right – she had remembered that moment when things had finally clicked into place for her about his guilt, but belatedly. She still chided herself about that.

Jackie was aware of all this, so there was no need to repeat every horrible detail of Martin's actions to her family, too. Clare found it helpful to talk about it with David, though. She'd also found it cathartic to talk about it with Jackie; the DCI had a helpfully dispassionate perspective.

Martin had deliberately slaughtered Tristan. And he'd taken a knife from Jess and Ahmed's kitchen to 'protect' others from Athena. His actions were premeditated. Athena had called out his propensity for violence – and had been so vehement that Martin assumed she knew what he'd done. He had decided to silence her, and had followed her to the rectory determined to do so.

But Martin continued to declare himself innocent of any attack on the hapless Rufus. He said he'd been as shocked as the rest of them about that.

While Clare pondered what exactly to tell them, Harriet spoke: 'He said at one point that it was for me.' She weighed each word carefully. 'He wrote to me. But that was a delusion, an excuse.'

'I don't understand how he could care about what's happening to refugees and also murder someone. It's horrible.' Anna bent forward to stroke Mia. 'I thought he was nice. Monty liked him.'

'We all liked him,' Harriet continued, 'and never imagined him capable of something like this.'

'He'd fought with Tristan before,' David offered. 'And he had his own issues, too – they were just well hidden.'

'He was a bit creepy about you, Harriet,' Clare added. 'Something didn't feel quite right there; it smelled off.'

'He isn't cheese, Mum.' Tom rolled a ball from side to side with his foot.

'Maybe he was simply jealous of Tristan, or hated him. He let all his feelings fester and then they exploded in an act of violence. I'm not sure we'll ever fully understand why he killed Tristan.'

David thought about what Clare said, and added, 'His willingness to let others take the blame had a clear motive, though – he wanted to get away with it.'

'I thought it was Athena,' said Harriet. 'Everyone did. Except for the people who thought it was me. Or thought it was Rufus who'd done it, and then Athena tried to cover it up by getting rid of Rufus.'

'That didn't work. We all suspected Athena. She behaved so oddly.'

'Was Martin going to kill her, too, Dad?' Tom asked.

'I think he realised she'd recognised the violence in him, she was a threat to him. He was afraid she'd identified him as Tristan's murderer. Perhaps he thought she'd seen him do something suspicious, but he won't say. He claims he was protecting Harriet and others from Athena that night. She accused him of violence when Harriet let him into Jess and Ahmed's flat that night, said she knew what he was capable of.'

David and Clare had reached their own conclusions about the dynamic between Athena and Martin that night, how each had recognised the other's capacity for malevolence and had responded accordingly.

'Is Athena OK, Mum?' Anna was gauging her parents' view

of the woman who had seemed ready to confide in her in the garden that strange night.

'I'm not sure. She's been through a lot.' Clare was reluctant to say too much.

'There's talk of Susan and Jim making a new role for her as their personal PA,' Harriet commented.

'How does Jess feel about that?' Clare asked, thinking it was a terrible idea.

'I think Athena's best left to fend for herself, away from my family.' Harriet was quick to agree with Clare's implied reservation.

'Dad, what does Jackie think happened to Rufus?' Anna had picked up her parents' ambivalence about Athena, and Harriet's hostility towards her.

'They're still sorting it out,' David said, playing for time.

When Clare had spoken to Jackie, they'd agreed that Athena had probably pushed Rufus into the quarry, believing he'd killed Tristan and wanting to be rid of him. However, nothing could be proven.

'Athena says he fell.' Harriet's voice was flat. 'She thought Rufus had killed Tristan, so she tried to get away from him, and he fell.'

'That doesn't make sense. People don't just fall over into a quarry,' Tom said. 'You stop yourself at the edge, even if you're being chased along a cliff and running at full speed.'

Clare wondered how her son had become an expert in such matters, then reassured herself that, right now, both her children were safe at home – Harriet and David, too.

'Maybe we'll never know exactly how it happened,' she said. 'Maybe Athena is confused about it too. The good thing is that

Rufus is continuing to recover. He's starting to eat again and to regain strength. His memory is patchy, but it looks like it will come back with time. His parents are thrilled.'

Athena perhaps less so. Clare thought it unsurprising that she was confused and troubled. Mistaking your partner for a murderer and belatedly realising your error would confuse anyone. Clare thought that Rufus had been sent on his way by Athena, but that Athena would weasel her way out of admitting it. But perhaps she was misjudging her. Perhaps Athena was innocent in all of this.

'Martin will stay in prison,' Tom said.

'Yes.' Clare knew Harriet had mixed feelings about Jim's decision to give Martin some support through the trial process, but possibly her uncle was feeling culpable in some way, for the whole sorry mess. Susan was steering clear.

'Will you still visit him, Mum?'

'We'll see.'

'You pray for him, don't you?' It wasn't clear whether Anna's comment was accusatory or simply factual.

'Your mum prays for all of us, and I'm grateful,' Harriet chipped in. 'My life would probably be even more of a mess if she didn't. And even I know that Jesus said, when people care for those in prison or visit them, it's as if they cared for him. Anyway, did I tell you that I'm painting Auntie Susan, after all?'

Clare appreciated how Harriet was trying to shift the children's attention. She knew the artist was starting to visualise this portrait, with new shadows of experience marking her aunt's face and surroundings. Harriet had told Clare it would be a deeper-toned painting than first envisaged: less gleamingly golden and more subtly coloured, now.

She'd also said she might show Clare her drawings of Tristan, or some of them. They'd discussed how she was still discovering him, re-evaluating him, after his death. Her drawings were part of that process and expressed her new feelings about him. She hadn't understood that a relationship could continue after death, as understanding and compassion deepened. Harriet felt differently about her dad now, as well – their dad.

'Will you paint Mia, one day?' Anna asked, as if subconsciously connecting the golden retriever with Harriet's musings about Susan and her aura.

'That's a great idea –' David sounded enthusiastic – 'but first let's find that cake for Harriet. And for us, too, of course.'

'Smooth change of subject, Dad,' said Tom.

'It's good to talk about things,' Clare added. 'But Dad is right – talking is always better with cake.'

CHAPTER 64

Later, David and the children relaxed on the sofa in front of the telly, with the dog spread across an assortment of their feet. Harriet and Clare were in the kitchen, sitting on two of the red chairs which circled the table. Harriet nursed a second mug of tea, and Clare got up to wipe the worktop surfaces and tidy cake remnants away.

'Athena will get away with it,' Harriet said, ruefully.

'Maybe. I do think it's worth you and Jess making a combined effort to ease Susan and Jim away from ongoing involvement with her.' Clare wanted to be proactive about this.

'So, you agree she pushed him?'

'Who knows for sure? It doesn't sound as if she'd be convicted. And she realised that Martin was violent. She helped Anna, whatever she may have done to Rufus.'

'Poor Rufus. And Tristan. Martin, even.'

'I hope he faces up to what he did, and the consequences.'

'We're all enduring those. I miss Tristan. Do you think he knows I miss him? That I'm sorry?'

Clare paused from wiping away the crumbs nestling around the toaster. 'I guess I think he knows what he needs to know. I just trust God with him. With all of us.'

Harriet responded to her sincerity. She didn't have much faith in God's love for Tristan, but she was glad that Clare did. 'Thanks for your help, Clare, and with Tristan's funeral when I was still prime suspect. Do you think Anna and Tom are OK?'

'They're resilient. But it's hard to know what's going on underneath. Tom was sad about Tristan, and still is. And it's a shock to see what people are capable of doing.'

'That's still unbelievable to me. It doesn't add up – that Martin did that, with no proper justification.'

'He was so jealous, Harriet. I suppose there was a lot going on in his head that we didn't see.' Clare sat down at the round table. 'As well as the awfulness, though, there have been positives. The way people have helped . . . friendships . . . Jess getting her work stuff resolved. Your mother having your support about the adoption and not hiding that anymore.'

'Yes, there are, but my brother is dead. The man I thought was my friend killed him. And Rufus may be recovering, but we don't know to what extent; and who knows what will happen to Athena?' Harriet sounded defeated, despite being exonerated of any crime.

'That's Jackie's problem, now. You and Jess can steer Susan and Jim into fresh things. Painting Susan sounds good.'

'I see her differently, now. She *is* different. We all are. Jess and Ahmed have had such a roller-coaster start to their marriage. Fabian has had a wake-up call, too.'

'You're closer as cousins again, I think?'

'Yes, and Jess is closer with her mum. Athena had edged Jess out and somehow became a surrogate daughter, or at least tried to.' Harriet's voice was more animated.

'And we're friends now,' Clare said. 'Anna and Tom are

adopting you as an extra aunt or godmother or something. Prepare yourself.'

On cue, Anna stood in the doorway, watching the two women. 'Dad says it's time to do something else. Do you want to play a board game, or cricket?'

Clare said she would join them in a moment; she just had to check whether the email about hymn choices for the following day's service had arrived OK. But, when she opened her laptop, an unexpected email in her inbox caught her attention.

Marked *Highly Confidential*, it had come from the priest in a Cornish parish, who wrote that their area dean had learned that Clare had recent experience of a high-profile police matter and thought that she would be well placed to assist them with addressing the consequences of tragedy in their own community.

This happened at a retreat held in our parish last year, with an inconclusive outcome, despite extensive police involvement. Sadly, the missing retreat participant, or their body, has never been found. I hope that you might be willing to hear more about this very challenging situation and to help us to manage the continuing fallout.

We'd also be very grateful for any assistance you can give in our preparations for this year's retreat, which is likely to go ahead but which will be very sensitive. Perhaps we can have a conversation, in confidence, to discuss this further?

Clare closed her laptop. She'd respond to that later; there was already more than enough on her plate for today. She wasn't looking for any more drama, although her interest was piqued – who had gone missing, and why? And what might be planned for this year's retreat? This might involve a visit to Cornwall, too, which sounded like a major plus.

CHAPTER 65

Six months later, Susan's voice was apologetic on the phone. Spring was underway, with trees coming into leaf and early daffodils flowering. The door to the garden was left open as Clare stood and listened.

'Fiona's mother is in a care home in Northumberland and fading. Fiona needs to be with her. Sunday is covered OK in the parish, but Clare . . . we were wondering . . . could you possibly?'

'Of course. No problem, Susan.'

'Thank you. It feels very different, this time.'

'Yes. But it's lovely to get together to do this.'

David had understood as soon as he heard Clare agreeing to do something for Susan, and adjusted his travel plans. They would take two cars tomorrow. Clare would want to be there ahead of time, and he didn't want the children to have to wait around. He was glad they had been included, but didn't want to expect too much of them.

So, the next day, here Clare was, in cassock-alb and stole, awaiting the arrival of Ahmed and Jess once again, at the church where they had been married. This time, Clare was conducting the ceremony.

The couple had invited family and close friends to a service of blessing of their marriage, and a renewal of their vows.

Things were simpler, this time. No hats, music or hymns – just a quiet, spoken service in the church. Fiona had planned the outline with Jess and Ahmed. It was an adaptation of the marriage service, marking a fresh beginning after the horrors and drama of their wedding, with the crime and its aftermath.

The trial had been straightforward, with Martin entering a guilty plea. The media had nevertheless salivated over every detail, their sensationalism a brutal reliving of events. Susan was now determined to work on legislation to curtail the impunity with which the press intruded on anyone connected with a story, however tangentially, or however vulnerable they might be. Jim was ready to sue for defamation, breach of privacy and anything else he could think of, but Fabian and Jess joined forces to dissuade him.

A text from Jess came soon after Susan's phone call to Clare about Fiona's absence. *Mum says you're doing the service for us. I'm sorry about Fiona's family, but it's perfect having you.*

And now, here came Jess in a lilac, patterned dress, arm in arm with Ahmed in his best jacket. There were no bridesmaids in attendance this time, but Anna sat smiling next to her dad, with Tom on the other side of him. Anna had told her mother that morning that she was glad Jackie wouldn't be there. She seemed to know her mum hadn't liked the police detective, and that Jackie's presence spelled trouble in some way.

Harriet sat in the next pew, wearing a pale green dress. Celeste was in dark purple. Peter and Fabian were with Susan and Jim, and Fatima and Suki were nearby. There was no Rufus or Athena, of course, no Trixie or Tinky or their parents, and no Martin. Just immediate family. No police, no caterers, no political allies or colleagues: everything was kept simple. After all the bruising revelations and experiences the previous summer, there was an atmosphere of tenderness and solace.

Clare spoke words of welcome. Then, as Fiona had planned, they began with a moment of silent reflection. Time to bring themselves together before God, to recognise all that they had been through and to offer their memories, their care for one another and for others, too. Time to bring their regrets and sorrow, as well as their gratitude and relief. Time to share their joy at Jess and Ahmed's marriage continuing. Their love, prayers and hopes for them, and for one another. This ongoing marriage was itself a symbol of God's blessing, and of hope.

The stones and arches of the nave seemed to hold them in hallowed space, with the prayers of centuries present with them. Jess and Ahmed stood together, their heads bowed, while others remained seated and quiet. From beyond came the sounds of the countryside, a hum of traffic and birdsong.

Anna and Tom planned to visit the horses in the field afterwards. They'd brought carrots. Maybe they'd stay there a little while, beside the water, as Tristan had liked to do, before they headed home.

ACKNOWLEDGEMENTS

Many people are involved in the creation of a book. My family have been so generous in their support – this novel is dedicated to Jonathan, Eleanor and Ben, with my love, and my thanks for all their good humour and their enthusiasm for this writing adventure. This book is a tribute to them. Matthew, Eleanor's partner and now husband, has been brilliant too – so his car gets a mention in the text!

Rev. Clare is a fictional character, but I took snippets of my own and clergy colleagues' experiences and fictionalised them. I am so fortunate to have worked with the wonderful clergywomen of the Church of England, whose steadfast work goes on without fuss and with great generosity of heart. My thanks to all my friends and clergy colleagues. Thank you to the vicar who brought round a bottle of something sparkly to celebrate the news of me being offered a publishing contract!

In the novel, Anna's nighttime wanderings owe something to stories read in childhood – Elizabeth Goudge's *The Little White Horse* and Philippa Pearce's *Tom's Midnight Garden*. My thanks to all who have encouraged me to discover the riches which books give us. I think of various English teachers, family members, librarians and friends – if any of you are reading this, I hope you have enjoyed the book! If any of my former pupils read this, sorry for any boring lessons, and thank you for all the good moments in classrooms in London and Antrim!

I have always loved reading crime fiction but only embarked on writing it a few years ago. The novelists Elly Griffiths and Lesley Thomson shared their expertise with their brilliant teaching during their course on crime writing which I attended at West Dean College. Their generosity and encouragement have been wonderful. Fiona Cummins also shared her skill, insights and experience on an evening course which I attended. I have benefitted so much from being taught by each of these wonderful, bestselling authors.

My experience of crime writers has been that they are welcoming and friendly to newcomers. I have very much enjoyed meeting several of them at a range of interesting crime fiction festivals and book signings over the last couple of years. It has been lovely to attend these in the company of other students from the courses I did. Thank you to each of those companions for their friendship and support – to Lisette, Anne, Annabel, Pam, Laura, Paula and Nic. Being alongside others who are also embarking on this crime writing process has meant so much – thank you, all you brilliant Agatha mates.

Alison Galbraith, Pam Hamilton and Lisette Teasdale read early versions (when Rev. Clare was still called Rev. Kate!) and helped improve things, as did Louise Voss who cast her very helpful, professional eye on a draft, and Victoria Goldman who copyedited the version which I sent to Quercus. Jane Wood is a legendary editor and she was so kind in her response, and tactful about how much work needed to be done!

Florence Hare has been completely brilliant as an editor. I cannot thank her enough for the way she undertook the mission to get this novel into better shape, with tact and great warmth, as well as rigour. I have also been very fortunate to have such an astute and experienced agent as Rebecca Carter, with her insightful support. Thank you both, very much, for your care and hard work.

My warm thanks too to Rebecca's colleagues at Rebecca Carter Literary – Tilda Butterworth, and also Margaret Halton and Alex Chernova, who look after translation rights.

Many thanks to Penelope Price who copyedited the text with such deft skill, it was amazing to see the improvements she made.

Thanks too to all who been involved in producing the audio version, Carrie Hutchinson and Helen Keeley who narrated it so expertly.

The whole Quercus team are brilliant, I have loved working with them as we have produced this book. It is surreal to have such a wonderful cover designed for it, I still don't quite believe this has all happened! My warm thanks to Andrew Smith and Alexandra Allden, for their fantastic work.

Myrto Kalavrezou and Katy Blott have been marvellously enthusiastic advocates for Rev. Clare's story in the marketing and publicity teams, and I am also very grateful for the work of Megan Schaffer and Kyla Dean in the sales team. It is such a pleasure to work with you all, thank you.

My thanks too to all the booksellers and librarians who will help make this book available to readers, and to Simon Appleby at Bookswarm for creating and managing my author website for me. Thank you for including photos of our golden retriever, too – and thanks to Danielle Keane for taking the pictures, and for making that process enjoyable rather than an ordeal!

So many friends and family have supported me in this project, my warm thanks to each of you, and to our crime fiction loving neighbours, too! Various communities and church congregations where I take services have also been so encouraging about my writing – thank you so much. I have been very fortunate to be with you in the parishes and hospices where I have worked, and with all at Rochester Cathedral.

The local community choir I now sing with also includes the

crime writer Laura Marshall, who has been very generous in her friendly encouragement. I have been extremely fortunate in every aspect of this writing and publishing process.

My wider family includes numerous crime fiction readers. Many thanks to my siblings and siblings-in-law, and to my wonderful nieces and nephews and their children – some of whose chickens have made it into the book!

Books are one way of connecting with others, and I have benefitted so much from the connections made through books over the years. Novels have often shaped my thinking and been a guide for me, as well as a means of entertainment and fun. I am very privileged to have been given the opportunity to write a novel, and I hope that readers will enjoy it. If not, I hope you can simply give it away, or give it back to the library, and enjoy reading something else!

So, thank you, very much, for reading the first of Rev. Clare's sleuthing adventures. When I attended my first meeting with Jane Wood and Florence Hare at Quercus to discuss the possibility of publishing it, we sat in the top floor café of the publishers' riverside office building in London. I tried to look serious, and not as if I was experiencing some kind of bizarre, wish-fulfilment dream. The view from the window included the sunlit dome of St Paul's Cathedral, where I was ordained back in the Summer of 1999. It felt like a reminder that life can hold many adventures and surprises, and that I could enjoy this one! I very much hope that you enjoy the novel, too.

Penny Stephens

April 2025